AN EARTH GIRL ON GOR

The Panther Girl carried herself arrogantly before the bound and helpless men, taunting them with her beauty and her spear. She jabbed at them, and a stain of blood showed on more than one tunic.

"Men!" she laughed contemptuously, and turned away from them. I saw the men struggle, but they could not free themselves.

Then she was standing before me. She appraised me, as might have a slaver. "Kajira," she said. "Slave!"

Without looking back, she strode from the camp. Her girls followed her. The choke leash slid shut on my throat. Stripped and gagged, my hands bound behind me, I was dragged after them toward the darkness of the forest.

By John Norman

THE CHRONICLES
OF COUNTER-EARTH

TARNSMAN OF GOR
OUTLAW OF GOR
PRIEST-KINGS OF GOR
NOMADS OF GOR
ASSASSIN OF GOR
RAIDERS OF GOR
CAPTIVE OF GOR

Published by Ballantine Books

CAPTIVE
OF GOR

John Norman

BALLANTINE BOOKS • NEW YORK

ISBN 0-345-25185-7-150

Manufactured in the United States of America

First Edition: December 1972
Eighth Printing: October 1976

First Canadian Printing: January 1973

Cover art by Boris Vallejo

Contents

Captive
of Gor

1 THE BRAND

THE FOLLOWING ACCOUNT IS WRITTEN at the command of my master, Bosk of Port Kar, the great merchant, and, I think, once of the warriors.

My name was Elinor Brinton. I had been independently wealthy.

There is much I do not understand. Let others find what meaning they can in this narrative.

I gather that my story is neither as unique, nor as strange, as it may seem. By the standards of Earth I was regarded as extremely beautiful. Yet on this world I am a fifteen-goldpiece girl, more lovely than many, yet far excelled by many whose stunning beauty I can only envy. I was purchased for the kitchens of the house of Bosk. Traders, I have learned, ply the slave routes between this world and Earth. Women, among other goods, are acquired and brought to the markets of this strange world. If you are beautiful, and desirable, you may fear.

Apparently they may do what they wish.

Yet I think there are perhaps worse fates that might befall a woman than to be brought to this world, even as a prize of men.

My master has told me not to describe this world in great detail. I do not know why that is, but I shall not do so. He has told me to narrate primarily what has occurred to me. And he has asked me to put down my thoughts and, particularly, my emotions. I wish to do so. Indeed, even if I did not wish to do so, I would have to obey.

Suffice it then to say but little of my background and condition.

I was expensively educated, if not well educated. I endured a succession of lonely years at boarding schools, and later at one of the finest women's colleges in the northeastern portion of the United States. These years seem to me now oddly empty, even frivolous. I had had no difficulty in obtaining fine grades. My intelligence, it seems to me, was good, but even when my work seemed to me inferior, it was rated highly, as, indeed, was that of my sorority sisters. Our parents were wealthy and substantial grants to the schools and colleges were often made following our graduations. Also, I had never found men, and many of my instructors were such, hard to please. Indeed, they seemed eager to please me. I was failed in one course, in French. My instructor in this case was a woman. The Dean of Students, as was his wont in such circumstances, refused to accept the grade. I took a brief examination with another instructor, and the grade became an A. The woman resigned from the school that Spring. I was sorry, but she should have known better. As a rich girl I had little difficulty in making friends. I was extremely popular. I do not recall anyone to whom I could talk. My holidays I preferred to spend in Europe.

I could afford to dress well, and I did. My hair was always as I wanted it, even when it appeared, deceptively, as most charmingly neglected. A bit of ribbon, a color on an accessory, the proper shade of expensive lipstick, the stitching on a skirt, the quality of leather in an imported belt and matching shoes, nothing was unimportant. When pleading for an extension for an overdue paper I would wear scuffed loafers, blue jeans and a sweatshirt, and hair ribbon. I would at such times smudge a bit of ink from a typewriter ribbon on my cheek and fingers. I would always get the extra time I needed. I did not, of course, do my own typing. Usually, however, I wrote my own papers. It pleased me to do so. I liked them better than those I could purchase. One of my instructors, from whom I had won an extension in the afternoon, did not recognize me the same evening when he sat some rows behind me at a chamber-music performance at the Lincoln Center. He was looking at me quizzically, and once, during an intermission, seemed on the point of speaking. I chilled him with a look and he turned away, red faced. I wore black, an upswept hairdo, pearls, white gloves. He did not dare look at me again.

I do not know when I was noticed. It may have been on a street in New York, on a sidewalk in London, at a cafe in Paris. It may have been while sun-bathing on the Riviera. It may even have been on the campus of my college. Somewhere. Unknown to me, I was noted, and would be acquired.

Affluent and beautiful, I carried myself with a flair. I knew that I was better than other people, and was not afraid to show them, in my manner, that this was true. Interestingly, instead of being angered, most people, whatever may have been their private feelings, seemed impressed and a bit frightened of me. They accepted me at the face value which I set upon myself, which was considerable. They would try to please me. I used to amuse myself with them, sometimes pouting, pretending to be angry or displeased, then smiling to let them know that I had forgiven them. They seemed grateful, radiant. How I despised them. How I used them! They bored me. I was rich, and fortunate and beautiful. They were nothing.

My father made his fortune in real estate in Chicago. He cared only for his business, as far as I know. I cannot remember that he ever kissed me. I do not recall seeing him, either, ever touch my mother, or she him, in my presence. She came from a wealthy Chicago family, with extensive shore properties. I do not believe my father was even interested in the money he made, other than in the fact that he made more of it than most other men, but there were always others, some others, who were richer than he. He was an unhappy, driven man. I recall my mother entertaining in our home. This she often did. I recall my father once mentioning to me that she was his most valuable asset. He had meant this to be a compliment. I recall that she was beautiful. She poisoned a poodle I had once had. It had torn one of her slippers. I was seven at the time, and I cried very much. It had liked me. When I graduated neither my mother nor my father attended the ceremony. That was the second time in my life, to that time, that I remember crying. He had a business engagement, and my mother, in New York, where she was then living, was giving a dinner for certain of her friends. She did send a card and an expensive watch, which I gave to another girl.

That summer my father, though only in his forties, died of a heart attack. As far as I know my mother still lives in New York City, in a suite on Park Avenue. In the settlement of the estate my mother received most everything, but I did receive some three quarters of a million dollars, primarily in stocks and bonds, a fortune which fluctuated, and sometimes considerably, with the market, but one which was substantially sound. Whether my fortune on a given day was something over a half million dollars or something over three quarters of a million dollars did not much interest me.

Following my graduation I took up my own residence, in a penthouse on Park Avenue. My mother and I never saw one another. I had no particular interest in anything following school. I smoked too much, though I hated it. I drank quite a bit. I never bothered with drugs, which seemed to me stupid.

My father had had numerous business contacts in New York, and my mother had made influential friends. I made a rare phone call to my mother a few weeks after my graduation, thinking it might be interesting to take up modeling. I had thought there might be a certain glamour to that, and that I might meet some interesting and amusing people. A few days later I was invited to two agencies for interviews, which, as I expected, were mere formalities. There are doubtless, many girls beautiful enough to model. Beauty, in itself, in a population numbering in the tens of millions, is not difficult to find. Accordingly, particularly with unexperienced girls, one supposes that criteria other than beauty and charm, and poise, often determine one's initial chances in such a competitive field. It was so in my case. I believe, of course, that I could have been successful on my own as well. But I did not need to be.

I rather enjoyed my career as a model, though it did not last more than a few weeks. I enjoy clothes, and wear them beautifully. I enjoy posing, though sometimes it is painful and wearying. The photographers and artists seemed intelligent, witty men, though sometimes abrupt. They were very professional. One of them once called me a bitch. I laughed. My assignments were frequent.

My most lucrative assignment was to be to model several pieces in a new line of swimwear being brought out by a rather well-known company, the name of which is, however, unimportant for purposes of this narrative.

I did not do so.

It was on a Monday afternoon that I received the assignment, and I was to report to the designated studio on Wednesday morning. I had no assignment for Tuesday. The evening before I had dismissed my colored maid and cook until Wednesday. I wanted the house to myself, to be alone, to read and play records.

I slept late Tuesday morning.

I was awakened by the sun streaming through the curtains. I stretched. It was a warm, lazy, lazy day. It was near noon. I sleep nude, between white satin sheets. I reached over to the ash tray on the night table near the bed and lit a cigarette. There was nothing unusual about the room. A stuffed toy, a fluffy koala bear, lay near the foot of the bed. The books lay on their tables. The lamp shade was tilted slightly as I remembered from the night before. The alarm clock, which I had not set, lay on the vanity. The cigarette did not taste well, but I had wanted it. I lay again on top of the sheets and stretched again, then swung my legs over the side of the bed and into my slippers. I pulled on a silken peignoir. I jammed the cigarette down into the ash tray and went to the bathroom to shower

I tied my hair up and slipped off the peignoir and slid back the door of the shower, and stepped inside. Soon I was luxuriating in the warm water of the shower. It was a good day, a warm, lazy, lazy day. I stood there for some minutes, head back, eyes closed, letting the warm water run over my body. Then I picked up the soap and began to soap my body.

As my fingers applied the soap to my left thigh, I was

suddenly startled. There was something there, that I had
never before touched.

I leaned to my left side, my left leg extended and straight.

Suddenly things went almost black. I could not catch my
breath. I looked in horror.

I had felt no pain.

But it had not been there the night before!

There was now a mark on my thigh. It was high on the
thigh. The mark itself was about an inch and a half high.
It was a graceful, cursive mark. In its way lovely. I knew
it could not have been the result of a natural wound. It
was in its way perfect, rather deep and clean. It was a deliberately, and precisely inflicted mark.

I gasped for breath, and felt for the wall to steady myself. Numbly, I washed the soap from my body and turned
off the shower. I left the bathroom, still wet, and walked
barefoot over the rug to stand before the full-length mirror
at one side of the room. There, again I gasped, and again
the room seemed to reel about me. On the mirror, which
I had not noticed before, there was another mark. It had
been drawn in my most scarlet lipstick on the surface of the
mirror. It was more than a foot high, but it was the same
mark that I wore on my thigh, that same graceful, cursive
mark.

Disbelievingly, I looked at myself in the mirror. I touched
again the mark on my thigh. I looked again at the red mark
drawn in lipstick on the surface of the mirror. I beheld
myself.

I knew almost nothing of these things, but there was no
mistaking the lovely, deep, incised mark on my thigh.

Everything went black, and I collapsed to the rug before
the mirror. I fainted.

I had been branded.

2 THE COLLAR

I DO NOT KNOW how long I lay on the thick rug before the mirror.

It was perhaps better than an hour, judging from the position of the sun coming through the curtains.

I rose to my hands and knees on the rug and looked at myself in the mirror.

I screamed.

I was going mad!

I threw my hands to my head, and shook my head.

I locked my fingers in the band at my throat, trying to tear it from my neck. It had been placed on me while I was unconscious!

About my throat, snugly, there was a graceful, gleaming band of steel.

Gathering my wits I simply reached behind my neck to release the catch, and remove it. My fingers fumbled. I could not find the release. I turned it slowly, carefully, because it fitted rather closely. I examined it in the mirror. There was no release, no catch. Only a small, heavy lock, and a place where a tiny key might fit. It had been locked on my throat! There was printing on the band, but I could not read it. It was not in a script I knew!

Once again the room seemed to go dark, and swirl, but I fought desperately to retain consciousness.

Someone had been in the room to place the band on my neck. He might still be here.

With my head down, hair falling to the rug, on my hands and knees, I shook my head. I tore at the pile on the rug. I would not lose consciousness. I must keep my wits.

I looked about the room.

My heart nearly stopped. It was empty.

I crawled to the telephone on the night table by the bed. I lifted it with great care, that not the slightest sound be made. There was no dial tone. The cord hung freely. Tears stung at my eyes.

There was another phone in the living room, but it was on the other side of the door. I was afraid to open the door. I glanced toward the bathroom. That room, too, frightened me. I did not know what might be within it.

I had a small revolver. I had never fired it. I thought of it only now. I leaped to my feet and darted to the large triple chest at the side of the room. I plunged my hand beneath the scarves and slips in the drawer and felt the handle. I cried out with joy. I looked at the weapon, disbelievingly. I could not even sob, or moan. I simply could not understand what had happened. Most of the weapon was a shapeless lump of metal. It was almost as if it were a piece of melted, steel chocolate. I dropped it back onto the silk. I stood up, numb, and looked at myself in the mirror. I was defenseless. But my terror was not a simple terror.

I sensed that more had occurred to me than could be accounted for simply in the terms of the world I knew. I was afraid.

I ran to the floor-length curtains before the huge window of my bedroom and flung them open.

I looked out on the city.

It hung dark with the gases of pollution, made golden in the sunlight. I could see thousands of windows, some with the sun reflecting from them, in the unreal golden haze. I could see the great walls of brick, and steel and concrete and glass.

It was my world.

I stood there for a moment, the sun streaming in upon me through the thick, dirty glass.

It was my world!

But I stood behind the glass nude, on my throat a band of steel, which I could not remove. On my thigh there was a mark.

"No!" I cried to myself. "No!"

I turned away from the window and, stealthily, made my way to the door to the living room, which was slightly ajar. I summoned all my courage, and opened the door slightly more. I almost fainted with relief. The room was empty. Everything was as I had left it.

I ran to the kitchen, which I could see from the living room, and threw open a drawer. I took out a butcher knife. I turned wildly, my back to the counter, holding the knife, but there was nothing.

With the knife in my hand I felt more secure. I returned to the living room, and the phone on the end table. I cursed as I saw that the cord had been severed.

I examined the penthouse. The doors were locked. The house was empty, and the patio on the terrace.

My heart was beating wildly. But I was elated. I ran to the wardrobe to dress, to leave the house and summon the police.

Just as I reached the wardrobe there was a heavy, firm knocking on the door.

I turned, grasping the knife.

The knocking was repeated, more insistently.

"Open the door," commanded a voice. "This is the police."

I almost fainted with relief. I ran toward the door, still holding the knife.

At the door I stopped, clutching the knife, terrified.

I had not called the police. In the penthouse it was not likely anyone had heard me scream. I had not tried to signal anyone when I had found the phones had been destroyed. I had only wanted to escape.

Whoever was on the other side of that door could not be the police.

The knocking was repeated again.

My head swam.

Then the knocking became even louder. "Open the door!" I heard. "Open the door. This is the police!"

I controlled myself. "Just a moment," I called, as calmly as I could. "I'll open the door in a moment. I'm dressing."

The knocking stopped.

"All right," said a voice. "Hurry."

"Yes," I called sweetly, sweating. "Just a moment!"

I ran into the bedroom and looked wildly about. I seized some sheets from a linen closet, feverishly knotting them together. I ran to the terrace. I felt sick, looking over the ledge. But some fifteen feet below me was a small terrace, one of hundreds projecting from the sides of the building. It opened into the apartment below me. In the sun, the air stinging my eyes, particles of soot and ash falling on me, I knotted one end of the rope of sheets securely about a small iron railing that surmounted a waist-high wall around the patio and terrace. The other end fell well down to the small terrace below. Had I not been terrified I would never have had the courage to do what I intended.

The knocking had now begun again on the door. I could sense the impatience in the sound.

I ran back into the bedroom to seize something to wear but as I entered the room I heard a man's shoulder strike at the heavy door.

I had seen on the patio that I could not carry the knife down the rope of sheets with me, for I would have to use both hands. Perhaps I should have held it between my teeth but, in my panic, I did not think of it. I was in the bedroom when I heard the door begin to splinter in, away from the hinges and the lock. Wildly I thrust the knife beneath the pillow on my bed and ran back to the patio. Not looking down, terrified, I seized the rope of sheets and, scarcely breathing, sick to my stomach, hand over hand, began to lower myself. I had disappeared over the ledge when I heard the door splinter fully away and heard men enter the apartment. As soon as I reached the terrace below, only a few feet away, I would be safe. I could attract the attention of the individuals in the apartment below or, if necessary, with a chair, or implement, or whatever might be found, break through the glass to their apartment.

Above me, from within the penthouse, I heard an angry cry.

I could hear noises from the street, far below. I did not dare look down.

Then my feet touched the tiles of the terrace below.

I was safe!

Something soft, folded and white slipped over my head, before my eyes. It was shoved deeply into my mouth. Another folded piece of cloth passed over my head. It was knotted tightly behind the back of my neck.

I tried to cry out but could not do so.

"We have her," I heard a voice say.

3   SILKEN CORDS

I STIRRED UNEASILY, shaking my head. It was a bad dream. "No, no," I murmured, twisting, wanting to awaken. "No, no."

It seemed as though I could not move as I wished. I did not like it. I was displeased. Angry.

Then, suddenly, I was awake. I screamed, but there was no sound.

I tried to sit upright, but I nearly strangled, and fell back. I struggled wildly.

"She's awake," said a voice.

Two men, masked, stood at the foot of the bed, facing me. I heard two others speaking in the living room.

The two men who had been at the foot of the bed turned and left the room, going to the living room to join the others.

I struggled fiercely.

My ankles had been bound together with light, silken cords. My wrists had also been bound together, but behind my back. A loop of the silken cord had been fastened about my neck, and by it I was bound to the head of the bed.

I could see myself in the mirror. The strange mark, drawn in lipstick, was still on the mirror's surface.

I tried to scream again, but could not. My eyes, I could see in the mirror, were wild over the gag.

I continued to struggle, but after some moments, hearing men returning to the room, stopped. Through the open door, I saw the backs of two men, in police uniforms. I could not see their faces. The two men with masks re-entered the room.

12

They looked upon me.

I wanted to plead with them, but I could make no sound.

I drew up my legs and turned on my side, to cover myself as well as I might.

One of the men touched me.

The other uttered a brief sound, abrupt. The other man turned away. The sound had been a word, doubtless of negation. I did not know the language.

The men had not ransacked the penthouse. The paintings remained on the walls, the oriental rugs on the floors. Nothing was touched.

I saw the man who had turned away, who seemed to be a subordinate, remove what appeared to be a fountain pen from a leather holder in his pocket. He unscrewed it, and I was startled. It was a syringe.

I shook my head wildly, no!

He entered the needle on my right side, in the back between my waist and hip.

It was painful. I felt no ill effects.

I watched him replace the syringe in its holder, and the holder in his inside jacket pocket.

The larger man looked at his watch. He spoke this time in English to the smaller man, he who had had the syringe. The larger man spoke with a definite accent, but I could not place the accent.

"We will return after midnight," he said. "It will be easier then. We can reach point *P* in five hours with less traffic. And I have other business to attend to this evening."

"All right," said the smaller man. "We'll be ready then." There had not been the slightest trace of an accent in the smaller man's response. I had no doubt that his native tongue was English. He perhaps had difficulty following the natural speech of the other. But when the other had spoken to him, curtly, in the strange tongue, he had obeyed, and promptly. I gathered he feared the larger man.

The room began to grow a bit dark at the edges.

The larger man came behind me and felt the pulse of one of my bound wrists.

Then he released me.

The room seemed to grow darker, and warmer. I tried to keep my eyes open.

The larger man left the room. The smaller lingered. He went to the night table and took one of my cigarettes and, with one of my tiny, fine matches, imported from Paris, lit it.

He threw the match into the ash tray. He touched me again, this time intimately, but I could not cry out. I began to lose consciousness. He blew smoke into my eyes and nose, leaning over me. I struggled weakly against the bonds, fighting to stay conscious.

I heard the larger man's voice, from the doorway it seems, but it seemed, too, from far away.

The smaller man hurriedly left my side.

The larger man entered the room, and I turned my head weakly to regard him. I saw the two men in the uniforms of police leaving the penthouse, followed by the smaller man, who, as he left the house, was drawing the mask from his head. I did not see his face.

The larger man was looking down at me. I looked up at him, weakly, almost unconscious.

He spoke to me matter-of-factly. "We will return after midnight," he told me.

I struggled weakly to speak, fighting the gag, the drug. I wanted only to sleep.

"You would like to know," he asked, "what will happen to you then?"

I nodded.

"Curiosity," he said, "is not becoming in a Kajira."

I did not understand him.

"You might be beaten for it," he said.

I could not understand.

"Let us say simply," he said, "that we will return after midnight." Through the mouth hole in the mask I saw his lips twist into a smile. His eyes, too, seemed to smile. "Then," he said, "you will be drugged again." "And then," he added, "you will be crated for shipment."

He left the room.

I pulled at the cords that bound me, and lost consciousness.

I awakened in the bed, still bound.

It was dark. I could hear the noises of the city's night traffic through the door open to the patio and terrace. Through the open curtains I could see the tens of thousands of bright rectangles of windows, many of them still illuminated. The bed was drenched in sweat. I had no idea of the time. I knew only it was night. I rolled over to see the alarm clock on the vanity, but the face had been turned to one side.

I struggled with my bonds, wildly. I must free myself!

But after a few precious minutes of futile struggle I lay bound as perfectly as I had been earlier in the afternoon.

Then suddenly new sweat broke out on my body.

The knife!

Before the men had burst into the penthouse I had thrust it beneath the pillow.

I rolled on to my side and, bound, lifted the pillow away with my teeth. I almost fainted with relief. The knife lay where I had left it. On the satin sheet I struggled to move the knife, with my mouth and the back of my head, toward my bound hands. It was a painful, frustrating task, but inch by quarter inch, I moved it downward. Once it fell to the floor and inwardly I cried out with anguish. Almost choking, from the loop on my throat, I slid half out of the bed and felt for the knife with my feet. My ankles had been crossed and lashed securely together. It was extremely difficult to pick up the knife. It fell again, and again. I cursed the neckrope that bound me to the head of the bed. I wept. Far below, in the streets, I heard the siren of a fire engine, and the other noises of the city night. I struggled, gagged and bound, silently, torturedly. At last I managed to get the knife to the foot of the bed. With my feet and body I managed to pull it up beneath me. And then I had the handle in my bound hands! But I could not reach the bonds. I held the knife but could not use it. Then, feverishly, I cried in-

wardly with joy, and pressed the point into the back of the
bed and braced it with my own body. I began to saw at the
cords with the knife. The knife, its handle braced against
my sweating back, slipped four times, but each time I put it
again in place and addressed myself again to my task. Then
my wrists were free. I took the knife and slashed the cord
at my throat and the cords at my ankles.

I leaped from the bed and ran to the vanity. My heart
sank. It was already a half past midnight!

My heart was pounding.

I pulled the gag down from my face, pulled the heavy
wad of soured packing from my mouth. Then I was suddenly ill, and fell to my hands and knees, and vomited on
the rug. I shook my head. With the knife I cut the gag from
where it lay about my neck.

I shook my head again.

It was now thirty-five minutes after midnight.

I ran to the wardrobe. I seized the first garments I
touched, a pair of tan, bell-bottomed slacks and a black,
buttoning, bare-midriff blouse.

I held them to me, breathing heavily. I looked across the
room. My heart almost stopped. There I saw in the shadows,
in the dim light in the room from the city outside, a girl.
She was nude. She held something before her. About her
throat there was a band of steel. On her thigh a mark.

"No!" we cried together.

I gasped, my head swam. Sick, I turned away from my
reflection in the full-length mirror across the room.

I pulled on the slacks and slipped into the blouse. I found
a pair of sandals.

It was thirty-seven minutes past midnight.

I ran again to the wardrobe and pulled out a small suitcase. I threw it to the foot of the triple chest and plunged
garments into it, and snapped it shut.

I seized up a handbag and ran, with the suitcase, into
the living room. I swung back a small oil, and fumbled with
the dial of the wall safe. I kept, usually, some fifteen thousand dollars, and jewelry, at home. I scrabbled in the opening and thrust the money and jewelry into the handbag.

I looked with terror at the splintered door.

On the wall clock it was forty minutes past midnight. I was afraid to go through the door. I remembered the knife. I ran back to the bedroom and seized it, shoving it into the handbag. Then, frightened, I ran to the patio and terrace. The rope of sheets that I had used to leave the penthouse had been removed. I ran again to the bedroom. I saw them lying to one side, separated, as though laundry.

I looked again in the mirror. I stopped. I buttoned the collar of the black blouse high about my neck, to conceal the steel band on my throat. I saw again the mark, drawn in lipstick, on the mirror. Seizing up my handbag and the small suitcase I fled through the broken door. I stopped before the tiny private elevator in the hall outside the door.

I ran back inside the penthouse, to get my wrist watch. It was forty-two minutes past midnight. With the key from my purse I opened the elevator and descended to the hall below, where there was a bank of common elevators. I pushed all the down buttons.

I looked at the dials at the top of the elevator doors. There were two that were already rising, one at the seventh floor and one at the ninth. I could not have called them!

I moaned.

I turned and ran toward the stairs. I stopped at the height of the stairs. Far below, on the steel-reinforced, broad cement stairs, ringing hollowly in the shaft, I heard the footsteps of two men, climbing.

I ran back to the elevators.

One stopped at my floor, the twenty-fourth. I stood with my back pressed against the wall.

A man and his wife stepped out.

I gasped, and fled past them.

They looked at me strangely as I pushed at the main-floor button.

As the door on my elevator slowly closed, I heard the door of the adjoining elevator open. Through the crack of the closing door I saw the backs of two men, in the uniforms of police.

Slowly, slowly the elevator descended. It stopped on four

floors. I stood in the back of the elevator, while three cou-
ples and another man, with an attaché case, entered. When
we reached the main floor I fled from the elevator but, in a
moment, regained my control, checked myself and looked
about. There were some people in the lobby, sitting about,
reading or waiting. Some looked at me idly. It was a hot
night. One man, with a pipe, looked up at me, over the top
of his newspaper. Was he one of them? My heart almost
stopped. He returned to his reading. I would go to the
apartment garage, but not through the lobby. I would go
by the street.

The doorman touched his cap to me as I left.

I smiled.

Outside on the street I realized how hot the night was.

Inadvertently I touched the collar of my blouse. I felt
the steel beneath it.

A man passed, looking at me.

Did he know? Could he know that there was a band of
steel on my throat?

I was foolish. I shook my head, trembling.

I threw my head back and walked hurriedly down the
sidewalk toward the street entrance to the apartmer' garage.

The night was hot, so hot.

A man looked me over thoroughly as I walked past. I
hurried past.

A few feet beyond I turned to look back. He was still
watching.

I tried to turn him away, with a look of coldness, of contempt for him.

But he did not look away. I was frightened. I turned
away, hurrying on. Why had I not been able to turn him
away? Why hadn't he looked away? Why hadn't he turned
away, shamefaced, embarrassed, and hurried on in the opposite direction? He hadn't. He had continued to look at me.
Did he know that there was a mark on my thigh? Did he
sense that? Did that mark make me somehow subtly different than I had been? Did it, somehow, set me apart from
other women on this world? Could I no longer drive men
away? And if I could no longer drive them away, what did

that mean? What had that small mark done to me? I felt suddenly helpless, and somehow, suddenly, for the first time in my life, vulnerably and radically female. I stumbled on.

I entered the apartment garage.

I found the car keys in my handbag and gave them hurriedly, smiling, to the attendant.

"Is anything wrong, Miss Brinton?" he asked.

"No, no," I said.

Even he seemed to look at me.

"Please hurry!" I begged him.

He quickly touched his cap and turned away.

I waited, it seemed for years. I counted the beatings of my heart.

Then the car, small, purring, in perfect tune, a customized Maserati, whipped to the curb, and the attendant stepped out.

I thrust a bill in his hand.

"Thank you," he said.

He seemed concerned, deferential. He touched his cap. He held open the door.

I blushed, and thrust past him, throwing my suitcase and handbag into the car.

I climbed behind the wheel, and he closed the door.

He leaned over me. "Are you well, Miss Brinton?" he asked.

He seemed too close to me.

"Yes! Yes!" I said and threw the car into gear and burned forward, only to stop with a shriek of rubber, skidding some ten feet.

With the electric switch he raised the door for me, and I drove out into the swift traffic, out into the hot August night.

Even though the night was hot the air rushing past me, pulling at my hair, refreshed me.

I had done well.

I had escaped!

I drove past a policeman and was almost going to stop, that he might help me, protect me.

But how did I know? Others had worn the uniforms of the police? And he might think I was insane, mad. And I might be detained in the city. Where they were. They might be waiting for me. I did not know who they were. I was not even clear what they wanted. They could be anywhere. Now I must escape, escape, escape!

But the air invigorated me. I had escaped! I darted about in traffic, swiftly, free. Other cars would sometimes slam on their brakes. They would honk their horns. I threw back my head and laughed.

I had soon left the city, crossing the George Washington Bridge, and taking the swift parkways north. In a few minutes I was in Connecticut.

I slipped my wrist watch on my hand, as I drove. When I did so it was one forty-six A.M.

I sang to myself.

Once again I was Elinor Brinton.

It occurred to me that I should not follow the parkways, but seek less traveled roads. I left the parkway at 2:07 A.M. Another car followed me. I thought little of it, but, after some four turns, the car still followed.

Suddenly I became frightened and increased speed. So, too, did the other car.

Then, as I cried out in anguish, I was no longer Elinor Brinton, the one always in control of herself, the rich one, the sophisticated one, she with such exquisite taste and intelligence. I was only a terrified girl, fleeing from what she knew not, a bewildered, confused girl, a terrified girl, one with a mark on her left thigh, a circle of steel locked snugly on her throat.

No, I cried to myself, no. I would be Elinor Brinton! I am she!

Suddenly I began to drive cooly, swiftly, efficiently, brilliantly. If they wanted a chase, they should have it. They would not find Elinor Brinton easy game! Whoever they might be, she was more than a match for them. She was Elinor Brinton, rich, brilliant Elinor Brinton!

For more than forty-five minutes I raced ahead of my pursuer, sometimes increasing my lead, sometimes losing it. Once, grinding and spurring about graveled side roads, they were within forty yards of me, but I increased the lead, yard by yard.

I thrilled to their pursuit, and would elude them!

Finally, when I was more than two hundred yards ahead of them, on a cruelly winding road, I switched off my head-lights and drove off the road into some trees. There were many turn-offs on the road, many bends. They would assume I had taken one.

I sat, heart pounding in the Maserati, with the lights off.

In a matter of seconds the following car raced past, skidding about a curve.

I waited for about thirty seconds and then drove back to the road. I drove lights off for several minutes, following the double yellow line in the center of the road by the moon-light. Then, when I came to a more traveled highway, a cemented road, well trafficked, I switched on my lights and continued on my way.

I had outsmarted them.

I continued generally northward. I assumed they would suppose that I had backtracked, and was returning south-ward. They would not suppose I would continue my journey in the same direction. They would suppose me too intelligent for that. But I was far more intelligent than they, for that was precisely what I would do!

It was now about four ten in the morning. I pulled into a small motel, a set of bungalows, set back from the road. I parked the car behind one of the bungalows, where it could not be seen from the road. No one would expect me to stop at this time. Near the bungalows, north on the highway, there was a diner, which was open. It was almost empty. The red neon lights of the diner loomed in the hot, dark night. I was famished. I had eaten nothing all day. I en-tered the diner, and sat in one of the booths, where I could not be seen from the highway.

"Sit at the counter," said the boy at the diner. He was alone.

"Menu," I told him.

I had two sandwiches, from cold roast beef, on dry

bread, a piece of pie left from the afternoon, and a small carton of chocolate milk.

At another time I might have been disgusted, but tonight I was elated.

Soon I had rented a bungalow for the night, the one behind which I had parked the Maserati.

I put my belongings in the bungalow and locked the door. I was tired, but I sang to myself. I was exceedingly well pleased with how well I had done. The bed looked inviting but I was sweaty, filthy, and I was naturally too fastidious to retire without showering. Besides I wanted to wash.

In the bathroom I examined the mark on my thigh. It infuriated me. But, as I regarded it, in fury, I could not help but be taken by its cursive, graceful insolence. I clenched my fists. The arrogance, that it had been placed on my body! The arrogance, the arrogance! It marked me. But beautifully. I regarded myself in the mirror. I regarded the mark. There was no doubt about it. That mark, somehow, insolently, incredibly enhanced my beauty. I was furious.

Also, incomprehensibly I found that I was curious about the touch of a man. I had never much cared for men. I put the thought angrily from me. I was Elinor Brinton!

Irritably I examined the steel band at my throat. I could not read the inscription on the band, of course. I could not even recognize the alphabet. Indeed, perhaps it was only a cursive design. But something in the spacing and the formation of the figures told me it was not. The lock was small, but heavy. The band fit snugly.

As I looked in the mirror the thought passed through my mind that it, too, like the mark, was not unattractive. It accentuated my softness. And I could not remove it. For an instant I felt helpless, owned, a captive, the property of others. The brief fantasy passed through my mind of myself, in such a band, marked as I was, naked in the arms of a barbarian. I shuddered, frightened. Never before had I felt such a feeling.

I looked away from the mirror.

Tomorrow I would have the steel band removed.

I stepped into the shower and was soon singing.

I had wrapped a towel about my hair, and, dried and re-freshed, though tired, and very happy, emerged from the bathroom.

I turned down the sheets on the bed.

I was safe.

My wrist watch, when I had prepared to shower, I had slipped into my handbag. I looked at it. It was four forty-five. I replaced the watch in the handbag.

I reached to pull the tiny chain on the lamp.

I then saw it. On the mirror across the room. At the base of the mirror lay an opened lipstick tube, mine, which had been taken from my handbag, while I had showered. On the mirror itself, drawn in lipstick, was again the mark, the same mark, cursive and graceful, which I wore on my thigh.

I tore at the phone. It was dead.

The door to the bungalow was unlatched. I had locked it. But the lock had been opened, and even the bolt with-drawn. I ran to the door and relocked it, holding myself against it. I began to sob.

Hysterically I ran to my clothes and dressed.

I might have time. They might have gone away. They might be waiting just outside. I did not know.

I fumbled in the handbag for the car keys.

I ran to the door.

Then, terrified, I feared to touch it. They might be wait-ing just outside.

I moved to the back of the bungalow. I switched off the light, and stood, terrified, in the darkness. I pulled back the curtains on the rear window of the bungalow. The win-dow was locked. I unlocked it. Noiselessly, to my relief, the window slid upward. I looked outward. No one was in sight. I had time. But they might be in front. Or perhaps they had gone, not expecting me to see the mark on the mirror until morning. No, no, they must be in front.

I crawled out of the window.

The small suitcase I left in the bungalow. I had the hand-bag, that was important. In it were fifteen thousand dollars and jewelry. Most important, I had the car keys.

Quietly I climbed into the car. I must turn on the ignition, put the car in gear and accelerate before anyone could stop me. The engine was still warm. It would start immediately.

Snarling and spurting the Maserati leaped into life, spitting stones and dust from its rear wheels, whipping about the corner of the bungalow.

I slammed on the brakes at the entrance to the highway and skidded onto the cement turning, and then with a scream of rubber, and the burning smell of it, roared down the highway. I had seen nothing. I switched on the car lights. Some traffic passed me, approaching me.

Nothing seemed to be behind me.

I could not believe that I was safe. But there was no pursuit.

With one hand I fumbled with the buttons on my black, bare-midriff blouse, fastening them. I then found the wrist watch in the handbag and slipped it on my wrist. It was four fifty-one. It was still dark, but it was August and it would be light early.

Abruptly, on an impulse, I turned down a small side road, one of dozens that led from the highway.

There would be no way of knowing which one I had taken.

I had seen no pursuit.

I began to breathe easier.

My foot eased up on the accelerator.

I glanced into the rear-view mirror. I turned to look. It did not seem to be a car, but there was something, unmistakably, on the road behind me.

For an instant I could not swallow. My mouth felt dry. With difficulty I swallowed.

It was several hundred yards behind me, moving rather slowly. It seemed to have a single light. But the light seemed to light the road beneath it, in a yellow, moving pool of illumination that coursed ahead of it. As it neared, I cried out. It was moving silently. There was no sound of a motor or drive. It was round, black, circular, small, perhaps seven or eight feet in diameter, perhaps five feet in thickness. It was not moving on the road. It was moving above the road.

I switched off the lights on the Maserati and whipped

off the road, moving toward some patches of trees in the distance.

The object came to where I had turned off the road, seemed to pause, and then, to my horror, turned gently in my direction, unhurried. In the yellow circle of light I could see the grass of the field, bearing the marks of my tires.

Hysterically I drove across the fields, twisting and turning, accelerating. I would get stuck, and would burn my way free.

Always the object, smoothly, not seeming to hurry, with the yellow light beneath it, approached more closely.

The Maserati struck a large stone. The engine stopped. Wildly I tried to start it again. There was a whine, then another. And then the ignition key only clicked meaninglessly, again and again. Suddenly I was bathed in yellow light and I screamed. It hovered over me. I fled from the car, into the darkness.

The light moved about, but it did not catch me again.

I reached the trees.

In the trees, terrified, I saw the dark disklike shape hover over the Maserati.

A bluish light then seemed, momentarily, to glow from the shape.

The Maserati seemed to shiver, rippling in the bluish light, and then, to my horror, it was gone.

I stood with my back against a tree, my hand before my mouth.

The bluish light then disappeared.

The yellowish light switched on again.

The shape then turned toward me, and began to move slowly in my direction.

I found that I clutched the handbag. Somehow I had seized it, instinctively, in running from the car. It contained my money, jewelry, the butcher knife I had thrust into it before leaving the penthouse. I turned and ran, wildly, through the dark woods. I lost my sandals. My feet were bruised and cut. My blouse was torn. Branches caught at my clothing and hair. A branch lashed my belly and I cried out in pain. Another stung my cheek. I fled. Always the light seemed

near, but it did not catch me. I ran from it, forcing my
way through the brush and trees, scraped and torn. Time
and time again it seemed on the verge of illuminating me,
yellow on the trees and brush only feet from me, but it
would pass by, or I would turn away from it and run again.
I stumbled on through the woods, my feet bleeding, gasping for breath. My hands, my right clutching the handbag,
fought the brush and branches that tore at me. I could run
no further. I collapsed at the foot of a tree, gasping, each
muscle in my body crying out. My legs trembled. My heart
pounded.

The light turned my way again.

I scrambled to my feet and ran wildly before it.

Then I saw some small lights beyond the trees and brush
some fifty yards in front of me, in a sort of clearing in
the woods.

I ran toward them.

I stumbled wildly into the clearing.

"Good evening, Miss Brinton," said a voice.

I stopped, stunned.

At the same time I felt a man's hands close on my arms
from behind.

I tried weakly to free myself but could not.

I shut my eyes against the reflection of yellow light from
the ground.

"This is point P," said the man. I now recognized his
voice. It was that of the larger man who had been in my
penthouse in the afternoon. He no longer wore his mask. He
was dark haired, dark eyed, handsome. "You have been very
troublesome," he said. Then he turned to another man. "Bring
Miss Brinton's anklet."

4   THE SLAVE CAPSULE

THE MAN HOLDING ME guided me from where I stood to a place at one side of the clearing. The other man accompanied him, and some others.

The yellow light flashed off, and the dark, disklike shape settled gently to the grass of the clearing.

It was still dark, but could not be long before morning.

In one of the lights I saw a hatch in the top of the disk open. A man crawled out. He wore a black tunic. The other men were dressed conventionally, those I saw then in the clearing.

Some further lights then, gradually, increased in intensity. I gasped.

In the center of the clearing there was a large, dark shape, much larger than the small one, but not particularly different in design or appearance. It might have been thirty feet in diameter, perhaps some seven or eight feet in thickness. It rested on the grass. It was made of black metal. There were various ports in it, and hatch apertures. A large door, in the side facing me, had been opened. It opened in such a way as to touch the ground and formed a sort of ramp, by means of which the ship could be loaded.

"Who are you? What is this?" I had whispered.

"You may release her," said the man to he who held me. He did so.

I stood among them.

I could now see there was a truck at another side of the clearing. Boxes of various sizes were being removed from it and being placed in the ship.

"Did you like your collar?" asked the man, pleasantly.

Inadvertently my fingers went to my throat.

He stepped behind me and tore open the top button of the black, bare-midriff blouse. I felt a small key being inserted into the small, heavy lock. The collar sprang open.

"You will doubtless have another," he said. He handed the collar to another man, who took it away.

He regarded me.

I still clutched the handbag.

"Let me go," I whispered. "I have money. Here. And jewelry. And much more. It's yours. Please."

I fumbled in the handbag and thrust the bills and the jewelry into his hands.

He handed the bills and jewelry to another man. He did not want them.

The men now began to bring, not gently, certain large square boxes from the truck, which they placed near the large, open hatch on the ship.

I clutched the handbag in my right hand, half-opened. Sick.

The large man took my left hand and removed the wrist watch from it.

"You will not need this," he said. He handed the watch to another man.

The time was five forty-two.

The men unloading the truck began to unsnap the sides of the large wooden boxes placed near the open hatch on the ship.

I watched with horror.

Inside each, secured with heavy straps and buckles, attached to rings in the box, was a girl. Each was unclothed. Each was unconscious. Each was gagged. Each wore a collar.

The men freed the girls, removing from them the gags and collars, and fastening on the left ankle of each what appeared to be a steel band.

They were then carried, unconscious, into the ship.

I screamed and turned to run. A man clutched at me. My hand tore the butcher knife from my handbag and I slashed wildly at him. He cried out with pain, holding his cut, bloody sleeve. I stumbled and got up to run. But they

were all about me, encircling me. I raised the knife to strike
at them, wildly. Then it seemed my whole hand and wrist
and arm was struck with some fantastic, numbing shock. The
knife fell from my fingers. My arm slowly fell, painfully. I
could not move my fingers. I sobbed with the pain. One of the
men picked up the knife. Another took me by the arm
and dragged me back before the large man. I was hunched
over, and looked up at him, sobbing, tears in my eyes.

The large man replaced a small implement in his jacket
pocket. It resembled a pocket flashlight. But the beam that had
struck me I had not seen.

"The pain will not last long," the man informed me.

"Please," I begged him. "Please."

"You were superb," he said.

I looked at him, numbly.

The man whom I had slashed with the knife stood behind
him, holding his arm, grinning.

"Have your arm attended to," said the large man. The
other grinned again and turned away, going toward the truck.

One of the men from the dark, disklike shape, the smaller
one, which had followed me, approached. "There is little
time," he said.

The large man nodded. But he did not seem perturbed,
nor hurried.

He looked at me, carefully. "Stand straight," he said, not
ungently.

I tried to stand straight. My arm still felt paralyzed from
the shock. I could not move my fingers.

He touched the bloodied cut on my belly, where the
branch had struck me. Then, with his hand, he lifted my
head, turning it, looking at the cut on my cheek.

"We are not pleased," he said.

I said nothing.

"Bring salve," he said.

An ointment was brought, and he smeared it across the
two cuts. It was odorless. To my surprise it seemed to be
absorbed almost immediately.

"You must be more careful," he said.

Again I said nothing.

"You might have marked yourself," he said, "or might have been blinded." He returned the ointment to another man. "They are superficial," he told me, "and will heal without trace."

"Let me go!" I cried. "Please! Please!"

"There is little time, little time!" urged the man in the black tunic.

"Bring her handbag," said the large man, calmly. It was brought to him, from where it had fallen when I had tried to escape.

He looked at me.

"Perhaps you are interested in knowing how you were followed?" he asked.

I nodded, numbly.

From the handbag he extracted an object.

"What is this?" he asked.

"My compact," I told him.

He smiled, and turned it over. He unscrewed the bottom. Inside there was a tiny cylinder, fused to a round, circular plate, covered with tiny, copperish lines. "This device," he said, "transmits a signal, which can be picked up by our equipment at a distance of one hundred miles." He smiled. "A similar such device," he said, "was concealed beneath your automobile."

I sobbed.

"It will be dawn in six Ehn," said the man in the tunic.

I could see that there was a lightness in the east.

I did not understand what he said.

The large man nodded at the man in the black tunic. The man in the black tunic then lifted his arm. The small disklike ship then slowly lifted and moved toward the large ship. A port in the large ship slid upward. The small ship moved inside. I could briefly see men, in black tunics, inside, fastening it to plates in a steel flooring. Then the port slid shut again. The remains of the boxes had now been replaced in the truck. Here and there, about the clearing, men were moving about, gathering up equipment. They placed these things in the truck.

I could now move my arm and, barely, the fingers of my hand.

"But your ship," I said, "the small one, could not seem to find me."

"It found you," he said.

"The light," I said, "it couldn't catch me."

"You think it was misfortune that you stumbled into our camp?" he asked.

I nodded, miserably.

He laughed.

I looked at him, with horror.

"The light," he said. "You ran always to avoid it."

I moaned.

"You were herded here," he said.

I cried out with misery.

He turned to a subordinate. "Have you brought Miss Brinton's anklet?"

The subordinate then handed him an anklet. I could see that it was steel. It was open. It had a hinged catch.

Then I stood before them as I had, in the tan slacks, in the black, bare-midriff blouse, save that I now wore a steel anklet.

"Observe," said the large man, indicating the black ship. As I watched it, it seemed that lights began to flicker on its surface, and then it seemed that tendrils of light began to interweave across its steel, and, before my eyes, it began to change in color, turning a grayish blue, streaked with white.

I could now see the first streak of light in the east.

"This is a technique of field-light camouflage," said the large man. "It is primitive. The radar-screening device, within, is more sophisticated. But the light camouflage technique has considerably reduced sightings of our craft. Further, of course, we do little more, normally, with the large craft than arrive and depart, at given points. The smaller craft is used more extensively, but normally only at night, and in isolated areas. It, too, incidentally, is equipped for light-camouflage and radar-screening."

I understood very little of what he said.

"Shall we strip her?" asked one of the subordinates.

"No," said the large man.

The large man stepped behind me. "Shall we go to the ship?" he asked.

I did not move.

I turned to face him.

"Hurry!" called the man in the black tunic, from within the large ship. "Dawn in two Ehn!"

"Who are you? What do you want?" I begged.

"Curiosity," he said, "is not becoming in a Kajira."

I stared at him.

"You might be beaten for it," he said.

"Hurry! Hurry!" cried the man in the black tunic. "We must make rendezvous!"

"Please," invited the large man, gesturing to the ship with one hand.

Numbly I turned and preceded him to the ship. At the foot of the ramp I trembled.

"Hurry, Kajira," said he, gently.

I ascended the steel ramp. I turned. He was standing back on the grass.

"In your time," he said, "dawn occurs at this meridian and latitude, on this day, at six sixteen."

I saw the sun's rim at the edge of my world, rising, touching it. In the east there was dawn. It was the first dawn I had ever seen. It was not that I had not stayed up all night, even many times. It was only that I had never watched a sunrise.

"Farewell, Kajira," said the man.

I cried out and extended my arms. The steel ramp swung upward and locked in place, shutting me in the ship. A sealing door then slid across the closed ramp, it, too, locking in place. I pounded on its plates, wildly, sobbing.

Strong hands seized me from behind, one of the men in a black tunic. There was a tniy, three-pronged scar on his right cheekbone. I was dragged weeping and kicking through the ship, between tiers of piping and plating.

Then I was in a curved area, where, fixed in racks on the wall, sloping to the floor, were several large, transparent cylinders, perhaps of heavy plastic. In these were the girls I had seen, those who had been taken from the truck.

One tube was empty.

Another man, clad as the first, unscrewed one end of the empty tube.

I could see that there were two small hoses, one at each end, fixed in each tube. They led into a machine fixed in the wall.

I struggled wildly, but the two men, one at my ankles, the other holding me under the arms, forced me into the tube. My prison was perhaps eighteen inches in diameter. The lid to the tube was screwed shut. I screamed and screamed, pushing and kicking at the cylinder. I turned on my side. I pressed my hands against the walls of the tube. The men did not seem to notice me.

Then I began to feel faint. It was hard to breathe.

One of the men attached a small hose to a tiny opening in the tube, above my head.

I lifted my head.

Oxygen streamed into the tube.

Another hose was attached at the other end of the tube, above my feet. There was a tiny, almost inaudible noise, as of air being withdrawn.

I could breathe.

The two men then seemed to brace themselves, by holding onto some rails, part of the racking of the piping. I suddenly felt as though I were in an elevator, and for the moment could not breathe. I knew then we were ascending. From the feeling of my body, pressing against the tube, I thought we must be ascending vertically, or nearly vertically. There was no peculiarly powerful stresses, and very little unpleasantness. It was swift, and frightening, but not painful. I heard no sound of motors, or engines.

After perhaps a minute the two men, holding to the railing, moved from the room.

The strange sensation continued for some time. Then, after a time, I seemed pressed against the side of the tube, rather cruelly, for perhaps several minutes. Then, suddenly, no forces seemed to play upon me, and, to my horror, I drifted to the other side of the tube. Then, after a moment of this, a very gentle force seemed to bring me back to the side of the tube on my right. Oddly enough, I now thought of this as down. Shortly thereafter one of the men in a black tunic, wearing sandals with metal plates on the bottoms, stepped carefully, step by step, across the steel plating. It had been the floor, but now it seemed as though it were a wall at my left, and he moved strangely on the wall.

He went to the machine into which the hoses from the tubes led, and moved a small dial.

In a moment I sensed something different in the air being conducted into my tube.

There were several other similar dials, beneath various switches, doubtless one for each of the containers.

I tried to attract his attention. I called out. Apparently he could not hear me. Or was not interested in doing so.

I was vaguely aware that now the gentle force seemed to draw my body against the tube differently. I was vaguely aware that now the ceiling and the floor seemed as they should be. I saw, not fully conscious of it, the man leave the room.

I looked out through the plastic. I pressed my hands against the heavy, curved, transparent walls of my small prison.

The proud Elinor Brinton had not escaped.

She was a prisoner.

I fell unconscious.

5 THREE MOONS

IT IS DIFFICULT FOR ME to conjecture what happened.

I do not know how long I was unconscious.

I know only that I awakened, stunned, bewildered, lying on my stomach, head turned to the side, on grass. My fingers tore down at the roots. I wanted to scream. But I did not move. The events of the August afternoon and night flashed through my memory. I shut my eyes. I must go back to sleep. I must awaken again, between the white satin sheets in my penthouse. But the pressing of fresh grass against my cheek told me I was no longer in the penthouse, in surroundings with which I was familiar.

I got up to my hands and knees.

I squinted toward the sun. Somehow it seemed not the same to me. I moved my hand. I pressed my foot against the earth.

I threw up with horror.

I knew I was no longer on my world, on the world I knew. It was another world, a different world, one I did not know, one strange to me.

And yet the air seemed beautifully clear and clean. I could not remember such air. The grass was wet with dew, and rich and green. I was in a field of some sort, but there were trees, tall and dark, in the distance. A small yellow flower grew near me. I looked at it, puzzled. I had never seen such a flower before. In the distance, away from the forest, I could see a yellowish thicket, it, too, of trees, but not green, but bright and yellow. I heard a brook nearby.

I was afraid.

I cried out as I saw a bird, tiny and purple, flash past overhead.

In the distance, near the yellowish thicket, I saw a small, yellowish animal moving, delicately. It was far off and I could not see it well. I thought it might be a deer or gazelle. It disappeared into the thicket.

I looked about myself.

Some hundred yards or so from me I saw a mass of torn metal, a ruptured structure of black steel, half buried in the grass.

It was the ship.

I noted that I no longer wore the anklet on my left ankle. It had been removed.

I still wore the clothing in which I had been captured, the tan slacks, the black, bare-midriff blouse. My sandals I had lost in the woods on Earth, while fleeing from the ship.

I felt like running from the ship, as far as I might. But there seemed to be no sign of life about it.

I was terribly hungry.

I crawled in the direction of the brook, and, lying on my stomach before it, scooped water into my mouth.

What I thought was a petaled flower underneath the swift, cold surface of the brook suddenly broke apart, becoming a school of tiny yellow fish.

I was startled.

I slaked my thirst.

I wanted to run from the ship. Somewhere there might be the men.

But the ship seemed still. I saw some small birds fluttering about it.

There might be food on the ship.

Slowly, frightened, I approached the ship, step by step.

I heard a singing bird.

At last, about twenty yards from the ship, I circled it, fearfully.

It was torn open, the steel plating split and bent, scorched and blistered.

There was no sign of life.

I then approached the ship, half buried in the grass. I

looked inside, through one of the great rents in the steel. Its edges seemed to have melted and hardened. In places there were frozen rivulets of steel, as though heavy trickles of paint had run from a brush and then hardened. The inside of the ship was black and scorched. The piping, in several places, had ruptured. Panels were split apart, revealing a complex, blackened circuitry within. The heavy glass, or quartz or plastic, in the ports was, in many places, broken through.

Barefoot, on the steel plating, buckled under my feet, the bolts broken, I entered the ship, holding my breath.

There seemed no one there.

The interior of the ship was compactly organized, with often only small spaces between tiers of tubing, piping and meters. Sometimes these small passages were half closed with bent pipes and tangles of wire erupted from the sides, but I managed to crawl where I wished to.

I found what seemed to be a control room, with two chairs and a large port before them. In this room there were also chairs about the side, four of them, before masses of dials, gauges and switches. There was no engine room that I could find. Whatever force drove the ship must have been beneath it, reached perhaps through the floor plating. The engines of the ship, and its weapons, if weapons it had, must have been operated from the control room. I found the area where the heavy plastic tubes had been kept, in one of which I had been confined. The tubes had all been opened. They were empty.

I heard a sound behind me and I screamed.

A small, furred animal scurried past me, its claws scrabbling on the steel plating. It had six legs. I leaned against a rack of piping, to catch my breath.

But now I was afraid.

I had found no one in the ship.

But where could they be? There had been a crash. But there were no bodies. But if there had been survivors, where had they gone? Might they return soon?

I returned to the main portion of the ship, and looked again at the great rents in the steel. It did not seem likely to me that they had been caused simply by the crash. There were four of them. One, rather on the bottom of the ship, was about five foot square. Two, on the left side, were smaller. The rent through which I had entered the ship was the largest. It was, at the point at which I had entered, as the metal had been torn open, like steel petals, more than nine feet in height, a vast gash which, irregularly, on the left, tapered downward to a tear in the steel of only some four inches in height. There were, of course, numerous other points of damage on the ship, both interiorly and exteriorly, pitted, buckled plating and such. Much of the buckled plating, I supposed, might have been done when the ship impacted. I looked once more at the great rents. It did not seem unlikely to me that the ship had been attacked.

Frightened, I ran through the ship, wanting to find food or weapons. I found the crew's quarters. There were lockers there, and six cots, three on a side, mounted one over the other on the two walls, a mirror. The lockers had been split open and were emptied. I found blood on one side of one of the cots.

I hurried from the room.

I found the tiny galley. In one corner, hunched over, nibbling, I saw an animal, about the size of a small dog. It lifted its snout and hissed at me, the hair about its neck and on its back suddenly bristling out with a crackle.

I screamed.

It seemed twice the size it had been.

It crouched over a metallic container, round, not unlike a covered plate, that had been sprung open.

The animal was silken. Its eyes blazed. It was mottled, and tawny. It opened its mouth and hissed again. I saw it had three rows of needlelike teeth. It had only four legs, unlike the small animal I had seen earlier. Two hornlike tusks protruded from its jaw. Another two hornlike projections emerged from its head, just over its black, gleaming, wicked eyes.

I was wild with hunger. I opened a cabinet. It was empty, save for some cups.

I screamed and began to throw the cups, which were metal, at the animal, hysterically.

It snarled and, the cups banging behind it on the metal of the wall, darted past me. Its silken body struck my leg as it ran from the galley. It had a long, whipping, hairless tail.

I shut the door of the galley, crying.

I opened all the cabinets, all the drawers and boxes. Everything edible, it seemed, had been taken. I would have to starve!

Then I sat down on the floor of the steel galley and wept. When I had cried, I went to the flat, metal container, that sprung open and exposed, that from which the ugly, terrible, silken animal had been feeding.

Choking, almost vomiting, I fed myself.

It was meat. It was thick, grainy, something like beef, but it was not beef.

With my hand and fingers I scratched and scraped every particle of food from the container. There was not enough. I devoured it. I sucked even my fingers, for every last bit of juice.

I stood up, refreshed and stronger. I looked about, dismally. In my search for food I had found some utensils, but no knives, nothing to use as a weapon.

Then it seemed to me that I had remained too long at the ship. I had not found bodies, though I had found, in one place, on a cot, a stain of blood. If there had been survivors, they might return. I became frightened. I had forgotten everything in my search for food, and my eating.

I opened the galley door.

I heard a bird twittering.

It was a small bird, about the size of a sparrow, but it looked a bit like a tiny owl, with tufts over its eyes. It was purplish. It looked at me quizzically. It was perched on some split piping.

It looked at me for a moment, and then, with a flurry of wings, darted out of the ship.

I, too, fled the ship.

Outside, everything seemed calm. I stopped. The dark forest was behind the ship, in the distance. The fields extended to the right. Somewhat more to the left, in the distance, in the fields was the yellowish thicket I had seen earlier.

The sun's position had altered, and the shadows were longer. I judged it to be in the afternoon, on this world. It was not cold. If this world had seasons, as I supposed it must, I would have guessed it was in the spring of their year. I wondered how long the year might be.

Outside, looking about more closely, I found some trampled grass, as though things had been placed there, perhaps earlier in the morning, boxes and such. In one place I found some strands of woman's hair. In another, there was a dark, reddish-brown stain on the grass.

I must get away!

I turned toward the forest, but its darkness frightened me.

Suddenly, from it, through the clear air, from far off, there drifted a roar, as of some large animal.

I turned away from the forest and began to run across the field, blindly toward the horizon, over the grass.

I had not run far when I stopped, for, in the sky, in the distance, I saw a swift, silverish, disklike object. It was moving rapidly and in my direction. I threw myself down in the grass. I covered my head with my hands.

In moments nothing had happened. I lifted my head.

The silverish disk had now landed near the rent, half-buried black ship.

The black ship itself glowed redly, but, in a few seconds, the glow faded.

Then hatches opened on the silverish ship and men leaped out. They carried tubes, or wands, of some sort, perhaps weapons. They, like the men of the black ship, wore tunics but these were of some shimmering, purplish material. Their heads were shaved. Some of the men deployed themselves about the ship; others, carrying their weapons, entered.

Then, to my horror, a large, golden creature, six-legged, supporting itself on its four long back legs, almost upright, stepped from the ship. It had large eyes and, I thought, antennae. It moved swiftly, delicately, almost daintily toward the ship and, bending down, disappeared inside. Some of the men followed it in.

In perhaps less than a minute the creature, and the men, emerged from the ship; they, together with their fellows, then swiftly re-entered the silverish ship. The hatches slid shut and the ship, almost simultaneously, lifted itself, silently, some hundred feet from the grass. Then it moved above the wreck of the black ship. There was a sudden, bluish flash, and a blast of almost incandescent heat. I put my head down. When I raised my head the silverish, disklike ship was gone. And so, too, was the wreck of the black ship. When I dared I went back to the site of the wreck. The depression in which it had lain, and the earth around, for some tens of feet, was scorched. But I could find nothing of the ship, not a bolt or a bit of quartz, not a thread of metal or a scrap of wire.

From the distant forest I heard again the roar of some great animal.

Once more I turned and fled.

When I came to the small stream, at which I had drunk earlier, I waded.

The water was waist deep.

Something struck, stinging at my ankle. I screamed and splashed across.

Then I was running again.

I must have run, and walked, and stumbled on for hours.

Once I stopped to rest. I lay, panting on the grass. My eyes were closed. I heard a rustle. I turned my head and opened my eyes. I watched it in terror. It was vinelike, and tendriled, leaved. A blind, split, podlike head was moving toward me, lifting itself slightly from the ground, moving from side to side. Inside the pod I could see, fastened in the upper surface, too long, curved, thornlike fangs. I screamed, leaping to my feet. The thing suddenly struck at me. It tore through the fabric of the slacks on my right leg. I pulled my leg away, tearing away the cloth. It struck again and again, as though sensing me by smell or heat, but it was rooted, and I was beyond its reach. I threw back my head, my hands to the sides of my head, and screamed. I heard another rustle, near me. I looked about, wildly. I saw the other plant, and then two others, too. And then another. Sweating, picking my way, I fled from the area. Then I was into the open grass again.

I continued running, and walking, for hours. At last it grew cool, and dark.

I could go no further.

I dropped to the grass.

It was a dark, beautiful, windy night. There were some white clouds scudding across the sky. I looked up at the stars. Never before had I seen stars look so beautiful, so bright and burning in the blackness of the night. "How beautiful is this world," I said to myself, "how beautiful!" I lay on my back and looked up at the stars, and the moons.

There were three moons.

I slept.

6 I ENCOUNTER TARGO, WHO IS A SLAVER

I AWOKE IN THE MORNING, near dawn. It was very cold, and gray and damp. I was terribly hungry. My body was stiff, and ached. I wept. I sucked dew from the long grass. I was alone. My clothes were wet. I was miserable. I was alone. I was alone. I was frightened. I was hungry. I wept.

As far as I knew I might be the only individual on this world. The ship had crashed here, but this may not have been its world. The other ship had come, to destroy the first, but this might not be its world either. And I had seen no survivors of the crash. And the other ship had departed. As far as I knew I might be the only living human being on this world.

I stood up.

Around me, soft, undulating, glistening with dew in the dim light, I could see nothing but grassy fields, seemingly endless fields, rolling and rolling, sweeping away from me on all sides toward horizons that might be empty.

I was lonely.

I walked on in the midst of the fields.

I heard the song of a bird, fresh in the morning. Near me, startling me, there was a tiny movement in the grass and a small, furry creature, with two large gnawing teeth, skittered past.

I continued on.

I would surely starve. There was nothing to eat. I cried.

Once, looking up, I saw a flight of large, white, broad-winged birds. They seemed lonely, too, high in the gray sky. I wondered if they, too, were hungry.

I trudged on.

I could not understand what had happened. There had been so much, that was so different. I remembered awakening on the August morning, showering. I remembered the men, my attempts to escape, my flight through the woods on Earth, the ship, the plastic tube in which I had been placed.

I remembered awakening again, in the grass, and then discovering the wreck of the black ship. And I remembered the second ship, the silverish one, that it had destroyed the first, and I remembered fleeing.

Now I was alone.

Elinor Brinton was alone, wandering across the fields of what world she even knew not.

I continued on.

About two hours, I would guess, after dawn, I came to a rock outcropping. Here, among the rocks, I found a tiny pool of rain water. I drank.

Nearby, to my delight, I found some berries to eat. They were good, and this filled me with some confidence.

The sun had now begun to climb in the sky and the air turned warmer. It showered once or twice but I did not much mind. The air was bright and clear, the grass green, the sky a full blue with bright, white clouds.

When the sun was overhead I found some more berries and, this time, I ate my fill. Not far away, in another outcropping of rock, I found another pool of trapped rain water. It was a large pool, and I drank as much as I wanted. And I washed my face.

Then I continued on.

I was not as frightened now, nor as displeased. It seemed to me not impossible that I might be able to live on this world.

It was beautiful.

I ran for a little ways, my hair flying behind me, laughing, and jumped and turned in the air, and laughed again. There was no one to see. I had not done that since I had been a little girl.

Then I stepped warily, for I saw, to one side, a patch of the dark, tendriled vinelike plants. I stood to one side and, fascinated, watched them rustle, sensing my presence. Several of the fanged seedpods lifted, like heads, sensing me, moving back and forth gently.

But I was no longer much afraid of them. I now knew their danger.

I continued on.

I saw no animals.

Here and there I found more berries, and, from time to time, more outcroppings of rock in which, almost invariably, I found water, doubtless trapped from recent rains.

But I was very lonely.

About the middle of the afternoon I sat down in the grass, in a gentle, sloping valley between two of the grassy hills.

I wonder what chance I might have of being rescued.

I smiled. I knew that this world was not mine. The ship that had brought me here, I knew, even with my limited knowledge of such matters, was far beyond the present capabilities of any of the civilizations of Earth. And yet the men who had captured me were surely human, or seemed so, as did those who manned the ship. Even those who had come from the silverish ship, with the exception of the tall, delicate golden creature, had seemed to be human, or much like humans.

But the black ship had crashed. And the silverish ship had departed, perhaps for another world.

But I wanted to be rescued! I would be rescued! I must be rescued!

But I was not particularly frightened.

I could live on this world.

But I was lonely.

There is nothing to be frightened of, I told myself. There is food here, and water. I had found berries, and there were doubtless other things to eat, fruits and nuts.

I laughed, so pleased I was.

Then I cried, for I was so lonely. I was all alone.

Then, startled, I lifted my head. Drifting through the air, unmistakable, though coming from some distance, was the sound of a shout, a human voice.

I leaped wildly to my feet and ran, stumbling up the hill. I came to its crest and looked wildly and cried out, and waved, and began to run down the side of the hill, stumbling and shouting and waving my arms. There were tears of joy in my eyes. "Stop!" I shouted. "Stop!"

They were humans! I would be rescued! They would have food and shelter, and water! I was saved! I would be safe! Safe!

"Stop!" I shouted. "Stop!"

There was a single wagon. About it were some seven or eight men. There were no animals at the wagon. At the front of it, standing on the grass, were some fifteen or twenty girls, unclothed. They seemed immeshed in the harness. Two men stood near them. The wagon itself seemed damaged, partly stained with black. Its cover, of blue and yellow silk, was torn. Near the front of the wagon, too, was a short, fat man, clad in a robe of broadly striped blue and yellow silk. Startled, they turned to face me.

I ran down the hill, stumbling and laughing, toward them.

Two of the men ran forward to meet me. Another two, flanking these, began to run toward the top of the hill. They passed me.

"I'm Elinor Brinton," I told the men who had come to meet me. "I live in New York City. I'm lost."

One of the men, with two hands, seized my left wrist. The other man, with two hands, seized my right wrist. They swiftly led me, pulling me, not gently, down the hill between them, toward the group at the wagon.

In a moment, they still holding me, I stood at the side of the wagon.

The small, fat, short man, he plump and paunchy in the robe of broadly striped blue and yellow silk, scarcely looked at me. He was more anxiously regarding the top of the hill, where his two men had gone. Crouching down, they were looking about, over the hill. Two others of his men had left the wagon and were looking about, some hundred yards or so, on other sides. The girls near the front of the wagon, immeshed in the harness, seemed apprehensive. The fat man wore earrings, sapphires pendant on golden stalks. His hair, long and black, did not seem well cared for. It was dirty, not well combed. It was tied behind his head with a band of blue and yellow silk. He wore purple sandals, the straps of which were set with pearls. The sandals were now covered with dust. Some of the pearls were missing. On his small, fat hands, there were several rings. His hands, and nails, were dirty. I sensed that he might be, in his personal habits, rather fastidious. But, now, surely he did not seem so. Rather he seemed haggard, apprehensive. One of the men, a grizzled fellow, with one eye, came back from searching the fields some hundred yards or so from the wagon. I gathered he had found nothing. He called the fat, pudgy little man "Targo."

Targo looked up to the top of the hill. One of the men there, standing a bit below its crest, waved to him, and shrugged, lifting his arms in the air. He had seen nothing.

Targo drew a deep breath. Visibly he relaxed.

He then regarded me.

I smiled my prettiest smile. "Thank you," I said, "for rescuing me. My name is Elinor Brinton. I live in New York City, which is a city on the planet Earth. I wish to return there, immediately. I'm rich, and I assure you that if you take me there, you will be well rewarded."

Targo regarded me, puzzled.

But he must understand English!

Another man came back, I suppose to report that he had found nothing. Targo sent him back, perhaps to stand watch. One of the men he then recalled from the top of the hill. The other remained there, also, I suppose, to watch.

I repeated, somewhat irritably, but with some patience, what I had said before. I spoke clearly, slowly, that I might be easier to understand.

I wished the two men would release my wrists.

I was going to speak further to him, to attempt to explain my predicament and my desires, but he said something abruptly, irritably.

I flushed with anger.

He did not wish to hear me speak.

I pulled at my wrists, but the two men would not release me.

Then Targo began to speak to me. But I could understand nothing. He spoke sharply, as one might speak to a servant. This irritated me.

"I do not understand you," I told him, icily.

Targo then seemed to reconsider his impatience. My tone of voice had seemed to startle him. He looked at me, carefully. It seemed he suspected he had been wrong in some way about me. He now came closer to me. His voice was oily, ingratiating. It amused me that I had won this small victory. He seemed kinder now, honeyed.

He would treat Elinor Brinton properly!

But I still, of course, could not understand him.

There seemed something, however, that was familiar about his speech. I could not identify what it was.

He seemed to refuse to believe that I could not understand him.

He continued to speak, finally very slowly, word by word, very clearly. His efforts, of course, were not rewarded in the least, for I could understand not even a word of what he had said. This seemed, for some reason, to irritate him. I, too, began to grow irritated. It was as though he expected anyone to be able to understand his strange language, whether it was their native language or not. How simple and provincial he was.

It was not even English.

He continued to try to communicate with me, but to no avail.

At one point he turned to one of his men and seemed to ask him a question. The fellow replied with a single word, apparently of negation.

Suddenly I was startled. I had heard that word before. When the small man, in my penthouse, when I had lain bound on my bed, had touched me, the large man, abruptly, angrily, had said that word to him. The smaller man had then turned away.

It struck me then what was familiar about the language Targo spoke. I had heard only a word or two of it before. My captors had conversed, almost entirely, in English. And I supposed they had been, at least on the whole, native speakers of English. But I recalled the accent of the large man, who had commanded them. In English, that accent had marked his speech as foreign. Here, however, a world away, I heard the same accent, or one similar, save that here it was not an accent. Here it was the natural sound, the rhythm and inflection, of what was apparently an independent, doubtless sophisticated, native tongue. I was frightened. The language, though it struck my ear as strange, was not unpleasant. It was rather strong, but in its way it seemed supple and beautiful. I was frightened, but I was also encouraged. Targo noted the difference in my attitude, and he redoubled his efforts to communicate with me. But, of course, I still could not understand.

I was frightened, because it had been the language, or rather like the language, of my chief captor, and perhaps others of his group. On the other hand, I was encouraged because it seemed to me then that these individuals, if they spoke the same language, must possess the technological skills to return me to my native world.

Yet it was hard to believe.

The men I now noted, held as I was, did not carry pistols and rifles, or even small weapons, such as my captor had had, or the wands, or silver tubes, which had been carried by the men from the silverish ship. Rather, to my surprise, even amusement, they wore at their sides small swords. Two, over their backs, had slung something like a bow, except that it had a handle, much like a rifle. Four of the others actually carried spears. The spears were large, with curved bronze heads. They seemed heavy. I could not have thrown one.

The men, saving the one called Targo, wore tunics, with helmets. They looked rather frightening. The opening in the helmets reminded me vaguely of a "Y." The swords they carried in scabbards slung over their left shoulder. They wore heavy sandals, laced with thick straps, more than a foot up their leg. Several of them, besides the small swords, carried a knife as well, this attached to a leather belt. They wore pouches also at the belt.

I was relieved that these men, apparently so primitive, could not be of the same group as my former captors, with their sophisticated equipment. But I was also apprehensive for, by the same token, surely men such as these did not have the technological capabilities essential for flights between worlds. These men, surely, could not, themselves, return me to Earth.

I had fallen in with them, however, and would have to make the best of it.

I was rescued, and that was the important thing. There were doubtless men on this world who did possess the capabilities for space flight and I would make inquiries and contact them. With my riches, I could pay well for my transportation back to Earth. The important thing was that I was now safe, that I had been rescued.

I noted the wagon.

It was rather large. It was also scarred in several places, as though it had been struck with sharp objects. In places the wood was splintered. I wondered where the draft animals, presumably oxen, were, who would draw the heavy wagon. I further noted that the boards of the wagon, besides being struck and splintered in certain places, were, in other places, darkened, as though by smoke. Further, looking more closely I could see that the paint on the wagon, which was red, had cracked and blistered considerably. It was reasonably clear that the wagon had been afire, or had come through a fire. As I mentioned, over the wagon, its cover, of blue and yellow silk, was torn. Further, as I could see now, it had been burned at the edges and was, in another area, stained from smoke and rain. It then occurred to me that Targo had seemed haggard, apprehensive, and that, although he seemed to be the sort of man who might be vain about his appearance, judging from the earrings, the sandals, the robe, the rings, that he had not kept up his appearance. I did not even think him the sort who would be likely to walk, but his sandals, with the pearled straps, with certain of the pearls missing, were stained with dust. I recalled, too, how apprehensive the men had been, when I had approached them, how they had examined the hill, the fields about, as though they feared I might not be alone.

Targo was running.

They had been attacked.

There were some objects in the wagon, some chests and boxes.

I looked to the girls near the front of the wagon, immeshed in the harness.

There were nineteen of them, ten on one side of the wagon tongue, and nine on the other.

They were naked.

I looked at them, irritably, and stunned. They were incredibly beautiful. I regarded myself as a fantastically beautiful woman, one among perhaps tens of thousands. I had even modeled. But here, to my amazement, and fury, I saw that at least eleven of these girls were unquestionably, clearly, more beautiful than I. On Earth I had never met a woman, personally, whom I had regarded as my superior in beauty. Here, uncomprehensibly, but obviously, there were at least eleven. I was puzzled how there could be so many in this one small place. I was shaken. But, I told myself, I am more than their equal in intelligence, and in riches, and in taste, and sophistication. They were doubtless simple barbarians. I felt pity for them. I hated them! I hated them! They looked on me as I had looked on other women, on Earth, casually, unthreatened. They looked on me as I had looked on plainer women, unimportant women, not to be taken account of, not to be considered seriously as a rival, simply as my inferiors in beauty. I could not remember ever having not been the most beautiful woman in any room I had entered. How I had relished the admiration of the men, the intake of their breath, their pleasure, their furtive glances, the irritation of the other women! And these women looked upon me, daring to, as I had upon those others. They regarded me curiously, I could see, but more importantly, I had seen, to my fury, that when I received their instantaneous appraisal, that which one woman gives always to another when first they meet, as natural and unconscious as a glance, that they had, at least to their own satisfaction, found themselves superior to me! To Elinor Brinton! I had seen that if I was to count with them I would have to have qualities other than my beauty to commend me to them, as if I were a plain girl, who must cultivate other qualities, who must struggle to be pleasing, rather than a beauty, whom others must strive to please! The haughty bitches! I was superior to them all! I was more beautiful! I was more rich. I hated them! I hated them!

But the important thing was that I was rescued, that I could soon buy my way home to Earth.

Surely someone would be found, if not here, in the next city, who spoke English, who could put me in contact with those from whom I might purchase passage in my return to Earth.

The important thing was that I had been saved, that I was safe.

I had been rescued.

I began to find Targo odious.

Further, I did not care for my wrists being held by the two men, one on each side.

I tried to pull my wrists away, angrily. I could not, of course, free myself.

I hated men, and their strength.

Targo himself had now grown more and more irritable.

"Let me go!" I cried. "Let me go!"

But I could not free myself.

Once again Targo tried to speak to me, patiently, slowly. I could tell that he was growing furious.

He was a fool, such a tiresome fool. They were all fools. None of them seemed to understand English. One, at least, of the men on the black ship had spoken English. I had heard him converse with the large man. There must be many, then, on this world, many!

I was tired of Targo.

"I do not understand you," I told him, sounding out each word, with great contempt and coldness. Then I looked away, loftily. I had put him in his place.

He said something to a subordinate.

Instantly I was stripped before him.

I screamed. The girls at the wagon tongue laughed.

"Kajira!" cried one of the men, pointing to my thigh.

Every inch of me blushed red.

"Kajira!" laughed Targo. "Kajira!" laughed the others. I heard the girls at the wagon tongue laughing, and clapping their hands.

Tears were running out of Targo's eyes, tiny in the fat of his face.

Then, suddenly, he seemed angry.

He spoke again, sharply.

I was thrown forward on my face and stomach on the grass. The two men who had been holding my wrists continued to do so, but they held them now apart and over my head, pressed down to the grass. Two other men came and held my ankles apart, they, too, pressed down to the grass.

"Lana!" cried Targo.

One of the other men went to the wagon tongue. I could not see what he did there. But I heard a girl laugh. In a moment she had left the wagon tongue and was standing somewhere behind me.

I had been a spoiled, pampered child. The governesses and nurses who had raised me had scolded me, and frequently, but they had never struck me. They would have been discharged immediately. In all my life I could not remember ever having been struck.

Then I was whipped.

The girl struck, with her small fierce strength, again and again, over and over, viciously, fiercely, as hard as she could, again and again. I cried out, and screamed and sobbed, and struggled. The handful of slender leather straps was merciless. I bit at the grass, I could not breathe. I could not see for tears. Again and again! "Please stop!" I cried. But then I could cry out no longer. There was only the grass and the tears and the pain of the straps, striking again and again.

I suppose the beating lasted actually for only a few seconds, surely not for more than a minute.

Targo said something to the girl, Lana, and the stinging rain of leather stopped.

The two men at my ankles released them. The two men who held my wrists pulled me up to my knees. I must have been in shock. I could not focus my eyes. I heard the girls laughing at the wagon tongue. I threw up on the grass. The men pulled me away from where I had vomited and another, from behind, holding my hair, pushed my face down to the ground, to the clean grass, and, turning my head, wiped the vomit from my mouth and chin.

Then I was pulled again up and placed, on my knees, the men holding my wrists, before Targo.

I looked up at him.

I saw that he now held my clothing in one hand. I scarcely recognized it. He was looking down at me. In his other hand I saw, dangling, the handful of straps with which I had been beaten. The girl was now being returned by one of the men to her position at the wagon tongue. The entire back of my body, my legs, my arms, my shoulders, was afire. I could not take my eyes from the straps.

The two men released my wrists.

"Kajira," said Targo.

He lifted the straps.

I shook.

I thrust my head to the grass at his feet.

I took his sandal in my hands and pressed my lips down on his foot, kissing it.

I heard laughter from the girls.

He must not have me beaten again!

I must please him.

I kissed his foot again, trembling, sobbing. He must be pleased with me, he must be pleased with me!

He spoke a brief word of command, and, with a swirl of his robe, turned away from me.

I sobbed, raising my head and looking after him.

I was seized from behind by the two men who had held my wrists. I watched Targo's retreating back. I did not dare call out to him. He was no longer interested in me. The two men dragged me to the wagon tongue.

There were ten girls on one side, nine on the other.

I saw the girl who had beaten me, Lana, some positions ahead of me. I noted, suddenly, that she was harnessed. There were buckled straps on her wrists, fastening her in place. And about her body, in a broad loop, passing over her left shoulder and across her right hip, was a wide, heavy leather strap, which was bolted into the wagon tongue. The other girls were similarly fastened. Buckled straps were placed on my wrists. Over my shoulder, about my body, was passed a heavy loop of leather.

I sobbed. I seemed scarcely able to stand. My legs trembled. The entire back of my body stung terribly. I tasted my tears.

The man began to adjust the strap on my body.

Near me, across from me, a short girl, with dark hair, very red lips, and bright dark eyes, smiled at me.

"Ute," she said, pointing to herself. Then she pointed at me. "La?" she asked.

I saw that the girls harnessed at the wagon tongue wore, on their left thighs, the same mark that I wore on mine.

I jerked at the straps on my wrists. I was secured.

"Ute," repeated the short, dark-eyed girl, pointing to herself. Then she again pointed to me. "La?" she inquired.

The man cinched the strap on my body. It was snug. Then he stepped away from me. I was harnessed.

"La?" persisted the dark-eyed girl, pointing at me with her strapped hand. "La?"

"Elinor," I whispered.

"El-in-or," she repeated, smiling. Then, facing the other girls, she pointed at me. "El-in-or," she said, pleased. She seemed delighted.

For some reason, I was utterly grateful, that this short, lovely girl should be pleased by my name.

Most of the other girls merely turned and regarded me, not much interested. The girl Lana, who had beaten me, did not even turn. Her head was in the air.

Another girl, a tall, blondish girl, some two positions ahead of me and on my left, smiled. "Inge," she said, indicating herself.

I smiled.

Targo was now crying out orders. He was looking about, apprehensively.

One of his men shouted.

The girls leaned forward into the traces, pulling at the wagon.

Two of his men thrust at the rear wheels.

The wagon began to move.

I leaned against the leather strap, pretending to push. They did not need me to pull the wagon. They had pulled it before. I dug my feet into the grass, as though straining. I grunted a little, to add to the effect.

Ute, at my right, cast me a glance, an unpleasant one. Her little body was straining at the strap.

I did not care.

I cried out with pain, and humiliation, as the switch struck my body.

Ute laughed.

I threw all my weight against the strap, sobbing, pushing with all my might.

The wagon was moving now.

In a minute or so I saw the girl Lana switched, as I had been, below the small of the back. She cried out with humiliation and pain, left with a stinging red stripe. The other girls, I among them, laughed. I gathered Lana was not popular. I was pleased that she, too, had been switched! She was a slacker! Why should the rest of us pull for her? Was she better than we?

"Har-ta!" cried Targo. "Har-ta!"

"Har-ta!" cried the men about us.

The girls began to push harder. We strained, to increase the speed of the wagon. From time to time the men would thrust, too, at the wheels.

We cried out with pain as two of the men, about the sides, one on each side, encouraged us with their switches.

We could pull no harder. And yet we were struck! I dared not protest.

The wagon lumbered over the grassy fields.

Targo walked beside us. I would have thought he would have ridden in the wagon, but he did not. He wanted it as light as it could be, even though it meant he, the leader, must walk.

How I dreaded it when he would cry "Har-ta!" for then we would be switched again.

I sobbed in the straps, under the switch.

But I was Elinor Brinton, of Park Avenue, of Earth! She had been rich, beautiful, smartly attired, tasteful, sophisticated; she had been well educated and traveled; she had been decisive, confident; she had carried her wealth and her beauty with *élan;* and she had deserved her position in society; it had been rightfully hers, for she had been a gifted, high-order, superbly intelligent individual, an altogether superior person! She *deserved* everything that she had had! Whatever she had had she should have had, for she was that kind of person! That was the kind of person she was!

So how was it that she now found herself on a distant world, alone and friendless, among barbarians, who could not even speak her language, choking with dust, sweating, unclothed, straining in a harness, under the switch of a master?

I glanced at Ute.

She regarded me, unpleasantly. She had not forgotten that I had shirked. She looked away, disgusted.

I was angry. I did not care. Who was she? A fool! On such a world as this it was every girl for herself! Every girl for herself!

"Har-ta!" cried Targo.

"Har-ta!" cried the men about us.

We cried out again, stung by the switches. I threw my full weight against the leather, digging my feet into the grass.

I sobbed.

I would not be permitted to shirk.

I had always had my way before, with both women and men. I could get extensions for my term papers. I could get a new fur wrap, when I wished. When I tired of one auto I would have another. I could always petition for what I wished, or wheedle for it, or look sad, or pout. I would always get what I wished.

Here I did not have my way.

Here I would not be permitted to shirk. The switch would see to that. If there were those here who might wheedle, or have their way, it would be those more beautiful, more pleasing than I. I would be expected, I realized, to my fury, for the first time, to do my share.

The switch struck again and I wept.

Sobbing, crying out inwardly, I pushed against the broad leather strap with all my might.

7 I, WITH OTHERS,
AM TAKEN NORTHWARD

TARGO, MY MASTER, WAS A SLAVER.

I cost him nothing.

Shortly before he made me one of his girls, some two or three days before, he had been attacked by outlaw tarnsmen, some four days journey north by northeast from the city of Ko-ro-ba, which lies high in the northern temperate latitudes of the planet Gor, which is the name of this world. He was bound, traveling over the hills and meadowlands east and north of Ko-ro-ba, for the city of Laura, which lies on the banks of the Laurius river, some two hundred pasangs inland from the coast of the sea, called Thassa. Laura is a small trading city, a river port, whose buildings are largely of wood, consisting mostly it seems of warehouses and taverns. It is a clearing house for many goods, wood, salt, fish, stone, fur and slaves. At the mouth of the Laurius, where it empties into Thassa, is found the free port of Lydius, administered by the merchants, an important Gorean caste. From Lydius goods may be embarked for the islands of Thassa, such as Teletus, Hulneth and Asperiche, even Cos and Tyros, and the coastal cities, such as Port Kar and Helmutsport, and, far to the south, Schendi and Bazi. And, from Lydius, of course, goods of many sorts, though primarily rough goods, such things as tools, crude metal and cloth, brought on barges, towed by tharlarion treading on log roads, following the river, are brought to Laura, for sale and distribution inland. The Laurius is a winding, long, gentle, slow river. It does not have the breadth and current which are the terrors of the titanic Vosk farther to the south, well below Ko-ro-ba, though well above Ar, which is said to be the greatest city of all known Gor. The Laurius, like the Vosk, flows in a generally westernly direction, though the Laurius inclines more to the southwest than the great Vosk.

Considering the nature of the goods commonly found in Laura, rough goods for the most part, one might have supposed it strange that Targo was bound for that city. It was not strange, however, for it was spring, and spring is the great season for slave raids. Indeed, the preceding fall, at the fair of Se'Kara, near the Sardar Mountains, he had contracted with a maurauder, Haakon of Skjern, for one hundred northern beauties, to be taken from the villages north of the Laurius and from the coastal villages, upward even to the edges of Torvaldsland. It was to collect this merchandise that Targo was venturing to Laura. He had already, at the fair, paid Haakon a deposit on this purchase, in the amount of fifty gold pieces. The balance of one hundred and fifty gold pieces would be due when the consignment was delivered. Two gold pieces is a high price for a raw girl, delivered in Laura, but, if the same girl can be brought safely to a large market city, she will probably bring five or more, even if untrained. Further, in offering as much as two gold pieces in Laura, Targo assured himself of first pick of Haakon's choicest captures. Beyond this, Targo had speculated that since no city had recently fallen, and the house of Cernus had been destroyed in Ar, one of the great slave houses, that the market would be high this spring. Moreover, it was his intention to have his girls receive some training, probably in the pens of Ko-ro-ba, before taking them southeast to Ar. Unfortunately for Targo, village girls are not of high caste. On the other hand, if worth a good deal less, they are much more easily acquired than a high-caste, free woman. When I was taken by Targo, he had only one high-caste girl on his chain, the tall girl, Inge, who was of the scribes. Ute, who had been harnessed next to me, had been of the leather workers. A slave, of course, in one sense, has no caste. In being enslaved, she is robbed of caste, as well as of her name. She belongs to her master in all respects, as an animal. He may call her what he wishes, and do with her what he pleases. It seemed not unlikely that one of Targo's village girls, if trained and brought to Ar, might net him from ten to fifteen, perhaps even twenty, gold pieces. His investment, in some respects an excellent one, was, however, not without its risks. It is not always easy to bring a beautiful girl to the market at Ar, where the highest prices are traditionally paid. It is not that the girl is likely to escape, for slavers seldom lose prisoners. It is rather that she may be taken from you. The female slave is prize booty.

Before Targo had acquired me, he had been making his way northward from Ko-ro-ba to Laura. Indeed, he had come all the way from the vicinity of Ar, buying and selling girls at various cities. He had purchased Inge, Ute and Lana, whom I hated, in Ko-ro-ba. Lana was our leader. We feared her. She was the strongest. She was also the most beautiful. Submissive, ingratiating and docile with the men, she was imperious with us. We did what she told us to, for otherwise she would beat us. As it is said, masters do not much interfere in the squabbles of slaves. She would have been severely beaten, of course, if she had disfigured us, injured us, or in any way lowered our value. But, beyond this, she might bully us, or beat us, as much as she pleased. We hated her. Also, we envied her. Not only was she the most beautiful, but she had been trained in the house of Cernus, the great slave house, in Ar, before its fall. Even more important she had once been sold even from the great block of the Curulean. Lana was always placed at the end of the display chain, that the most attractive merchandise be glimpsed last. We were hoping that she would be sold, but Targo was holding out for an extremely high price for her. Doubtless he would have received it many times, except that she had not been of high caste. She treated the rest of us as slaves. Targo, and some of the guards, sometimes, would give her candies, and sweetmeats. My own position in the display chain, at the beginning, was fourth. I was taught to kneel in a certain way, and, when inspected, to lift my head, smile, and utter a certain phrase. Targo, and the guards, made me practice it many times. I later learned that its meaning was "Buy me, Master." In displaying a girl, an ankle ring is placed on her left ankle. This locks on the ankle. There is also a smaller ring, projecting from the larger ring, which also locks. This smaller ring can either be snapped into a particular link in a chain, thus allowing the girls to be spaced at certain intervals, or it can be closed about the chain as a whole, thus permitting the chain to run freely through the ring without injuring or burning the girl's ankle. In the "display chain," we were spaced on the chain, and the chain stretched rather taut and fastened at both ends, sometimes to trees, sometimes to two large metal screws, more than two feet in length, which screwed into the ground, beyond the reach on each end of the first and last girl. Thus, not only would we be secured, but we were unable to crowd together, as girls, particularly unexperienced girls, have a tendency to do when not prevented. In the display chain, it might be mentioned, as would be expected, we are exhibited unclothed. A Gorean saying has it that only a fool would buy a woman clothed. I suppose it is true.

Targo had set forth from Ko-ro-ba with forty girls and five wagons, ten bosk, and many other goods. His men, at that time, had numbered more than twenty. Two days out of Ko-ro-ba, crossing the fields northward toward Laura, the sky had darkened with a flight of outlaw tarnsmen, more than a hundred of them, under the command of the terrible Rask of Treve, one of the most dreaded warriors on all Gor. Fortunately for Targo he had managed to bring his caravan to the edge of a vast Ka-la-na thicket just before the tarnsmen struck. I had seen several such thickets when I was wandering alone in the fields. Targo had divided his men expertly. Some he set to seize up what gold and goods they could. Others he ordered to free the girls and drive them into the thicket. Others he commanded to cut loose the great bosk that pulled the wagons, and drive them, too, into the brush and trees. Then, but moments before the transmen struck, Targo, with his men driving the girls and the bosk, fled into the thicket. The transmen alighted and ransacked the wagons, setting fire to them. There was sharp fighting in the thicket. Targo must have lost some eleven men, and some twenty of his girls were taken by the tarnsmen, but, after a bit, the tarnsmen withdrew. Tarnsmen, riders of the great tarns, called Brothers of the Wind, are masters of the open sky, fierce warriors whose battleground is the clouds and sky; they are not forest people; they do not care to stalk and hunt where, from the darkness of trees, from a canopy of foliage, they may meet suddenly, unexpectedly, a quarrel from the crossbow of an invisible assailant.

Rask withdrew his men and, in moments, the captured girls bound across their saddles, the goods of Targo thrust into their packs, they took flight.

Targo gathered his men and goods. Nineteen of his girls, separately, taken deep into the thicket, had had their wrists bound together, either before their body or behind their back, about small trees. These were the ones he had managed to keep. Lana, Ute and Inge had, of course, been among them. The bosk, unfortunately for Targo, had either broken free or been cut free. They had disappeared over the grassy fields. When he emerged from the thicket he found left only one usable wagon, and that damaged by smoke and fire. He had lost a good deal, but he had saved some goods, and, most importantly, his gold. He camped that night in the thicket. In the morning a harness was jerry-rigged. The girls looked at one another. Not now, indolently, would they ride chained to the ankle bar in the wagon. Then Targo had set out again for Laura. Some two or three days later, in the trackless fields, wandering, they had encountered a young barbarian girl, strangely clad, whom they had made their slave.

It took many days to reach Laura.

Fortunately, not more than two days after I had been added to Targo's chain, we encountered a caravan of Bosk wagons, traveling southeast toward Ko-ro-ba from Laura. Targo sold two girls, and, with some extra gold, purchased two wagons and two teams of bosk, as well as supplies of water and food. He also purchased certain articles of slavers' equipment, a display chain, various other sorts of chains, slave bracelets, ankle rings, neck collars, binding fibers, branding irons and whips. I was more pleased to note that he also purchased some silks, perfumes, and combs and

brushes, and boxes of cosmetics. He also purchased a large
quantity of rough cloth. From this, as I later saw, camisks
were made, a simple slave garment. When chained in a
wagon, to the ankle bar, girls are commonly unclothed. When
the tarnsmen had struck, the girls had been freed from the
wagons, to be driven into the thicket. The camisks had been
burned with most of Targo's other goods. The camisk is a
rectangle of cloth, with a hole cut for the head, rather
like a poncho. The edges are commonly folded and stitched
to prevent raveling. Under Targo's direction the girls, happily, cut and stitched their own camisks. The camisk, I am
told, normally falls to the knees, but Targo made us cut ours
considerably shorter. I made mine poorly. I had never
learned to sew. Targo was not satisfied with its length, and
he made me shorten it still more. Mine was then no longer
than Lana's, or the other girls'! But I remembered my beating. I did not wish another. I feared the straps terribly. And
so I was dressed as they. The camisk, I am told, was at one
time commonly belted with a chain. However, the camisks
that I have personally seen, and those we were given, were
belted with a long, thin strap of leather binding fiber. This
passes once around the body, and then again, and then is
tied, snugly, over the right hip. When Targo inspected me, he
made me tighten the belt, to accentuate my figure. Already
I had learned, for the first time in my life, to stand straight,
truly straight. I was cuffed, or kicked, when I forgot. Soon
it was natural for me to do so. The belt of binding fiber not
only makes it easier to adjust the camisk to a given girl, but,
of course, the binding fiber serves to remind her that she is
in bondage. In a moment it may be removed, and she may
be secured with it, leashed, or bound hand and foot. I wondered why Targo permitted us camisks. I think there were
probably two reasons. The first is that the camisk, in its way,
is an incredibly attractive garment. It displays the girl, but
provocatively. Moreover, it proclaims her slave, and begs to
be torn away by the hand of a master. Men thrill to see a
girl in a camisk. Secondly, I think Targo gave us camisks to
make us even more his slaves. We desperately wanted to
have something to cover ourselves, be it only a camisk. That

he might take it away if irritated, or dissatisfied with us, made us that the more eager to please him. None of us wished to be unclothed among others clothed, that we, nude, might seem more the slave than they.

Our lives became a great deal easier after Targo encountered the caravan wagons.

The two wagons he bought were merchant wagons, with red rain canvas. The back wheels were larger than the front wheels. Each was drawn by two bosk, large brown creatures with spreading, polished horns, hung with beads. Their hoofs were also polished and their long, shaggy coats groomed to a shine. One of the wagons had an ankle bar, and the other one was fitted with the ankle bar from Targo's damaged wagon, which he then abandoned and burned on the grass. Ten girls, commonly, ride in such a wagon, five to a side. Lana's wagon was the first wagon; my wagon was the second. Each wagon held nine girls. Targo had sold two girls. We were fitted with ankle rings joined by a short length of chain. One ankle ring is closed on the girl's ankle, the chain passed about the bar and then, on her other ankle, the second ankle ring is closed, securing her. I did not care. I did not even care that we were not permitted camisks in the wagon. Moments after lying down on the canvas, spread over the polished floor boards of the wagon, in spite of the movement and the bumping and jostling, I fell asleep. To be relieved of the agony of the harness and the strain of drawing the wagon was simply in itself an exquisite delight.

When I awoke, many hours later, I was stiff and sore in every muscle of my body.

We were taken from the wagon and, chained outside, kneeling, were fed. In the two days since I had been captured, prior to our encountering the caravan, we had had only berries and water, and bits of small game, cooked by the guards and thrown to us in scraps. Now, chained, kneeling in a circle, we passed about, one to the other, a bowl of hot soup; then each of us was given a sixth of a round yellow loaf of bread, which we ate with our hands; then, before each of us, on the grass, the guards threw a large piece of cooked meat. I was famished and, burning my fingers, I clutched at it, and, half-choking, thrust it half into my mouth, tearing at it with my teeth and hands, the juices running at the sides of my mouth. I think few of my friends would have recognized the sophisticated, tasteful Elinor Brinton in the naked Gorean slave girl, chained, kneeling on the grass, thrusting meat into her mouth, tearing at it, her head back in ecstasy, feeding, the juices of the meat running on her body. It was only roast bosk, and half raw, but I devoured it. No delicate, sauced portion of filet mignon which I had savored in any Parisian restaurant compared to that hot, steaming chunk of bosk, half raw, running with juices, that I had seized from the grass of a Gorean field, beside the wagon of a slaver.

Following our meal we were taken to a nearby stream where we washed ourselves. I was reluctant to enter the water but, at a word from Targo, I immersed myself, shuddering, teeth chattering, in the swift, chill stream. In a few moments I became accustomed to the water, and soon was reluctant to leave it. I, following the other girls, washed my hair, as well as by body. Some of the girls, to my amazement, began to play, splashing water on one another. They were laughing. No one paid me attention, save that I, like the others, was always under the eye of a guard. I was lonely. I approached Ute, but she turned away. She had not forgotten that I had tried to shirk in the harness. When I was permitted I left the water and sat on the grass, my chin on my knees, alone.

On the bank Targo beamed. He liked to see his girls happy. I supposed, idly, that a happy girl was easier to sell. The guards, too, seemed in a good humor. They called out things to the girls which made them squeak and fume, and the girls, laughing, called back things to them, uncomplimentary I gathered, which made them laugh, and slap their knees in amusement. One girl splashed water on the one-eyed, grizzled guard and he plunged into the water and, to the laughter of all, gave her a good ducking. When she came up sputtering and he, shivering, soaking wet in his clothes, emerged from the stream, even I laughed. Then the girls were called from the water, to dry their hair. They knelt in a circle, laughing and talking.

They did not notice me. I had been forgotten.

When the grizzled, one-eyed guard returned to the bank, now clad in dry clothes, the girls cried out to him, pleading with him, and he leapt into the center of the circle and began, wildly, to regale them with some narrative, which seemed to require much gesticulation. It must have been hilarious, for they squealed with amusement. Even I smiled, to see him leaping about, his arms waving, his face first transformed with mock horror and then, at last, after a wild stroke, as though with a spear, transfigured with a mock triumphal ecstasy.

The girls howled with laughter, and slapped their left shoulders with the palms of their right hands. He bowed to them and, gravely, left the circle. They continued to slap their shoulders with pleasure. He shook his head regally, however, and would not re-enter the circle. I saw Lana glance in my direction. Then, she leapt to her feet, to the center of the circle, and she cried out to Targo, oh so prettily, and held out her hands to him. He smiled, and said something to one of his grinning men. To my anger, the clothes that had been taken from me were brought to the circle.

Lana, not without some difficulty, drew them on.

How beautiful she was in my clothing! She wore them better than I!

Then Targo, protesting, was pulled by two squealing girls to the center of the circle. Then, Lana, imperiously, began to upbraid him. I did not care for her performance. The girls, however, seemed to relish it with uncontrolled glee. Lana walked about Targo, crying out at him and gesturing. And she addressed herself, too, to the other girls, as though laughing at them and mocking them. Her voice was as haughty and supercilious, as cold, as amused, as commanding, as that of an empress. She treated them all as though they might be less than the dirt beneath her feet. She had a way of lifting her head, putting her nose in the air, turning her face to one side, as though bored, and making a slight movement of her entire body and especially the right hand, as though she were irritated beyond all patience, but would try to control herself. The girls shrieked with laughter. Lana was an excellent mimic. I was furious.

Then the two girls who had pulled Targo to the circle leaped on Lana and stripped her, throwing her to the grass before Targo. Another girl leaped up and pretended to beat her while Lana wiggled, and squirmed and howled, in mock pain. Then, when she was released she crawled rapidly to Targo, shuddering, thrust her head to his feet, seized his foot and began to cover his sandal with kisses.

The girls howled with amusement.

Several of them looked at me, to see my reaction. I looked away.

Targo clapped his hands twice and, once again, there were masters and slave girls.

A box of combs and brushes was brought. Then the girls, in pairs, began to comb and brush one another's hair. Several vied to comb and brush Lana's hair. I was given a comb.

Timidly I went to Ute. There were tears in my eyes. I could not even speak her language. I could not tell her I was sorry that I had shirked in the harness, trying to let others work for me. I could not even tell her I was desperately unhappy, that I was lonely. I could not tell her that I wanted her, more than anything, to be my friend.

In the stream she had rejected me, turning away from me.

I went to Ute, and she turned and looked at me. Timidly, fearing that she might turn away again, I indicated that I wished to be allowed to comb her hair, if I might, if it might please her for me to do so.

She looked at me, coldly.

Sobbing, I fell to my knees before her, unable to speak to her, and put my head to her feet.

Then she was kneeling before me, and lifted my head. There were tears, too, in her eyes.

"El-in-or," she said, and kissed me.

I wept, and kissed her.

Then she turned, still kneeling, and permitted me to comb

her hair. When I had finished, she took the comb, and combed mine.

My two favorites among the girls were Ute and Inge, who was of the scribes. These two names are, in sound at least, German names. Neither of the girls, however, spoke German, of which I had learned a few words, or French, which I can speak with some fluency. Both were Gorean girls, totally. Neither, of course, knew English. Many Gorean names are apparently of Earth origin.

Almost immediately Ute, and Inge, as well, began to teach me Gorean.

It took many days to reach the banks of the Laurius.

We encountered four more caravans, and, at each, Targo put forth his display chain. I was fourth on the chain. I wished that Lana would be sold. I hoped that Ute and Inge would not be.

With these caravans there were slave girls, who would sometimes come to look at us, with their masters. How I envied them their freedom, unchained, to run and laugh and walk as they pleased. How beautiful they were in their brief slave tunics, with the loop on the left shoulder. How smug they were, in their lock collars, on the arms of their masters, regarding us. How they looked down on us, kneeling on the grass, fastened in the display chain, naked, unbought girls.

Strangely I gave little thought to the possibility that I might be sold. Once, however, after I had lifted my head, smiled prettily, and uttered the ritual phrase of the inspected slave girl, "Buy me, Master," my heart nearly stopped. The man had not continued on. He was still regarding me. Further, with horror, I realized that he was regarding me with some interest. I could tell by his eyes. I had a terrible, sinking feeling. I turned white. I wanted to get up and cry out, and run, dragging wildly at the chain. Then, to my unspeakable relief, he was no longer in front of me, but was inspecting the next girl. I heard her "Buy me, Master." I began to shudder. He also stopped before another girl, the ninth on the chain. When he had traversed the chain, he returned to stand before me. It was as though I was made

of wood. I could not meet his eyes. I was terrified. I could
not even repeat, "Buy me, Master." He was then further
down the chain again, before the ninth girl. He purchased
her. Targo sold two girls that afternoon. I saw moneys exchange hands. I saw the ninth girl released from the chain.
I saw her kneeling before her buyer, back on her heels, head
down, arms extended, wrists crossed, as though for binding.
It was the submission of the girl to her new master. He
put slave bracelets on her, fastening her wrists together,
and put a leash on her throat. I saw him lock the leash
to a ring on the side of his wagon. She wanted
to touch him, but he cuffed her away. She seemed timid,
but happy. It had been a long time since she had been
owned by a master. I wondered what it would be like to
belong to a man. I shuddered. The girl knelt in the shade of
the wagon until the caravan moved, and then, getting up,
leashed, walked beside the wagon. She turned once, lifting
her braceleted wrists. We waved to her. She seemed happy.

Twice we stopped at palisaded villages, those of simple
bosk herders. I liked these stops, for there we would have
fresh bosk milk, still hot, and would have a roof over our
heads for a night, be it only of grass. These villagers would
always spread fresh straw in the hut in which we would be
chained for the night. It smelled clean, and was dry. I loved
to lie on it, after the canvas spread over the hard boards
of the wagons.

Ute and Inge, and Ute in particular, were patient, inde-
fatigable teachers. They taught me Gorean for hours a day,
and, of course, I heard nothing but this language. I soon
found myself saying things in Gorean without thinking about
it. I was taught the language as a child is taught, who has
no language at his disposal. Accordingly I learned the language directly and immediately, fluidly, not as an archi-
tecture of grammatical cases and a series of vocabulary lists,
in which foreign terms stood matched with English terms.
Ute and Inge, not knowing English, could not have presented me with an abstract structure of transformations
and linguistic equations if they had wished. Knowing no
English themselves, they had no choice but to teach me a

living language, in life, as practical and concrete as a tool, as expressive and beautiful as flowers and clouds. It was not long before I caught myself, upon occasion, thinking in Gorean. And, only some ten days after my lessons had begun, I had my first dream in which intelligible Gorean was spoken to me and I responded, spontaneously, without thinking, in the same tongue. Interestingly, it was a dream in which I had managed to steal a candy and blame Lana, and she was beaten for it. I enjoyed the dream, but then it seemed Targo was coming for me, with the straps swinging in his hand. I awakened in a cold sweat, but safely chained in the wagon, on the canvas. It was raining outside, and I could hear the rain beat on the squarish roof of red rain canvas stretched over our heads. I could hear the breathing of the other girls in the wagon. I snuggled down again on the folded canvas beneath my body and, with a rustle of chain, listening to the rain, soon fell asleep again. In the beginning my grammer was not particularly good, but Inge helped me improve it. After a time, I could even detect certain regional differences in the dialects of the girls and the guards. My vocabulary would gradually become far more extensive, but I was pleased with myself. In only a few days, under the intensive tutelage of Ute and Inge, I had, to my delight and surprise, learned to speak passable Gorean. There was a special reason, of course, why I was so eager to learn the language. I wished to make contact with men who could return me to Earth. I was certain that I could, with my resources on Earth, purchase swift passage back to my home planet.

Once I noted, speaking to Inge, that Ute, regularly, made certain grammatical errors.

"Yes," said Inge, matter-of-factly, "she is of the leather workers."

I then felt superior to Ute. I myself would not make those mistakes. I was Elinor Brinton.

"I will speak high-caste Gorean," I told Inge.

"But you are a barbarian," said Inge.

Briefly I hated her.

I told myself that Inge, with all her pretensions, she

of the scribes, would still be a chained slave girl, at the beck
and call of a master, when I, Elinor Brinton, was safe on
Earth, once again in my snug penthouse. And Ute, too!
Foolish, stupid little Ute, who could not even speak her own
language correctly! What could that meaningless little thing,
pretty as she was, ever be but a man's toy? She was a natural
slave girl! She belonged in chains. And Inge, too, for she was
arrogant! They would remain on Gor, mastered girls, while
I, Elinor Brinton, rich and clever, secure and safe, laughed
in my penthouse a world away! How amusing that would
be!

"Why does El-in-or laugh?" asked Ute, looking up.

"Elinor," I corrected her.

"Elinor," smiled Ute.

"It is nothing," I said.

We heard one of the guards shouting outside. We also
heard, in the distance, some bosk bells.

"A retinue!" shouted one of the guards.

"There is a free woman with the retinue!" shouted another.

I heard Targo crying out. "Slaves out!"

I was thrilled. I had never seen a Gorean free woman.
A guard hastily unlocked one end of the ankle bar and lifted
it. One by one, we slid along the bar and to the back edge
of the wagon, where the gate had been dropped. My ankles,
and those of the other girls, were still joined, of course, by
about a foot of chain and two ankle rings. As we left the
wagon, each of us, one by one, we were thonged in a line,
by binding fiber, in throat coffle. Then, craning for a look,
we lined up beside the wagon. The girls from the other
wagon, ahead of us, Lana among them, were already on
the grass, looking.

We could see a large, flat wagon, drawn by four huge,
beautifully groomed black bosk.

On the wagon, under a fringed, silken canopy, on a
curule chair, there sat a woman.

The wagon was flanked by perhaps forty warriors, with
spears, twenty to a side.

We could hear the bosk bells, on the harness of the bosk,

quite clearly now. The retinue would pass close by. Targo had gone out, his blue and yellow robe swirling, part way to meet it.

"Kneel," said one of the guards.

We did so, as in the display chain.

A Gorean slave girl in the presence of a free man or woman always kneels, unless excused from doing so. I had even learned to kneel when addressed by the guards and, of course, always, when approached by Targo, my master. A Gorean slave, incidentally, always addresses free men as "Master," and all free women as "Mistress."

I watched the flat wagon rolling closer.

The woman sat regally on the curule chair, wrapped in resplendent, many-colored silks. Her raiment might have cost more than any three or four of us together were worth. She was, moreover, veiled.

"Do you dare look upon a free woman?" asked a guard.

I not only dared, but I was eager to do so. But, nudged by his foot, as the wagon approached, I lowered my head to the grass, as did the other girls.

The wagon, and the retinue, stopped only a few feet opposite us.

I did not dare to raise my head.

I suddenly then understood that I was not as she. For the first time in my life I suddenly understood, kneeling in the grass in a Gorean field, the thundering, devastating realities of social institutions. I suddenly understood, as I had not before, how on Earth my position and my wealth had created an aura about me, that made lesser people respect me and move aside when I wished to pass, that made them deferential to me, eager to please me, fearful should they fail to do so. How naturally I had carried myself differently than they, better, more arrogantly. I was better! I was their superior! But now I was taken from my world.

"Lift your head, Child," said a woman's voice.

I did so.

She was no older than I, I am sure, but she addressed me as a child.

The guard's foot nudged me again.

"Buy me, Mistress," I stammered.

"A barbarian," smiled the woman. "How amusing."

"I picked her up in the fields," said Targo. He was anxious that my presence on his chain not be taken as evidence of his poor judgment. He wished to assure the woman that he had had me for nothing, that he would not have purchased such an inferior girl for his chain.

I looked into her eyes. How steadily she regarded me, over her veil, her eyes amused. How beautiful she seemed. How splendid and fine! I could no longer meet her eyes.

"You may lower your head, Girl," she said, not unkindly.

Gratefully I put my head again, swiftly, to the grass.

I was furious with how I acted, how I felt, but I could not help myself.

She was so magnificent. I was nothing. The other girls, too, had their heads to the grass, kneeling before the free woman. They, like I, were only slaves, stripped, their ankles chained, their throats in leather coffle, branded girls, nothing before one who was free.

I wept. I was a slave girl.

There was a rustle of bosk bells and a creak of wheels. Targo moved back, bowing deeply, and the wagon slowly moved past us. The feet of the flanking guards passed within a yard or two of us.

When the wagon, and the retinue, had passed us, Targo straightened up. He had a strange expression on his face.

He was pleased about something.

"Into the wagons," said Targo.

"Into the wagons!" called the guards.

We were returned to the wagons.

"Who was she?" asked the grizzled, one-eyed guard.

"The Lady Rena of Lydius," said Targo, "of the Builders."

Once again I found myself, with the other girls, chained in our wagon, moving slowly across the Gorean fields toward Laura.

That night, at a stream, we stopped early to camp. In the evening, the girls, under guard, attend to various tasks. They tend the bosk, clean the wagons, draw water and gather firewood. Sometimes they are permitted to cook. Ute and

I, tied together by the throat, but otherwise unimpeded, wearing our camisks, like the other girls, under a guard, went off with two buckets to gather berries. There were not many berries, and it was not easy to fill our buckets. I stole berries from Ute's bucket, and had mine filled first. We were not supposed to eat the berries, and I do not think Ute did, but I would slip them inside my mouth when the guard was not looking. If one was careful to keep the juices inside there was no telltale sign on the lips and chin. Ute was such a sweet, precious little fool.

When we returned to the camp it was near dark. I was surprised to see, glowing near our wagon, a small, hot fire, banked with stones. From the fire there protruded the handles of two irons.

When we had been fed, we were allowed to sit near the wagons. We wore our camisks. Our only fetter was a length of binding fiber, fastening us together, at intervals of about a yard. It was tied about the left ankle of each girl.

For some reason the girls did not talk much.

Suddenly the guards leaped to their feet, seizing their spears.

Out of the darkness came two men, warriors. Between them, face-stripped, was a woman, stumbling. Her arms, over her resplendent robes, were bound to her sides with a broad leather strap. She was thrown to the feet of Targo. I, and the other girls, crowded about, but the guards pushed us back with their spears. The woman struggled to her knees, but was not permitted to rise. Her eyes were wild. She shook her head, no. Targo then, piece by piece, from the leather pouch at his belt, handed forty-five pieces of gold to the chief of the two men. The girls cried out in amazement. It was a fantastic price. And he had not even assessed her! We realized then that she had been contracted for in advance. The two men took Targo's gold and withdrew into the darkness.

"You were foolish to hire mercenaries to guard you," said Targo.

"Please!" she cried.

I recognized her then. She was the woman with the retinue.

I felt pleasure.

"Please!" wept the woman. I admitted to myself that she was beautiful.

"You have an admirer," Targo told her, "a Captain of Tyros, who glimpsed you in Lydius last fall. He has contracted to buy you privately in Ar, to be taken to his pleasure gardens on Tyros. He will pay one hundred pieces of gold."

Several of the girls gasped.

"Who?" asked the captive, plaintively.

"You will learn when you are sold to him," said Targo. "Curiosity is not becoming in a Kajira," said Targo. "You might be beaten for it."

I remembered that the large man, on the planet Earth, had said to me this thing. I gathered that it was a Gorean saying.

The woman, distraught, shook her head.

"Think!" urged Targo. "Were you cruel to someone? Did you slight someone? Did you not grant someone the courtesy that was his due?"

The woman looked terrified.

"Strip her," said Targo.

"No, no!" she wept.

The strap was removed from her body, and her clothing cut from her.

She was bound tightly over the large rear wheel of our wagon. Her right thigh, particularly, was lashed tightly to it, with several straps of binding fiber. I myself wore my brand on the left thigh.

I watched her being branded.

She screamed terribly, her head back. Then she was sobbing, her cheek pressed against the rim.

We girls crowded about her.

Her head was down on the rim.

"Lift your head, Child," I told her.

She lifted her head and gazed at me, her eyes glazed. She was naked. I wore a camisk! In fury I struck her face. "Slave!" I screamed. "Slave!" I struck her again. A guard pulled me away. Ute went to the girl and put her arms about her shoulders. Comforting her. I was furious.

"Into the wagons," called Targo.

"Into the wagons!" repeated the guards.

The binding fiber was removed from our ankles and soon we were chained again in the wagons.

The new girl was placed in our wagon, near the front. She was bound hand and foot and tied on her side, that she might not tear at her brand. A slave hood, with gag, was placed on her, that her weeping and cries might not disturb our rest.

Soon, to my interest, the guards had hitched up the bosk, and, by the light of the three moons, we were moving slowly again over the fields.

Targo did not wish to remain too long in this place.

"Tomorrow," I heard him say, "we reach Laura."

8   WHAT OCCURRED NORTH
OF LAURA

WE REACHED THE BANKS OF THE LAURIUS shortly after dawn
the following morning.

It was foggy, and cold. I, and the other girls, with the
exception of the new girl, freshly branded, hooded and
gagged, bound on her side, had crawled between the layers
of canvas on which we rode in the wagon. I, and some of
the other girls, lifted up the side canvas of the square-
canvassed wagon and peeped out, into the early morning
fog.

We could smell fish and the river.

Through the fog we could see men moving about, here
and there, some low wooden huts. Several of the men must
be fishermen, already returning with a first catch, who had
hunted the river's surface with torches and tridents at night.
Others, with nets, were moving down toward the water. We
could see poles of fish hanging to the sides. There were
some wagons, too, moving in the direction that ours was. I
saw some men, too, carrying burdens, sacks and roped
bundles of fagots. In the doorway of one of the small
wooden huts I saw a slave girl, in a brief brown tunic, regarding us. Where the tunic parted, at her throat, I caught
the glint of a steel collar.

Suddenly the butt of a spear struck at the canvas where
we were looking and we quickly put down the side wall.

I looked about at the other girls, in the early light. They
were awake now. They seemed excited. Laura would be my
first Gorean city. Would there be someone here who would
send me home? How frustrated I was, chained in the wagon.
Even the back flap of the wagon had been tied down. The

canvas was damp, and stained from the dew and fog, and an early morning rain. I wanted to cry out and scream my name, and cry for help. I clenched my fists and did not do so.

The wagon began to tilt forward then and I knew we were moving down the slope toward the river bank. I could also tell that the wheels were slipping in the mud, and I heard the creak of the heavy brake being thrown forward, backing the shoe against the front left wheel rim. Then, bit by bit, releasing the brake and applying it, the wagon, jolting, slipped and slid forward and downward. Then I heard pebbles beneath the wheels and the wagon was level again.

We sat there for several minutes, and then, eventually, we heard Targo haggling with a barge master for passage across the river.

The wagon then rolled forward onto a wooden pier. The bosk bellowed. The smell of the river and the fish was strong. The air was cold and damp, and fresh.

"Slaves out," we heard.

The back flap of the wagon was tied up and the back gate of the wagon swung downward.

The grizzled, one-eyed guard unlocked the ankle bar, lifting it.

"Slaves out," he said.

As we slid to the back of the wagon our ankle rings were removed. Then, naked, unchained, we were herded to the river edge of the wooden pier. I was cold. I saw a sudden movement in the water. Something, with a twist of its great spine, had suddenly darted from the waters under the pier and entered the current of the Laurius. I saw the flash of a triangular, black dorsal fin.

I screamed.

Lana looked out, pointing after it. "A river shark," she cried, excitedly. Several of the girls looked after it, the fin cutting the waters and disappearing in the fog on the surface.

I huddled back from the edge of the pier, between Inge and Ute. Ute put her arms about me.

A broad, low-sided barge began to back toward the pier. It had two large steering oars, manned by bargemen. It was drawn by two gigantic, web-footed river tharlarion. These were the first tharlarion that I had ever seen. They frightened me. They were scaled, vast and long-necked. Yet in the water it seemed, for all their bulk, they moved delicately. One dipped its head under the surface and, moments later, the head emerged, dripping, the eyes blinking, a silverish fish struggling in the small, triangular-toothed jaws. It engorged the fish, and turned its small head, eyes now unblinking, to regard us. They were harnessed to the broad barge. They were controlled by a bargeman, with a long whipping stick, who was ensconced in a leather basket, part of the harness, slung between the two animals. He would also shout at them, commands, interspersed with florid Gorean profanity, and, slowly, not undelicately, they responded to his cries. The barge grated against the pier.

The cost for transporting a free person across the Laurius was a silver tarsk. The cost for transporting an animal, however, was only a copper tarn disk. I realized, with a start, that that was what I would cost. Targo was charged twenty-one copper tarn disks for myself, the other girls, the new girl, and his four bosk. He had sold four girls before reaching the banks of the Laurius. The bosk were disengaged from the wagons and tied forward on the barge. Also forward on the barge was a slave cage, and two guards, with the sides of their spears, herded us onto the barge, across its planking and into the cage. Behind us I heard one of the bargemen slam the heavy iron door and slide the heavy iron bolt into place. I looked back. He snapped shut a heavy padlock. We were caged.

I held the bars, and looked across the river to Laura. Behind me I could hear the two wagons being rolled onto the barge and then, with chains, being fastened in place. They were mounted on large circles of wood, which could rotate. Thus the wagon may be brought forward onto the barge and, when the circle is rotated, be removed the same way. The fog had begun to lift and the surface of the river, broad, slow-moving, glistened here and there in patches. A few dozen yards to my right a fish leaped out of the water and disappeared again, leaving behind him bright, glistening, spreading circles. I heard the cry of two gulls overhead.

The bargeman in the leather basket shouted out and slapped the two tharlarion on the neck with the whipping stick.

There must be someone in Laura who could return me to the United States, or who could put me in touch with those who could!

There were other barges on the river, some moving across the river, others coming toward Laura, others departing. Those departing used only the current. Those approaching were drawn by land tharlarion, plodding on log roads along the edges of the river. The land tharlarion can swim barges across the river, but he is not as efficient as the vast river tharlarion. Both sides of the river are used to approach Laura, though the northern shore is favored. Unharnessed tharlarion, returning to Lydius at the mouth of the Laurius, generally follow the southern shore road, which is not as much used by towing tharlarion as the northern.

On these barges, moving upriver, I could see many crates and boxes, which would contain such goods, rough goods, as metal, and tools and cloth. Moving downstream I could see other barges, moving the goods of the interior downriver, such objects as planking, barrels of fish, barrels of salt, loads of stone, and bales of fur. On some of the barges moving upstream I saw empty slave cages, not unlike the one in which I was secured. I saw only one slave cage on a barge moving downstream. It contained four or five nude male slaves. They seemed dejected, huddled in their cage. Strangely, a broad swath had been shaven lengthwise on their head. Lana saw this and shrieked out, hooting at them across the water. The men did not even look at us, moving slowly across the current toward Laura.

I looked at Ute.

"That means they are men who were taken by women," said Ute. "See," she said, pointing up to the hills and forests north of Laura. "Those are the great forests. No one knows how far they extend to the east, and they go north

as far as Torvaldsland. In them there are the forest people,
but also many bands of outlaws, some of women and some
of men."

"Women?" I asked.

"Some call them the forest girls," said Ute. "Others call
them the panther girls, for they dress themselves in the
teeth and skins of forest panthers, which they slay with
their spears and bows."

I looked at her.

"They live in the forest without men," she said, "saving
those they enslave, and then sell, when tiring of them. They
shave the heads of their male slaves in that fashion to humili-
ate them. And that, too, is the way they sell them, that all
the world may know that they fell slave to females, who then
sold them."

"Who are these women?" I asked. "Where do they come
from?"

"Some were doubtless once slaves," said Ute. "Others were
once free women. Perhaps they did not care for matches
arranged by their parents. Perhaps they did not care for the
ways of their cities with respect to women. Who knows? In
many cities a free woman may not even leave her dwelling
without the permission of a male guardian or member of
her family." Ute smiled up at me. "In many cities a slave
girl is more free to come and go, and be happy, than a free
woman."

I looked out through the bars. I could now see, fairly
clearly, the wooden buildings of Laura. The water was wet
and glistening on the backs of the two tharlarion drawing
the barge.

"Do not be so sad and miserable, El-in-or," said Ute.
"When you wear a collar and have a master, you will be
more happy."

I glared at her. "I will never wear a collar and have a
master," I hissed at her.

Ute smiled.

"You want a collar and a master," she said.

Poor stupid Ute! I would be free! I would return to Earth!

I would be rich again, and powerful! I would hire servants! I would have another Maserati!

I restrained myself. "Were you ever happy with a master?" I asked, acidly.

"Oh yes!" said Ute, happily. Her eyes shone.

I looked at her, disgustedly. "What happened?" I asked.

She looked down. "I tried to bend him to my will," she said. "He sold me."

I looked away, out through the bars. The fog had now dispelled. The morning sun was bright on the surface of the river.

"In every woman," said Ute, "there is a Free Companion and a slave girl. The Free Companion seeks for her companion, and the slave girl seeks her master."

"That is absurd," I said.

"Are you not a female?" asked Ute.

"Of course," I said.

"Then," said Ute, "there is a slave girl in you that wants her master."

"You are a fool," I told her, savagely. "A fool!"

"You are a female," said Ute. "What sort of man could master you?"

"No man could master me!" I told her.

"In your dreams," she asked, "what sort of man is it who touches you, who binds you and carries you away, who takes you to his fortress, who forces you to do his bidding?"

I recalled how, outside the penthouse, hurrying to the garage, a man had looked at me, and had not looked away, and how, fleeing, branded, frightened, helpless, I had felt, for the first time in my life, vulnerably and radically female. I recalled, too, how in the bungalow, when I had examined the mark on my thigh, and the collar that was then at my throat, how I had felt, briefly, helpless, owned, a captive, the property of others. I recalled the brief fantasy which had passed through my mind of myself, in such a band, marked as I was, naked in the arms of a barbarian. I had shuddered, frightened. Never before had I felt such a feeling. I recalled I had been curious for the touch of a man—perhaps for that of a master? I could not rid my mind of the brief feeling I had felt. It had recurred in my mind, from time to time, particularly at night in the wagon. Once it had made me feel so lonely and restless that I had wept. Two times I had heard other girls crying in the wagon. Once, Ute.

"I do not have such dreams," I told her.

"Oh," said Ute.

"El-in-or is a cold fish," volunteered Lana.

I glared at her, tears in my eyes.

"No," said Ute, "El-in-or is only sleeping."

Lana looked across the cage. "El-in-or wants a master," she said.

"No!" I screamed, weeping. "No! No!"

The girls then, except for Ute, but even including Inge, began to laugh and cry out, mocking me, in a singsong voice, "El-in-or wants a master! El-in-or wants a master!"

"No!" I cried, and turned away, putting my face against the bars.

Ute put her arms about me. "Do not make El-in-or weep," she scolded the other girls.

I hated them, even Ute. They were slaves, slaves!

"Look!" cried Inge, pointing upward.

Far away, through the sky, from the east of Laura, following the forest line, there came a flight of tarnsmen, perhaps forty of them, mounted on the great, fierce, hawklike saddlebirds of Gor, the huge, swift, predatory, ferocious tarns, called Brothers of the Wind. The men seemed small on the backs of the great birds. They carried spears, and were helmeted. Shields hung on the right sides of the saddles.

The girls, thrilled, pressed against the bars, crying out and pointing.

They were far off, but even from the distance I found myself frightened. I wondered what manner of men such men might be, that they could master such winged monsters. I was terrified. I shrank back in the cage.

Targo came forward on the barge, and, shielding his eyes against the early morning sun, looked upward. He spoke to the one-eyed guard, who stood behind him. "It is Haakon of Skjern," he said.

The one-eyed guard nodded.

Targo seemed pleased.

The tarnsmen had now, somewhere behind Laura, brought their great birds to the earth.

"The compound of Haakon is outside of Laura, to the north," said Targo.

Then Targo and the one-eyed guard returned toward the stern of the barge, where two of the bargemen handled the great steering oars. There were six in the crew of the barge, the man who directed the two tharlarion, the two helmsmen, the captain, and two other bargemen, who attended to matters on the barge, and handled mooring and casting off. One of the latter had locked the slave cage.

We were now better than two thirds of the way across the broad river.

We could see stone, and timber and barrels of fish and salt stored on docks on the shore. Behind the docks were long, planked ramps leading up to warehouses. The warehouses seemed constructed of smoothed, heavy timbers, stained and varnished. Most appeared reddish. Almost all had roofs with wooden shingles, painted black. Many were ornamented, particularly above the great double doors, with carvings and woodwork, painted in many colors. Through the great doors I could see large central areas, and various floors, reached by more ramps. There seemed many goods in the warehouses. I could see men moving about, inside, and on the ramps, and about the docks. Various barges were being loaded and unloaded. Except for villages, Laura was the only civilization in the region. Lydius, the free port at the mouth of the Laurius, was more than two hundred pasangs downstream. The new girl had been Rena of Lydius, of the Builders, one of the five high castes of Gor. She still lay, secured, in the wagon. I expected Targo would keep her hooded and gagged in Laura, for it was possible she might be known there. I smiled to myself. She would not escape Targo. Then I shook the bars with rage.

The tharlarion now turned slowly in the broad river, near Laura, and, under the stick, and cries, of their driver, began to back the barge against its pier. The helmsmen, at their steering oars, shouting and cursing, brought the barge to its mooring. There was a slight shock as the heavy, wet, rolled hides tied at the back of the barge struck the pier. The two extra crewmen, standing on the deck, threw great looped ropes over heavy iron mooring cleats, fastened in the pier. Then they leaped to the pier and, with smaller ropes, fastened to the same cleats, began to draw the barge close to the pier. There is no rear railing on the barges and the barge deck matches the pier in height. Once the ropes are secured the wagons may be rolled directly onto the pier.

A man came forward and untied the straps leading to the nose rings of the bosk from the bosk ring on the deck. He led them back toward the stern of the barge and onto the pier. The broad cricles of wood on which the wagons were mounted were now rotated, so that the wagon tongues faced the pier. The bosk, now, bellowing and snuffing, and skuffing at the wood with their hoofs, were being backed toward the harness. The two extra crewmen were unchaining the wagon.

Some men came down to the pier to watch us land. Others stopped, too, for a time, to regard us.

The men wore rough work tunics. They seemed hardy.

There was a strong smell of fish and salt in the air.

There is little market in simple Laura for the more exquisite goods of Gor. Seldom will one find there Torian rolls of gold wire, interlocking cubes of silver from Tharna, rubies carved into tiny, burning panthers from Schendi, nutmegs and cloves, spikenard and peppers from the lands east of Bazi, the floral brocades, the perfumes of Tyros, the dark wines, the gorgeous, diaphanous silks of glorious Ar. Life, even by Gorean standards, is primitive in the region of the Laurius, and northward, to the great forests, and along the coast, upward to Torvaldsland.

Yet I had little doubt that the strong, large-handed men of Laura, sturdy in their work tunics, who stopped to regard us, would not appreciate the body of a slave girl, provided she is vital, and loves, and leaps helplessly to their touch.

"Tal, Kajirae!" cried one of the men, waving.

Ute pressed against the bars, waving back at him.

The men cheered.

"Do not smile at anyone," warned Lana. "It would not be well to be sold in Laura."

"I do not care where I am sold," said Ute.

"You are high on the chain," said Inge to Ute. "Targo will not sell you until he reaches Ar." Then Inge looked at me, frankly. "He might sell you," she told me. "You are an untrained barbarian."

I hated Inge.

But I feared she was right. I suddenly became afraid that I might be sold in this river port to spend the rest of my life as the slave of a fisherman or woodsman, cooking and tending his hut. What a fate for Elinor Brinton! I must not be sold here! I must not!

One of the extra bargemen came and, with his heavy key, unlocked the large padlock that secured the gate of our slave cage. With a creak, he swung open the gate.

Our own guards were behind him. "Slaves out," said one of them. "Single file."

We saw that the bosk had now been harnessed.

When we emerged from the cage, one by one, we were given our camisks, and placed in throat coffle, fastened therein with a long length of binding fiber, the fiber looped about the neck of each, knotted, and then passed on to the next girl. Our hands and feet were free. Where would one run in Laura? Where would one run anywhere?

Barefoot we left the barge and stepped out onto the pier, walking along the left sides of the wagons.

I could see a long wooden ramp leading up from the pier to a long wooden road winding between the crowded warehouses. We, in coffle, followed this road. I liked the smell of Laura, the fresh fields before the forests, even the smell of the river and the wood. We could smell roast tarsk from somewhere. We, and the wagons, passed between wooden

sleds, with leather runners, on which there were squared
blocks of granite, from the quarries east of Laura; and between barrels and hogsheads of fish and salt; and between
bales of sleen fur and panther hides, from the forests beyond.
I put out my hand and touched some of the sleen fur as I
passed it. It was not unpleasing to my touch. There were
men who came to stand along the edge of the road to
watch us pass. I gathered that we were good merchandise. I
walked very straight, not looking at them. Then one of them,
as I passed him, reached out and seized my leg, from the
back, behind the knee. I cried out with alarm, leaping away.
The men laughed. One of the guards stepped between us,
with his spear. "Buy her," he said, not pleasantly. The man
bowed low to the guard in mock apology. The other men
laughed, and we continued on our way. I could feel his hand
on my leg for several minutes. For some reason I was
pleased. No one had reached out to touch Lana!

The smell of roast tarsk became stronger and, to our
delight, the wagons turned and rolled into one of the huge
warehouses. The floor was smooth. When we were inside the
doors were closed. Then, kneeling, delighted, we were fed
bread and roast tarsk, and hot bosk milk.

I became aware of Targo standing over me.

"Why did the docksman touch you?" he asked.

I put down my head. "I do not know, Master," I said.

The one-eyed, grizzled guard stood near Targo. "She now
walks better than she did," he said.

"Do you think she might become beautiful?" asked Targo.

That seemed to me a strange question. Surely a girl is
either beautiful or not beautiful.

"She might," said the guard. "She has become more beautiful just since we have owned her."

This pleased me, but I did not undertand it.

"It is hard for a white silk girl to be beautiful," said
Targo.

"Yes," said the guard, "but there is a good market for
white silkers."

I did not understand this.

When I looked at Targo again, he said, "Put her six on the chain."

I looked down, flushed with pleasure. When I looked up again Targo and the guard were elsewhere. I began to chew my bread and roast tarsk. I glanced at the former five and six girl, now four and five. They were not much pleased. "Barbarian," said the six girl. "Five girl," I said to her.

But Targo did not display his chain in Laura, to my relief. He wanted higher prices.

After we had eaten we continued on our way, climbing the wooden streets, tied together by the neck beside the wagons. Once we passed a paga tavern, and, inside, belled and jeweled, otherwise unclothed, I saw a girl dancing on a square of sand between the tables. She danced slowly, exquisitely, to the music of primitive instruments. I was stunned. Then there was a jerk at my neck, on the binding fiber, and the guard prodded me ahead with the butt of his spear. Never had I seen so sensuous a woman. About noon we arrived at a slave compound north of Laura. There are several such. Targo had rented space in one compound, adjoining others. Our compound shared a common wall of bars with another, that of Haakon of Skjern, whom Targo had traveled north to do business with. The compounds are formed of windowless log dormitories, floored with stone on which straw is spread; the dormitory then opens by one small door, about a yard high, into the barred exercise yard. This yard resembles a large cage. Its walls are bars, and its roof, too. The roof bars are supported at places in the yard by iron stanchions. There had been rain recently in Laura and the yard was muddy, but I found it more pleasant than the stuffy interior of the dormitory. We were not permitted our camisks in the compound, perhaps because of the mud in the yard.

In the compound adjoining ours, crowded, there were some two hundred and fifty to three hundred village girls. Some of these, not too many, did a good deal of wailing, which I did not much care for. I was pleased that the guards, with whips, kept them silent at night. That way we could all get some sleep. They were stripped and slaves, but, each morning, they would still braid one another's long, blond hair. That seemed important to them, and they were permitted to do it, for some reason. Targo's other girls, of whom I was one, all wore their hair long and combed, straight. I was hoping my hair would grow swiftly. Lana had the longest hair of all of us. It fell below the small of her back. I had fantasies of putting my hands in it and shaking her head until she screamed for mercy. Most of the village girls had not been branded as yet. None wore collars. They were generally blue-eyed, though some were gray-eyed. They were girls taken by the raiders of Haakon of Skjern, in the villages to the north of the Laurius, and from the coastal villages, upward even to the borders of Torvaldsland. Most did not seem too distressed about their slavery. I gathered that life in the villages must be hard for a young girl. Targo would have his pick of one hundred of these women. He had paid a deposit of fifty golden tarn disks, and on our first morning in the compound, I had seen him pay one hundred and fifty more to the huge, bearded, scowling Haakon of Skjern. I had watched Targo, not hurrying, with his expert eye and quick, delicate hands, examining the women. Sometimes they would try to pull away from him. When they did they were held by two guards. I recalled that he had once similarly examined me, shortly after we had encountered our first caravan. At one point I had cried out and my body had leaped, uncontrollably. He had seemed pleased. "Kajira," he had said. I noted that girls who responded similarly were invariably selected, sometimes over their more beautiful sisters in bondage. I thought, however, that none of them had responded as I had responded. Targo took more than two days to make his choices. When he did make a choice the girl was removed to our compound. They did not mix with us but, with their northern accents, kept to themselves. A full day was spent in the heating of irons and the branding of them. These were not pleasant days, incidentally, for the new girl, Rena of Lydius. She was kept within the dormitory, her wrists behind her back, fastened with slave bracelets, her neck chained to a heavy ring set in the wall. Further, except when she was fed, she was kept in a gag and slave hood. She would sit against the wall, knees drawn up, head down, the leather slave hood, with its gag, drawn over her head and features. I was given the task of feeding her. When I first unhooded her and removed the gag, she had pleaded with me that I help her escape, or tell others of her plight. What a fool she was! I would be beaten for such an act, perhaps even impaled! I told her "Be silent, Slave!" and rehooded and regagged her. I did not even feed her then, that she might learn her lesson. I ate her portion that morning, and again in the evening. I had two extra portions that day. The next morning when I freed her head she had tears in her eyes but did not try to speak to me. I fed her in silence, thrusting food into her mouth, telling her to eat swiftly, and then giving her a drink from the leather water bag. Then I resecured her. She had been of high caste. I hated her. I would treat her as what she was, a slave.

Beyond the compound of Haakon of Skjern I could see the compound of his tarns, where, hobbled, the great birds beat their wings, threw back their heads and screamed, and tore at the great pieces of bosk thrown before them. Sometimes they tore at their hobbles and struck at their keepers with their great yellowish, scimitarlike beaks. The wind driven by their pounding, snapping wings, with hurricanes of dust and small stones, could hurl a man from his feet. Those great rending beaks and pressing, ripping talons could tear him in two as easily as the great thighs of bosk on which they fed. Even separated as I was by three walls of bars, that of their compound, that of the far wall of Haakon's compound, and that of our common wall, these birds terrified me. The northern beauties of Haakon, too, I was pleased to see, cowered away from that side of their compound. Sometimes when one of the great birds screamed, several of them would scream, too, and run, huddling away against our bars, or flying into their log dormitory. I do not know why it is that women fear tarns so terribly, but we do. But most men do, too. It is a rare man who will approach a tarn. It is said that the tarn knows who is a tarnsman and who is not, and if one approaches him who is not, he will seize him and rip

him to pieces. It is little wonder that few men approach the
beasts. I had seen tarn keepers, but, except for Haakon of
Skjern, I had seen no tarnsmen. They were wild men, of the
caste of warriors, who spent much of their time in the
taverns of Laura, fighting and gambling and drinking, while
slave girls, excited and with shining eyes, served them and
pressed about them, begging to be noticed and ordered to
the alcoves. It was no wonder that some men, even warriors, hated and envied the arrogant, regal tarnsmen, one
night rich, the next impoverished, always at the elbow of
adventure, and war and pleasure, wearing their pride and
their manhood in their walk, in the steel at their side and the
look in their eyes.

But Haakon was a tarnsman, and he frightened me. He
was ugly, and he seemed treacherous.

Targo seemed nervous in doing business with him.

We remained six full days in Targo's rented compound
outside of Laura. On five of these days, in the morning, I
was taken with four other girls into Laura, leashed with
them, to bring back supplies. Two guards accompanied us.
But, interestingly, at a given building, one guard would separate me from the others and together, the guard and I, we
would go into the building, while the others continued on to
the market. Returning from the market they would call at
the building, at which time I and my guard would go outside. There I would be leashed with the others again, the
burdens would be redistributed, I would take up my share,
and, carrying my burden as a slave girl, on the head, balancing it with one hand, I and the others, under guard, would
return to the compound. The last two times I begged to do
so, and was permitted to carry a jar of wine on my head. Ute
had taught me to walk without spilling it. I enjoyed the men
watching me. Soon I could carry wine as well as any girl,
even Ute.

The building where I would wait on these days was the
house of a physician. I was taken through a corridor to a
special, rough room, where slaves were treated. There my
camisk would be removed. On the first day the physician, a
quiet man in the green garments of his caste, examined me,

thoroughly. The instruments he used, the tests he performed, the samples he required were not unlike those of Earth. Of special interest to me was the fact that this room, primitive though it might be, was lit by what, in Gorean, is called an energy bulb, an invention of the Builders. I could see neither cords nor battery cases. Yet the room was filled with a soft, gentle, white light, which the physician could regulate by rotating the base of the bulb. Further, certain pieces of his instrumentation were clearly far from primitive. For example, there was a small machine with guages and dials. In this he would place slides, containing drops of blood and urine, flecks of tissue, a strand of hair. With a stylus he would note readings on the machine, and, on the small screen at the top of the machine, I saw, vastly enlarged, what reminded me of an image witnessed under a microscope. He would briefly study this image, and then make further jottings with his stylus. The guard had strictly forbidden me to speak to the physician, other than to answer his questions, which I was to do promptly and accurately, regardless of their nature. Though the physician was not unkind I felt that he treated me as, and regarded me as, an animal. When I was not being examined, he would dismiss me to the side of the room, where I would kneel, alone, on the boards, until summoned again. They discussed me as though I were not there.

When he was finished he mixed several powders in three or four goblets, adding water to them and stirring them. These I was ordered to drink. The last was peculiarly foul.

"She requires the Stabilization Serums," said the physician.

The guard nodded.

"They are administered in four shots," said the physician. He nodded to a heavy, beamed, diagonal platform in a corner of the room. The guard took me and threw me, belly down, on the platform, fastening my wrists over my head and widely apart, in leather wrist straps. He similarly secured my ankles. The physician was busying himself with fluids and a syringe before a shelf in another part of the room, laden with vials.

I screamed. The shot was painful. It was entered in the small of my back, over the left hip.

They left me secured to the table for several minutes and then the physician returned to check the shot. There had been, apparently, no unusual reaction.

I was then freed.

"Dress," the physician told me.

I gratefully donned the camisk, fastening it tightly about my waist with the double loop of binding fiber.

I wanted to speak to the physician, desperately. In his house, in this room, I had seen instrumentation which spoke to me of an advanced technology, so different from what I had hitherto encountered in what seemed to me a primitive, beautiful, harsh world. The guard, with the side of the butt of his spear, pressed against my back, and I was thrust from the room. I looked over my shoulder at the physician. He regarded me, puzzled.

Outside the other four girls and their guard were waiting. I was leashed, given a burden, and, together, we all returned to Targo's compound.

I thought I saw a small man, garbed in black, watching us, but I was not sure.

We returned, similarly, to the physician's house on the next four days. On the first day I had been examined, given some minor medicines of little consequence, and the first shot in the Stabilization Series. On the second, third and fourth day I received the concluding shots of the series. On the fifth day the physician took more samples.

"The serums are effective," he told the guard.

"Good," said the guard.

On the second day, after the shot, I had tried to speak to the physician, in spite of the guard, to beg him for information.

The guard did not beat me but he slapped me twice, bringing blood to my mouth. Then I was gagged.

Later, outside, the guard looked at me, amused.

I stood facing him, head down, gagged.

"Do you wish to wear your gag home to the compound?" he asked.

I shook my head vigorously, No. If I did wear it back Targo would surely inquire, and I would doubtless be beaten. I had seen him, once or twice, tell a girl to ask a guard to beat her. The girl is then strung up by the wrists. And the guard uses not the handful of leather straps with which Lana, only with her woman's strength, had struck me, but the five-strap Gorean slave whip, wielded with the full, terrible strength of a man. I had no desire to feel it. I would be compliant, swift to obey and be pleasing in all things. No, I shook my head, no!

"Does the little slave beg her guard's forgiveness?" he asked, teasing me.

I nodded vigorously, Yes. It is hard to be a slave girl. Men tease you, but, in an instant they may change, and their eyes may grow hard. You must be careful what you say, what you do. They hold the power of the whip. I knelt to him, putting my head down to his feet. Then, as I had seen Lana once do, I gently took his leg in my hands and put my cheek, head down, against the side of his leg.

"All right," he said.

He untied the gag. I looked up at him, gratefully, my hands at his hips, as I had seen Lana do.

He suddenly seized me by the arms and lifted me to face him.

Suddenly, with terror, I realized I was going to be raped.

"Ho!" said a voice, that of the other guard. "It is time to return to the compound."

Angrily, my guard released me and I staggered back.

"She is white silk!" said the other guard, laughing uproariously.

The other girls, leashed behind him, were laughing.

My guard, however, with a great laugh, seized me and, like a naughty child, threw me across his knee. He then beat me, soundly, with the stinging flat of his hand, until I cried for mercy and wept.

I was only too happy to be leashed again and carry a burden.

The girls, even Ute, were laughing.

I was annoyed, humiliated.

"She's a lovely, isn't she?" said the guard who had interfered.

"She is learning the tricks of the slave girl," said my guard, grinning, breathing heavily.

The other guard looked at me. "Stand straight," he said. I did so. "Yes," he said, "she makes a lovely wench." And he added, "I would not mind owning her."

I walked back to the compound, proudly, with the deliberate, taunting, insolent grace of the slave girl. I knew then that men wanted me, the leashed animal carrying her burden, Elinor Brinton.

I did not, of course, try to speak again to the physician.

On the fourth day I received the last shot in the Stabilization Series. On the fifth day the physician had taken his tests and pronounced the serums effective.

When I left his house on the fifth day I heard him tell the guard, "An excellent specimen."

The fourth and fifth days I was permitted to carry wine back to the compound.

It was true that I had never felt as healthy in my life as I did then, nor had the air seemed as clear and pure, the sky so blue, the clouds so sharp and white. I suddenly realized, climbing the ramps of Laura toward the compound, leashed, under guard, carrying a jar of wine on my head, balancing it with my right hand, among my sisters in bondage, breathing the fantastic air of Gor, that I was happy. Though barefoot, though thonged by the throat, though branded, though clad in a camisk, though a degraded slave, at the mercy of men, I felt, perhaps for the first time in my life, paradoxically, vitally and joyously happy. I now thought more often of men. I knew now that they found me attractive. And, startlingly, for the first time in my life, I, too, began to find them attractive, deeply and sensuously attractive, even excitingly so. One would carry his head in a certain way; another laughed well, openly, heartedly; another had sturdy legs; another had long, fine arms and strong hands, a fine chest and head. I found I wanted to look upon them, to stand near them, as if by accident, to touch them, as if inadvertently, perhaps in brushing past them. Sometimes

they would discover me looking upon them, and I, responding
to their grin, would look down, swiftly, shyly. Sometimes I
would be pleased when, among the other girls, they would
throw me their leather or sandals to clean. I did so, excel-
lently. I did not object either, at the stream on stones, near
the compound, to washing their garments. I liked to handle
them, to feel the strong fabric that had clung to their sweet
strength. Once Ute caught me holding the tunic of the
guard who had watched me at the physician's against my
cheek, my eyes closed. She squealed with delight and leaped
to her feet, standing between the flat rocks in the water,
pointing to me. The other girls, too, looked, laughing, slapping at their knees. "El-in-or wants a master!" squealed Ute.
"El-in-or wants a master!" I pursued her into the stream
splashing water at her, and she fled away, stumbling, and
then turned and fled back to the bank. Ute, and the others,
stood there, laughing and pointing at me. I stood knee deep
in the swift stream. "El-in-or wants a master!" they cried,
laughing.

I stood in the stream, furious, fists clenched. "Yes," I
cried, "I want a master!"

Then, angrily, I returned to my laundry, and so, too, did
the other girls. But I felt there was now something different.
I listened to them chat gaily together, pounding and rinsing
the fabrics, in the sunlight, at the edge of that swift stream.
And I, too, Elinor Brinton, worked with them. My hands
were in the cold water, immersing the fabric, and lifting it
and wringing it, and pounding it on the rock, and immersing
it again, in simple, ancient rhythms. What was it that was
different? I wore my camisk, belted with binding fiber,
naught else. I knelt as they. I worked as they. There was no
penthouse here, no Maserati, no wealth, no mighty buildings, no roar and drone of engines, no scream of planes, no
clouds of choking smoke. There was only the laughter of the
girls, the bubbling of the stream, the work, the blue sky and
white clouds, the wind and the bending grass, clean air and,
somewhere, the call of a tiny horned gim, the tiny purplish owllike bird.

I stopped working for a moment and took a deep breath.

I was no longer angry. I felt the binding fiber, in its double loop, tight against my body. I stretched. I felt my body luxuriously protesting the rough fabric of the camisk. I wondered what man would tear it from me.

"Work," said a guard.

I returned to my work, Elinor Brinton, one slave girl among others, primitively washing the clothes of masters at the edge of that swift stream on a beautiful, distant world.

I knelt there on the flat rock, pounding and rinsing the fabric, in the fresh air with the bright blue sky overhead. I listened to the sound of the stream. I looked up and saw the sky. I put down the wet fabric and suddenly stood up on the rock, throwing my arms into the air and laughing. The girls looked at me, bewildered. "Yes! Yes," I cried. "I am a female!"

I stood on the rock in the sun before the rushing stream, my arms raised, eyes closed.

Then I opened my eyes to the blue skies.

"Yes! Yes! Yes!" I cried, to all the skies of Gor, and all the stars and all the worlds. "I want a master! I want a master!"

"Return to your work," said a guard.

Swiftly, lest I be beaten, I knelt again on the rock and returned to my washing.

I laughed.

The other girls, too, laughed.

I was happy.

Ute, slapping fabric on the flat rocks and rinsing it in the cold water, began to sing.

I was happy. I was one with them.

I found myself looking forward eagerly to my sale. I found myself wondering, curiously, what it would be like to be owned by a man. Sometimes, when the other girls were not looking, I put my hand to my throat, as though his collar were there. I pretended to trace the lettering on the collar, which proclaimed me his. I did not even have an objection to being sold in Laura. It seemed to me a simple, wild, lovely place, with the glorious air and sky, the forest to the north, the river to the south. I loved its ramps going down to the river and winding among the warehouses, the painted, carved wood on its buildings, the black shingles, the smell of bosk on the ramps and the creak of wagons, the smell of fish and salt, and glistening tharlarion, from the river, the smell of hides and fur, and sawed lumber, at the docks. And her men I liked, in their rough cloaks and tunics, vital, supple, strong men, large-handed and laughing, men who worked with their hands and backs in the clean air and on the river. I wondered if I might, as I had seen other girls, ride beside them on their wagons, or, as I had heard, fish with them at night with torches on the river. I wondered if I could bargain shrewdly with his coins at the market, if he would like my cooking. I smiled to myself that I would try to please him well in the furs. And I smiled again to myself, for I knew he would beat me if I did not. I wondered if he would take me with him on journeys and sometimes, where no one could see, walking in the fields, though I were slave, hold my hand. I had seen a master and his girl kissing in a doorway in Laura. I had seen her eyes. How I had envied her! She loved him. I hoped, for her sake, that he would not sell her. It is strange. Not until I had become a slave girl, and understood that men might own me, did I become so devastatingly, thrillingly, aware of them, the rude beauty and strength of their bodies, and their power.

Interestingly, for the first time in my life, I found that I was not displeased to be a woman. I was pleased, rather, indeed, thrilled, that they were men. It is joyous to be a woman on Gor, even though slave, with such men. I would not have exchanged my sex, though I was only a girl in bondage, for the throne of Ar.

That afternoon, Targo called me aside. "Slave," he called. I, frightened, not knowing what I might have done, ran to him and knelt at his feet, head down. I trembled.

"Lift your head," he said.

I did so.

"When the display chain is put forth again," he said, "you are Eleven Girl."

I could not believe my ears. "Thank you, Master," I whispered.

There were sixteen girls in the chain now, for Targo had sold four before coming to Laura. The hundred village girls were not included in the display chain. They were to be sold in Ar.

"You are high on the chain now," said Targo.

I put my head down.

"You are almost beautiful," he said.

When I lifted my head he had gone.

I was much pleased.

I ran to the barred gate of the compound and the guard unlocked it, and I went inside, and then he closed the gate, relocking it.

He did not make me remove my camisk before entering. We were now permitted to wear our camisks in the compound. Even the village girls, yesterday, under the eyes of guards, had cut and sewn camisks for themselves. They wore them happily. It was the first clothing they had been permitted since they had been taken by the maurauders of Haakon of Skjern. I do not know why, for certain, we were permitted clothing in the compound. It may have been, of course, because the weather had now cleared and the compound was no longer muddy, but I do not really think so. I think it was rather because Targo was, simply, rather pleased with the lot of us. His older girls, among whom I numbered myself, were excellent goods. His new girl, the Lady Rena of Lydius, would net him fifty-five gold pieces if she could be delivered in Ar to her captain from Tyros. And his hundred village girls, bought for only two gold pieces a girl, could well stand to make him rich, if they could be brought to Ar before the Love Feast. Targo was in a good mood. That is why, I think, Targo permitted us clothing in the compound.

I ran to tell Ute and Inge that I was now Eleven Girl. We hugged and kissed one another.

Lana was high girl, of course, Sixteen. Inge was second, even though she had been of high caste, Fifteen. Ute was Fourteen.

It is not only prestigious to be high on the chain, but, of course, then one's price is commonly higher as well, and, accordingly, one's master is somewhat more likely to be well fixed.

I strutted before Ute and Inge, in the rough camisk. "I do not object," I told them, loftily, "if my master chooses to dress me in silk."

We laughed.

"Let us hope," said Inge, "you are not purchased by the master of a paga tavern.

I looked at her, irritably.

"They can often afford fine girls," said Inge, "paying more than many private masters can."

I swallowed.

"Of all the slave girls sold, however," observed Inge, "very few are purchased for taverns."

I looked at her gratefully.

"Perhaps you will be purchased for a serving slave or a tower slave," said Inge.

I stretched luxuriously in the camisk. "No," I said, lazily, "I think I will be purchased for a pleasure slave."

Ute clapped her hands with pleasure.

"But you are untrained," pointed out Inge.

"I can learn," I informed her.

"All of us, I have heard," said Ute, "will receive training in the pens of Ko-ro-ba."

I had heard this, too.

"I will doubtless train superbly," I told them.

"How different you are," exclaimed Ute, "since you have come to us!"

"Do you think, El-in-or," asked Inge, "that I, though of the Scribes, might give pleasure to a man?"

"Take off your camisk," I told her, "and I will assess you."

She laughed.

"What of me?" howled Ute.

We laughed at her. Neither of us had the least doubt that Ute would be a treasure for any man.

"You will be superb," I told her.

"Yes," said Inge, warmly, "superb!"

"But what," wailed Ute, "if we are all purchased by the same master?"

I leaned forward, menacingly toward them. "I will scratch your eyes out!" I cried.

We all laughed, and hugged and kissed again.

Later that afternoon there was an entertainment at the compound. A mountebank, with pointed hat, with a tuft on it, in silly robes, with his painted clown's face, leading a strange animal, arrived at the compound. For a copper tarn disk he would give a performance at the compound. We all begged Targo, even the village girls, that he be permitted to do so. Targo consented, to our delight, and the small mountebank with the strange animal cleared a small space near the bars on the far side of the compound, away from the bars forming the common wall with the compound of Haakon of Skjern. We, and the hundred village girls, delighted, pressed against the bars to watch. Vaguely, the small mountebank, in his swirling, silly robes, with his painted face, seemed somehow familiar, but I knew he could not be. How absurd that would be! He danced and turned somersaults, and sang silly songs, before the bars. He was a small, thin man, agile. He had quick eyes, and hands. And he told funny stories and jokes. He also performed magic tricks, with silks and scarves, and juggled colored hoops he wore at his belt. Then he would reach through the bars and pretend to find coins in the hair of the girls. From my hair, to my delight, he seemed to draw forth a silver tarsk. The girls cried out in envy. It was the most expensive coin he found. I blushed with pleasure. Lana was not much pleased. I laughed. We laughed and clapped our hands with pleasure. During this time his beast slept, or seemed to sleep, behind him, curled on the grass, a guard holding its chain.

Then the mountebank, with a bow, turned to the animal and, taking its chain from the guard, spoke to it, abruptly and authoritatively. "Awaken, Sleepy One!" he said. "Stand straight!"

The beast frightened us. We were pleased it was so tame, so much under the control of its master.

Slowly the beast lifted itself to its hind legs, and lifted its paws and opened its mouth.

Several of the girls screamed. I, too, shrank back from the bars.

It was an incredibly hideous, large-eyed, furred thing. It had wide, pointed ears. It stood perhaps eight or nine feet high. It may have weighed seven or eight hundred pounds. It had a wide, two-nostriled, leathery snout. Its mouth was huge, large enough to take a man's head into it, and it was rimmed with two rows of stout fangs. There were four larger fangs, long and curved, for grasping, in the position of the canines. The upper two fangs protruded at the side of the jaws when its mouth was closed. It had a long, dark tongue. Its forelegs were larger than its hindlegs. I had seen it move, shambling on its hind legs, and on the knuckles of its forelegs, but now I saw that what I had taken as forelegs were not unlike arms and hands. Indeed, they had six digits, several jointed, almost like tentacles, which terminated in clawlike growths, which had been blunted and filed. It also had claws on its hindlegs, or feet, which were retractable, as the mountebank demonstrated, issuing sharp voice commands to the beast. The hindlegs, or feet, like the forelegs, or hands, if one may so speak, were also six-digited and multiply jointed. They were large and spreading. The claws, as I saw when they were exposed, upon the order of the mountebank, were better than four inches long, curved and sharp. I could not even determine in my mind whether to think of it as a four-footed animal, with unusual prehensile forelegs, or as something manlike, with two legs and two arms, with hands. It was tailless.

Perhaps most horrifying were the eyes. They were large and black-pupiled. For an instant I thought they rested upon me, and saw me, but not as an animal sees, but as something might see that is not an animal. Then, again, they were simple and vacant, those of a mountebank's performing beast.

I dismissed the sensation of uneasiness from my mind.

With the other girls I applauded, striking my left shoulder in Gorean fashion, as the mountebank put his beast through its paces.

Now it was sitting comically on its rump with its paws fluttering in the air. Now it was rolling over and over. Then it was whining, begging piteously.

Frequently, from a large pocket in his robes, the mountebank would throw the animal a tiny piece of bosk meat, when it had performed well. Sometimes he would scold it, and withhold the meat. Then the animal would put down its head, and turn it to the side, like a reprimanded child. And then the mountebank would give it its piece of meat. The guards enjoyed the performance as well as the girls. I saw that even Targo laughed, holding his belly in his blue-and-yellow slaver's robes. Sometimes the mountebank would give pieces of meat to the girls to throw to the beast. Lana begged hardest and was given the most pieces of meat. She threw me a look of triumph. I threw only one piece of meat to the animal and that quickly. The beast frightened me. Lana did not seem afraid at all. The piece of meat disappeared into that vast, fanged orifice and the large, round eyes blinked sleepily, contentedly. The girls laughed. And I saw the eyes look at me once again. I put my hand before my mouth, terrified. But then I saw that they were again vacant and stupid, those of a beast. Soon, once again, telling myself how silly I had been, I was laughing again with the other girls.

At the conclusion of the mountebank's performance he gave a great, deep bow, bending at the waist and doffing his hat in a great, sweeping arc. We might even have been free women! How pleased we were! We leaped up and down, we clapped our hands with pleasure, we struck our left shoulders, we cried out, we thrust our hands through the bars to him, and, to our delight, though we were slave, he came to the bars and kissed and touched our hands. Then he stood back and waved at us.

Then, to our sorrow, his performance was over.

He stepped back.

There was a silence.

The beast then rose to its hind legs, sleepily, and regarded us. Then, suddenly, it gave a hideously terrifying roar and sprang toward the bars, its great clawed appendages grasping towards us, its huge, fanged hole of a mouth wild with its white traps of teeth, howling and hissing. It struck the bars, reaching through them, its teeth grating on them, its chain striking against the iron, its claws scraping towards us. We stumbled back, terrified and screaming, trying to flee, but impeding one another. I found myself thrown from my feet and helpless, tangled and pressed in upon by the bodies of my sisters in bondage. And as I could not free myself so could not those whom I and others pressed in upon. I screamed and screamed. Then we became aware that the guards, and Targo, were laughing. They had been warned. It had been part of the performance, but scarcely one to our liking. How comical we must have seemed in our rout, our terror. How comical to the guards and Targo, and the mountebank, must have seemed that undignified pile, that squirming, panic-stricken heap, that helpless, terrified, screaming tangle of slave girls. The monster was now sitting quietly beside the mountebank, licking its jaws, half-asleep, its eyes empty and vacant, blinking. The guards were still laughing, and Targo was still smiling. Body by body, the tangle of slave femininity unraveled itself. I think we were all humiliated and embarrassed, so fooled we had been, so miserable and precipitate had been our flight. But, too, we were still frightened. Some of us stood near the tiny door to the heavy log dormitory, ready to run within. Others had fled to the opposite wall of bars. Most of us stood near the bars, but back some feet from them. I angrily, but still frightened, smoothed down my camisk, as though it had been a dress. I looked at the men laughing. How clever they thought they were! They were beasts, all of them! I suppose they were big, brave men, with their spears and swords, and if the beast charged at them, they would just stand there and kill it, while we, only women, fled like screaming children. I looked at the men. I hated them. They thought they were so clever, so brave, so great, so different from us! But then I blushed red, every bit of me not covered by the camisk. We had fled like screaming children. We had fled like women! We were women! I was still terrified of the beast, even separated from it by bars. What did they expect! I did not care for their lesson. But I have never forgotten it. We learned it well. We were different! I recalled how a guard had once given me his spear, and it had been so heavy, I could throw it only a few feet. He had then taken it from me and hurled it into a block of wood, head deep, more than a hundred feet away. He sent me to fetch it for him and I had scarcely been able to work it free of the wood. His shield I had barely been able to lift. On Earth I had not thought much of the strength of men. Strength had not seemed important. It had seemed unimportant, irrelevant. But on Gor I realized that strength was important, very important. And that we were weaker than they, far, far weaker, and that, on such a world, if they chose, we were theirs. That night I had cleaned his leather and sandals, as a slave girl, kneeling to one side, while he conversed with men. When I had finished, I remained kneeling there, waiting for him. When he had finished he arose and, without thanking me, put on the leather and sandals, then gestured that I should precede him to the compound. He unlocked the barred gate and opened it. In the threshold I turned to face him. "I, too, am a human being," I told him.

He smiled. "No," he said. "You are a Kajira." Then he turned me about and, with a proprietary slap, sped me through the gate. He then closed the gate and locked it.

I pressed against the bars putting my hands through, trying to touch him.

He came back to the bars and took my hands, holding me against the bars.

"When will you use me?" I asked.

"You are white silk," he had said, and turned away.

I had moaned, leaning against the bars, lonely. I was filled with strange sensations. The three moons were bright in the sky. I shook the bars, but I was locked within. I saw him disappear in the darkness, toward the wagons. I held the bars, and pressed my cheek against them, and wept.

Ute, and several of the girls, I realized, were laughing at themselves, and us. It had been a splendid joke on us, the charge of the animal! What a jolly conclusion to the mountebank's performance. I could not laugh, but I did smile. The girls were now waving to the mountebank and he, smiling and bowing, acknowledged our attention and then, with his large, strange animal on its chain, turned and left.

How precious and delightful Ute was!

Soon we were all laughing with her. Several of the girls began to sing. My sense of pleasure returned. I raced Inge to the end of the compound and back, and beat her. Some of the girls began to play tag, and games. Even some of the northern girls joined with us. We had a cloth ball, stuffed with rags, and, laughing, we threw this about. Some of the girls sat in circles, telling stories. Others faced one another, kneeling, and, with string and their fingers, played an intricate cat's-cradle game. Others played "Stones," where one player guesses the number of stones held in the other's hand. I tried the cat's-cradle game but I could not play it. I always became confused, trying to copy the intricate patterns. How beautifully they would suddenly, in all their complexity, appear. The other girls laughed at my clumsiness. The northern girls, incidentally, were very skilled at this game. They could beat us all.

"It takes much practice," said Ute.

"There is nothing much else to do in the villages," said Lana, who refused to try the game.

At "Stones," however, I was genuinely pleased with myself. It has two players, who take alternate turns. Each player has the same number of "Stones," usually two to five per player. The "Stones" are usually pebbles or beads, but in the cities one can buy small polished, carved boxes containing ten "stones," the quality of which might vary from polished ovoid stones, with swirling patterns, to gems worth the ransom of a merchant's daughter. The object of the game is simple, to guess the number of stones held in he other's hand or hands. One point is scored for a correct guess, and the game is usually set for a predetermined number of paired guesses, usually fifty. Usually your opponent tries to outwit you, by either changing the number of stones held in his hand or, perhaps, keeping it the same. I was quite successful at this game, and I could beat most of the girls. I could even beat Inge, who was of the scribes. I challenged Lana to "Stones," but she would not play with me. Ute, however, of all those I played with, I could not beat. This irritated me, for Ute was stupid. She even made mistakes in speaking her own language. She was only of the leather workers, too! But it was hard to remain angry with Ute. I was pleased with the afternoon. I was now Eleven Girl. I had seen the mountebank's performance, and I had enjoyed myself afterward.

I saw that a cart, loaded with jugs of paga, arrived at the compound. It was greeted with cheers by the guards. Tonight was a night for celebration. Tomorrow we would leave the compound and begin the overland journey across the river and southeast to Ko-ro-ba, and from thence to Ar.

Targo's wagons, now in the number of sixteen, the additional wagons and teams purchased in Laura, were scattered about at various distances from the compound, forming, in groups of twos and threes, small, isolated camps for the guards. Besides the nine guards who had been with him when I had been captured, he had now eighteen additional men. They had been hired in Laura, known men, vouched for, not drifting mercenaries. Targo, in his way, may have been a gambler, but he was not a fool.

Ute came rushing to me, happily, and seized my arm.

"Tonight," she laughed, "when the food is served, you and I, and Lana, are not to go to the food line."

"Why not?" I asked, in dismay. On Earth I had been a very finicky eater. On Gor, however, I had developed a fantastic appetite. I was not at all pleased with the prospect of losing my supper. What had we done?

Ute pointed through the bars at one of the groups of

wagons, some hundred yards from the compound, toward the forests. Some five guards camped there.

"They have asked Targo to permit us to serve them," she said.

I flushed with pleasure. I liked to be outside the compound, and I enjoyed being near to the men. Never before had I served so small and intimate a group. Moreover, I knew the guards, for they had been with Targo since my capture. I liked them.

That evening, as it was growing dark, Ute and I, and Lana, did not go to the food line. A girl, however, was given a pan of food to give me for the new girl, chained in the dormitory. I took this food, and a water bag, within the darkened log enclosure.

It had been a beautiful day, and I was pleased. Moreover, I was looking forward to the evening.

This time, when I fed the new girl, the former Lady Rena of Lydius, I permitted her to eat at her own pace, and gave her the water bag more than once.

When she had finished she looked at me. "May I speak?" she asked.

I saw that the hood, her gag and the bonds had taught her slavery. "Yes," I said.

"Thank you," she said.

I kissed her, and then regagged and rehooded her.

When I went outside I returned the water bag to its hook outside the door of the dormitory, and gave the pan back to the girl who had given it to me. She was doing kitchen work that night. She was one of the village girls. The kitchen was an open, roofed shed abutting on the log dormitory, outside the bars. She was gathering pans inside the compound. Then she was released to go to the kitchen, where, with some other of the northern girls, their arms immersed to the elbows in wooden tubs of heated water, she set about washing the pans. Targo had not had his older girls subjected to this kitchen work. We were pleased by this. It was surely work more fit for the blond, northern girls.

I knelt with Ute and Lana inside the gate, leading from the girl cage.

I was hungry, and it was now dusk.

"When do we eat?" I asked Ute.

"After the masters," said Ute, referring to the guards in the plural, "if we please them."

"If we please them?" I asked.

"I am always fed," said Lana.

"Do not fear," said Ute, laughing at me, "you are white silk!"

I looked down.

"You will please them," Ute reassured me. "We all will. Why do you think they asked for us?"

"Perhaps we should have eaten in the food line," I said.

"And be beaten?" asked Lana.

"No," I said, confused.

"A hungry girl often serves better," said Ute. Then she laughed at me. "Do not fear," she said. "If they like you, they will throw food."

"Oh," I said.

I was irritated. Elinor Brinton, of Park Avenue, of Earth, did not care to be thrown food like an animal, provided she pleased her masters!

"Wenches!" boomed a voice.

We jumped. I flushed with pleasure. We leaped to our feet. Our guards had come for us!

The gate was unlocked.

"Come out," said one of them, their leader.

We ran outside. We had been fetched by our masters of the evening.

The gate was then relocked.

We knelt on the grass. How pleasant it was not to be behind the bars of the girl cage.

Three guards had come for us. I knew them, and the other two, with whom they camped. They were among my favorites. I was excited. Sometimes, before falling asleep, or even in my dreams, I had fancied myself in their arms. I could imagine the pleasure of being held, helpless, in their strong arms. But beyond this I had only the white silk girl's dim sense of the changes they could bring about in my body, only the vague instinctual sensing, deep in my femaleness, of the fantastic pleasures to which a slave girl may be subjected by her master, pleasures by means of which he may, if it pleases him, totally and completely dominate her, making her helplessly, irreservedly his, naught but a yielded slave girl.

The men were in fine humor.

One of them pointed across the grass to the fire between the wagons.

It was more than a hundred yards off, glowing in the darkness, away from the compound.

The men then removed their sword belts, holding the short swords and scabbards in their left hand, the belts in their right.

"No!" laughed Ute. "No!"

"Run!" cried the guard.

Ute and Lana sprang to their feet and raced toward the fire. I was slower than they. I was suddenly stung, smartly, with the fierce slap of a sword belt. "Oh!" I cried, in pain, and leaped to my feet, and ran stumbling toward the fire. They were swifter than we, of course. Ute, Lana and I ran, laughing and stumbling, barefoot, squealing in protest, crying out in pain, through the darkness over the grass toward the fire.

Ute reached it first, laughing, falling to her hands and knees and putting her head down to the grass, her hair falling over the sandal of one of the two guards waiting there. "I beg to serve you, Masters!" she gasped, laughing.

Lana was but an instant behind her and she, too, fell to her hands and knees, head down. "I beg to serve you, Masters!" she cried.

I was stung once more and then, like Ute and Lana, I too was on my hands and knees, head down, touching the grass. "I—I beg to serve you, Masters!" I cried.

"Then serve!" cried one of the fellows at the fire, he whose sandal was lost in Ute's dark hair.

Suddenly there were three more sharp slaps of the sword belts and, crying out, protesting, begging for mercy, laughing, we leapt to our feet to busy ourselves.

Lana, Ute and I knelt in a line, facing the players. Our hands were bound behind our backs with binding fiber.

The men, wagering, tossed us pieces of meat.

We caught them, in the firelight. A catch was two points. A piece which was dropped was fair game for any. We fought for the dropped pieces. The retrieval of such a piece was one point. Ute dropped a piece and Lana and I fought, each holding to a part of the fallen prize, rolling and tearing. I struggled back to my knees, tearing my head to one side. "Mine!" I cried, swallowing the meat, almost choking, laughing.

"Mine!" cried Lana, gorging the other half ot the meat.

"Point for each," adjudicated one of the guards.

We were excited, and wanted to play further.

"We are weary," said one of the guards. We saw copper tarn disks being exchanged.

Elinor Brinton had done well for her guard. He was pleased with her. She suffused with pleasure as he snapped his fingers for her to approach him.

She leaped to her feet and ran to him, where he shook her head roughly, and unbound her.

"Fetch me paga," he said.

"Yes, Master," she said.

I went to the wagon to fetch a large bota of paga, which had been filled from one of the large jugs.

Lana and Ute, too, went to the wagon, to fetch other botas, so commanded by other guards.

Soon I returned to the firelight, the heavy bota of paga, on its strap, slung over my shoulder, Ute and Lana, with theirs, behind me.

The grass felt good to my bare feet. It seemed I could feel each blade. I felt the rough fabric of the camisk on my body as I moved, the pull of the strap on my shoulder, the heavy, swaying touch of the bota as, in the rhythm of my walk, it touched my side.

Beyond the fire, in the distance, like an irregular margin, a torn, soft, dark edge hiding the bright stars of Gor, I could see the lofty, still blackness of the borders of the northern forests. Far off, I heard the scream of a hunting sleen. I shivered.

Then I heard the laughing of the men, and turned again toward the fire.

Back away toward the compound, here and there on the meadow, I could see other fires, and clusters of wagons. This was a night for paga, for celebration. Tomorrow, Targo, and his men and his merchandise, would make their way to Laura and, crossing the river there, begin their long, overland journey to Ko-ro-ba, called by some the Towers of the Morning, and from thence to luxurious Ar itself. The journey would be not only long and hard but dangerous.

"Paga!" called the guard.

I hurried to him.

"Let Lana dance," whimpered Lana.

The guard handed me a piece of meat and I took it in my teeth kneeling beside him, where he sat cross-legged, I lifting and squeezing the bota of paga, filled from one of the large jugs, guiding the stream of liquid into his mouth. I bit through the charred exterior of the meat, into the red, hot, half-raw, juicy interior.

The guard, with one hand, gestured that he had had enough.

I laid the bota aside on the grass.

I closed my eyes, running my tongue about the inside of my mouth, and over my teeth and lips, savoring the juice and taste of the externally charred, hot, half-raw meat.

Tomorrow we would begin the journey to Ko-ro-ba, and from thence to luxurious, glorious Ar.

I opened my eyes.

The fire was very beautiful, and the shadows on the wagon canvas.

Ute was humming.

"I want to dance," said Lana. She was lying beside one

of the guards, her head at his waist. She bit at his body through the fabric of the tunic. "I want to dance," she teased. Her body was beautiful in the parting of the camisk.

"Perhaps," he encouraged her.

The guards had liked us, muchly, and had apparently expected that they would for, to our delight, they had purchased a small bottle of Ka-la-na wine, in a wicker basket, which they had permitted us, swallow by swallow, to share. I had never tasted so rich and delicate a wine on Earth, and yet here, on this world, it cost only a copper tarn disk and was so cheap, and plentiful, that it might be given even to a female slave. I remembered each of the four swallows which I had had. I tasted them even still, with the meat and bread which I had eaten. It was the first Gorean fermented beverage which I had tasted. It is said that Ka-la-na has an unusual effect on a female. I think it is true.

I took the hand of the guard near whom I knelt, and placed it at my waist, slipping his fingers inside the double loop of binding fiber that belted my camisk, that he might hold me.

His fist suddenly tightened the loop, and I gasped, being suddenly drawn toward him.

We looked at one another.

"What are you going to do with me, Master?" I asked.

He laughed. "You silken little sleen," he said. He removed his hand from the binding fiber. I reached out for him. He thrust a huge piece of the yellow Sa-Tarna bread into my hands. "Eat," he said.

Looking at him, smiling, holding the bread in both hands, I began to eat it.

"She-sleen," he smiled.

"Yes, Master," I said.

"Targo would take my hide off to the backbone," he muttered.

"Yes, Master," I smiled.

"She is only white silk," said Lana. "Lana is red silk. Let Lana please you."

"Lana," I told her, loftily, "could not please an urt."

Lana screeched with rage as Ute, and the men, laughed, and leaped toward me. The fellow over whom she leapt seized her by one ankle, and she fell short of me, crying out in fury. He dragged her back and pulled her up to her feet, where he held her by the arms, kicking and squirming.

Another of the guards, laughing, untied the double loop of binding fiber which belted her camisk and, drawing the fiber about her body, as she cried out, threw it aside. Then he tore her camisk from her. The guard who held her then threw her to the grass at their feet. She looked up at them, frightened. Would she be beaten?

"If you have so much energy," said the guard who had torn away the camisk, "you may dance for us."

Lana looked up, her eyes bright with pleasure. "Yes," she cried, "let Lana dance." Then she threw me a look of hatred. "We shall see who can please men!" she cried.

Another of the guards had gone to one of the wagons, and, as he returned, I heard the sound of slave bells.

Lana stood proudly beside the fire, her head back and arms down, and extended, at her sides, while the bells, mounted in their double rows, on their straps, were fastened on her wrists and ankles.

Meanwhile the Ka-la-na bottle was brought forth again by another guard. He held it for Lana to drink, and then passed it to Ute and myself. There was a bit left and I gave it back to him, and he handed it to the now-belled Lana. With a barbaric jangle of bells she threw back her head and finished the bottle.

She threw the bottle to one side and put down her head, and then brought her head up and back, shaking her head back and forth, her hair flying, and she stamped down on her right foot.

Ute and the men began to sing and clap, one of them slapping at the leather of a shield.

I thought I saw a movement in the darkness, beyond the wagons.

Lana, for an instant, stopped, her hands lifted over her head. "Who is beautiful?" she demanded. "Who pleases men?"

"Lana!" I cried, in spite of myself. "Lana is beautiful! Lana pleases men!" I could not help myself. I was stunned, and then overwhelmed. I had not realized that my sex was capable of such beauty. Lana was incredibly beautiful, extraordinarily, utterly and incredibly beautiful.

I could scarcely speak, so thrilled I was.

Then with a tempestuous flash of the slave bells Lana again danced in the firelight, before the men.

I became aware, suddenly, that the hand of the guard near whom I knelt, his fist, was in the binding fiber that belted my camisk.

I sensed a furtive movement, to one side.

"Master?" I asked.

He was not watching Lana. He was lying on his back, looking up at me, kneeling near him.

I could hear the slave bells, the song of Ute and the men, their clapping, the slapped rhythm on the leather shield.

"Kiss me," said the man.

"I am white silk," I whispered.

"Kiss me," he said.

I bent toward him, a Gorean Kajira, obeying her master. My hair fell about his head. My lips, delicately, obediently, lowered themselves toward his. I was trembling.

My lips parted, paused but an inch above his.

No, something in me cried, no! I am Elinor Brinton! I am not a slave girl! I am not a slave girl!

I tried to draw away, but his hands on my arms held me.

I struggled, terrified, trying to pull away.

I was held, his prisoner.

He seemed puzzled at my struggles, my terror. But then, too, I felt helpless, and furious. I hated him. I hated all men, and their strength. They exploited us, they dominated us, they forced us to serve them, and do their bidding! They were cruel to us! They did not acknowledge our humanity! And mixed with my anger and terror were the instinctual fears of the white-silk girl, dreading to be made a woman. And most, perhaps, mixed therein were the fury and the frustration, and terror, of the spoiled, rich Earth girl, Elinor

Brinton, resenting her station, repudiating the role that had been given her so undeservedly on this barbaric world. I am Elinor Brinton, I cried to myself! She is no slave! She obeys no man! She is free! Free! The girl who had worn the black, buttoning, bare-midriff blouse, the tan slacks, who had owned the Maserati, who had had three quarters of a million dollars, who had had a penthouse, who had modeled, and traveled, struggled. The exquisite, beautiful, educated, sophisticated, smartly attired, tasteful girl struggled. The Earth girl struggled, finding herself in the arms of a barbarian on a distant world.

"Do not touch me," I hissed at him.

He turned me about, easily, placing me on my back on the grass.

"I hate you! I hate you!" I wept.

I saw a look of anger come into his eyes. He held me very tightly. Then, too, to my dismay, I saw another look, which I, even white silk, understood. I would not be simply used, and discarded. I had irritated him. I moaned. I would be used with patience, and care, and delicacy and thoroughness, and efficient mastery, until I had yielded myself to him, on his terms, not mine, until I, proud and angry and free, had been reduced to a surrendered female slave.

I tried to struggle. I heard the bells of Lana, the singing and clapping of Ute and the men, the slapping of the rhythm of Lana's dance on the leather of the shield.

His large head bent toward my throat. I turned my head to one side, weeping.

Suddenly there was a rush about us of bodies, the sound of blows. Lana began to scream, but the scream was muffled. Ute cried out, but then her cry, too, was abruptly terminated. The men tried to climb to their feet, shouting in anger. There were blows, heavy blows from the darkness. The man who had held me leaped half to his feet, crying out, when something large and heavy struck him on the side of the head. He fell to one side in the grass. I tried to dart to my feet but two bodies, those of girls, thrust themselves on me. Another girl snapped a choke leash on my throat, twisting it, so that I almost strangled. As I opened my mouth, gasping for air, a wadding was thrust into it by another girl. Then I was gagged. The pressure on my throat then eased. I as thrown onto my stomach and, with binding fiber, my wrists were tied behind my back. Then, by the choke leash, half strangling, I was dragged to my feet.

"Build up the fire," said the leader of the girls, a tall, blondish girl. How startling she seeemd. She carried a light spear. She was dressed in skins. There were barbaric golden ornaments on her arms, and about her neck.

Another of the girls threw wood on the fire.

I looked about.

Girls knelt beside the last two of the guards, fastening them in bonds.

Then they stood up.

I saw that Lana, and Ute, were already bound and gagged.

"Shall we enslave the men?" asked one of the girls.

"No," said the tall, blond girl.

The girl who had asked the question gestured to Ute and Lana. "What of them?" she asked.

"You saw them," said the tall, blond girl. "Leave them here. They are Kajirae."

My heart leapt. These were forest girls, sometimes called panther girls, who lived wild and free in the northern forests, outlaw women, sometimes enslaving men, when it pleased them to do so.

Doubtless they had seen me struggle! I was no Kajira! Doubtless they wanted me to join them! Now I would be free! Perhaps, somehow, they could even help me return to Earth. In any case, they would free me! I would be free!

But I stood there on the grass, gagged, my hands bound behind my back, a choke leash on my throat, held by one of the girls.

It did not seem that I was free.

"Drag the men about the fire," said the tall girl.

"Yes, Verna," said one of the other girls.

Together, in pairs, the girls dragged the men back to the fire. The men, too, by now, had been gagged. Only one of them had regained consciousness. One of the girls in the skins knelt before him, holding a knife at his throat, her hand in his hair.

Some of the girls threw aside their clubs. They looked at the men, their hands on their hips, and laughed.

How elated I was, that they had come swiftly from the darkness, with clubs, and had made captives of men, taking them as simply as girls. But I, too, had been bound.

The tall girl, the blond girl, their leader, called Verna, lithe in the skins of forest panthers, in her golden ornaments, with her spear, strode to where Lana lay on the grass, on her side, bound and gagged. With her spear, Verna rolled Lana onto her back. Lana looked up at her in terror. Verna's spear was at her throat.

"You danced well," said Verna.

Lana trembled.

Verna looked at her with contempt, and then drew aside the spear. She kicked Lana savagely in the side. "Kajira!" she scorned.

The tall girl then went to Ute and kicked her as well, again saying "Kajira!"

Lana whimpered, but Ute made no sound. There were tears in her eyes over the gag.

"Tie the men in sitting positions about the fire," ordered Verna.

Her girls, perhaps fifteen of them, complied. They used a heavy chest, and a wagon tongue, to do so.

From a distance it would appear that they sat about the fire.

Verna approached me.

She frightened me. She seemed tall, and strong. There was a feline arrogance in the barbarian beauty. She seemed magnificent and fierce in the brief skins and golden ornaments. She put her spear point under my chin and lifted my head.

"What shall we do with the slaves?" asked one of the girls.

Verna turned about, to regard Lana and Ute. She gestured to Ute. "Remove that one's camisk," she uaid. Then she said, "Tie them at the feet of their masters."

Ute was stripped of her camisk, and then she and Lana, with a loop of binding fiber fastened to the ankles of two of the guards, were tied by the throat at their feet.

Again I felt the point of Verna's spear under my chin, forcing up my head.

She looked at me for a long time. Then she said, "Kajira."

I shook my head in denial, No, No!

Some of the girls were rifling in the wagons, gathering food, coins and drink, cloth, knives, whatever they wished.

They were now ready to depart.

The men were now conscious, and struggled, but they were helpless.

From a distance it might appear they were merely sitting about the fire, celebrating, two Kajirae at their feet.

I could see other fires, other wagon clusters about the meadow. From one of them came the sound of singing.

The men pulled at their bonds.

I supposed they might not be discovered until morning.

"Strip her," said Verna to one of her girls. I shook my head, No! My camisk was cut from me. I stood as only a bound slave among them.

"Burn the camisk and binding fiber," said Verna.

I watched the garment and fiber thrown on the flames. It would not be used to give my scent to domesticated sleen, trained to hunt slaves.

"Put more wood on the fire," commanded Verna.

More logs were thrown on the fire.

Then Verna turned away from me, and strode before the men.

How beautiful she was, and proud and fierce, in the brief skins and golden ornaments. She was beautifully figured and she carried herself arrogantly before them, taunting them with her beauty, and spear.

"I am Verna," she told them, "a Panther Girl, of the High Forests. I enslave men, when it pleases me. When I tire of them I sell them." She walked back and forth before them. "You are tarsks and beasts," she told them. "We despise you," she said. "We have outwitted you, and captured you.

We have bound you. If we wished, we would take you into the forests and teach you what it is to be a slave!" As she spoke she jabbed at them with her spear, and a stain of blood was brought through the fabric of more than one tunic. "Men!" laughed Verna, contemptuously, and turned away from them.

I saw them struggle, but they could not free themselves. They had been bound by Panther Girls.

Then Verna was standing before me. She appraised me, as might have a slaver.

"Kajira," she said, contemptuously.

I shook my head, No!

Without looking back she then strode, spear in hand, from the camp, toward the dark forests in the distance.

Her girls followed her, leaving the fire, and the bound men, and Ute and Lana, whom they had tied at the feet of two of the guards.

The choke leash slid shut on my throat and, half strangling, stumbling, stripped and gagged, my hands bound behind my back, I was dragged after them, toward the darkness of the forest.

9 THE HUT

I WAS TERRIFIED to enter the forest, but I had no choice.

The choke leash is a useful device for controlling a bound slave. I must follow perfectly. I could not offer the least resistance without strangling myself.

The girls moved swiftly, single file, through the brush and small trees at the edge of the forest. I could feel leaves and twigs beneath my feet. They stopped only long enough to lift aside some branches and take up the light spears, and bows and arrows, which they had hidden there. Each girl wore, too, at her waist, a sheathed sleen knife.

The tall, blond girl, Verna, beautiful and superb, led the file, her bow and a quiver of arrows now on her back, her spear in hand. Sometimes she would stop to listen, or lift her head, as though testing the air, but then she would resume her journey. Bound as I was, and without the protection of skins, I could not protect my body from the lashings of branches. If I should stop in pain, struck, or stumble, the merciless choke leash, closing on my throat, impelled me forward again.

Then, after perhaps an hour of this torture, Verna lifted her hand, and the girls stopped.

"We will rest here," she said.

It had been difficult making our way through the brush and thickset trees. To reach the high trees of the forest, the great Tur trees, would be perhaps better than another hour's trek.

"Kneel," snapped the girl who held my leash.

I did so, breathing heavily.

"As a Pleasure Slave!" snapped the girl.

Gagged, I shook my head, No!

"Cut switches and beat her," said Verna.

I shook my head, begging, eyes wild, no, no!

I knelt as I had been ordered.

They laughed.

The girl who held my leash looped it over my back.

I pulled at the binding fiber on my wrists.

The girl bound my ankles cruelly, using the end of the choke leash, making the strap taut between my throat and ankles. My head was strapped back. I could barely breathe.

One of the girls scrambled up a nearby tree. In a moment, in the moonlight, she was throwing down water gourds and strips of meat.

Sitting cross-legged on the leaves, the girls passed about the gourds and began to chew on the meat.

When they had drunk and eaten, they sat about in a half circle, looking at me.

"Untie her ankles," said Verna.

The girl did. This released the pressure of the choke leash. My head fell forward.

When I lifted it, Verna stood before me, her knife at my face.

"Scar her," said the girl who had held my leash.

I looked at Verna in terror.

"Are you afraid you will not be so pretty?" asked Verna. "That men will not like you?"

I closed my eyes.

I felt the blade move between my cheek and the gag, cutting the gag free. I almost fainted. With my tongue I forced the packing from my mouth. I almost vomited.

Verna's knife was again in its sheath.

When I could look at her, I said, as evenly as I could, "I am hungry, and thirsty."

"Your masters fed you," said Verna.

"Indeed she was fed!" cried one of the girls. "She was fed by hand, like a beast." The girl snorted. "She even, bound, leaped to catch meat in her teeth."

"Men must find you very pleasing," said Verna.

"I am not a slave girl," I told them.

"You wear a man's brand," said Verna.

I blushed. It was true that I wore the brand of a man.

"She even had Ka-la-na wine," sneered one of the girls.

"Fortunate slave," said Verna.

I said nothing. I was furious.

"It is said," said Verna, "that Ka-la-na wine makes any woman a slave, if but for an hour." She looked at me. "Is it true?"

I said nothing. I recalled with shame how I had, near the fire, placing my guard's hand in my binding fiber, encouraged my own ravishment as a slave girl, and how I had knelt, my hair falling about his face, to kiss him.

I knew that I had provoked him, and then that I had fought him.

"I fought him!" I cried.

The girls laughed.

"Thank you for saving me," I said.

They laughed.

"I am not a slave," I repeated.

"You wore a camisk," said one of the girls. "You were in the girl cage. You served as a slave!"

"You wanted them to touch you," cried another.

"We know the movements of the body of a slave girl," said another, "and your body betrays you! You are a slave!"

"You want to belong to a man!" cried Verna.

"No, No, No!" I wept. "I am not a slave! I am not!"

The girls, and I, were quiet.

"You saw that I struggled," I whispered, desperately.

"You struggled prettily," said Verna.

"I want to join you," I said.

There was a silence.

"We do not accept slave girls among the women of the forest," said Verna proudly.

"I am not a slave girl!" I cried.

Verna regarded me. "How many of us do you count?" she asked.

"Fifteen," I told her.

"My band," said Verna, "consists of fifteen. This, it seems

to me, is a suitable number, for protection, for feeding, for concealment in the forest." She looked at me. "Some groups are smaller, some larger, but my band," she said, "as I wish, numbers fifteen."

I said nothing.

"Would you like to be one of us?" she asked.

"Yes!" I cried. "Yes!"

"Untie her," said Verna.

The choke leash was removed from my throat. My wrists were unbound.

"Stand," said Verna.

I did so, and so, too, did the other girls. I stood, rubbing my wrists.

The girls put down their spears, unslung the bows and quivers from their shoulders.

The light of the three moons filtered through the trees, speckling the glade.

Verna removed her sleen knife from her belt. She handed it to me.

I stood there, holding the knife.

The other girls stood ready, some half crouching. All had removed their knives from their sheaths.

"The place of which of these," asked Verna, "will you take?"

"I do not understand," I said.

"One of these," said Verna, "or myself, you will fight to the death."

I shook my head, No.

"I will fight you, if you wish," said Verna, "without my knife."

"No," I whispered.

"Fight me, Kajira!" hissed the girl who had held my leash. Her knife was ready.

"Me!" cried another.

"Me!" cried yet another.

"Whose place will you take?" asked Verna.

One of the girls cried out and leaped toward me, the knife flashing in her hand.

I screamed and threw the knife from me, and fell to my knees, my head in my hands.

"No, no!" I cried.

"Bind her," said Verna.

I felt my hands pulled again behind my back. The girl who had held my leash lashed them together, mercilessly. I felt again the snap of the choke collar on my throat.

"We have rested," said Verna. "Let us continue our journey."

The girl, clad like the others in the skins of forest panthers, who had held my leash, and now again held it, she who had bound me, her sleen knife again in its sheath, thrust her face toward mine. It was she who had leaped at me with her knife. She twisted her hand in the metal and leather choke collar. "Kajira!" she said, with contempt. I gasped, choking. I was terrified of her.

Verna regarded me. She wiped the dirt and cumbled leaves from her sleen knife, which I had thrown from me, on the skins of her brief garments, and then replaced it in her sheath. She slung again about her shoulders her bow and quiver, and took up again her light spear. The other girls similarly armed themselves, preparing to depart. Some gathered up the water gourds and what meat was left from their meal.

Verna approached me.

I knelt.

"What are you?" she asked.

"Kajira, Mistress," I whispered.

I looked up at her.

"May I speak?" I asked.

"Yes," she said.

I knew I was not as these other women. I was not as they were.

"Why," I asked, "was I taken?"

Verna looked at me, for a long time. And then she said, "There is a man."

I looked up at her, helplessly.

"He has bought you."

The girls, led by Verna, again began to make their way through the dark, moonlit forest.

Again the metal and leather collar slid shut on my throat, and with a gasp of anguish, wrists bound behind my back, not permitted clothing, I followed at my tether, not as they, the proud women of the forest, but only as I could be among them, Kajira.

We continued on, for perhaps another hour. Once Verna lifted her hand, and we stopped.

We stood silently.

"Sleen," said Verna.

The girls looked about.

She had smelled the animal, somewhere.

One of the other girls said, "Yes."

Most of them merely looked about, their spears ready. I gathered few could smell the animal. I could not. The wind was moving softly from my right.

After a time the girl who had said, "Yes," said, "It is gone now." She looked at Verna.

Verna nodded.

We again continued on our way.

I had sensed nothing, and I gathered that most of the other girls had not either.

As we continued our journey, we could see the bright moons above.

The girls seemed restless, short-tempered, irritable. I saw more than one looking at the moons.

"Verna," said one of them.

"Quiet," said Verna.

The file continued its journey through the trees and brush, threading its way through the darkness and branches.

"We have seen men," said one of the girls, insistently.

"Be silent," said Verna.

"We should have taken slaves," said another, irritably.

"No," said Verna.

"The circle," said another. "We must go to the circle!"

Verna stopped and turned.

"It is on our way," said another.

"Please, Verna," said another, her voice pleading.

Verna regarded the girls. "Very well," she said, "we shall stop at the circle."

The girls relaxed visibly.

Irritably, Verna turned, and again we continued on our way.

I understood nothing of this.

I was miserable. I cried out, suddenly, when a branch, unexpectedly, struck me across the belly. With a cry of rage the girl who held my leash expertly, with a twist of her wrist, threw me choking from my feet. Then her foot was on the leash a few inches from my neck, pinning me, choking, to the ground. With the free end of the leash she struck me five times across the back.

"Silence, Kajira!" she hissed.

Then I was pulled again to my feet, and we continued our journey. Again branches struck me, but I did not cry out. My feet and legs were bleeding; my body was lashed, and scratched.

I was nothing with these proud, free, dangerous, brave women, these independent, superb, unfearing, resourceful, fierce felines, panther girls of the northern forests of Gor. They were swift, and beautiful and arrogant, like Verna. They were armed, and could protect themselves, and did not need men. They could make men slaves, if they wished, and sell them later, if they were displeased with them or wearied of them. And they could fight with knives and knew the trails and trees of the vast forests. They feared nothing, and needed nothing.

They were so different from myself.

They were strong, and unfearing. I was weak, and frightened.

It seemed they were of a sex, or breed, other than, and superior to my own.

Among such women I could be but the object of their scorn, what they despised most, only Kajira.

And among them I felt myself to be only Kajira, one fit to be tethered and led, scorned as an insult to the beauty and magnificence of their sex.

I was other than, and less than, they.

"Hurry, Kajira!" snapped the girl who dragged on my leash.

"Yes, Mistress," I whispered.

She laughed.

I was being taken at night through the forest, a bound slave. Verna had told me that there was a man. I had been told that I had been bought. I was being delivered by women, another woman, but a weakling, one who was only a piece of merchandise, one who, on this harsh world, could be only merchandise, to my master.

I wept.

Then, after perhaps another hour, we came, almost abruptly, suddenly, to a stand of the high trees, the Tur trees, of the northern forests.

It was breathtakingly beautiful.

The girls stopped.

I looked about myself. The forests of the northern temperate latitudes of Gor are countries in themselves, covering hundreds of thousands of square pasangs of area. They contain great numbers of various species of trees, and different portions of the forests may differ considerably among themselves. The most typical and famous tree of these forests is the lofty, reddish Tur tree, some varieties of which grow more than two hundred feet high. It is not known how far these forests extend. It is not impossible that they belt the land surfaces of the planet. They begin near the shores of Thassa, the Sea, in the west. How far they extend to the east is not known. They do extend beyond the most northern ridges of the Thentis Mountains.

We found ourselves now in a stand of the lofty Tur trees. I could see broadly spreading branches some two hundred feet or more above my head. The trunks of the trees were almost bare of branches until, so far above, branches seemed to explode in an interlacing blanket of foilage, almost obliterating the sky. I could see glimpses of the three moons high above. The floor of the forest was almost bare. Between the lofty, widely spaced trees there was little but a carpeting of leaves.

I saw two of the girls looking up at the moons. Their lips were parted, their fists clenched. There seemed to be pain in their eyes.

"Verna," said one of them.

"Silence," said their leader.

It was no accident that we had stopped at this place. One of the girls whimpered.

"All right," said Verna, "go to the circle."

The girl turned and sped across the carpeting of leaves.

"Me, Verna!" cried another.

"To the circle," said Verna, irritably.

The girl turned and sped after the first.

One by one, with her eyes, Verna released the girls, and each ran lightly, eagerly, through the trees.

Then Verna came to me and took my leash from the hand of the girl who had held it. "Go to the circle," she told the girl.

Swiftly, not speaking, the girl ran after the others.

Verna looked after them.

We stood alone, she in her skins, I unclothed, she free, I bound, my leash in her grasp.

Verna regarded me, for some time, in the moonlight.

I could not meet her eyes. I dropped my head.

"Yes," said Verna. "You would be pleasing to men. You are a pretty little Kajira."

I could not lift my head.

"I despise you," she said.

I said nothing.

"Are you a docile slave?" she asked.

"Yes, Mistress," I whispered, "I am docile."

Then, to my amazement, Verna unsnapped the choke leash from my throat and then unbound my wrists.

She looked at me, and still I could not meet her eyes.

"Follow the others," she said. "You will come to a clearing. At the edge of the clearing, you will find a post. Wait there to be bound."

"Yes, Mistress," I said.

Verna laughed, and stood behind me. I could imagine her,

straight in her skins and golden ornaments, with her spear and weapons, watching me.

Each step was torture.

"Posture!" snapped Verna, from yards behind me.

I straightened my body and, tears in my eyes, walked between the trees, in the moonlight.

After some hundred yards I came to the edge of a clearing. It was some twenty-five to thirty yards in diameter, ringed by the lofty trunks of Tur trees. The floor of the clearing was lovely grass, thick and some inches in height, soft, and beautiful. I looked up. Bright in the dark, starstrewn Gorean sky, large, dominating, seemingly close enough to touch, loomed the three moons of Gor.

The girls of Verna's band stood about the edge of the circle. They did not speak. They were breathing deeply. They seemed restless. Several had their eyes closed, their fists clenched. Their weapons had been discarded.

I saw, at one side of the clearing, the post.

It was about five feet high, and seven inches thick, sturdy, sunk deep into the ground. In its back, there were two heavy metal rings, one about two feet from the ground, the other about three and a half feet from the ground. It was a rough post, barked. On its front, near the top, carved, cut into the bark with the point of a sleen knife, was a crude representation of opened slave bracelets. It was a slave post.

I went and stood before it, Elinor Brinton, the slave.

Briefly, through my mind flashed the memory of my former riches, of the penthouse, the Maserati, my luxuries, and education and travels, my former status and power, and then of my capture and my transportation to this rude world.

"Kneel," snapped Verna.

I did so.

Verna resnapped the leather and metal choke collar on my throat. She then threaded the leash through the ring, about three and a half feet high, behind the post, brought the leash about and looped it, from the left to the right, about my neck and then rethreaded it through the ring, pulling it tight. I was bound by the neck to the post. Then she threaded

the free end of the leash through the lower of the two
rings, passed it about my belly, and rethreaded it again
through the same ring, keeping it tight, fastening me at the
waist to the post. With the free end of the leash, keeping
it taut, she then lashed my ankles together behind the post.
I was bound, save that my hands were free.

Verna took the length of binding fiber from her skins,
that which had formerly bound my wrists.

"Place your hands above your head," she said.

I did so.

She tied the binding fiber securely about my left wrist,
took the fiber behind the post, threaded it through the highest of the two metal rings, and then, jerking my right wrist
back, bound it, too, fastening me to the post.

I knelt, secured.

"Docile slave," sneered Verna.

"Verna!" spoke one of the girls.

"Very well!" said Verna, irritably. "Very well!"

The first girl to leap to the center of the circle was she
who had first held my leash.

She had blond hair. Her head was down, and shaking.
Then she threw back her head, moaning, and reached up,
clawing for the moons of Gor. The other girls, too, responded
to her, whimpering and moaning, clenching and unclenching
their fists.

The first girl began to writhe, crying out, stamping in the
circle.

Then another girl joined her, and another, and another.
And then another!

Stamping, turning, crying out, moaning, clawing at the
moons, they danced.

Then there were none who had not entered that savage
circle, save Verna, the band's leader, proud and superb,
armed and disdainful, and Elinor Brinton, a bound slave.

The first girl, throwing back her head to the moons,
screamed and tore her skins to the waist, writhing.

Then, for the first time I noticed, in the center of the
circle, there were four heavy stakes, about six inches in
height, dark in the grass. They formed a small, but ample,

square. I shuddered. They were notched, that binding fiber might not slip from them.

The first girl began to dance before the square.

I looked up into the sky. In the dark sky the moons were vast and bright.

Another girl, crying out, tore her own skins to the waist and clawing, moaning, writhing, approached the square. Then another and another!

I did not even look upon Verna, so horrified I was at the barbaric spectacle. I had not believed that women could be like this.

And then the first girl tore away her skins and danced in her golden ornaments beneath the huge, wild moons, on the grass of the circle, before the square.

I could not believe my eyes. I shuddered, fearing such women.

Then suddenly, to my amazement, Verna cried out in anguish, a wild, moaning, anguished cry, and threw from herself her weapons and tore away her own skins and leaped into the circle, turning, and clawing and crying out like the others. She was not other than they, but first among them! She danced savagely, clad only in her gold and beauty, beneath the moons. She cried out and clawed. Sometimes she bit at another girl or struck at her, if she dared approach the square more closely than she. Writhing, enraged, but fearful, eyes blazing, dancing, they fell back before her.

She danced first among them, their leader.

Then, throwing her head back, she screamed, shaking her clenched fists at the moons.

And then, helplessly, she threw herself to the grass within the square, striking at it, biting and tearing at it, and then she threw herself on her back and, fists clenched, writhed beneath the moons.

One by one the other girls, too, violently, threw themselves to the grass, rolling upon it and moaning, some even within the precincts of the square, then throwing themselves upon their backs, some with their eyes closed, crying out, others with their eyes open, fixed helplessly on the wild moons, some with hands tearing at the grass, others pounding the

earth piteously with their small fists, sobbing and whimpering, their bodies uncontrolled, helpless, writhing, under the
moons of Gor.

I found myself pulling at my bonds, suddenly aching with
an inexplicable loneliness and desire. I pulled at the fiber
that bound my wrists, so cruelly back; my throat pressed
against the straps on my throat, almost choking me; my
belly writhed under its strap; my ankles moved against one
another, helpless in the leather confinement of the knotted
strap. I looked up at the moons. I cried out in anguish. I
wanted to be free, too, to dance, to cry out, to claw at
the moons, to throw myself on the living, fibrous, flowing
grass, to writhe with these women, my sisters, to writhe with
them in the frenzy of their need.

No, I cried out to myself, no, no! I am Elinor Brinton!
I am of Earth! No, no!

"Kajirae!" I screamed at them. "Kajirae!" "Slaves! Slaves!"

There was no fear in my voice, but almost hysterical
triumph! "Slaves!" I screamed at them. "Slaves!" I then knew
myself better than they! I was superior! I was above them!
Though I was bound and branded I was a thousand times
greater and finer than they. I was Elinor Brinton! Though
I might be stripped, though I might be tied to a slave post, I
was greater and finer, and of nobler stock, than they. They
were naught but slaves.

"Kajirae!" I screamed at them. "Kajirae!" "Slaves! Slaves!"

They paid me no attention.

I cried out at them hysterically, and then was quiet. My
limbs ached, particularly my arms, tied so cruelly back, but
I was not too displeased. The moons fled across the black
sky, burning with its bright stars. The girls lay now quietly
on the grass, some still whimpering slightly, many with their
eyes closed, some lying on their stomachs, their face pressed
against the grass, the stain of tears on their cheek, mingling
into the grass. It was colder now, and I felt chilly, but I
did not mind. I was now, though bound and stripped, well
pleased with myself. I had regained my self-respect. I now
knew myself superior to such women, to such despicable
things, as these.

At last the girls, one by one, rose from the grass, drew on again their skins, and took up their weapons.

Then, Verna at their lead, they approached me.

I knelt by the post, very straight.

"It seemed to me," I said, "that your bodies moved as might have those of slave girls."

My head leaped to the side, stinging, as Verna, with all her might, slapped me.

Then she looked at me. "We are women," she said.

There were tears in my eyes. I tasted a bit of blood in my mouth, where my lip had been struck against my teeth. But I did not cry out or whimper. I smiled. Then I looked away.

"Let us kill her," said one of the girls, she who held my leash before, who had been the first to enter the circle of the dance.

"No," said Verna.

Verna looked about at the other girls.

They were ready to depart.

"Bring the slave," said Verna.

"I am free," I told her.

Verna strode from the area wherein was found the circle of the dance.

The other girls followed her, with the exception of the blond girl, who had held my leash. She untied my hands and then, behind my body, but not behind the post, rebound them, cruelly. I did not complain. Then she untied the strap at my ankles, freeing them, and, drawing the strap about the post and through the two rings, released me from the post. By the choke leash she pulled me to my feet. I looked at her and smiled. She said nothing, but turned angrily away, and led me from the post, following Verna and her band.

Verna suddenly lifted her hand.

"Sleen," she whispered.

The girls looked about.

I was apprehensive. I wondered if it were the same animal which Verna, and one of the other girls, had detected earlier. The girls, too, seemed apprehensive. I hoped that it was not the same animal. If it was, it had been following us. There are, of course, many sleen in the forests.

The girls remained still for a long time, scarcely breathing.

"Is it still there?" asked one of the girls, the one who had been able to detect the sleen earlier. Her nostrils were flared, testing the air.

"Yes," said Verna. She gestured in a direction somewhat forward of the band and to its oblique right. "It is there," she said. I could see nothing but the darkness of the trees, and the shadows.

We continued to stand still for some time.

Then, after this time, Verna said, "It is gone."

The girls looked at one another. I could tell the difference in their breathing. I took a deep breath, and shuddered. I looked again into the darkness, the trees and shadows, to the right. Then I felt the leather and metal choke collar again slide shut on my throat and, choking, I followed hurriedly at my tether.

After the trek of perhaps an hour we came to a clearing in the forest. In the clearing, there was a small hut, a stave house, with a single door and window. Inside there was a light.

I was led to the door of this house.

"Kneel," said Verna.

I did so.

I was apprehensive. I knew this must be the house of the man who had purchased me.

But I could not be purchased, for I was Elinor Brinton, a free woman, of Earth. No matter what bonds I might wear, no matter what transactions in which I might figure, I could not be purchased, for I was free!

There was a leather bag, on two leather strings, which hung from a hook outside the door.

There was no sound from within the house.

Verna removed the bag from its hook and knelt down on the ground, the other girls around her. She shook the contents of the bag out on the ground. It contained steel arrow points. She counted them in the light of the moons. There were one hundred of them.

Verna gave six points to each of her girls. Ten she kept for herself. She, and they, put the points into the pouches they wore at their belts.

I looked at her, shaking my head, not believing what I had seen. Could it be that this, and this alone, was my price, that I had been purchased for only this, the points for one hundred arrows? But I reminded myself that I could not be purchased, for I was Elinor Brinton, for I was free!

"Rise, Slave," said Verna.

I rose to my feet and she unsnapped from my throat the hated choke leash.

I looked at her. "I am free," I told her.

"Let us kill her," urged the blond girl, she who had held my leash.

"All right," said Verna.

"No!" I cried. "No! Please!"

"Kill her," said Verna.

Uncontrollably I fell to my knees before her. "Please don't kill me!" I cried. "Please! Please!" I trembled. I wept. I pressed my head to her feet. "Please!" I begged. "Please! Please! Please! Please!"

"What are you?" asked Verna.

"A slave," I cried out. "A slave!"

"Do you beg for your life?" asked Verna.

"Yes," I whimpered. "Yes, yes!"

"Who begs for her life?" asked Verna.

"A slave begs her mistress for her life," I wept.

"Is it only slaves who so beg for their lives?" asked Verna.

"Yes!" I cried out. "Yes!"

"Is it only slaves who so beg and grovel?" asked Verna.

"Yes," I said. "Yes!"

"Then you are a slave," said Verna.

"Yes!" I cried.

"You then acknowledge yourself a slave?" Verna inquired.

"Yes!" I cried. "Yes! I acknowledge myself a slave! I am a slave! I am a slave!"

"Spare the slave," said Verna.

I almost collapsed. Two of the girls lifted me to my feet. I could scarcely stand.

I was shattered.

I then knew as I had not known before, that I was a slave. I was not free. I knew then that the body of Elinor Brinton, even when she had been in college, even when she had concerned herself with the trivia of term papers, even when she had eaten in Parisian restaurants, when she had strolled the boulevards of the continent, when in New York she had stepped from and into taxis, had been the body of a slave girl. That body, attired in its evening gowns, its cocktail dresses, its chic tweeds, might perhaps have been more appropriately clad in the brief silk of a Gorean slave girl, fit only for the controlling touch of a master. I wondered if men had realized that. If there had been Gorean men who had looked upon me I had little doubt that they might, smiling, have seen me thus. But I hated men!

I wondered what price my body would bring in a market. I wondered what price I would bring.

I was shattered.

My eyes met those of Verna.

"Slave," she sneered.

"Yes, Mistress," I whispered, and looked down. I could not meet her eyes, those of a free woman.

"Are you a docile slave?" she asked.

"Yes, Mistress," I said, quickly, frightened, "I am a docile slave."

"Docile slave," she sneered.

"Yes," I said, "yes, Mistress."

The girls laughed.

Suddenly it seemed so foolish to me that it had seemed that I was free. I almost choked with misery. It was only too obvious that I was not free. I knew then that I might indeed figure in transactions, and knew that I would do so as mere property. I could figure in commercial exchanges, for I was goods. I could indeed be purchased, and bought and sold. In the moment of my misery my vanities, my pretenses, had been swept away. I knew then, as I had not before, that I was a slave girl.

"Through that door," said Verna, gesturing with her head "is your master."

I stood and faced the door, stripped, wrists lashed behind my back.

Suddenly, unaccountably, I turned and faced her. "A hundred arrow points," I pouted, "is not enough!" I was startled that I had said this, and more with how I had said it. It was surely not Elinor Brinton who could have said this. It was the remark of a slave girl. But it had been Elinor Brinton who had said it. With horror I suddenly realized that she was a petty slave girl.

"It is all that you are worth to him," said Verna.

I pulled futilely at the binding fiber on my wrists.

She regarded me, as might have a man. I stood in fury, scrutinized. "I myself," said Verna, "would not have paid as much."

The girls laughed.

I shook with fury, a humiliated slave girl. My action seemed uncontrollable, and I hated myself for it.

"The girl fancies," said the blond girl, who had held my leash, "that she should have fetched a higher price."

"I am worth more!" I pouted.

"Be silent," said Verna.

"Yes, Mistress," I said, frightened, putting down my head.

A ripple of amusement passed through the girls.

I did not care. I was angry, and I was humiliated. I should have brought far more.

I suddenly knew that I would be a clever slave. I was highly intelligent. I could undoubtedly scheme and wheedle, and obtain my way. I could smile prettily, and would, to obtain what I wished. I felt petty and sly, but justifiably, proudly so. Was I not a slave? I knew that I could well employ the wiles of a slave girl to make my life pleasant and easy.

But only a hundred arrow points! It was not enough!

The door to the hut swung open.

Suddenly terrified I faced the opening.

I felt the point of Verna's spear in my back.

"Enter, Slave Girl," said Verna.

"Yes, Mistress," I whispered.

I felt the point of Verna's spear again against my back. It pressed forward. I stumbled into the room, crying out with anguish.

The door shut behind me, two beams falling into place, barring it.

I looked about, and then I threw back my head and screamed in uncontrollable terror.

10　WHAT TRANSPIRED
IN THE HUT

THE LARGE-EYED, FURRED THING blinked at me.

"Do not be afraid," said a voice.

The animal was fastened to a ring in the wall by a stout, spiked leather collar, fastened to a heavy chain.

I stood with my back to the opposite wall of the hut, shrinking against it, terrified. I felt the rough boards at my back. My head was lifted and back, eyes wide. The back of my head pressed back against the boards. I felt the boards, too, pressed against the fingertips of my bound hands. I could not breathe.

The beast looked at me, and yawned. I saw the two rows of white fangs. Then, sleepily, it began to nibble at the fur of its right paw, grooming it.

I saw that the chain was short, that it would not reach even to the center of the room.

"Do not be afraid," again said the voice.

I took a breath, with difficulty.

Across the room, his back to me, bending over a shallow pan of water, with a towel about his neck, was a small man. He turned to face me. His face was still the painted clown's face, but he had put aside his silly robes, the tufted hat. He wore a common Gorean male house tunic, rough and brown, with leggings, such as are sometimes worn by woodsmen, who work in brush.

"Good evening," he said.

I shuddered. I did not move.

His voice seemed different now, no longer the voice of the comical mountebank. Too, somehow the voice seemed familiar to me, but I could not recall if, or where, I had once heard it. I knew only that I was terribly frightened.

He turned again to the pan of water on the table and began to wash the paint from his face.

I could not take my eyes from the beast.

It regarded me, sleepily, and returned to the grooming of its paw.

It seemed incredibly huge, even more so in the small hut than earlier outside of Targo's compound. It was like a glistening, somnolent boulder of fur, alive, hundreds of pounds in weight. The eyes were large, black, round, the snout wide, two-nostriled and leathery. I shuddered at its mouth, and fangs, the upper two protruding downwards at the sides of its jaws. Its lips were wet from the saliva from its long, dark tongue, which, with its teeth, it was using to groom the fur on its right paw. The strike of those jaws could, with one wrenching twist, have torn away the shoulder of a man.

I trembled, terrified, my back pressed against the rough boards.

Elinor Brinton trembled, terrified, naked and bound, her back pressed against the rough boards, a cowering slave girl.

"Good evening, Miss Brinton," said the man. He had spoken in English.

"You!" I cried.

"Hello, Cookie," he said.

"You!" I whispered. It was the smaller man, one of those who had originally captured, and had bound me on my own bed in my penthouse. It was he who had entered the syringe in my right side, in the back, between my waist and hip, drugging me. It was he who had touched me intimately, who had been warned away from me by the larger man. It was he who had taken my matches and cigarettes, who had leaned over me, and had blown smoke, as I had lain nude before him, bound and gagged, into my face.

His ferret eyes regarded me, looking me over.

"You're a pretty little cookie," he said.

I could not speak.

"Kajira!" he snapped in Gorean. Every muscle in my body tensed.

He suddenly snapped his fingers and, in the swift double gesture of a Gorean master, pointed to a place on the dirt floor before him, almost simultaneously turning his hand, spreading his first and index fingers, pointing downwards.

I fled to him and knelt before him, my knees in the dirt, in the position of the pleasure slave, my head down, trembling.

"It is interesting," he mused, "the effect of slavery on a woman."

"Yes, Master," I whispered.

"Excellent," he said.

"The proud, arrogant, rich Miss Brinton," he remarked, speaking in English.

"No, Master," I whispered, in English.

"Are you not Miss Brinton?" he asked.

"Yes," I whispered, "I am Elinor Brinton."

"What is she?" he asked.

"Only a Gorean slave," I said.

"I never thought to have you at my feet," he said.

"No, Master," I whispered.

"It is not unpleasant," he said.

"No, Master," I whispered.

He went to a side of the room and picked up a small bench, which he brought forward and set before me. He then sat on this bench and, for some time, regarded me. I did not move.

Then he rose from the bench and went again to the side of the room, where there was a pile of cut logs. He took one and put it on the fire at the side of the room, in a shallow, rimmed, stone hearth. There was a shower of sparks. Smoke found its way upward through a rudely fitted stone venting.

I was tense, frightened. I did not move. He returned and sat again before me.

Then he said, "Stand."

Immediately I leaped to my feet.

"Turn," he said.

I did so.

To my surprise, he unbound my wrists. My hands were numb. I could scarcely move my fingers.

He sat on the bench, and I stood before him. I rubbed my wrists and moved my fingers, trying to restore their circulation.

He did not speak to me.

I stood before him for a long time.

"Step back," he said.

Terrified, because it brought me nearer the beast, I did so, trembling.

"Attack!" he shouted in Gorean to the beast.

It howled and lunged for me, jaws snapping, great black, furred arms gasping.

I screamed hysterically and found myself in the corner of the room, screaming, wedged in the corner, on my knees, my hands in front of me, scratching at the boards with my fingernails, weeping, screaming and weeping.

"Do not be afraid," he said.

I screamed and screamed.

"Do not be afraid," he repeated.

"What do you want with me!" I cried. "What do you want with me!" I shuddered, and shook with tears, and fear. "What do you want with me?" I begged. "What do you want with me?"

"Miss Brinton," he said, kindly.

I tried to breathe.

"Goreans are barbarians," he said. "They have compromised your modesty." His voice was solicitous, apologetic, concerned, kindly.

Numbly I turned to face him.

He stood near the bench. In his arms he held a red-silk, full-length, belted lounging robe, with a high, throat-inclosing, figured, brocade collar.

"Please," he invited.

I approached him numbly, and turned. He held the robe for me, as might have an escort. He helped me slip it on.

"It's mine," I whispered. I remembered the robe.

"It was yours," he said.

I looked at him. What he said was true. I could own nothing. It was rather I, who was owned.

I belted the robe.

"You are lovely," he commented.

I fastened the high, figured, brocade collar about my throat.

I regarded him, once again my own woman.

"Yes," he said, "you are very lovely, Miss Brinton."

I watched him as he went again to the side of the room, and brought forward a small table, and another small bench. He gestured that I should join him at the table. He seated me.

I sat at the table, and watched him as he threw another log on the fire. Again there was a shower of sparks, and the smoke climbing upward through the venting.

The beast now lay curled in its place, on straw. Its eyes were closed, but it did not seem to be asleep. It would move occasionally, or yawn or change its position.

"Cigarette?" asked the man.

I looked at him. "Yes," I whispered.

He produced two cigarettes from a flat, golden case. They were my brand. With a small match, he lit my cigarette for me, and then his. He threw the match into the fire.

I fumbled with the cigarette. My hand shook.

"Are you nervous?" he asked.

"Return me to Earth!" I whispered.

"Are you not puzzled as to why you were brought to this world?" he asked.

"Please!" I begged.

He regarded me.

"I will pay you anything," I whispered.

"Money?" he asked.

"Yes!" I said. "Yes!"

"Money is unimportant," he said.

I looked anguished.

"Smoke your cigarette," he said.

I drew on the cigarette.

"Were you startled the morning you awakened and found yourself branded?" he inquired.

"Yes," I whispered. My hand inadvertently touched the mark on my thigh, under my robe.

"Perhaps you are curious as to how it was done?"

"Yes," I whispered.

"The device," said he, "is not much larger than this." He indicated the small, flat box of cigarettes. "A handle, containing the heating element, is fixed into the back of the marking surface. It switches on and off, much like a common flashlight." He smiled at me. "I generates a flesh-searing heat in five seconds."

"I felt nothing," I said.

"You were fully anesthetized," he said.

"Oh," I said.

"I personally think a girl should be fully conscious when being branded," he said.

I looked down.

"The psychological impact is more satisfactory," he said.

I could say nothing.

"Salve was applied to the wound. It healed quickly and cleanly. You went to bed a free woman." He looked at me, unpleasantly. "You awakened a Kajira."

"The collar?" I asked.

"You were lying unconscious before the mirror," he said. "We re-entered your apartment by means of the terrace." He smiled. "It is not hard to collar a girl."

I recalled the collar had been later removed at the location referred to as point P, before the black ship had fled the earth, through the gray skies of that August dawn.

The man who had removed the collar had said that doubtless I would have another.

I shoved the cigarette irritably down on the table, breaking it, grinding it out.

I knew that I could be collared, when it pleased a man to do so.

"May I have another cigarette?" I asked.

"Of course," he said, and solicitously, as I bent forward, he lit me another.

I drew on the fresh cigarette. "Do you often bring women to this world as slaves?" I asked.

"Yes," he said, "and sometimes men, too, if it should serve our purposes."

"I see," I said.

I was irritated.

I remembered the two men thrusting me into the narrow, transparent slave capsule, in its rack, its lid being screwed shut. I remembered my pressing my hands against its sides, the beginning of the flight from Earth, the sedating gases.

I had indeed been brought to this world as a slave.

We smoked together for some time without speaking.

I remembered awakening, lying in a Gorean field, some hundred yards or so from the black wreckage of the slavers' ship. I remembered, too, that on Earth, at the location called point P, before I had boarded the ship, a heavy steel anklet, doubtless an identification device of some sort, had been locked on my left ankle. When I had awakened in the field, it had been gone.

I looked at him. "Why was I brought to this world?" I asked.

"We bring many women to this world," he remarked, "because they are beautiful, and it pleases us to make them slaves."

I regarded him.

"Also, of course," he said, "they are valuable. They may be distributed or sold, as we please, to further our ends or increase our profits."

"Was I brought to this world as such a girl?" I asked.

"It may interest you to know," he said, "that you were marked for abduction at the age of seventeen. In the intervening five years we watched you carefully, maturing into a spoiled, rich, highly intelligent, arrogant young woman, exactly the sort that, under whip and collar, becomes a most exquisite slave."

I drew on the cigarette, in fury.

"So I was simply brought to Gor to be a female slave?" I asked.

"Let us say," he remarked, carefully, "you would have been brought to Gor as a female slave, regardless."

"Regardless?" I asked.

"Yes," he said.

"I do not understand," I said.

"We lost you briefly," he said. His eyes clouded. "The ship crashed," he explained."

"I see," I said.

"After the crash," he said, "we detected the approach of an enemy craft. We abandoned our ship and scattered, fleeing with our cargo."

"But," said I, "was I not part of your—your cargo?"

His eyes narrowed. I could tell he would choose his words carefully.

"We have enemies," he said. "We did not wish you to fall into their hands. We feared pursuit. We removed your identification anklet and hid you in the grass, some distance from the ship. Then with the other girls, we fled, intending to rendezvous later, if possible, and return for you. There was, however, no pursuit. The enemy was apparently content only to destroy the ship. When we returned there was little more than a crater. You, of course, were gone."

"How did you find me?" I asked.

"As an unprotected female on Gor, particularly a beautiful one, there was little doubt that the first male you encountered would make you his slave."

I looked down, irritated.

"I went to Laura," he said. "It is the largest city in the area. I expected that it would be there that you would be put up for sale."

"And you would have bought me?" I said.

"Yes," he said. "Simple." He smiled. "But, unfortunately for us, your capture was effected by slavers, and they wished to take you south for a better price. Accordingly we used panther girls, Verna and her band, to acquire you." He smiled again. "It was, incidentally, must less expensive."

I looked at him in irritation.

"You cost only one hundred arrow points."

I shook with anger.

"That bothers you, doesn't it?" he asked.

"No," I said.

"It would bother only a natural slave girl," he said.

I looked down, shaking with fury. I was not a slave. I was not a slave!

I sat there in the belted, red-silk lounging robe, with the high brocade collar enclosing my throat. I drew again on the cigarette. I was not a slave!

"How did you know that I was in Targo's compound?" I asked.

"Doubtless," said he, "I would have investigated, and found you there, but, earlier, I saw you in Laura. You were in coffle, throat-leashed, fetching supplies, with other slaves."

I looked down in irritation.

"You carry wine beautifully," he commented.

"I am not a slave," I told him.

"I see," he said.

"I am free," I told him.

"I see," he said.

I remembered now that once, in Laura, I had seen a man, garbed in black. I had thought that he might have been watching us. But I had not been sure. I now realized that it had been he.

"And so," I said, "you found me."

"I confirmed your identity at the compound," said he, "during the performance of the mountebank, and, of course, surveyed the entire area and planned, in effect, the raid of the panther girls.

"It was your good fortune," I told him, haughtily, "that I was not caged that night."

He smiled. "I had spoken with Targo and the guards," he said, "and knew the celebrations planned for the evening. Further, I had even spoken with the guards, ostensibly jesting with them, as to their choices for the evening. I knew even at which wagon you would serve."

"You are thorough," I said.

"One must be," he said.

"And so I am here," I said. I lowered the cigarette. "What are you going to do with me?" I asked.

"Perhaps feed you to the beast," he said.

I stiffened. It was true that he could do that, if he wished.

I drew again on the cigarette. "What are you going to do with me?" I asked.

"In some respects," said he, "it was your good fortune to fall in with a slaver."

"Oh?" I asked.

"Yes," said he. "Doubtless you have not yet served fully as a slave girl."

I looked at him with apprehension.

"You will doubtless find it an interesting experience," he said, "to serve, not as a free woman, but as a slave girl, fully, for a master who will exact his full dues and more, from his property."

"Please," I said.

"Few Earthwomen," he said, "have that exquisite pleasure."

"Please," I said. "Do not speak to me so."

"Smoke your cigarette," he said, kindly.

I drew on the cigarette.

"Have you never been curious," he asked, "what it would be like, to be forced to yield yourself, utterly, to a master?"

"I hate men," I told him.

"Superb," he said.

I looked at him with irritation.

"You might be interested to know," he said, "that all indications are that you will be a fantastic pleasure slave for a master."

"I hate men!" I cried.

"Excellent," he commented.

I looked at him with fury.

I drew again on the cigarette. "What do you want with me?" I asked.

Suddenly the beast made a noise. It was a rumble, a growl. I stiffened, and turned.

It had lifted its head. Its wide, pointed ears lifted. It was listening.

The man, and I, watched the beast, I, frightened, he, alert, cautious.

His eyes seemed to meet those of the beast, and the beast seemed to look at him. Then it had lifted its lips away from its teeth, and looked away, its ears still lifted. It growled again.

"It is a sleen outside," said the man.

I trembled.

"When I was brought here," I said, "twice the band caught the scent of a sleen."

The man looked at me. "It was stalking you," he said, "you, and the others."

"Perhaps there were different sleen," I whispered.

"Perhaps," he said.

The beast now crouched on the straw, its nostrils wide in the leathery snout, its eyes bright and black, the ears lifted.

"It is close," said the man. He looked at me. "Sometimes the sleen will follow a quarry for pasangs, before making its strike, lurking, approaching, withdrawing, then at last, when satisfied, attacking from the darkness."

The beast growled menacingly.

To my horror I heard a snuffling behind the door, and then a whining, a scratching.

The man smiled. "It is the sleen," he said.

I looked at him.

"Do not be frightened," he said. "We are safe in the hut."

I heard a scratching, as of heavy claws, at the door.

The small hairs on the back of my neck rose.

"The door is stout," said the man. "We are safe within."

I looked to the boards, shuttered across the window. It was a small window, not more than a foot in diameter.

"The sleen was probably following the band," he said. "The trail led here."

"Why doesn't he follow the panther girls?" I whispered.

"He might have," said the man, "but he did not." He gestured with his head to the beast. "Also, he may smell the beast. Sleen are sometimes curious, and not infrequently resentful of the intrusion of strange animals into what they choose to regard as their territory."

There was an angry whine behind the door. This was answered by a throaty snarl from the collared beast within.

"Why doesn't he go away?" I asked.

"He may smell the beast," said the man.

I took another draw on the cigarette.

"Or," said the man, "he may smell food within."

"Food?" I asked.

"You and I," said he.

My hand shook with the cigarette, spilling ashes.

"We are safe within," he said.

"Don't you have weapons, powerful weapons," I asked, "with which you might kill it?"

The man smiled. "It is unwise to carry weapons of power on the surface of Gor," he said.

I did not understand this.

"But," he smiled, "we are safe within."

I hoped that he was right.

"You are lovely in your robe," he said.

"Thank you," I said.

I could no longer hear the sleen now.

I ground out the cigarette on the table, and looked at him, cooly.

"I was not brought to Gor, was I," I asked, "to be a simple female slave, simply to be given, or sold, to a master?"

"I told you," he reminded me, "that at the age of seventeen you were marked for abduction. In any event, you would have been brought to Gor as a female slave."

"But in my case," I pressed, "there were, were there not, additional considerations?"

"Yes," he said.

I leaned back. I suddenly felt sharp, and cool. There was something they needed of me. I now could bargain. I now could negotiate. I might yet be able to arrange for my return to Earth. I must be clever. I must be shrewd. I had power.

"Would you like to discuss business with me?" I asked.

"You are very beautiful in your robe," he said.

"Thank you," I said. I felt a certain sense of triumph now.

"Would you like another cigarette?" he asked.

I did not want one.

"Yes, thank you," I said.

He gave me another cigarette, and I took it. He closed the small, flat golden cigarette box and struck a small match. I leaned forward, and he bent forward to light the cigarette. The flame from the match was but an inch short of the cigarette. He looked at me. "You are prepared to negotiate?" he asked.

I smiled at him. "Perhaps," I said.

He brought the match toward the cigarette, and I bent forward for the light.

The match dropped.

I looked at him, startled.

Suddenly, with fury, he, with his full strength, slapped me across the side of the face, literally knocking me from the bench and against the wall.

Instantly he was on me and tore the robe from my body. Then, insolently, brutally, he threw me on my belly in the dirt. He knelt across my body and I felt my hands jerked behind my body. With the binding fiber he had earlier removed, he lashed them with ferocious cruelty behind my body. Then he sprang to his feet and kicked me in the side. Terrified, in pain, I rolled to my side, looking up at him in horror. He bent down and seized me by the hair and the left arm and thrust me toward the beast.

"Feed!" he cried.

I screamed, thrust toward the wide, fanged jaws of the beast.

He jerked me back, cruelly, on my knees, and I saw the jaws snapping at me, saw the curved teeth, the hideous tongue and eyes. Again and again the jaws snapped at me, once grazing my body, as I was held just outside the perimeter of the beast's chain. It pulled against the chain and collar, trying to reach me.

Then, angrily, the man threw me backward in the dirt, across the room, on my side.

"Do not feed!" he cried to the beast.

Then, from a hook on the wall, he took a large piece of meat, bosk meat, and threw it to the animal.

It began tearing at it with its fangs and claws. It could have been my body.

The man approached me.

I lay on my side in the dirt, naked and bound, looking up at him in horror. In his hand he held an uplifted slave whip.

"You told me you were free," he said.

"No! No!" I cried. "I am a slave! A slave!"

"A hundred arrow points is too much for such a slave," he said.

Terrified, I struggled to my knees and put my head down, to his feet.

"Kiss my feet," said he, "Slave."

I did so.

"The proud Miss Brinton," he said.

I trembled at his feet.

"Are you prepared to negotiate?" he asked.

I put my forehead against his feet, to the straps of his sandals, my hair falling across his sandals.

"Command me," I begged.

He stepped away from me. I lifted my head. I saw that he took the red-silk robe, and cast it into the fire. Kneeling in the dirt, naked and bound, tears in my eyes, I watched it burn.

He regarded me.

I put down my head. "Command me, Master," I begged, Elinor Brinton, a cowering Gorean slave girl.

"It is our intention," he said, "to have you trained as a slave girl, to give exquisite pleasures to a master. And then you will be placed in a certain house."

"Yes, Master?" I asked.

"And," he said, "in this house, you will poison its master."

I looked at him with horror.

Suddenly there was a horrifying squeal and a splintering of wood.

I screamed.

The head of a sleen, eyes blazing, its long needlelike teeth snapping, thrust through the small, broken window, the shutters splintered to the side. Snarling, it began to wiggle its shoulders, like a cat, through the opening.

The beast at the side of the wall went wild.

The man, suddenly distraught, cried out in fear, backing away from the window.

I was on my feet, backed against the wall.

The large, wide, triangular head of the sleen, its nocturnal eyes blinking against the sudden light of the fire, thrust further into the room, followed by its shoulders, then its right, clawed paw.

The beast bellowed in fury, leaping up.

The man, as though brought to his senses by the maddened cry of the beast, picked up the slave whip and ran to the window, striking the sleen, trying to drive it back through the window. But, as I watched in horror, I realized the sleen could not retreat. It now had two paws through the window and a third of its body. It squealed and hissed in fury, struck by the whip, and then it caught it in its teeth and tore it away from the man. I, bound, screamed and pressed against the wall. Then the man picked up a piece of wood, kindling, from near the fire, and struck the sleen. The wood broke across its neck. Another paw and leg, clawed, scrabbled through the window. The sleen has six legs. It is long, sinuous; it resembles a lizard, save that it is furred and mammalian. In its attack frenzy it is one of the most dangerous animals on Gor. Wildly the man bent down to the fire and picked up a piece of wood from the fire, burning, and thrust it toward the sleen. It squealed in pain, blinded in one eye. Then it caught the wood in its teeth and wrenched it away. Then another leg came through the window, and almost half of the animal's body thrust into the room. The man then screamed and fled to the door. He threw up the beams, unlocking it. The beast roared at him and he turned, terrified. I screamed. I could not understand. It was almost as though the beast had commanded him to remain.

The sleen, hissing, one eye blazing, the other seared by the torch, maddened with pain, began to wiggle and squirm through the aperture.

Then to my horror I observed the beast. It lifted its large paws to its throat. The paws were six-digited, several jointed, almost like furred tentacles, surmounted by clawlike growths, blunted, filed. It unfastened the buckled collar at its throat and cast it aside.

Then, with a cry of rage, it leapt toward the sleen. The two animals locked in combat. The sleen came through the window, scrambling through, biting and tearing. The beast seized it about the throat, its great jaws biting at the throat and vertebrae. The two animals rolled in the small hut, twisting, squealing, hissing, scattering the benches and table. Then, with a horrifying snap of bone and tearing of flesh and fur the jaws of the beast bit through the back of the sleen's neck. It stood there then, holding the body of the sleen in its claws, its mouth dropping fur and blood. The body of the sleen twisted compulsively. The beast turned to regard us.

"It's dead," cried the man. "Put it down."

The beast looked at him, uncomprehendingly, and I was suddenly terrified. The man, too, seemed terrified.

Then the beast threw back its head and uttered a wild, horrifying scream, and fell to feeding on the sleen's carcass.

"No, no!" cried the man. "Do not feed! Do not feed!"

The beast raised its head, half buried in the sleen's body, meat hanging from its jaws.

"Do not feed!" whispered the man.

I was terrified.

The beast was in its feeding frenzy. I suspected it could not then be controlled. Surely the man, who knew more than I of such matters, was almost beside himself with terror.

"Stop!" cried the man.

The beast looked at him, eyes blazing, its face drenched in blood.

"Obey your master!" I cried. "Obey your master!"

The beast looked at me. I shall never forget the horror I felt. "I am the master," it said.

The man cried out and fled from the hut. I, forgotten by the beast in its feeding, inched toward the door, and then, hearing the feeding of the beast behind me, fled, naked and bound, into the darkness.

11   SORON OF AR

I KNELT ON THE LOW WOODEN PLATFORM, while one of the leather workers, with a long needle, approached my face.

"See," said Targo, to the other girls, "El-in-or is brave."

Many of them were whimpering.

I closed my eyes. No anesthetic was used, for I was a slave, but it was not particularly painful.

It was said to be a Turian custom, from the far south, which was spreading north.

The leather worker then went to the other side of the platform.

There were tears in my eyes, for my eyes smarted.

I felt the second pain, sharp, followed by an unpleasant burning sensation.

The leather worker stood up.

My ears had been pierced.

The girls, in line, kneeling, cried out, whimpering and shuddering. Guards stood on either side of the line.

"See how brave El-in-or is," said Targo.

The leather worker wiped away the bit of blood with a cloth.

He then fixed two tiny steel rods, with threaded ends, through the wounds. To each end of each of the rods he threaded a tiny steel disk, that the tiny rods might be held in the wounds. The disks and rods would be removed in four days.

"Next," he said.

None of the girls moved.

I left the platform.

Ute, biting her lip, tears in her eyes, said, "I will go next."

The other girls gasped, and shuddered.

Ute knelt on the platform.

I stood to one side. My hand went to my right ear. "Do not touch your ear, Slave," snapped the leather worker.

"No, Master," I said.

"Stand against the wall, El-in-or," said Targo.

"Yes, Master," I said, and went to one side of the large slave room in the public pens of Ko-ro-ba.

"I, too, am of the leather workers," Ute told the leather worker, with the needle.

"No," he said, "you are only a slave."

"Yes, Master," she said.

I saw her kneel, very straight, on the wood, and watched the needle pass through her right ear lobe. She did not cry out. Perhaps she wished to show courage before one who was of the leather workers.

The lady Rena of Lydius flung herself naked, on her knees, before Targo. She lifted her hands to him.

"You took me on contract," she said. "You captured me for another! Surely you will not do this to me! My master would surely object! Do not do this cruel thing to me! My master would not wish it!"

"Your master," said Targo, "he who arranged for your capture and delivery, instructed that you be delivered to him with the pierced ears of a slave girl."

"No," she wept. "No!"

A guard dragged the distraught Lady Rena of Lydius, a slave girl, back to her place in the line.

Inge then knelt before Targo. "I am of the scribes," she said, "of high caste. Do not permit this to be done to me!"

"Your ears will be pierced," said Targo.

She wept, and was dragged back to her place in line.

Lana then approached Targo.

I hated her.

She knelt before him, ingratiatingly, and put her head down. "Please, Master," she wheedled. "Let it be done to the other girls, if you wish, but not to Lana. Lana would not like it. It would make Lana sad. Lana would be happy if master would not have it done to her."

I stood against the wall, in fury.

"Your ears will be pierced," said Targo.

I smiled.

"It will lower my price!" cried Lana.

"I do not think so," smiled Targo.

Ute had now had her left, as well as her right, ear lobe pierced, and had had the tiny steel rods and disks fixed in her ears. She was trying not to cry. She came and stood next to me.

She looked at me. "You are so brave, El-in-or," she said.

I did not answer her.

I was watching Lana and Targo.

"Please!" wept Lana, now genuinely frightened, and distressed, fearing that Targo would not yield to her entreaties. "Please!"

"Your ears will be pierced," said Targo.

"No," cried Lana, terrified, weeping. "Please!"

"Take this slave away," said Targo.

I smiled as Lana was dragged, weeping, by a guard to her place in line.

The lady Rena of Lydius now left the platform, the rods fixed in her ear wounds. She could scarcely walk. A guard, holding her by the arm, half carried her to the wall, where he left her. She fell to her knees and covered her face with her hands, weeping.

"I am a slave girl," she wept. "I am a slave girl."

Inge, terrified, was now thrust onto the wooden platform.

I had no impulse to comfort the Lady Rena of Lydius. She was a fool. So, too, were Ute, and Inge, and the others.

It was interesting to me that the girls so objected to the piercing of their ears. What fools they were. I had never had my ears pierced on Earth, of course, but I had contemplated having it done. I might have had it done, if I had remained on Earth. Surely a great many of the girls and women I knew on Earth had had their ears pierced. How else could one wear the finest earrings? What fools these girls were.

Inge shrieked, more with humiliation than pain, as the needle thrust through her right ear lobe.

"Be quiet, Slave," said the leather worker.

Inge stifled her sobs.

"Do not move," he cautioned her.

"Yes, Master," she whimpered.

The piercing of the ears of women, only of slave girls, of course, was a custom of distant Turia, famed for its wealth and its nine great gates. It lay on the southern plains of Gor, far below the equator, the hub of an intricate pattern of trade routes. Some two or three years ago it had fallen to barbarians, nomadic warriors, and many of its citizens, in flight from the city, had escaped north. With them had come certain articles, techniques and customs. One could tell a Turian because he insisted on celebrating the New Year at the summer solstice, for instance. They also used very sweet, syrupy wines, which were now, in many cities, available. The Turian collar, too, a looser ring of steel, large enough for a man's fist to grasp on the girl's throat, was occasionally seen now in the northern cities. The piercing of the ears of slave girls, that they might have earrings fastened in them, was another Turian custom. It had been known on Gor before, but it was only with the flight of the escaping Turians that it had become more widespread recently.

The Turian camisk was also now occasionally seen. It is rather like an inverted "T," the bar of the "T" having beveled edges. It passes from the girl's throat, in front of her body, between her legs, and is then lifted, pulled tight, and wrapped about the thighs. Its single cord fastens the garment behind the girls's neck, behind her back and then, after passing about her body once or twice, ties in front. It conceals her brand but exposes her back. The cord makes it possible to adjust the garment to a given girl. Tightening the cord accentuates her figure. The Turian camisk is worn tightly. Turians are barbarians. In private pens in Ko-ro-ba, where we were taken daily for training, we were taught to wear the garment. A master might require it of us. It is said that only a man knows how to tie a Turian camisk on a girl properly. There are many such sayings on Gor.

Inge was thrown, forcibly, against the wall, weeping. In her ears were the tiny metal rods. She tried to pull them from her ears and the guard, angrily, cuffed her, and, with a foot of binding fiber, lashed her wrists behind her body.

Inge was such a fool.

She knelt against the wall, the side of her face thrust against the boards, staining them with tears, her entire body shaking.

Ute was kneeling beside the Lady Rena of Lydius, who seemed uncontrollable. She had her arms about her shoulders, trying to soothe her.

Ute looked up at me. "You are so brave, El-in-or," she whispered.

"You are a fool," I told her.

Lana crept to the wall and knelt there, her face in her hands.

"I hate Turians," screamed the Lady Rena of Lydius.

Ute held her more closely. She kissed her. The Lady Rena put down her head, weeping.

Turia, I had heard, had not been destroyed. Indeed, I had heard that it now stood once again, much as before, the sovereign city of the southern plains, and that much of its wealth, by exchanges and trading, had been regained. It was fortunate, I gathered, for the economy of Gor, particularly the south, that the city had not been destroyed. Much of the hides, the horn and leather which found its way northward came from Turia, obtained from the Wagon Peoples of the treeless, southern plains, and many of the manufactured goods, and goods of price, which found their way to the far south, and even to the Wagon Peoples, were produced in, or passed through, Turia. Perhaps the Tuchuks, one of the fierce Wagon Peoples, traditional enemies of Turia, her conquerors, had spared her for such reasons, that they might have outlet for their goods and a source for goods they could not well manufacture, or acquire, for themselves. It was still dangerous, however, to take caravans to Turia. For whatever reasons, Turia, though once conquered, had been spared. It was the best known of the Gorean cities below the equator, sometimes called the Ar of the south.

"I hate Turians!" screamed the Lady Rena of Lydius. "I hate them!"

"Be silent, Slave," said I to her.

"Do not scold her, El-in-or," chided Ute. "She is sad." "Do not cry so, Lady Rena," said Ute to the girl. She again held her and kissed her.

I looked away. I was hungry. The last of the girls, her ears pierced, fled from the low, wooden platform, running to crouch among us, weeping, at the wall.

I hoped that we would have a good lunch. The food was better in the private pens, where we were trained, than in the public pens of Ko-ro-ba, areas of which were available for rent to passing slavers, where we were housed at night. In the public pens, state slaves are kept as well as the merchandise of slave caravans passing through the city. A master of the city, of course, who might be leaving the city temporarily, could also rent space in the public pens, to board his slaves there. Most masters, however, if inclined to board their slaves, would do so at the private pens, where the food and facilities were better. Another reason for a master to board a slave at the private pens, of course, is that she might, while there, be given training, or further training, that she might be a more delicious slave to him upon his return. Indeed, even if a master does not leave the city, it is not unknown for him to send a girl to the private pens, that her value to him, and to others, if she be sold, might be improved. Girls, incidentally, do not care to be boarded. Life in the pens, intentionally, is made hard. When released from the pens a girl is almost always desperately eager to please her master, that she not be returned to them, for further training.

We trained, during the day, commonly in private facilities, under the tutelage of pleasure slaves, but in the evening we would be returned to the long tiers of cages in the public pens. These cages are heavily barred, and the bars are rather, irritatingly, widely set, but we cannot squeeze between them. The cages are strong enough to hold men, which, doubtless, sometimes they do. Straw is spread on the metal plating which is the floor. There are four girls to a cage. I shared mine with Ute, Inge and Lana. We are supposed to keep our own cage clean, but Lana and I let Inge and Ute do this work. We are too valuable to do such work.

I did not care particularly for the wooden bowls of stew and bread we commonly had at the public pens, but I was hungry and ready to eat even such, and with enthusiasm. In the private pens we were given better food, lean meats and vegetables and fruits, and, if our group had trained acceptably, after the evening meal, before being returned, hooded, to the public pens, we would be given candies or pastries, or, sometimes, a swallow of Ka-la-na wine. Once Inge had broken down in training, and wept, and we had been denied our little delicacies. When we reached the cage at the public pens Lana and I had beaten her, preventing Ute from interfering.

"El-in-or," snapped Targo.

I gathered he must have called once before, and I had not heard.

I ran to him and knelt before him.

"To the platform," he said.

I looked up at him. "Why?" I asked.

He looked at me.

Quickly I leaped up and ran to the low wooden platform, and knelt again upon it.

I did not understand.

The leather worker had not left the room. He was reaching into his leather bag.

I was puzzled. Then it occurred to me that he must want to check the rods in my ears, to see that they were fixed properly.

I knelt quite straight, but impatiently. I wanted my lunch. I wished that he would hurry.

"Put your head back," he said.

I looked at him with sudden apprehension. In his hand he held something which looked like a pair of pliers, except that the claws were extremely slender, and bent in such a way as to touch one another, at the tips scarcely more than a needle's width.

"What is that?" I asked.

"A punch," said Targo.

"Put your head back," said the leather worker.

"No," I whispered. "What are you going to do?"

"Do not be afraid, El-in-or," called Ute. "It is nothing."

I wished she would be quiet.

"What are you going to do?" I asked, frightened.

"Someday a master may wish to put a nose ring on you," expained Targo. "This way you will be ready."

"No!" I screamed. "No! No!"

The other girls looked up, from their own misery, puzzled, watching me.

"No!" I wept. "Please! Please!"

"Put your head back," repeated the leather worker, irritated.

Targo looked at me, puzzled. He seemed genuinely disappointed. "But you are brave," he said. "You are the brave one."

Suddenly I went to pieces, horrified, hysterical. "No!" I screamed. I tried to scramble from the platform. The leather worker seized me. "Hold her!" he said.

"Bind her," said Targo.

I, held by the leather worker, cast wild eyes on Targo. "No, Master!" I implored. "Please!" But already my ankles were being tied together. Another guard pulled my hands behind my back and my wrists were lashed together.

"No!" I screamed. "No!"

Two guards held me by the arms on the platform. Another guard put his left arm about my throat, from behind, and with his right hand in my hair, pulled my head back, holding it still.

I could not scream. The guard's arm on my throat was tight.

"Do not move," commanded the leather worker.

I felt the back of the claws of the punch enter my nostrils, distending them. There was a tiny, sharp click. Tears burst into my eyes. I felt acute pain for an instant, and then a prolonged, burning, stinging sensation.

Everything went black, but I did not faint, held in position by the guards.

When I opened my eyes, blinded with tears, I saw the leather worker approaching my face with a tiny, steel ring, partly opened, and a pair of pliers.

As I was held he inserted the ring in my nose. It was painful. Then, with the pliers, he closed the ring, and turned it, so that its opening, where the closed edges met, was concealed within, at the side of the septum.

I began sobbing with pain, with misery and degradation. The guards released me. One untied my ankles.

"Gag her," said Targo.

I was gagged. My wrists were not unbound, they fearing perhaps I would have torn at the ring. Perhaps I might have.

A guard, not much pleased with me, dragged me stumbling, eyes filled with tears, moaning with misery, from the platform. He threw me, half stumbling, into the wall, among the other girls. I struck the wall, and slid down it, to my knees. I could not believe what had been done to me. Everything almost went black again. I shuddered and shook, tears running from my eyes, leaning against the wall.

"Next!" had called the leather worker.

Ute, who was looking at me with puzzlement, as were the other girls, rose to her feet and went obediently to the block.

When she returned, she, too, wore a tiny, steel ring in her nose. There were tears in her eyes. "It smarts," she said to Inge.

I looked at Ute, piteously. Could she not see what had been done to me, to me!

Ute came to me and took me by the shoulders, and I sobbed against her, uncontrollably.

"Do not cry, El-in-or," she said.

I pressed my head against her shoulder.

She held my head to her shoulder.

"I do not understand, El-in-or," she said. "The most terrible thing you do not mind. You are then very brave. And then you cry about a little nose ring. It is not like having your ears pierced."

"El-in-or is a coward," said Rena of Lydius.

"Next," called the leather worker.

Rena rose to her feet and went to the platform.

"The piercing of the ears is far more terrible," said Ute. "Nose rings are nothing. They are even pretty. In the south even the free women of the Wagon Peoples wear nose rings." She held me more closely. "Even free women in the south," she insisted, "the free women of the Wagon Peoples, wear nose rings." She kissed me. "Besides," she said, "it may be removed, and no one will ever know that you wore it. It will not show." Then Ute's eyes clouded with tears. I looked at the tiny steel rods holding open the wounds in her ears. "But only slave girls," she wept, "have their ears pierced." She wept. "How can I ever hope to become a Free Companion," she wept. "What man would want a woman with the pierced ears of a slave girl? And if I were not veiled, anyone might look upon me, and laugh, and scorn me, seeing that my ears had been pierced, as those of a slave girl!"

I shook my head, and again pressed my head into her shoulder. I understood nothing. I knew only I, Elinor Brinton, once of Park Avenue, once of the restaurants and boulevards of New York and the continent, now wore in my nose a tiny ring of steel.

Inge went next to the platform, her hands still bound behind her back, that she not disturb the tiny rods in her ears. She submitted to the fixing of the ring gracefully.

She did say to Targo, "But I am of the scribes."

He said to the leather worker, "Put the ring in her nose."

She did not protest.

Lana went next to the platform. When she returned, she threw back her head, and placed her hands behind her head. "Is it not pretty?" she asked.

"It would be more beautiful if it were of gold," said Rena of Lydius.

"Of course," said Lana.

"But it is pretty," said Inge to Lana. "You are so beautiful, Lana," she said.

Lana smiled.

Inge looked at her timidly. "Am I pretty?" she asked.

"Yes," granted Lana, "the ring is pretty—and you are pretty."

Inge looked at her gratefully.

"What of me?" asked the Lady Rena of Lydius.

"You are beautiful," said Inge.

I did not lift my head from Ute's shoulder. I did not want anyone to see.

One after the other of the girls went to the platform.

Afterwards we were fed. Inge and I were unbound, and I was ungagged.

We knelt in a circle, eating from the wooden bowls of bread and stew. We were given no utensils. Our fingers served to pick out meat and bread, and the gravy we drank. The girls chatted, and most seemed to have forgotten the ordeal of the morning. If they had not forgotten it, there was very little they could do about it. Further, they knew that with their ears pierced, they might bring a somewhat higher price, and thus, perhaps, obtain a somewhat better-fixed master. Some prudish slavers, scandalized by ear piercing, refused to have it done to their girls, but Targo, doubtless because of the gold involved, had insisted upon it. Many Gorean men apparently find pierced ears in a girl extremely provocative. Craftsmen of the metal workers, men specializing in the working of gold and silver, were concerned to work out new forms of jewelry for slave females. It was said that a year ago in Ar, Marlenus, Ubar of that city, had created a sensation at a banquet given for his high officers, by presenting a slave-girl dancer before them who, though she was not in his private pleasure gardens or compartments, he had had put in earrings. Today, however, better than a year later, it was not uncommon to see a slave girl wearing, and insolently, such jewelry, even in public.

I had no objection to earrings. Indeed, if I could find an attractive pair, or pairs, I was confident I could wear them to my advantage, to please a master, to perhaps obtain my way, to perhaps help me dominate him. If I could engage his affections, I would have him then, would I not, at my mercy? I would bend my efforts to do so, and when

I had done so then. I might, by granting, or refusing to grant, my favors, or the fervor of my favors, control him and, though I wore the collar, own him! How else could a woman fight on Gor? She is not as strong as a man! She is at their mercy. The entire culture puts her at his feet. Well I was beautiful enough, and intelligent enough, to fight, and surely to win! I was truly a slave girl, and that I knew, but my master would learn that a slave girl could be a dangerous foe. I would conquer him. So I mused. The only thing that I did not take into my considerations was the Gorean male. He is unlike the men of Earth, on the whole so weak and pliable, so reasonable, so compromising, so much in need of recognition and affection, or its pretense. The only thing I failed to take into my calculations was that the Gorean male, whether by culture or genetic endowment, is unlike the typical man of Earth. He, unlike the typical man of Earth, though not unlike all, is a natural master of women. There was a time in my life when I would not have understood this, or how it could be. There was surely a time in my life when I could not have believed this, when I would have found it preposterous, absurd, incomprensible, false. But at that time I had not been brought to this world. At that time I had not been in the arms of a Gorean male.

"Eat," urged Ute.

I had scarcely touched the stew in the wooden bowl.

"We will wear the nose rings," said Ute, "until our training is finished. Then, when we leave Ko-ro-ba, they will be removed."

"Where did you hear this?" I asked. There are often rumors carried about the pens and cages.

"I heard Targo telling one of the guards," she whispered, looking about.

"Good," I said. I reached into the bowl. No one ever need know that Elinor Brinton, of Park Avenue, had once had a steel ring fixed in her nose.

Pleased, I joined Ute in eating.

Afterwards, after we had been hooded and taken to our private training pens in Ko-ro-ba, I trained well.

It was well that I had eaten, for the work was difficult.

Perhaps Targo wished to take our minds from the events of the morning. In the evening, at the private pens, we were fed well and our group, myself, Ute, Inge and Lana, were among those groups given pastries following their meal.

I was pleased with my performance. It was right that we should be rewarded.

I was, indeed, rather pleased with my performance in general.

Sometimes I was irritated by the instructor, herself a slave, when she would commend me. "See," she would say to the other girls. "That is how it is done! That is how the body of a slave girl moves!" But I wanted to learn, that I might use my skills to enhance my fortunes on Gor. As a warrior applies himself to the arts of his weapons, so I applied myself to the arts of the female slave, which I was. I became sleek and more beautiful from the diet and the exercises. I learned things of which I had not dreamed. Our training, because it was limited to a few short weeks, did not include many of the elements that are normally included in a full training. I remained ignorant of Gorean cooking and the cleaning of Gorean garments. I learned nothing of musical instruments. I remained ignorant even of the arrangements of small rugs, decorations and flowers, things that any Gorean girl, slave or free, is likely to know. But I was taught to dance, and to give pleasure, and to stand, and move, and sit and turn, and lift my head and lower it, and kneel, and rise. Interestingly, and sometimes not altogether to my pleasure, I found the training becoming effective. In the early evening of the day on which our nose rings had been affixed I was returning to my cage, after having run an errand for Targo in the pens. I was one of his favorites, and he often used me for his errands.

As I passed by a guard, as a slave girl passes a man, he seized me by the arm and held me, almost jerking me off my feet, pulling me to him. "You are learning to move, Slave," he said. I was frightened. Then I was not frightened. I pulled slightly against his arm as though I might be frightened, but could not hope to elude him. And indeed, of course, I could not have, in fact, eluded him, even had I cared to do so. He, being a man, was quite strong enough, as I knew, to do with me what he might please. How I resented the strength of men! I looked up at him, timidly. "Perhaps, Master," I whispered, lips timidly parted, slightly smiling, keeping my ankles together, and moving my body slightly away from him, but my shoulders pointing towards him.

"She-sleen," he said.

He grinned.

He took the nose ring between his thumb and first finger and lifted it. I stood painfully on my toes.

"You are a pretty slave," he said.

"I am white silk," I whispered, now frightened, truly frightened.

He released the ring and reached for me. "What does it matter?" he asked.

I backed away from him, and turned and, stumbling, striking into the wall of cages, fled down the hall. I am afraid I did not flee as a lovely slave girl. I fled clumsily, terrified, as an Earth girl fleeing from a Gorean male.

I heard him laugh behind me, and stopped. He had been having sport with me.

I turned and looked at him in irritation.

He clapped his hands and took a step toward me, and I turned and fled stumbling away again, hearing his laughter in the hallway behind me.

But in a moment or two I had regained my composure.

When I reached the cage I was well pleased with myself. I had attracted the guard. He had wanted me. He, of course, would not have taken me, for fear of the wrath of Targo, but I had no doubt of his desire. I shuddered. If it had not been for Targo he doubtless would have taken me, on the cement flooring, before the bars. But still, on the whole, I was quite pleased. I knew that I was desirable. I knew that I was very desirable. I was an exciting slave. I was proud. I was much pleased.

Ute and Inge asked Lana and I to help clean the cage that night but we, as usual, refused. That was the work of lesser girls. Lana and I were more valuable than Ute and

Inge, or so we thought. The three of us might have forced
Lana to help, but then I would have had to work, too. I
realized that if I joined with Lana, though I did not care for
her, they could not force either of us to work. Since Ute
and Inge were insistent that the cage be cleaned, this unpleasant task thus fell regularly on them. I liked a clean
cage. I just did not wish to clean it. Lana and I, that night,
thought them fools, and, satisfied with ourselves, went to sleep
on the straw.

I was pleased that I was exciting. I touched the nose
ring. I resented it. In the morning I would have even more
reason to resent it. I became drowsy. I was pleased that I
was exciting, and was pleased, too, that the hated nose ring
would be removed before we left Ko-ro-ba. I rolled over,
closing my eyes. Ko-ro-ba, I thought, Ko-ro-ba. I was drowsy.
We had approached the city in the early morning and Targo
had permitted us to leave the wagons to look upon it, in
the morning sun. The city, the sun reflecting on its walls
and towers, was very beautiful. It is sometimes called The
Towers of the Morning, and perhaps justifiably so. I rolled
again to my other side, shutting my eyes. But there was
little beauty in the pens, with their heavy blocks of stone
and stout bars, and straw, and the smells. I then fell asleep,
pleased that I was exciting, forgetting even the nose ring.
As I fell asleep I thought that Ute and Inge were busying
themselves in the cage, cleaning it.

Ute was such a sweet, stupid little thing. And Inge, too.

But, as it turned out, they did not clean the cage that
night.

"Awaken, Slaves!"

I felt a sharp pain in my nose, excruciating.

I was instantly awake. I heard Lana cry out with pain.
I jerked my head and felt another sharp pain.

"Keep your hands at your sides," commanded Ute.

Lana and I had been thonged together by the nose rings.
In our sleep it had been done. A thong had been passed
through the two rings and then knotted. The knotted, double
thong that fastened us together was only about a foot long.

Lana and I faced one another. Ute's small fist was securely fastened on the thong.

Lana tried to reach the thong. Ute twisted it. Lana squeaked with pain. I, too, cried out, for the same thong bound me. Then Lana, tears in her eyes, had her hands down at her sides, obediently. I did, too. We dared not move.

"Ute!" I protested.

She twisted the thong, and I cried out in misery.

"Be silent, Slave," said Ute, pleasantly enough.

I was silent, and so, too, was Lana.

Ute jerked us to our feet and we wept with pain. Our hands, our clenched fists, reamained at our sides.

"Place your hands behind your backs," recommended Ute. Lana and I looked at one another.

Ute gave the thong a twist.

We cried out and did as we were told.

Inge then came forward with two small thongs, probably wheedled from a guard.

I felt my wrists tied behind my back. Then Lana's wrists were similarly secured.

"Kneel, Slaves," said Ute.

Lana and I looked at one another in fury. There was a sharp tug on the nose thong and the two of us, crying out, knelt before Ute and Inge.

"The cage," said Ute, "needs cleaning." Her fist never left the thong. "You may call the guard," she said, "for brushes and water, and fresh straw."

"Never!" said Lana.

There was a sharp twist on the thong.

"I'll call him," I cried. "Please! Please!"

"Which of you chooses to work first?" asked Ute.

Lana looked at me. "Let El-in-or," she said.

"Let Lana," I said.

"El-in-or will work first," said Ute.

The guard brought fresh straw, and water in a leather bucket, and a heavily bristled brush.

My hands were unbound and, on my hands and knees, I began to gather the soiled, stinking straw.

"Be careful!" cried Lana. It had hurt me, too.

Lana was left bound, and we were left thonged by the nose rings. It was clumsy work.

I cleaned one half of the cage, taking out the used straw and scrubbing the plating. Ute would not let me shirk. I had to scrub my section of the plating twice. My knees hurt. At last my half of the cage was clean and I spread fresh straw there. Then I was rebound and Lana was unbound, and set to her work, cleaning the other half of the cage. On my hands and knees, wrists tied behind my back, my nose ring linked to Lana's by the thong, I followed her about, as she had me. At last her work was done. She, too, was forced to scrub her portion of the cage twice. Her wrists were then re-bound. Ute then took us to the bars at the front of the cage and, unknotting the thong, passed it around two of the bars and reknotted it, over one of the crossbars, about two and a half feet above the floor plating. She then left us there.

"Ute," I begged, "please let us go."

"Please," wheedled Lana.

We squirmed, but were secured.

On the outside of the bars, slave girls, and guards, passed by, on their way to the morning feeding. They laughed at us. It was well known in the pens that we had shirked the cleaning of our cage. I was humiliated. Even Lana, then, did not seem so lofty and clever, kneeling bound by the bars, for the inspection of all, thonged to them by a nose ring.

When the cage was unlocked, Ute and Inge went to break-fast. Lana and I remained behind.

When Ute and Inge returned Lana and I had had enough of this misery.

"Lana will work," promised Lana.

"If you do not," warned Ute, "next time it will not go so easily with you."

Lana nodded. She was strong, but she knew that in a slave cage, one is at the mercy of one's cage mates. Ute and Inge had demonstrated their power.

"And you, El-in-or?" inquired Ute, pleasantly.

I hated Ute!

"El-in-or, too, will work," I said.

"Good," said Ute. Then she kissed Lana and myself. "Let us now release these slaves," she said to Inge. Ute and Inge freed us.

"It is time to leave for the private pens, for morning training," said a guard, passing by.

Lana and I got to our feet and looked at Ute and Inge. We would not again shirk our work.

One day slipped into another in the pens of Ko-ro-ba. Four days after we had had our ears pierced the leather worker returned to the pens and removed the tiny threaded rods with the disks from our ears. Behind remained the tiny, almost invisible punctures in our ear lobes, ready for whatever jewelry a master might decide to fix in them. The nose rings would not be removed until the day before our departure from the pens. We were pierced-ear girls, among the most exciting of slaves.

Day followed day, and round followed round of feedings, exercisings and training periods. One day seemed much like another, save that our lessons increased in length and complexity. I found it necessary now to apply my full attention and intelligence to master the increasingly subtle and intricate skills of the female slave. The slave mistress would switch me, and the others, when we failed. I noted the change and the improvement in the other girls. We were learning, we were increasing our skills. Even Inge! I watched her, in the training sand, dancing to hide drums, naked, in slave bracelets and jeweled dancing collar. She did not then appear to be of the blue-robed, studious scribes. She was only a naked, dancing slave girl, exciting, writhing in the sand, her body throbbing to the beat of a man's pleasure drums. I wondered if a scribe would buy her. I supposed if one did, she would pretend to be a shy girl, once of the scribes herself. But what if he should command her to perform? Would he not then be astonished to find what he had purchased, a girl suddenly forced to reveal herself as a wild slave, exquisitely trained to please the senses of a master? I now saw Inge as a rival. But I resolved to best her. I could be even a more superb slave than she! Ute, of course, was incredible, superb. She would doubtless bring a high price. But I thought that I would bring a higher. It also interested me, even astonished me, to see the fervor and skill brought to her training by the refined Lady Rena of Lydius. She knew that she had already, in effect, been purchased, but she did not know who her master might be. Since her ears had been pierced she was terrified that she might not please him. She trained with almost piteous ardor. She had been a free woman; she was now a female slave, the ease of whose life and whose fortunes would now depend entirely on her capacity to be pleasing to those who might capture or purchase her, those who would own her. Lana and I, incidentally, were, by general admission, and the indications of our instructor, the finest of the slaves in our lot. Try as I would I could never best her. I hated her. But though I was not as good as Lana, I had little reason to be ashamed of my advances in the arts of the female slave. I was almost flawlessly superb. I would bring a high price. I was proud. In acknowledgement of my skills, perhaps, Lana began to take me into her confidence, and though I hated her, I became her friend. We spent more time together, and I talked less with stupid Ute and skinny Inge. Lana and I were the best, the very best!

I was much pleased.

Subconsciously now, from day to day, my body began to reveal me truly as a slave girl. I was no longer even aware of it. There are dozens of subtle movements, tiny things, almost indiscernible, but which one notices, almost without noticing, about the movements of a slave girl, things which, cumulatively, distinguish, and very obviously, her movements from those of a free woman.

I now no longer moved as a free woman, even a beautiful one, of Earth. I now moved, and naturally, as what I was, uninhibited and shameless, taunting, catlike, insolent, a Gorean slave girl.

Once, when I got to my feet in the cage and walked across the straw, Inge, who was kneeling nearby, said, unexpectedly, suddenly, "You *are* a slave, El-in-or!" I leaped at her and slapped her. Tears sprang to her eyes. "Slave!" she screamed.

I seized her by the hair and kicked her. Then, scratching
and cursing, we began to roll and fight in the straw. Lana
laughed. Ute tried to separate us. "We are all slaves," she
said. "Do not quarrel!" Suddenly it felt like the top of my
head was being yanked off and I heard Inge scream with
pain.

A guard was now in the cage and had each of us, separated, bent over, held by the hair.

Inge and I then did not move so much as a muscle.

I was suddenly afraid that I would be beaten. I had been
beaten only once, when first enslaved, by Lana, with straps,
at the side of the slave wagon. Never had a man beaten me.
I was terrified of having the full five-strap Gorean slave
lash, wielded with the full strength of a man, used on me. I
was too sensitive to pain. The other girls, common girls,
might be beaten, but not I. It would hurt me too much.
They could not understand how it would feel to me, how
much it would hurt!

"She started it!" I cried out.

"She slapped me!" cried Inge. Inge was frightened, too.
She was only of the scribes, and, too, feared the lash. But
she would not have felt it as cruelly as I would have, for
she was more common than I, less sensitive, less delicate.

"She started it!" I cried. "She slapped me first!"

Ute gasped.

"Don't beat me," I wept. "She started it! She slapped
me first!"

"Liar!" screamed Inge.

"Liar!" I screamed at her.

Ute was looking at me with disappointment. Lana was
laughing.

"The guard was outside," said Lana. "He saw!"

Held by the hair, bent over, my heart sank. I was a slave
girl who had been caught in a lie. I trembled.

But neither I, nor Inge, was beaten.

The guard grinned.

It had not surprised him, as it apparently had Ute, that
I was a lying slave girl. He had, apparently, to my irritation,

not expected anything else of me. I realized then how I was regarded in the pens.

I was angry.

Our hands were tied behind our backs. The guard, then, pulling me by the hair, dragged me to one side of the cage. He stood me there, facing the interior of the cage, and took my hair and knotted it about one of the crossbars of the cage, about a foot above my head. He then took Inge to the opposite side of the cage, put her standing against the wall of bars there, facing me, and similarly fastened her in place. She winced.

The guard then left the cage, locking the gate behind him. "Sleep well, Slaves," he said.

Lana rolled luxuriously on the straw. "Good-night, Master," she called.

"Good-night, Wench," said he.

He looked at Ute. Ute lay down on the straw. "Good-night, Master," she whispered.

He nodded. Then he looked at me. "Good-night, Master," I said.

When he looked at Inge, she, too, responded so.

Then he left.

Some hours later, some hours before dawn, Inge looked at me, hatred in her eyes. "You are a liar, El-in-or," she said.

"You are a fool," I said.

The next morning, when the guard unbound our hair from the crossbars, Inge and I collapsed to the steel plating that floored our cage. In our misery we scarcely noticed that he had unbound our wrists. I lay in the straw, my face pressed into it, feeling the obdurate steel beneath it.

Then, after some time, I crawled to Inge. "I am sorry," I said, "Inge."

Inge looked at me, her eyes hard. Her body, too, was in pain, from the miseries of the night.

"Forgive me, Inge," I asked.

Inge looked away.

"El-in-or is sorry, Inge," said Ute.

I was grateful to Ute.

Inge did not look upon me.

"El-in-or was weak," said Ute. "She was afraid."

"El-in-or is a liar," said Inge. Then she looked at me, directly, with hatred. "El-in-or is a slave," said Inge.

"We are all slaves," said Ute.

Inge put her head down on her knees.

Tears came to my eyes. Ute put her arms about me. "Do not weep, El-in-or," she said.

I pulled away from Ute, suddenly angry. Ute went to her own portion of the cage.

What Inge had said was true. I was a slave.

I rolled over on my back in the straw and stared at the ceiling, more steel plating, the flooring of the cage in the tier above us.

But, unlike Inge, I was a superb, and exciting, slave!

I heard the sandals of the guard approaching, outside, on the grating before the tier of cages. I leapt to my feet and pressed against the bars.

"Master!" I called.

He stopped.

I thrust my hand through the bars, toward him.

He took a hard candy from his pouch, and held it, outside of my reach.

I struggled to reach the candy. I could not. Then he handed it to me.

"Thank you, Master," I said. I put the candy in my mouth. I had known his step. Few of the guards carried candies. I was pleased with myself. I did not think Inge would have succeeded in winning a candy from him.

I sat in the straw and sucked the candy.

"I forgive you, El-in-or," said Inge. Her voice sounded weary.

I did not answer her, for I feared she might want to taste the candy, that it would be a trick on her part.

I heard Lana approach. She thrust out her hand. "Give it to me," she said.

"It's mine," I said.

"Give it to Lana," said Lana. "I am first in the cage."

She was stronger than I.

I gave her the candy and she put it in her mouth.

I crawled to Inge. "Do you really forgive me, Inge?" I asked.

"Yes," said Inge.

I crawled away from Inge, and lay down on my belly in the straw.

What Inge had said was true. I was a slave.

I rolled over on my back in the straw and again stared at the ceiling, that obdurate steel plating, the flooring of the cage in the tier above us. I lay there naked in the straw, feeling the steel plating beneath my back. Yes, I was a slave. "Yes," I said to myself, "you are a slave, Elinor." The panther girls taught you that, and the man in the hut. You are a natural slave. I lifted one knee. But you are a beautiful slave, and a clever slave, I told myself.

I rolled onto my belly in the straw and picked up a bit of straw and poked at the floor with it.

Odd, I thought, how Elinor Brinton, she who had been so rich, so elegant, so arrogant, she who had been of Park Avenue, she who had owned the Maserati, was now, on a distant world, only this, a common slave, naked, on her belly in straw, steel plating beneath it, behind heavy bars, caged, merchandise.

I had no hope of returning to Earth. The men in the silver ship had doubtless been of another world, not this one. I had seen no ships, nor men, such as they, on this world. Besides, for all I knew, they might be even more terrible, and fierce, than those of the black ship. I had no desire to meet them. I was also frightened by the memory of the huge golden creature who had accompanied them. Such men, and such a creature, I was sure, would not be likely to return me to Earth. I had seen their power, when they had destroyed the black ship. I was frightened. And, I mused, the men of the black, disklike ship, who had brought me here, were not such that I would expect them, even if they should find me, which I regarded as unlikely, to return me to Earth. I had learned I could not bargain with them. In the hut I had learned what I was to them, only the most

abject of female slaves, a girl fit only to kneel at their feet
and beg to be commanded. And even if I should serve
them, might I not then, that I might not fall into the hands
of their enemies, or reveal their plans and plotting, be slain?
And even if I did serve them, and they, in their lenience,
spared me, I knew that I would be kept by them only as a
girl, another slave, to be sold or disposed of as they saw fit.
I was pleased that I had escaped in the forest. They would
have little hope of finding me again. The chances that I
might have found my way back to Targo's chain, or be returned to him, were not high. Indeed, it would have been
probable that I, naked and bound, alone, defenseless in the
forest, would have died of exposure or fallen prey to panthers or sleen.

My thoughts strayed back to that terrible night, when
I fled from the hut, into the darkness, leaving the beast
feeding on the carcass of the destroyed, bloodied sleen.

I shuddered.

I had run madly away, through the dark trees, stumbling,
falling, rolling, getting up and running again. Sometimes I
ran between the great Tur trees, on the carpeting of leaves
between them, sometimes I made my way through more
thickset trees, sometimes through wild, moonlit tangles of
brush and vines. I even found myself, once, when passing
through the high Tur trees, at the circle, where the panther
girls had danced. I saw the slave post to one side, where I
had been tied. The circle was deserted. I fled again. At times
I would stop and listen for pursuit, but there was none. The
man, too, fearing the beast in its feeding frenzy, had fled.
I most was afraid that the beast itself might follow me.
But I was sure that it would not soon do so. I do not think
it was even aware I had fled the hut. I expected it to feed
until it was gorged, and then perhaps it would sleep. Once
I nearly stumbled on a sleen, bending over a slain Tabuk, a
slender, graceful, single-horned antelopelike creature of the
thickets and forests. The sleen lifted its long, triangular jaws
and hissed. I saw the moonlight on the three rows of white,
needlelike teeth. I screamed and turned and fled away. The
sleen returned to its kill. As I fled I sometimes startled small

animals, and once a herd of Tabuk. I tried, in the moonlight, to run in the same direction, to find my way from the forest, somehow. I feared I would run in circles. The prevailing northern winds, carrying rain and moisture, had coated the northern sides of the high trees with vertical belts of moss, extending some twenty to thirty feet up the trunks. By means of this device I continued, generally, to run southward. I hoped I might find a stream, and follow it to the Laurius. As I ran through the darkness I suddenly saw, before me, some fifty or sixty yards away, four pairs of blazing eyes, a pride of forest panthers. I pretended not to see them and, heart pounding, turned to one side, walking through the trees. At this time, at night, I knew they would be hunting. Our eyes had not met. I had the strange feeling that they had seen me, and knew that I had seen them, as I had seen them, and sensed that they had seen me. But our eyes had not directly met. We had not, so to speak, signaled to one another that we were aware of one another. The forest panther is a proud beast, but, too, he does not care to be distracted in his hunting. We had not confronted one another. I only hoped that I might not be what they were hunting. I was not. They turned aside into the darkness, padding away. I nearly fainted. I felt so helpless. I pulled at my bound wrists, but they were uncompromisingly secured behind my back.

Then, to my joy, I felt a drop of rain on my naked body, and then another. And then, suddenly, with the abruptness of the storms of the Gorean north, the cold rains, in icy sheets, began to pelt downwards. In the forest, tied, bound, in the icy rain, I threw back my head and laughed. I was overjoyed. The rain would wipe out my trail! I might escape the beast! I doubted that even a sleen, Gor's most perfect hunter, could follow my trail after such a downpour. I laughed, and laughed, and then, crouching, hid in some brush, trying to protect myself from the rain.

After some two hours the rain stopped and I crawled out from the brush and again continued my way southward.

I no longer feared pursuit, but I was now more aware than I had been of my predicament in the forest itself.

I tried to rub through the binding fiber that held my wrists, rubbing it against the trunk of a fallen tree, but I could not loosen it, or rub through it. Gorean binding fiber is not made to be so easily removed from a girl's wrists. After an hour I was bound as securely as before.

I decided I had better keep moving.

I felt helpless, vulnerable and futile. I was like an animal without hands, a four-footed animal, save that I had no hide to protect me, but only the softness of my flesh, and I did not have the delicate senses, the smell and the hearing of such animals to protect me, and I did not have their swiftness, the fleetness of their flight. I was ripe quarry.

I pulled at my wrists, helplessly.

I fled southward.

I was hungry.

At bushes I stopped and nibbled at berries.

Then, shortly before noon, I stumbled onto a small stream, which could only be a tributary of the Laurius.

I flung myself down on the pebbles of its shore and lapped the fresh water, slaking my thirst.

Then, rising, I entered the stream, feeling its cold waters on my ankles, and waded downstream. I wished to take this further precaution against leaving a trail behind me, a stain of odor on a twig, a dampness of perspiration on a leaf.

I followed the stream for an Ahn, sometimes stopping to lift my head to overhanging branches, to nibble at hanging fruit.

Then the stream joined a larger stream, and I followed that further. I had little doubt that this larger stream would join the Laurius.

As I waded in the water, bound, I asked myself if I should try to make my way to the Laurius, and thence to Laura. There I would be fed. There, too, I would be re-enslaved. I asked myself if I should not rather try to find a hut in the forest, where there might be a slave girl, who would unbind me, and give me food. She surely would not want her master to see me, for I was beautiful. Then I was frightened, for what if the girl would slay me, or sell me herself secretly, to hunters, or give me to panther girls, who would make me their slave, or sell me. They might even return me to the man and the beast in the hut, for more arrowpoints!

I did not know what to do. I was in misery.

Also, recalling that I had been sold for only one hundred arrowpoints, for some reason, irritated me. It made me furious. Surely I was worth much more. As girls went, I was valuable. I should have brought pieces of gold! Not arrowpoints!

In my anger I did not notice the man, standing back in the brush, near the shore of the stream.

Suddenly a leather loop fell about my neck. I was startled, and turned. It drew tight. I was snared.

Bound, naked, helpless as a Tabuk, I was snared.

He drew me toward him.

I was pulled from the edge of the stream, where I had waded. I felt the pebbles of the shore under my feet, and then grass, and then, whether from hunger, or exhaustion, or fear, everything went black, and I fainted.

I awakened sometime later. I was being carried in a man's arms. I wore his shirt. It was longer than a common female slave tunic. The sleeves had been rolled back. It was warm. My hands were no longer cruelly bound behind my back. A loop of binding fiber had been tied about my belly and knotted in back. My hands were confined in front of me by slave bracelets. The binding fiber, in its center, had been knotted about the chain of the bracelets, so that my hands were held close to my belly. The loose ends of the binding fiber had then been knotted together behind my back, so that I could not reach the knot. The bracelets were not tight, but I could not slip them. I did not care.

"You are awake, El-in-or," he said.

It was one of Targo's guards, he who had guarded me at the physician's.

"Yes, Master," I said.

"We thought that we had lost you."

"I was stolen by panther girls," I said. "They sold me to a man. There was a beast. He fled. I escaped."

I was conscious of the strength of his arms. They frightened me.

"I am still white silk," I told him.

"I know," he said.

I reddened.

"Fortunately for you," he said.

I looked down.

Suddenly he dropped me.

"You are awake," he said. "You can walk."

Sitting on the grass, in pain, displeased, I looked up at
him.

"No, I cannot walk," I said. "I cannot even stand."

He tied up the shirt in the back, sticking it into the
binding fiber. He then went and cut a switch.

When he returned I was on my feet.

"Good," he said. He pulled down the shirt and threw
away the switch.

I walked before him.

"Targo has already left Laura," he said. "We will join
him across the river, at the night's camp."

We walked on.

"If you had left Laura with Targo," he said, "you might
have seen Marlenus of Ar."

I gasped. I had heard of the great Ubar.

"In Laura?" I asked.

"Sometimes he comes north, with some hundred tarnsmen, for the hunting in the forests," said the guard.

"What does he hunt?" I asked.

"Sleen, panthers, women," said the guard.

"Oh," I said.

"He hunts for a week or two," said the guard, "and then
returns to Ar." He pushed me ahead with the flat of his
foot. I had been dallying. "The duties of a Ubar," said he,
"are pressing, and Marlenus looks forward to his hunting."

"I see," I said.

"When he is finished he sends his catch back by caravan,"
he said.

"Oh," I said.

We walked on.

"Is he after anything in particular?" I asked.

"Yes," said the guard, "Verna, an outlaw girl."

I stopped.

"Do not turn around," he said.

I was irritated. I knew him, and he liked me, but he was my captor. He had not given me permission to face him. In his shirt, I pulled at the slave bracelets, tied against my belly with the binding fiber.

"It was Verna and her band who captured me," I said.

"It is said she is beautiful," said the guard. "Is it true?"

"Ask," I said, "the men at the camp, whom she captured and bound, when she stole me."

His fist was in my hair, bending my head back. "Yes," I said, "she is beautiful. She is very beautiful!"

He released me.

"Marlenus will capture her," he said, "and send her in a cage to Ar."

"Oh?" I asked, archly.

"Yes," he said, "and in his pleasure gardens, she will feed from his hand."

I put my head back. "You seem to think any woman can be tamed," I said.

"Yes," he said, from behind me. I felt his hands on my shoulders.

I was not displeased that Marlenus was hunting Verna, and her girls. I hoped that he would capture her, and them, and strip them, and put the blazing iron to their bodies, and lock them in collars, and whip them, and make them slave girls!

"Any woman," he said.

"I am white silk," I whispered. I pulled against his hands, and he released me. I hurried on.

I continued to walk ahead of him, in his shirt, my wrists confined before my body.

"Stop," he said.

I did.

He came behind me and, lifting the shirt some inches,

tucked it into the binding fiber that was knotted about my waist. He wanted to see more of my legs.

"Continue," he said. He pressed me forward again with the flat of his foot. I stumbled forward, and was now again walking before him.

"Posture," he said.

And so I walked well, as he wished, before him.

From time to time, as we walked, he gave me food from his pouch, which he shoved into my mouth.

In the late afternoon, we rested for an Ahn. Then, at his command, I rose to my feet, and we continued on our journey to Laura, I preceding him, as before.

I was acutely conscious of his watching me. I could not turn to look, of course, but I knew that every movement of my body was his to see.

"I shall be interested to see," he said, "how you train as a pleasure slave in Ko-ro-ba."

"You find me pleasing, do you not?" I asked. Then I was sorry I had asked.

"You have interesting possibilities as a female slave," he said. "I find myself curious to taste you."

I hurried on. "We must hurry," I said. "We must join the wagons!"

"White-silk, She-sleen," he said. "Wait until you are red silk!"

I hurried ahead.

Actually I was not displeased. When, that night, after taking a barge across the Laurius, loaded with lumber, we found Targo's encampment, I was happy. Ute and Inge were there and the other girls I knew. Even Lana. Targo was pleased that I had been returned to his chain. That night, stripped in the slave wagon, lying on the canvas, my ankles chained to the ankle bar, fed, I slept soundly, happily.

We were on our way to the city of Ko-ro-ba, where we would receive training, and from thence we would journey in a southeastern direction toward the great city of Ar.

"What are you thinking, El-in-or?" asked Ute.

I lay on my belly, in the straw, in the cage in Ko-ro-ba, poking with a bit of straw at the steel plating.

"Nothing," I said.

I wondered of the man in the hut and the beast. They would not have been able to follow my trail after the rain. They would probably not suppose I could have been returned to Targo. Indeed, Targo had left Laura before I could have reached the city. I supposed that the man and the beast would look for me, if at all, in the vicinity of Laura, or northward, or even in the forest. I supposed they would regard it as likely that I had never escaped the forest. They would regard it as likely that I had fallen to beasts, perhaps, or perhaps had died of exposure.

I was safe.

A slave girl in a pen in Ko-ro-ba.

I had no hope now of returning to Earth. I knew now that on this world I would wear a collar and serve a master.

Further, I had now come to see myself as a slave girl. The panther girls in the forest, and the man in the hut, had taught me that I was slave. I now knew that even on Earth, even when I had been rich, even when I had dwelled in Park Avenue, when I had owned the Maserati, my body had been that of a slave girl, the body of a wench who, from the Gorean point of view, was fit only, and rightly so, for silk, and the whip. I had been found out. The Goreans had found me out, and would treat me accordingly. They have a way with such women. I struck the steel plating in fury, with my small fist. They bring them to heel, teach them to obey, and to serve, and deliciously. I wished that I was on Earth again, where slave girls might go free, live luxuriously, pamper themselves, and even, should it please them, command the weak men of Earth. I heard the step of a guard outside. I knew several of them by their step. It was one of whom I was frightened. I pretended to be asleep in the straw. When he had passed I rolled again on my belly and put my chin on the back of my hands, their palms resting on the plating. I would be a clever slave, a beautiful slave, an exciting one. I was a slave. I would be a superb one. I would use my intelligence and my beauty to make my life on Gor an easy one. I had learned a great deal in my training. I was eager to learn more. Already my body moved as that of a slave girl, and unconsciously, naturally! I smiled. I would bring a high price on the block. I glanced over at Inge. Poor sticklike Inge! What man would want her? And Ute was so little and stupid. Even Lana seemed dull to me. But I was superb. I recalled the man in the hut had said that the indications were that I would make a fantastic pleasure slave for a master. My brow wrinkled and my lip curled. I was irritated. It was I who would conquer. I remembered the panther girls, dancing under the moons of Gor, and how they had writhed helplessly beneath those wild moons. I despised them for their weakness. I did not have such weaknesses. I was a slave, but I did not have such weaknesses. Inside I was cold and hard, and hated men. I would conquer them.

And so I mused, an illiterate barbarian slave girl in a Ko-ro-ban pen.

Some four days before we were to depart Ko-ro-ba for Ar, the news swept like tarns through the pens.

"Verna the outlaw girl!" we heard the cry. "She has been taken by Marlenus of Ar!"

"Marlenus has captured Verna, the outlaw girl!"

I rushed to the bars of the cage, thrilled. I wept with joy. How I hated that proud woman, and her band! Let them be slaves! Let them be slaves!

"Poor Verna," said Ute.

Inge was silent.

"Let her be a slave!" I cried. "Like us!" I whirled to face them on the straw, my back against the bars. "Let her be a slave like us!" I cried.

Ute and Inge watched me.

I turned about again, grasping the bars, filled with a sense of triumph, with vindictive victory. Let Verna kneel to men, and fear the whip!

"Poor Verna," said Ute.

"Marlenus will tame her," I said. "In his pleasure gardens he will have her feeding from his hand."

"I hope she will be impaled," said Lana.

I did not hope that. But I hoped she would be put in slave rouge, and silk, and bells! Let her know slavery! How I hated the proud Verna! How pleased I was that she, as I, had fallen prey to men!

I looked about the cage, flushed, furious. I shook the bars. I stamped on the plating beneath the straw with my heel. I cried out with rage, and picked up straw and flung it about the cage. I had been captured, and must be a slave girl!

"Please, El-in-or," cried Ute. "Do not behave so."

"Let Verna be a slave!" I screamed down the long hall between the cages.

I wept, holding the bars. "Let her know what it is to be a slave," I whispered.

A guard looked at me, curiously.

I shrieked with misery and ran across the cage, flinging myself into its back wall, pounding on it, and then I sunk to my knees by the wall and, in rage and frustration, weeping and screaming, pounded on the steel plating of the floor.

"Weep, El-in-or," said Ute. "Weep."

I lay on the floor, naked in the straw, a helpless slave girl, the property of men, who must do as they commanded her, and wept, and wept.

I mention two other bits of news, which, from the outside world of laughter and daylight, filtered into the straw-strewn, barred pens.

Haakon of Skjern, from whom Targo had purchased his hundred northern beauties, now concluding their training, was in Ko-ro-ba.

This news, for no reason I clearly understood, rendered Targo apprehensive.

The other news dealt with the bold raids of Rask of Treve.

All Ko-ro-ba seemed aflame with fury.

Four caravans had fallen spoils to the fierce, swiftly striking tarnsman of Treve. And his men had fired dozens of

fields, destroying Sa-Tarna grains. The smoke of two of
these fields had been visible even from the high bridges of
Ko-ro-ba herself.

Ko-ro-ban tarnsmen flew at all hours, in the high sun,
in the cold morning, at dusk, even when the beacon fires
burned upon the lofty walls, flew patterned sorties, and irregular sorties, but never did they find the elusive, maraud-
ing band of the terrible Rask of Treve.

I mused to myself.

I had some reason to know that name, Rask of Treve.
Targo, and others, had even more reason. It had been he,
Rask of Treve, who had raided Targo's slave caravan, before,
in the fields northwest of Ko-ro-ba, on the route to Laura, a
wandering, strangely clad, barbarian girl had been enslaved,
whose name was El-in-or. Indeed, it was because of Rask
of Treve that Targo, who became that El-in-or's master,
had lost most of his women and wagons, and all of his bosk.
It was because of him that El-in-or, the barbarian girl, with
the other girls, had been harnessed to his one remaining,
partially burnt wagon, and had been forced, and under the
switch, to draw it, as draft animals. Targo, as I knew, had
fled into a Ka-la-na thicket with his men, saving his gold
and nineteen of his girls, Inge, Ute and Lana among them.
Rask of Treve, as a raider true to the codes of Treve, that
hidden coign of tarnsmen, that remote, secret, mountainous
city of the vast, scarlet Voltai range, had not, in these circumstances, much pushed pursuit. In the shadows of the
forest the crossbow quarrel can swiftly touch, and slay.
The element of the tarnsman is not the green glades, and
the branches; it is the clouds, the saddle and the sky; his
steed is the tarn, his field of battle, strewn with light and
wind, higher than mountains, deeper than the sea, is the
very sky itself. Such men do not care to venture creeping
into the shadows of forests, pursuing scattered game. Vic-
torious, they roar with laughter and, hauling on the one-
straps of their tarn harness, take flight. There is always
other gold, and other women. And, the Priest-Kings willing, a coin that is lost today, or a woman, may, at a later
time, in a more convenient place, be found, and more! A

woman who escapes your collar this afternoon may, by nightfall, find herself chained at your feet. If the coin is to be yours, argue such men, it will be; and if the woman is destined, some night, on this or another, in your tent, on your rugs, by the light of your fire, to feel your chains locked on her body, she will. Flee though she might, that fate will be hers, and she, on the rugs spread over the sand, will be yours.

There was little known of Rask of Treve.

Indeed, there was little known even of the city of Treve. It lay somewhere among the lofty, vast terrains of the rugged Voltai, perhaps as much a fortress, a lair, of outlaw tarnsmen as a city. It was said to be accessible only on tarn-back. No woman, it was said, could be brought to the city, save as a hooded, stripped slave girl, bound across the saddle of a tarn. Indeed, even merchants and ambassadors were permitted to approach the city only under conduct, and then only when hooded and in bonds, as though none not of Treve might approach her save as slaves or captive suppliants. The location of the city, it was said, was known only to her own. Even girls brought to Treve as slaves, obedient within her harsh walls, looking up, seeing her rushing, swift skies, did not know wherein lay the city in which they served. And even should they be dispatched to the walls, perhaps upon some servile errand, they could see, for looming, remote pasangs about them, only the wild, bleak crags of the scarlet Voltai, and the sickening drop below them, the sheer fall from the walls and the cliffs below to the valley, pasangs beneath. They would know only that they were slaves in this place but would not know where this place in which they were slaves might be. It was said no woman had ever escaped from Treve.

And little more seemed known of Rask of Treve than of his remote and mysterious city.

It was said that he was young, audacious and ruthless, that he was powerful, and brutal and bold, that he was resourceful, brilliant, elusive, a master of disguises and sub-terfuges. It was said that a woman might not even know when she was in the presence of Rask of Treve, being casually examined, to see whether or not she was later to be acquired by him.

It was said that he was a fierce, long-haired man, a tarnsman, a warrior.

It was said that he was one of the master swords of Gor.

It was said, too, that he was incredibly handsome, and merciless to women.

Men feared his sword.

Women feared the steel of his slave collars.

Women, it was said, had special reason to fear Rask of Treve. It was said he had a gargantuan contempt, and appetite, for them. It was said that when he used a woman, he then branded her, with his name, as though she, once used, no matter to whom she might afterwards be given or sold, could truly belong only to him. It was also said that he would use a woman only once, claiming that he had, he, Rask of Treve, in once using her, emptied her, exhausted her, taken from her all she had to give, and that, thus, she could no longer be of interest to him. No man on Gor, it was said, could so humble, or diminish, a woman as Rask of Treve. And yet, it was said, there were few women on Gor, strangely enough, to the fury of their own men, or guardians, who were not willing to be used, and branded and spurned by Rask of Treve, that young, audacious, ruthless warrior, only that they might helplessly know his touch.

Rask of Treve, it was said, had never purchased a woman. He would capture, and take by force, those that pleased him. Rask of Treve, it was said, like many Gorean warriors, preferred free women, enjoying the delicious agonies of his prey, as he reduced them to the utterness of the surrendered female slave. On the other hand, if it should please him, it was said he could take a girl who was already slave and make her more a slave than a slave.

I was later furious with myself that I had wept in the cell.

Of course I was a slave girl!

I had been taught that!

I knew it well!

But I would be a superb one!

Sometimes I thought angrily of girls on Earth, many of them, who, too, were slave girls, but who had not learned this, and who, presumably, would never do so. I thought of them, dressing for men, trying to please them, though not much caring for them, to advance themselves in powers and luxuries, using their bodies and minds, their smiles, and glances and words, and touches, clumsily perhaps, not having been trained, to obtain their desires of foolish, starved men. These were girls, not caring for men, who employ the needs of men, without penalty, intelligently to their own profit. Smile at a man of Earth and he will be grateful; pretend to be willing to please a man of Earth and he will do anything for you. You may then use them, such needful weaklings, to rise in the million strata of your intricate society, to climb, to ingratiate and insinuate yourself swiftly, expertly, into the high, warm, comfortable, luxurious places in your busy, impersonal, complex, loveless, anxious world. You will make them pay well for your favors. I held the bars. How different it was on Gor. Such an exploitative, indifferent girl, on Gor, might be simply carried off, and enslaved. Of such women the Goreans enjoy making slaves. She would find her favors were not hers to dispense, at her own pleasure and to her own profit, but his to command, as he was pleased to do so. Gorean men were not so easily fooled as the men of Earth. Gorean men do not choose to be dominated, but to dominate, to be the master. I wished, sometimes, that such girls, of Earth, might find themselves, as I was, found out, and find themselves naked, branded, helpless in a Gorean slave cage, forced to be the slave girls they unknowingly were. I was taught. They were not. I was angry. But they were free. And I was caged. They, though as slave as I, had escaped; I had not; I had been captured, and, by Gorean men, would be forced to pay my price! I had no hope of freedom. I was furious. I had hope only that, though on this world, I could use my inclinations and training, those of a slave girl, to win myself an easy life. That I did not think would be difficult to do, for a girl as clever and beautiful as I. My training, I suspected, as well as my intelligence, would make me more than a match for any man, even the strangely attractive, powerful men of Gor.

Our training continued.

Once, there was a visitor to the pens, a tall stranger, partially hooded, who wore robes of blue and yellow silk, those of the Slavers. He had, over his left eye, a strip of leather, which was wound about his head. He was shown through our section of the pens by Targo.

"This is Soron, of Ar," said Targo, stopping before our cage. Then he said, "El-in-or."

I was apprehensive. I did not wish to be sold until we reached Ar. I wished to be sold from the great block of the Curulean Auction House. It was in that place that there were to be found the highest placed, richest buyers of Gor. It was my hope to become the preferred pleasure slave of a wealthy master, and to reside in one of the high towers of Ar, Gor's largest and most luxurious city, and to have silks and jewels wherewith to deck myself, and no work to do, saving perhaps pleasing my master or guests to whom he might, if he pleased, give me for the evening.

"El-in-or!" snapped Targo.

I went to the bars, and knelt before them. "Buy me, Master," I said.

"Does this girl know how to present herself?" asked the man.

Targo was angry. "Again!" he snapped.

I was frightened now. I leapt to my feet, and went again to the rear of the cage. Then I turned, this time a slave girl, and approached the bars, as a slave girl approaches the bars, behind which a master observes her. I smiled, slightly, insolently, and knelt again before him. I felt the steel plating beneath the straw. I lowered my eyes to his sandals, which were of black, polished leather, with wide straps, and then, still smiling, tauntingly, lifted my head. I regarded him. "Buy me, Master," I whispered.

"No," he said.

I rose to my feet, irritated, and backed away. He need not have been so curt. I had tried to present myself well.

I had! But he had expressed no interest whatsoever. I felt the humiliation of the spurned slave girl.

"Buy me, Master," said Inge, now at the bars, whom Targo had gestured forward.

I did not like the way Inge had said "me," as though to contrast herself with me, and my failure! Did she think herself superior to me? Further, I was furious with how she had approached the bars. She had done so superbly, sinuously. Was she not only of the scribes! Could she, sticklike Inge, be more attractive to a man than I?

The man regarded her, appreciatively, sizing her up, as a master appraises truly high-quality feminine merchandise.

"Were you truly of the scribes?" asked the man.

"Yes," said Inge, startled.

"The refinement of your accent," he said, "suggested the scribes."

"Thank you, Master," said Inge, lowering her head.

"She is excellent merchandise," said the man. "She has the intelligence, and education, of the scribe, and yet she is obviously an exquisite and well-trained female slave."

Inge did not raise her head.

"She should be sold to a scribe," said the man.

Targo spread his hands, and smiled. "To whomever pays the most gold," he said.

"You may return to your place," said the man.

As lightly and beautifully as a cat, Inge leapt to her feet and returned to the straw at the back of the cage. I hated her.

"Buy me, Master," said Ute, coming forward in her turn.

"A beauty," said the man.

Ute, though a slave, blushed with pleasure. She lowered her head. How her blush, and smile, became her! I hated her!

"I am Lana," said Lana, and she came forward, and, in her turn, knelt before the bars. "Buy Lana, Master," she said.

"I did not ask to hear the name of a slave," said the man.

Lana looked at him in surprise.

"Return to your place, Slave," said the man.

Angry, Lana did so.

"You may now approach again," said the man.

Lana did so. She knelt sinuously, and excitingly, before him, and looked up at him. "Buy me, Master," she whispered.

"Return to your place, Female Slave," said the man. He then turned to talk with Targo. Furious, dismissed, Lana again rose to her feet and returned to the back of the cage. She looked about, but neither Ute, Inge nor myself would meet her eyes. I looked away, and smiled.

The man, and Targo, were now prepared to go to the next cage.

I stood at the back, right-hand corner of the cage, on the steel plating, on the straw. I looked out, through the bars. The man had turned and was regarding me. I tossed my head, and, angrily, looked away. I could not, however, in a moment, resist looking again, to see if he might still be looking at me. He was. My heart skipped a beat. I felt frightened. And then he had turned away with Targo, and was then before the next cage. I heard a girl move on the straw in the next cage, approaching the bars. I heard her "Buy me, Master." I turned away, feeling uneasy. I looked about the cage. It was so strong. There was no escape for me. I felt helpless.

That evening, at our meal, I managed to steal a pastry from Ute. She did not even know who it was that removed it from her pan.

Our training in the pens of Ko-ro-ba now began to move toward its conclusion.

Our bodies, superbly trained, even those of Inge and Ute, now became unmistakably those of slave girls. We had had trained into our bodies mysteries of movements of which even we, for the most part, were no longer aware, subtle signals of appetite, of passion and of obedience to a masculine touch, movements which excited the fierce jealousy, the hatred, of free women, particularly ignorant free women, who feared, and perhaps rightly, that their men might leave

them for the purchase or capture of such a prize. Most
slave girls, incidentally, fear free women greatly. Some of
these movements are, in standing, as obvious as the turning of a hip; in reclining, as obvious as the partial extension of a leg, the pointing of toes. But many are more subtle, tiny, almost undiscernible movements, which yet, in their
total effect, brand a female body as being incredibly sensuous, things like a way of glancing, a way of holding the
head, subtle things like the almost invisible, sudden flexion
of the diaphragm, the tiny fear movement of the shoulders,
which signals that the girl, as she is, is helpless quarry. Incidentally, we also learned our own responsiveness to certain
signals. For example, we could become curious, uneasy,
simply by turning an open palm, perhaps unnoticeably, toward a male. It made us feel vulnerable. I did not like to do
this. And, of course, we came to understand, too, the movements of men, and how to read their interest and desire. It
is not really a mystery that the Gorean slave girl, who is
trained, seems to anticipate her master's moods, and that
he scarcely need ever speak of desire to her. She knows
when he does not desire her, and when he does desire her,
and when he does desire her, she signals her responsiveness
to him, and goes to him. I smiled to myself. Men pay higher
prices for trained slave girls. Some of them do not even
understand fully the training the girl receives. They think
commonly only in gross terms, such as her being trained in
the dances of various cities, and in the arts of love, as
practiced in various cities. They often do not know she is
trained to read his desires, like an animal, from his body,
and to serve them promptly, subtly and fervently. The
trained girl is well worth her price. I intended to use my
training to enslave my master. I had little doubt I could do
so. I would have an easy life. Even though a token collar
might be locked on my throat, it would be I who would be
master!

Sometimes, at night, lying in the straw of the cage, I
would think of Verna, and when I did so, knowing her
captured, destined for brand and collar, I would laugh to

myself. I wished that I might have some opportunity to show my lack of fear of her, my contempt for her, that slave!

In these days, as our training in the Ko-ro-ban pens drew to its conclusion, I forgot both about Haakon of Skjern and Rask of Treve. Rask of Treve, it was said, had at last been driven from the environs and claims of the city of Ko-ro-ba. Certain of the tarnsmen of Ko-ro-ba boasted of having driven him from the lands of the state, but others, as I learned from guards, were only silent. At any rate, it seemed that Rask of Treve, and his raider's band, had left the lands of the Towers of the Morning. Sa-Tarna fields ripened in their yellow beauty, and caravans passed with safety. The skies remained clear of the thunder and screams of the tarns of Treve, the war cries of her spear-bearing warriors. Rask of Treve, it seemed, now sought elsewhere for the weight of gold and the flesh of women. Haakon of Skjern, it seemed, still remained in Ko-ro-ba. Skjern is an island in Thassa, muchly distant from Ko-ro-ba. It lies west of bleak, rocky Torvaldsland, substantially above even the vast, green belt of the northern forests. The men of Skjern seldom ventured as far south, or as much inland, as Ko-ro-ba, the Towers of the Morning. Haakon, with his tarnsmen, it seemed, came in peace. They paid for their entry into the city, claiming to need supplies for ventures in trading. Their weapons, for they were a goodly number of warriors from a distant state, were surrendered at the great gate, to be returned to them upon their departure. In Ko-ro-ba the scabbards of Haakon of Skjern and his men would, by the order of the city, be empty. What was there to fear of a Haakon of Skjern with an empty scabbard? I could not understand the uneasiness of Targo, and certain of his men. Haakon had done business with them, and might wish to do so again. He might not even know we were in Ko-ro-ba. Besides, rumors had it that he would be remaining in Ko-ro-ba for days following our departure, and would then be flying northward, returning to Laura. Furthermore, in Ko-ro-ba Targo had purchased additional girls, and guards, and his caravan southeast to Ar would be a substantial one, one surely not to be endangered by some forty to fifty tarnsmen. Too, there seemed nothing menacing in the way in which Haakon spent his time in Ko-ro-ba. He seemed truly to be arranging for supplies, and his men, in their leisure, gambled and drank in the inns and taverns of the city, spending their time striking up acquaintances with men here and there, other tarnsmen, mostly men like themselves, from other cities, now, too, by coincidence within the walls of Ko-ro-ba. There was nothing to fear from Haakon of Skjern, and his men.

"Slaves out," said the guard, turning the key in the heavy lock and swinging back the barred gate of the cage.

In a few minutes I, pleased, knelt, naked, on the wooden platform in the large room in the public pens of Ko-ro-ba. This time I needed not be bound hand and foot, nor held by guards.

I put my head back and the leather worker again reached toward my face.

His instrument was rather like a pair of closed, long-handled pliers. He inserted the tip of this instrument, consisting of a pair of small, hinged rods, like opposing crescents, into the steel nose ring and then, with his two hands, pulling outwards on the handles, slowly, carefully, opened the instrument, spreading the ring. Then, with his fingers, he slipped it free, and dropped it on the platform.

I ran joyfully from the platform to the wall. I felt my face and laughed. I no longer wore the hated nose ring! Elinor Brinton was free of the hated nose ring!

"El-in-or," said Targo.

I knelt immediately.

"You are very beautiful when you are happy," he said.

I blushed, looking down. "Thank you, Master," I said.

Ute then came to the wall. She, too, now, was free of her ring.

I wanted Ute to hold me and kiss me. I was so happy.

"Ute," I said, "I am happy."

"Good," she said, and turned away.

I was hurt. When Inge came to the wall, I looked to her. She was my friend.

"Inge," I cried, "I am happy!"

But Inge, too, turned away, and went to kneel beside Ute.

I felt alone, terribly alone.

When Lana came to the wall I approached her, timidly. I put out my hand to touch her. "I want to be your friend," I said.

"Find out when we are leaving for Ar," said Lana.

"I might be beaten," I whispered.

"No," said Lana. "Targo likes you. He will not beat you."

"Please, Lana," I begged.

Lana looked away.

"I will try," I whispered.

I went to Targo, trembling, and knelt at his feet, my head to the boards of the floor.

"May a slave speak?" I asked.

"Yes," he said.

But I could not form the words, so frightened I was.

"Speak," he said.

"When," I asked, in a whisper, terrified, "—when do we leave for Ar, Master?"

There was a silence.

"Curiosity," he said, "is not becoming in a Kajira." His voice was not pleasant.

I moaned.

I crossed my wrists beneath me and touched my head to the floor, exposing the bow of my back. It is the submissive posture of a slave girl who is to be punished. It is called Kneeling to the Whip. I shook, visibly, at his feet. I whimpered. I waited for him to call a guard, to bring the lash.

"El-in-or," said Targo.

I looked up.

"In the morning," said Targo, "slaves will be fed before dawn. Then, at dawn, we will leave Ko-ro-ba for Ar."

"Thank you, Master," I breathed.

He smiled, releasing me.

I leaped to my feet and fled back to Lana's side. "We will leave at dawn tomorrow," I told her, excitedly.

"I had thought so," said Lana.

I reached out to touch Lana's arm, and she permitted me to do so. "I want to be your friend," I said.

"All right," said Lana.

"I am your friend," I said.

"Yes," said Lana.

"And you," I begged, "you, too, are my friend?"

"Yes," said Lana, "I am your friend."

"You are the only friend I have," I told her. I felt very alone.

"That is true," said Lana.

How lonely it was, to have only one friend. But I had at least one friend, someone who liked me, someone to whom I might talk, someone whom I might trust and in whom I might confide.

"Tonight," said Lana, "if you are given a pastry, you must give it to me."

"Why is that?" I asked.

"Because we are friends," said Lana.

"I do not want to do that," I said.

"If you wish to be my friend," said Lana, "you will have to please me."

I said nothing.

"Very well," said Lana, looking away.

"Please, Lana," I whispered.

She did not look at me.

"I will give you the pastry," I said.

That night, before our departure, I had great difficulty in getting to sleep. Ute, Inge and Lana, all, slept soundly. I lay awake in the straw, looking up at the steel plating above me, dim, metallic, in the flicker of a lantern hung outside the cage, on a peg fixed into the wall on the opposite side of the corridor.

Tomorrow we would leave for Ar.

I was not much pleased with the evening feeding. Lana had taken the pastry, which I had agreed to give her.

And when I had attempted to steal that of the Lady
Rena of Lydius, unseen by Rena, Ute's hand had closed on
my wrist. Her eyes were very hard. I released the pastry.
And Ute and I returned to our food pans. I had had no
pastry this night! I was angry.

I hated Ute, the smug, ugly, stupid little thing.

And I hated Inge, too, for she was skinny and ugly, and
stupid.

And I hated Lana, though she was my friend. I did not
think her much of a friend.

I hoped that I would sell for a higher price than any
of them. That would show them!

I got to my knees in the cell and watched my shadow on
the back wall, from the lantern outside. I stretched, and
threw my hair up and back, arranging it on my back. I was
beautiful. I wondered what a man would pay to own me. I
wondered what I would bring on the great block at Ar,
when I stood there naked for the buyers, Elinor Brinton, a
nude female slave to be auctioned to the highest bidder.

The thought of Verna, the outlaw girl, passed through my
mind. She had captured me, and sold me for a hundred arrow points!

How humiliating, and insulting!

I was worth gold! Gold!

Perhaps Marlenus, her captor, would choose to put her on
the block! Perhaps she would sell for a hundred arrow
points!

But I would bring gold, much gold!

I looked about at the slave flesh in the straw, that of
Ute, and Inge, and Lana. They were slaves. I hated them
all. I wanted to be free of them! I wanted to be free of
them! I did not need friends. I was better than all of them!
I wanted only to be rid of them!

I lay there in the straw, and recollected the forest north
of Laura.

I recalled Verna, and the panther girls, dancing in the
circle. I recalled them, when they could no longer restrain
themselves, throwing themselves to the grass, writhing in
their helpless need, even the proud, arrogant Verna!

They were all weak.

I was hard, and strong. I was Elinor Brinton. I was a slave girl, and a true slave girl, that I knew, but I was not weak. I was hard, and strong. I would enslave some man, and exploit him, and make a fool of him. I would conquer. Elinor Brinton, though only a female, and a slave, would conquer!

Now, satisfied with myself, I began to grow drowsy. For some reason my thoughts strayed back, to the time when the slaver, Soron of Ar, had passed through the pens, in the company of Targo.

"Buy me, Master," I had said to him, as I had had no choice but to do.

"No," he had said.

I twisted in the straw, angrily. Then I lay still, looking up at the steel plating of the ceiling.

He had purchased no girls.

That seemed to me strange, but it was not what bothered me, as I lay there.

To me he had simply said, curtly, "No."

How offended I had been.

With every other girl, as far as I knew, in our cage, and further along the tier of cages, as far as I could hear, he had either spoken with them, or dismissed them, or told them to return to their place. It was only, as far as I knew, to my "Buy me, Master" that he had said, simply, "No."

He had rejected the purchase of all of us, and yet only I, as far as I knew, had been rejected in precisely that way. It was only to my "Buy me, Master," that he had said, with such crude bluntness, "No." I did not care that he did not buy me! Indeed, I did not want him to buy me! So he would not purchase me? What was that to Elinor Brinton? She was pleased! She did not want to belong to him! But I recalled that I had seen him looking at me, afterwards. I had tossed my head and, angrily, insolently, had looked away. When I had looked again, his eyes were yet upon me, yet appraising me. I had been frightened. I had known myself helpless, held captive in the cage. I must wait there, behind bars! There had been no escape for me! Men might do with me what they pleased. I was their prisoner. I was theirs, their slave!

But after I was sold, then could I, though slave, conquer!

What could a girl do locked in a cage with other girls, some of them perhaps almost as beautiful as she?

I was a slave girl.

Very well!

I would make my master suffer, as only a woman can make a man suffer. I would humble him, and, using his needs, would bring him to his knees before me, to beg for my pleasures. I would wring from his weakness whatever I might wish to please my will!

I would conquer!

Men are beasts!

I hated them!

"Buy me, Master," I had said to Soron, the Slaver of Ar.

"No," he had said.

I think of all men, at that time, I most hated Soron of Ar. How he had appraised me, as I had stood helpless, naked, behind the bars, on the straw of the slave cage, his to be seen as he wished; how he had examined me, candidly, objectively, every inch of me, Elinor Brinton, female slave merchandise! How I hated him! How I hated men! How I hated most Soron of Ar!

I fell asleep.

I had a strange dream, turning and moaning in the straw. I dreamed that I had escaped, and that I was free, running and walking in the high grass of a Gorean field. How pleased I was to be free!

And then suddenly I turned and, behind me, some eight or ten feet away, standing, not speaking, tall in the blue and yellow robes of the slaver, still partially hooded, the band of leather across his left eye, was Soron of Ar.

I fled.

But then it seemed he was ahead of me. I turned, and ran again, back, and then to the left, and the right, but each time, as I thought myself escaped, I saw his tall figure, standing there, in the grass.

I was naked.

I ran and ran.

And then, once again, I turned.

Again, some eight to ten feet away, not speaking, he stood. We were alone, in the high grasses of the field.

"Buy me, Master," I said to him. I did not kneel.

"No," he said.

"Purchase me!" I begged. "Purchase me!"

"No," he said.

I now saw, in his hand, coiled, several slender loops of braided leather.

I screamed, and turned and fled.

The leather loop suddenly dropped about me and jerked tight, pinning my arms to my sides.

I screamed.

"Be silent," cried Lana, shaking me, in the straw. "Be silent!"

I awakened, crying out. Then I saw Lana, and the straw, and the lantern on its peg on the other side of the bars, on the wall across the corridor. Ute had risen to her hands and knees, and Inge was on one elbow. Both were looking at me. Then they lay down again, sleepily, in the straw.

I reached to Lana. I was terrified. "Lana," I begged.

"Go to sleep," said Lana, and she lay down in the straw.

I crawled to Ute. "Ute," I begged. "Please hold me, Ute."

"Go to sleep," said Ute.

"Please, please!" I begged.

Ute gave me a kiss, and put her arm about my shoulder. I pressed my head against her shoulder.

"Oh, Ute!" I wept.

"It is only a dream," said Ute. "We will sit up for a time, and then we will go to sleep."

After a time we lay down, side by side, and I, holding to Ute's hand, kissing it, fell asleep.

12   I GATHER BERRIES

HOW GOOD IT WAS to be out of the slave wagon!

Standing in the grass, in the sunlight, I stretched, and laughed.

I wore my new camisk. I was much pleased.

I had sewn it in the wagon, the first day out of Ko-ro-ba. My old camisk, long ago, had been burned near the compound of Targo.

I suppose girls of Earth might find the camisk a shameful, scandalous garment, but I was much pleased to have it. We had not been permitted camisks in the pens of Ko-ro-ba. In the stinking straw they might have been soiled. Also, it is thought by slavers that it is, upon occasion, good for a girl to find herself naked and behind bars. But now the dimly lit cells, the steel and cement, the stomach-wrenching heat and dampness, the close, foul air, the soiled straw, the stink, the crowding, the heavy bars, were behind us. Sometimes free women fall desperately ill when brought to the pens. Inge and I had vomited for more than an hour after we had been forced into the pens, and locked in our cell. But now the pens were behind us.

I stretched again.

It was a day in the early summer, the second day of En'Var. In the chronology of Ar, that city for which we were bound, it was said to be the year 10,121.

I could feel the grass at my calves, the sun on my face and arms and legs, the warm, fresh, root-filled earth beneath my bare feet.

I was happy.

I lifted my face to the sun and closed my eyes, letting its warmth and light bathe my face and closed my eyes.

Elinor Brinton, the rich girl of Earth, was happy.

I felt the pull of a strap on my throat, and opened my eyes. By a long, leather strap, some ten feet in length, I was fastened by the neck to Ute. We were picking berries.

Elinor Brinton, the Gorean slave girl, quickly bent down and, with her fingers, pulled berries from the twigs of a small bush, and put them in her leather bucket.

Ute had her back to me, and the guard, too. He, drowsy, was leaning on his spear.

We were perhaps a pasang from the caravan. I, by standing on my tip toes in the grass, on the low hill on which we were gathering berries, could see the squarish tops of the wagons, with their blue and yellow canvas coverings.

We were nine days out of Ko-ro-ba.

It would be weeks before we could reach Ar, where we would be sold.

I was pleased with the summer's day, and the breezes.

Surreptitiously, I moved, picking berries here and there, closer to Ute.

She was not facing me, nor was the guard.

My hand darted into her leather bucket and seized a handful of berries, and quickly put them in my own. Neither she nor the guard noticed. Ute and the guard were stupid.

I slipped one of the berries into my mouth, taking care that no juices showed on my lips or face.

How clever I was.

How good it was to have the stench of the pens behind us!

I bent down and rubbed my ankles, and then stretched my legs. I ached from riding in the slave wagon. Girls are given only about a foot of chain fastened to their ankle rings, which is looped about the central bar, locked in place, in the slave wagon. There are only some folds of canvas to serve as a cushion between your body and the hard boards of the wagon. But now I was out and, save that I was tethered to Ute, could move as I wished.

How good it was to have the stench of the pens behind us! How good it was to be out of the slave wagon!

I, Elinor Brinton, formerly a rich girl, now a slave on a distant planet, was happy.

I had more than one reason, too, I reminded myself, to be happy.

I laughed.

I recalled the morning we had left Ko-ro-ba.

We had been called from our cells well before dawn. Each of us had then been forced to eat a large bowl of heavy slave gruel. We would not be fed again until that night. In the courtyard of the pens, under torchlight, with brushes, we were forced to scrub the stink of the pens from our bodies. We were then admitted to the wagons. We sat in the wagons, five to a side, our feet toward the center. The central slave bar was then locked in place. A guard then entered the wagon, with ten sets of chains and ankle rings over his shoulder. Beginning at the front of the wagon, backing toward the back, girl by girl, he fastened us to the bar. He then slipped from the wagon, and lifted up the back gate of the wagon, shoving its bolts in place, securing it. The canvas was then tied down. We found ourselves alone with ourselves, in the darkness, chained in the wagon.

"Hi!" cried our driver, and we felt the wagon, creaking, begin to move.

We were merchandise on our way to Ar.

The caravan, wagon by wagon, made its way slowly toward Ko-ro-ba's Street of the Field Gate, which is the southernmost gate of the city.

But we had been unable to move as rapidly as we had wished. The streets, even at that hour, were crowded. We could sense that there was a holiday atmosphere.

"What is it?" I had asked Inge.

"I do not know," she had said.

We heard the drivers cursing and shouting at the crowds, but we could make little progress.

Indeed, other wagons, we gathered, merchant wagons and those of peasants, too, were blocked in the streets.

Foot by foot we moved toward the Street of the Field Gate, and then, at last, came that street.

In the wagons, with the canvas tied down, chained, we listened to the crowds.

By this time it was full daylight outside, and much light filtered through the wagon canvas. We could see one another quite clearly.

The girls were excited.

"What is it?" I asked.

"I do not know," said Inge angrily.

I cursed the canvas.

We heard music in the distance, trumpets, drums and cymbals. We looked at one another, scarcely able to restrain ourselves.

"Move to one side and stop," said a voice from outside, one who spoke with authority.

Our wagon pulled over to one side of the broad avenue, Ko-ro-ba's Street of the Field Gate.

We felt crowds surge about the wagon. The music was coming closer.

There was much shouting.

"It is the catch of Marlenus!" cried a man.

My heart leapt.

I turned about, kneeling, twisting the ankle chain, and dug with my fingers under the edge of the rain canvas.

The drums, the cymbals, the trumpets, were now quite close.

I lifted up an edge of the rain canvas and peeped through.

A hunt master, astride a monstrous tharlarion, holding a wand, tufted with panther hair, preceded the retinue. He wore over his head, half covering his face, a hood formed of the skin of the head of a forest panther. About his neck there were twined necklaces of claws. Across his back there was strapped a quiver of arrows. A bow, unstrung, was fastened at his saddle. He was dressed in skins, mostly those of sleen and forest panthers.

Behind him came musicians, with their trumpets, and cymbals and drums. They, too, wore skins, and the heads of forest panthers.

Then, on carts, drawn by small, horned tharlarion, there came cages, and poles of trophies. In certain of the cages, of heavy, peeled branches lashed together, there snarled and hissed forest sleen, in others there raged the dreadful, tawny, barred panthers of the northern forests. From the poles there hung the skins and heads of many beasts, mostly panthers and sleen. In one cage, restlessly lifting its swaying head, there coiled a great, banded horned hith, Gor's most feared serpentine constrictor. It was native only to certain areas of the forests. Marlenus' hunting must have ranged widely. Here and there, among the wagons, leashed, clad in short woolen skirts, heavy bands of iron hammered about their throats, under the guard of huntsmen, cowled in the heads of forest panthers, there walked male slaves, male outlaws captured by Marlenus and his hunters in the forest. They had long, shaggy black hair. Some carried heavy baskets of fruits and nuts on their shoulders, or strings of gourds; others bore wicker hampers of flowers, or carried brightly plumaged forest birds, tied by string to their wrists.

The other girls, too, watched excitedly, all of them coming to my side of the wagon, wedging among us, lifting up the rain canvas, peeping out.

"Aren't the male slaves exciting," said one of the girls.

"Shameless!" I scorned her.

"Perhaps you will be hooded and mated with one!" she hissed back.

I struck at her. I was angry. It had not occurred to me, but what she said was true. If it should please my master, I could, of course, be mated, as easily as a bosk or a domestic sleen.

"Look at the huntsmen!" breathed Lana, her eyes bright, her lips parted.

Just at that moment one of the cowled huntsmen, a large, swarthy fellow, looked our way and saw us peeping out. He grinned.

"I wish such a man would hunt me," said Lana.

"I, too," said the Lady Rena, excited.

I was startled that she had spoken so. Then I recalled that she, too, was only a female slave. The Lady Rena of

Lydius, like the rest of us, was only a naked girl, a slave, chained in a wagon, destined for the touch of a master.

I rejoiced that I did not have their weaknesses.

I peeped again through the tiny opening between the canvas and the wooden side of the wagon.

More carts were going by, and more huntsmen and slaves. How proud and fine seemed the huntsmen, with their animals and slaves. How grandly they walked. How fearful they appeared, in skins, cowled in the heads of forest panthers, with their hunting spears. They did not bear burdens. They led or drove those that did, inferior, collared, skirted men, slaves. How straight walked the huntsmen, how broad their backs, how straight their gaze and high their head, how large their hands, how keen their gaze! They were masters! They had made slaves even of men! What would a mere woman be in their hands?

I detested them. I detested them!

"Ute," said Inge, "how would you like such a master?"

"I am a slave," said Ute. "I would try to serve him well."

"Ah, Ute," breathed Inge. "You have never forgotten your leather worker, who sold you."

Ute looked down.

"What of you, El-in-or?" taunted Inge, though she was of the scribes.

"I detest them," I told her.

"You would serve such a one well," Inge informed me. "He would see to that."

I did not answer her.

Inge was now looking again, out of the tiny opening between the canvas and the wood. "I want to be owned," she said. "I want to be owned."

"You are of the scribes," I whispered to her.

She looked at me. "I am a slave girl," she said. "And so, too," she added, not pleasantly, "are you." She looked at me. "Slave," she said.

I struck at her, but she caught my hair and pulled my head down to the canvas. I could not reach her hair, nor could I disengage her fists from mine. I was helpless, and held painfully.

"Who is most slave in the wagon?" challenged Inge.

I wept, trying to pull her hands from my hair.

"Who is most slave in the wagon?" repeated Inge, angrily. She gave my hair a vicious yank, twisting my head on the canvas. I lay twisted among the other girls, chained. Inge knelt. "Who is most slave in the wagon?" repeated Inge, again, again yanking my hair, twisting it.

"El-in-or," I whispered. "El-in-or!"

"Let us all hear who is most slave in this wagon," said Inge.

"El-in-or!" I cried out, in pain, weeping. "El-in-or!"

When Inge released me, I scrambled back from her. I had no desire to fight her. I looked at her. There was triumph in her eyes. Every muscle in her body seemed vital and alive. I sensed then, knew then, that she had been waiting a long time for such an encounter. She had wanted a pretext to fight me. I now knew I could no longer bully Inge.

"Let us fight!" she challenged.

"No," I said. "No." I shook my head.

I had thought myself stronger than Inge. I now realized that I was not. I had, as I thought I could with impunity, struck at her. Then, suddenly, cruelly, decisively, she had bested me. I looked at her. The shining eyes, the vital body, her eagerness to fight. I lowered my eyes, my head. Inge's days of being bullied by me were now at an end. Suddenly I was afraid of her. I had thought myself able to beat her, if I might choose, but now I knew that she, if she chose, could beat me. I had been clearly bested, and I sensed I could be again, if she wished. I was now frightened of Inge. I hoped that she would not bully me. Almost immediately I sensed the shift of power in the wagon, among the girls. I no longer ranked as high as I had, and Inge ranked higher. I sensed that Inge was regarded with a new respect, suddenly, and that I, who had often been the bully, the aggressor, would henceforth be regarded with little or no respect.

That made me angry.

Then we heard more music from outside, as more musicians, near the end of the retinue, approached.

A girl from the other side of the wagon squeezed between Ute and I.

"Get back," I snapped at her.

"Be quiet," she said.

"Look!" cried Ute.

There was, outside, the snap of a whip.

There was a great shout from the crowd.

I pressed closer to the opening, looking out. More carts of sleen and panthers, with huntsmen and slaves, were passing.

Then I heard the snap of the whip again.

The crowd gave another shout.

"Look!" cried Inge.

And then we saw it.

A cart was passing, flanked by huntsmen and slaves, bearing their burdens of gourds, flowers, nuts and fruits. On the cart, horizontally, parallel to the axles, there was a high pole, itself supported by two pairs of diagonally crossed poles, lashed together at the point of their crossings. It was a trophy pole, with its stanchions, peeled, formed of straight branches, like the other trophy poles, from which had hung the skins of slain animal. Only standing below this pole, alone on the cart, her skins knotted about her neck, her wrists bound behind her back, her hair fastened over the pole, holding her in place, was a beautiful panther girl, stripped, her weapons, broken, lying at her feet. I recognized her as one of the girls of Verna's band.

I cried out with pleasure.

It was the first of five carts. On each, similarly, wrists bound behind her back, stripped, her hair bound cruelly over a trophy pole, stood a panther girl, each more beautiful than the last.

I heard the blare of the trumpets, the clash of the cymbals, the pounding of the drums. The men shouted. Women cursed, and screamed their hatred of the panther girls. Children cried out and pelted them with pebbles. Slave girls in the crowd rushed forward to surge about the carts, to poke at them with sticks, strike them with switches and spit upon them. Panther girls were hated. I, too, wished I could rush out and strike them and spit upon them. From time to time, guards, huntsmen, with whips, would leap to the cart and crack their whips, terrifying the slave girls, who knew that sound well, back from the carts, that they might pass, but then the slaves would gather again, and rush about the following cart, only to be in turn driven back again. Standing outside the range of the whip they would then spit, and curse and scream their hatred of the panther girls.

"Slaves are so cruel," said Ute.

Cart by cart passed.

"Look!" cried Inge.

We now heard the snap of whips again, but this time the leather blades fell upon the naked backs of girls.

"Look!" cried Lana, pleased.

A huntsman came now, holding in his hand five long leather straps, dragging behind him five panther girls. Their wrists were bound before their bodies, lashed tightly. The same strap that lashed their wrists, I saw, served, too, as their leash, that held in the huntsman's grip. Like the girls bound by the hair to the trophy poles, on the carts, these were stripped, their skins knotted about their necks.

Behind them there walked another huntsman, with a lash. He would occasionally strike them, hurrying them forward.

I saw the lash fall across the back of the blond girl, she who had held my leash in the forest, who had been so cruel to me. I heard her cry out, and saw her stumble forward, bound, in pain. I laughed.

Behind this first group of five girls there came a second group, it, too, with its huntsman holding the leashes, dragging his beautiful captives, and another following behind, occasionally lashing them forward.

How pleased I was. There had been fifteen girls, five on the carts, and two of the tethered groups! All of Verna's band had fallen captive!

There now came a great shout, and I squeezed even further forward in the wagon, to peep out.

Then the crowd became suddenly quiet.

One last cart approached. I could hear its wheels on the stones before I could see it.

It was Verna.

Beautiful, barbaric Verna!

Nothing, save her weapons, had been taken from her. She still wore her brief skins, and about her neck and on her arms, were barbaric ornaments of gold.

But she was caged.

Her cage, mounted on the cart, was not of branches, but of steel. It was a circular cage, between some six and seven feet in height, flat-bottomed, with a domed top. Its diameter was no more than a yard.

And she was chained.

Her wrists were manacled behind her body, and a chain led from her confined wrists to a heavy ring set in the bottom of her cage.

Her head was in the air.

She was manacled as heavily as might have been a man. This infuriated me. Slave bracelets would hold her, as they would any woman!

How arrogant and beautiful she seemed!

How I hated her!

And so, too, must have the other slave girls in the crowd, with their switches and sticks.

"Hit her!" I screamed through the canvas.

"Be quiet!" cried Ute, in horror.

"Hit her!" screamed Lana.

The crowd of slave girls swarmed forward toward the cart with their sticks and switches, some of them even leaping upon it, spitting, and striking and poking through the bars of the high narrow cage.

I saw that the domed top of Verna's cage was set with a ring, so that the cage might be, if one wished, hung from the branch of a tree, or suspended from a pole, for public viewing. Doubtless Marlenus had given orders that she be exhibited in various cities and villages on the route to Ar, his prize, that she might thus, this beautiful captive, an outlaw girl well known on Gor, considerably redound to his prestige and glory. I supposed that she would not be enslaved until she reached Ar. Then, I supposed, she would be publicly enslaved, and perhaps by the hand of Marlenus himself.

The slave girls swarmed about the cage, poking, and striking with their switches, and spitting and cursing. Their abuse was endured by Verna. It seemed she chose to ignore them. This infuriated them and they redoubled their efforts. Verna now flinched with pain, and her body was cut and marked, but still she would not lower her head, nor did she deign to speak to, or recognize in any way, her foes.

Then there was a roar of anger from the crowd and, to my fury, men began to leap, too, to the cart, but to hurl the slave girls from the cage. And huntsmen, too, angrily, now leaped to the cart, striking about them with their whips. The slave girls screamed, and fled from the cart. Men seized them, and disarmed them of their sticks and switches, and then threw the girls to the stones at their feet, where they cowered, at the sandals of free men, and then the men ordered them from the street. The girls leapt up and, weeping, terrified, fled away, humiliated, chastened slaves.

I was angry. I wished that I might have had a stick or switch. How I would have beaten Verna! I was not afraid of her! I would have beaten her well, as she deserved!

How I hated Verna!

Her cart was now moving away, drawn by the small, horned tharlarion.

In her cage, manacled, Verna still stood proudly. Her head was still in the air, her body straight, her gaze level and fixed. She gave no sign that she had noticed either those who had so rudely assailed her, or those who had protected her from them. How arrogant and superior she seemed!

How I hated her, and hated her!

A spear butt struck at the wood of the wagon, near where we peeped out. We drew back, frightened. The canvas was then tied down again. We were alone with ourselves again, closed in the wagon.

We heard the drums, the trumpets and clashing cymbals growing fainter, down the street, as the retinue continued on its way.

"Hereafter," said Inge, "El-in-or will address each of us in this wagon as Mistress."

I looked at her in anger.

"No," said Ute, to Inge.

"Yes," said Inge.

"That is being cruel to El-in-or," said Ute.

"We shall treat El-in-or exactly as she deserves," said Inge.

The other girls, except Ute, and Lana, who perhaps feared she might be similarly treated, agreed.

"You will be treated exactly as you deserve, won't you?" asked Inge, looking at me.

I did not answer her.

"Is that not true, El-in-or?" asked Inge, sweetly.

I bit my lip.

"Is it not true?" pressed Inge. Her voice was not pleasant.

"Yes," I whispered.

"Yes, what?" asked Inge. Her voice was hard.

"Yes—Mistress," I said.

The other girls, even Lana, laughed.

"Move your feet," said the girl across from me.

I looked at Inge. Her eyes were hard.

"Yes, Mistress," I said. I moved my chained ankles. I hated Inge, and Lana, and Ute, and all of them!

The girls laughed.

We felt the wagon again begin to move, once again resuming its journey toward the Field Gate. Once again we were goods, female slaves, on our way to be sold in Ar.

But I had been forced to acknowledge myself most slave in the wagon. I was more slave than they!

I was forced even to address them as Mistress!

I was furious.

Angrily, in the field, in the sunlight, more than a pasang from the wagons, on the route to Ar, I picked berries, snapping them from their twigs and throwing them into the bucket.

The sun and the grass, and the breezes, were doubtless as pleasant as they had been, but I was not now in much of a mood to enjoy them. I recollected with satisfaction my witnessing of the captivity of Verna, the Panther Girl, but I recollected with much less satisfaction what had occurred in the slave wagon, when Inge had so decisively bested me;

when I had learned that she could beat me, if she pleased, and would, should it please her; when I, a former bully among them, had so suddenly lost my status with them; when Inge, whom I now feared, forced me, and cruelly, to address her, and the others, with the exception of Ute, though slaves themselves, by the title of Mistress, as though it was only I among them who might be the slave! Moreover, to my fury, the other girls of the caravan, hearing of this, and thinking it a great joke, were quick to demand of me the same dignity.

"Address them as Mistress," said Inge, "or I will beat you."

I wanted to be sold in Ar, to be free of them! I wanted to be a pampered, perfumed girl, with jewels and cosmetics and silks, the pet and favorite of an indulgent master, whom I might control. I wanted the luxuries, and the sights and pleasures of Ar! I wanted to be an envied slave!

I had bowed my head to Inge.

I would have a very pleasant life, as a manipulative, kept female. The only difference between myself and the kept girl of Earth, I speculated, was that I would not be able to choose who it was that would keep me. I would be purchased.

What a fool I was! I did not yet know what it was to be a Gorean slave girl.

"Yes, Mistress," I had said to Inge, humbly, hating her.

"You may now kiss my feet," she informed me.

My fists clenched. Her eyes flashed.

I did so. I was much afraid of her. The other girls about laughed. And so I called them Mistress. I wanted to be free of them all!

I was miserable.

But two girls I did not address as Mistress, Ute, who did not wish it, and Lana, in whose case, for reasons of her own, Inge did not insist upon it.

I wanted to get swiftly to Ar, and to be sold, to be free of them all!

I wanted to begin my new and pleasant life.

I looked at Ute.

"Ute," I said.

Ute turned, in the strap, from picking berries.

"Yes, El-in-or?" she said.

"When will we reach Ar?" I asked.

"Oh, not for many days," she said. "We have not yet even come to the Vosk."

The Vosk is a great river, which borders the claims of Ar, on the north.

Ute then returned to her picking of berries. Neither she nor the guard were watching, so I stole some more of her berries for my bucket. Two I placed in my mouth, carefully, that no sign that I had tasted them be evident.

I looked up. The sky was bright and blue, and the white clouds scudded swiftly by. I was wearing a camisk. I was out of the pens, out of the slave wagon. The air was warm and clear. I was not particularly displeased.

Moreover, I had had an opportunity to be revenged on Verna, before whom I had demonstrated my superiority and lack of fear.

It had happened five days out of Ko-ro-ba.

The Merchants have, in the past few years, on certain trade routes, between Ar and Ko-ro-ba, and between Tor and Ar, established palisaded compounds, defensible stockades. These, where they exist, tend to be placed approximately a day's caravan march apart. Sometimes, of course, and indeed, most often, the caravan must camp in the open. Still, these hostels, where they are to be found, are welcome, both to common merchants and to slavers, and even to travelers. Various cities, through their own Merchant Castes, lease land for these stockades and, for their fees, keep their garrisons, usually men of their own cities, supplied. The stockades are governed under Merchant Law, legislated and revised, and upheld, at the Sardar Fairs. The walls are double, the interior wall higher, and tarn wire is strung over the compound. These forts do not differ much, except in size, from the common border forts, which cities sometimes maintain at the peripheries of their claims. In the border forts, of course, there is little provision for the goods of merchants, their wagons, and such. There is usually room for little more than their garrisons, and their slaves. I hoped I would not be a slave girl in a distant border fort. I wanted to reside in a luxurious city, where there would be many goods, and sights and pleasures. I wanted to wear my collar in great Ar itself.

Five days out of Ko-ro-ba, we had stopped at one of these Merchant Fortresses.

Inside the interior wall, girls are sometimes permitted to run free. They cannot escape, and it pleases them.

One wagon at a time, for a given interval, Targo permitted his girls, in wagon sets, to enjoy freedom of movement. How I ran inside the large fortress.

Then I cried out, "Lana! Lana!"

"What?" she asked.

"Look!" I cried.

Over against one long wall of the stockade was the camp of the huntsmen of Marlenus. They had left Ko-ro-ba after us, but they had traveled more swiftly.

Lana and I, and some of the other girls, ran to look at the cages of sleen and panthers, and the trophies. Lana laughed at the cages of male slaves.

She and I went to them, with others, too, to taunt them.

We would come close to the cages, and when they would reach for us, we would jump back.

"Buy me!" I laughed.

"Buy me! Buy me!" laughed the others.

One of the men reached his hand to Lana. "Let me touch you," he begged.

She looked at him, contemptuously. "I do not permit myself to be touched by slaves," she said. She laughed scornfully. "I will belong to a free man, not a slave."

Then she walked away from him, as a slave girl, taunting him.

He shook the bars in anger.

"I, too," I informed him, "will belong to a free man, not a slave."

Then I, too, walked away from him, showing him the contempt of a slave girl.

I heard him cry out with rage, and I laughed.

We looked, too, at the sleen and the panthers, and the skins, and the great, captive hith.

Verna's girls, the fifteen of them, stripped, were housed, crouching and kneeling, in small, metal slave cages. We threw dirt on them, and spat at them.

I was particularly pleased to abuse the blond-haired girl, who had held my leash in the forest. I found a stick and poked her through the bars.

She snapped and snarled at me, like an animal, and reached, clawing, through the bars for me, but I was too quick for her.

I poked her again and again, and threw dirt on her, and laughed.

"Look!" said Lana.

I left the blond-haired girl.

We stopped before Verna's cage.

There were some of the huntsmen about, but neither Lana nor I much feared them. They were not, we noted, much interested in what we did.

That gave us courage.

"Greetings, Verna," said I, boldly.

She was no longer manacled, but she was, I noted, securely confined in the cage.

The cage itself was now hung from a pole, rather like a high trophy pole. Its floor was about six inches off the ground.

I looked up at her.

She looked down at me.

I would have preferred to have looked down upon her, but she was a taller woman than I, and, of course, the cage was suspended somewhat off the ground.

"Perhaps you remember me?" I asked.

She looked at me, saying nothing.

"It was I, incidentally," I informed her, "who, in Ko-ro-ba, first cried out to the slave girls to strike you. It was I who instigated their attack."

She said nothing.

"It is to me," I informed her, "that you owe that beating."

Her face was expressionless.

I still held the stick with which I had poked the blond-haired girl, she who had held my leash in the forest.

I struck out with it, upsetting the pan of water in her cage, emptying it. The water ran over the small, circular floor of the cage, and some of it dripped out, falling to the ground.

Still Verna made no move.

I walked about the cage. Verna could not watch both myself and Lana.

She did not turn to follow me. Behind the cage I reached in and stole the food she had in the cage, two larma fruit lying, split, on its metal floor. I bit into one and tossed the other to Lana, who, too, ate it.

When we had finished the fruit, Lana and I discarded the skin and seeds.

Verna still watched us, not moving.

I was angry.

Suddenly I struck at her with the stick, and she flinched, but did not cry out.

Lana threw dirt on her.

Then I seized the cage and, on its chain, spun it about. The chain twisted, and then the cage turned. Lana and I, laughing, spun the cage back and forth, and when I could I struck Verna through the bars. We struck her, and spat on her, and threw dirt on her.

There were huntsmen nearby but they did not restrain us. We had much sport.

Then we let the cage hang still. Verna had her eyes closed. She held the bars. She swallowed.

After a time she opened her eyes.

We, for some minutes more, continued to abuse her, with sticks, and dirt, and our spittle and our insults. She made no response.

I was not afraid of her. I had never been afraid of her.

Then we heard one of Targo's guards calling us. It was time for us to be returned to our wagon, and for another set of girls to be freed, to enjoy the liberty of the compound.

I gave Verna another blow with the stick.

"Can't you say anything?" I screamed. I was infuriated that she had not cried out, that she had not groveled, that she had not wept for mercy.

We heard the guard call again.

"Hurry," said Lana, "or we will be beaten!"

I gave Verna one last blow, a stinging stripe across the shoulder, with the stick.

"Can't you say anything?" I screamed at her.

"You have pierced ears," she said.

I cried out in anger, and turned, throwing away the stick, and ran back to the wagon.

I threw another berry into the bucket.

"Ute," I said.

Ute turned again, to regard me.

"Speak to Inge," I said to her. "Tell her not to be cruel to me." I did not wish to address the girls of the chain as Mistress.

"Why do you not speak to her yourself?" asked Ute.

"She doesn't like me," I said. "She would beat me."

Ute shrugged.

"She likes you, Ute," I pressed. "Speak to her for me. Ask her not to make me call the other girls Mistress. I do not wish to do so. They are only slaves!"

"We are all slaves," said Ute.

"Please, Ute," I begged.

"All right," said Ute. "I will ask her."

Ute then turned away, and continued to pick berries. It was now late in the afternoon. We were perhaps a pasang and a half from the distant wagons. From the hill on which we now picked berries I could see them. It would be time for the evening meal soon.

I looked about to see if the guard was watching. He was not.

My bucket was no more than half full.

Ute had put her bucket behind her and was picking ber-ries about a yard ahead of it. Her back was to me. Ute was such a stupid little thing. I put my finger under the wide strap knotted about my throat, which tethered me to her. Then I crept close and took two handfuls of berries from her bucket and put them in mine.

I kept some to put in my mouth.

Then, as I put the berries in my mouth, I thought I heard something. I looked up, and back. Ute, too, and the guard, at the same time, heard it. He cried out and, angrily, began to run back toward the wagon.

Ute saw them before I did, in the distance. I had heard only the sound, vague, from far off, like a myriad snappings, and shrill, wind-borne screams.

"Look!" cried Ute. "Tarns!"

In the distance, in a set of four, long, narrow, extended "V's," there came a flight of tarnsmen. The first "V" was lowest in altitude, and in advance of the other three; the second was second lowest, and in advance of the other two, and similarly for the third and fourth. There were no tarn drums beating. This was not a military formation.

"Raiders!" cried Ute.

I was stunned. What seemed most clear to me, and most incomprehensible, was that our guard had left us. He had run back toward the wagons. We were alone!

"There must be more than a hundred of them!" cried Ute.

I looked up.

"Down!" she cried, and dragged me by the arms to a kneeling position on the grass.

We watched them strike the caravan, in waves, and turn and wheel again, discharging their bolts.

The bosk were being cut loose and stampeded. There was no effort to turn the wagons in a single defensive perimeter. Such a perimeter has little meaning when the enemy can strike from above. Rather, men, hauling on the wagon tongues and thrusting with their shoulders, were putting the wagons in a dense square, with spaces between them. This formation permits men to conceal themselves under the wagons, the floors of the wagons providing some protection above them. The spaces between the wagons provides opportuniy for the defenders to fire their crossbows upward at the attackers, and gives some protection against the spreading of fire, wagon to wagon. In many of the wagons there were still girls chained, screaming. Men there tore back the coverings of blue and yellow canvas, that they might be seen.

"Unchain them!" cried Ute, as though someone might hear. "Unchain them!"

But they would not be unchained, unless the day went badly for the caravan, in which case they would be freed and, like the bosk, stampeded.

In the meantime their bodies served as partial cover for the defenders under and between the wagons.

The raiders wanted the girls. Indeed, that was the object of their enterprise.

Accordingly, unless they wished to destroy the very goods they sought, their attack must be measured, and carefully calculated.

Swiftly the formation of tarnsmen wheeled and withdrew.

"The attack is over," I said.

"They will now use fire," said Ute.

I watched with horror as, in a few moments, again the sky filled with tarns, and the beating of wings and the screams of the great birds.

Now, down from the skies rained fiery quarrels, tipped with blazing, tarred cloth wound about the piles.

Wagons caught afire.

I saw defenders unchaining screaming girls. One's hair was afire.

The girls huddled under the wagons, many of them burning.

I saw a defender forcing the head of the girl whose hair burned into the dirt, extinguishing the flames.

I saw two girls now fleeing across the grass, away from the wagons.

Tarnsmen now struck the earth, leaping from their birds, to the east of the wagon square and, swords drawn, rushed among the burning wagons.

The clash of steel carried dimly to the hill, where Ute and I watched.

"Unbind me!" cried Ute.

The straps we wore about our throats were broad, and the strap, too, that joined us. But, about the throat, the broad strap, for each of us, was perforated in two places, and it was by means of narrow binding fiber, passed several times through the performations and knotted, that it was fastened on our throats. The guard had knotted the binding fiber, tightly.

My fingers fought at the knot, futilely, picking at it. I was upset. I could not loosen it.

"I cannot see to untie the knot," cried Ute. "Untie it!"

"I can't!" I wept. "I can't!"

Ute pushed me away and began to chew at the leather strap, desperately, holding it with her hands.

I wept.

Not all the tarnsmen had dismounted. Some still rode astride the great birds, though the birds stood now on the grass.

I saw men fighting between the wagons, some falling.

I saw one of the tarnsmen, yet mounted on his tarn, remove his helmet and wipe his forehead, and then replace the helmet. He was their leader. I could not fail to recognize him, even at the distance.

"It is Haakon!" I cried. "It is Haakon of Skjern!"

"Of course it is Haakon of Skjern!" said Ute, biting at the strap, tearing at it with her fingers.

Now Haakon of Skjern stood in the stirrups of the tarn saddle, and waved his sword toward the wagons. More warriors dismounted now and rushed among the wagons.

Several of the wagons were now flaming. I saw men rushing about. Two girls fled from the wagons, across the fields.

There must have been more than a hundred tarnsmen with Haakon. When he had come to Ko-ro-ba, he had had little more than forty men, if that many. Others, mercenaries, he must have recruited in the city.

His men outnumbered those of Targo, considerably.

The sounds of blades carried to where we knelt. I was terrified. Ute was savagely tearing at the strap with her teeth.

Then, suddenly, from under the burning wagons, across

the fields, there fled dozens of girls, running in all directions.

"He's driven the girls out," cried Ute, furiously. She jerked at the strap. She had not been able to chew it through. She looked at me, savagely. "They have not seen us," she said. "We must escape!"

I shook my head. I was afraid. What would I do? Where would I go?

"You will come with me or I will kill you!" screamed Ute.

"I'll come, Ute!" I cried. "I'll come."

I now saw the tarnsmen returning from the burning wagons, racing to their tarns. They had no interest, or little interest, in the wagons or the supplies. In Targo's gold they might have had interest but they would have to spend men to obtain it. Meanwhile the real treasure was escaping.

Targo, a rational man, and a brilliant slaver, had chosen to purchase his own life, and that of his men, and the safety of his gold, by the flight of the slave girls.

It had been a desperate measure, and one not willingly adopted by a merchant. It was clear evidence that Targo had recognized the seriousness of his predicament, and the odds by which he was outnumbered and the probable result of continuing the engagement.

"Come, El-in-or!" screamed Ute. "Come!"

Ute pulled with both her hands on the strap that bound us together and I, choking, stumbling, fled after her.

We turned once.

We saw tarnsmen, in flight, riding down running girls, the tarns no more than a few feet from the grass, beating their wings, screaming.

Often a tarn would clutch the girl in its talons and alight. The tarnsman would then leap from the saddle and force the bird's talons from its prey, binding the hysterical girl's wrists and fastening her to a saddle ring, then remounting and hunting another. One man had four girls bound to his saddle. Another would fly low and to the side of the running girl, and a beat of the tarn's great wings would send her rolling and sprawling for a dozen yards across the grass. Before she could arise, the tarnsman would be upon her,

binding her. Another would strike the victim in the small
of her back with the butt of his spear, felling her, numbing
her, for the binding fiber. Others, flying low and to the side,
roped the girls as they ran, using their slender ropes of
braided leather, familiar to all tarnsmen. Such warriors do
not even deign to dismount to bind their fair prisoners.
They haul them to the saddle, in flight, there securing them,
stripping them and fastening them to the binding rings.

It is a favorite sport of tarnsmen to streak their tarn
over an enemy city and, in such a fashion, capture an enemy
girl from one of the city's high bridges, carrying her off,
while the citizens of the city scream in fury, shaking their
fists at the bold one. In moments her garments flutter down
among the towers and she is his, bound on her back across
the saddle before him, his prize. If he is a young tarnsman,
and she is his first girl, he will take her back to his own
city, and display her for his family and friends, and she will
dance for him, and serve him, at the Collaring Feast. If he
is a brutal tarnsman, he may take her rudely, should he
wish, above the clouds, above her own city, before even
his tarn has left its walls. If he should be even more brutal,
but more subtly so, more to be feared by a woman, he will,
in the long flight back to his city, caress her into submission,
until she has no choice but to yield herself to him, wholly,
as a surrendered slave girl. When he then unbinds her from
the saddle rings, she, so devastatingly subdued, well knows
herself his.

I saw Rena of Lydius running, frantic, from the wagons,
in her camisk.

I saw a tarnsman wheel his tarn after her.

She fled.

Rena of Lydius was being hunted!

I put my hand before my mouth.

The wide, swiftly closing loop of braided leather fell
about her running body. The tarn streaked past her, only a
few feet overhead. The rope jerked tight. She screamed.
She was jerked from her feet into the air, screaming, a dozen
feet above the rushing grasses beneath her, and then was
dragged to the saddle. I saw her clutching the tarnsman,

terrified. With a small knife he cut the binding fiber that belted her camisk. The camisk now flew behind her, like a cape, about her neck, whipped by the wind. He resheathed his knife. He then threw the camisk from her. He gestured that she should lie on her back across the saddle in front of him, crossing her wrists and legs. She, terrified, did so immediately. He then secured her.

I screamed.

The strap that bound me to Ute jerked on my neck, and I fell.

"Hurry!" cried Ute. "Hurry!"

I scrambled to my feet and, following Ute, fled.

13   I FEEL THE CAPTURE LOOP

I STOOD IN THE SWIFT STREAM, the water coming to somewhat above my knees. I had tied the camisk up about my waist, with the binding fiber.

Hands poised, I scrutinized the silver form turning in the clear water.

It swam near the fence of small wands which Ute had thrust into the bottom of the stream, and turned back, as though puzzled.

My hands dove for it, clutching. I touched it. There was a churning of water. I drew back my hands, with a cry of disgust. With a spattering of water and a flurry of pebbles the swift, squirming body twisted away.

I stood up again.

It was not likely to escape.

I stood within Ute's structure of wands. It consisted of two parts. The first, a few feet upstream, was in the form of a "V," which had an open bottom, which pointed downstream. This formed a funnel of wands, such that a small swimming creature could easily enter it, but would not so easily find again the opening to escape. The second part of the structure was a simple, curved fence of wands a few feet downstream of the first, forming the downstream wall of the trap.

Ute was hunting. She had also set snares. She had used the pieces of binding fiber which had, by means of the perforations, fastened our throat straps on us.

I again began to stalk the silver body in the trap.

Ute and I, to our astonishment, had escaped. Separated as we had been from the wagons, and doubtless, too, in virtue of the confusion, it had been our fortune not to have been noticed in our flight.

I had shaken my head. I had been afraid. What could we do? Where would we go?

"You will come with me or I will kill you!" had screamed Ute.

"I'll come, Ute!" I had cried. "I'll come."

Dismayed, terrified, bound to her by the throat strap, I had stumbled after her.

We had run for perhaps an Ahn, when, gasping, exhausted, scarcely able to move, we had reached the edge of a large Ka-la-na thicket.

In this thicket, still tethered one to the other, we had thrown ourselves down on the grass.

"Ute, I am afraid," I had whispered to her. "I am afraid!"

"Do you not understand," she whispered, her eyes filled with joy, "we are free! We are free!"

"But what will we do?" I asked.

Ute crawled over to me, and began to work, with her small strong fingers, at the knot that bound the collar on my throat. "We will need this binding fiber," she said.

After a time, she managed to undo the knot. "Now," she said, "unbind me."

"I cannot," I told her. I had tried before, and could not do it.

"Do it," said Ute, her eyes hard.

I again tried. I could not, with my small fingers, loosen it.

"Bring me a tiny stick," said Ute.

I did so.

She then chewed at the end of the tiny stick, sharpening it, putting a point on it.

She handed it to me.

With this tool, wedging it between the strands, I managed, after a time, to loosen them, and removed Ute's throat strap.

"Good," she said.

"What will we do, Ute?" I begged.

She coiled the heavy strap and put it about her shoulder.

The two smaller pieces of binding fiber she thrust in the belt of her camisk, itself of binding fiber.

She then stood up.

"Come along," she said. "We must go deeper into the thicket."

"I cannot move," I told her. "I am too tired."

Ute looked at me.

"If you wish to leave now," I told her, "you must go on without me."

"All right," said Ute. "Farewell, El-in-or," said she. She then turned and began to move away.

"Ute!" I had cried.

She did not turn.

I had leaped to my feet, running after her. "Ute!" I had wept. "Ute, take me with you!"

My hands now poised themselves over the silverish body in the water before me.

I clutched again. This time I caught the thing, squirming, horned, scaly. It thrashed about. I could not hold it. It was too terrible to feel! With a slap of its tail it slithered free and darted away, downstream, but then, halted by the barrier of wands, turned and, under the water, motionless, faced me.

I backed away, toward the open end of the "V," which pointed downstream.

I could keep the thing in the trap. Ute would be back soon.

We had been free for five days. We had stayed in Ka-la-na thickets by day, and had moved across the fields at night. Ute was heading south and westward. The tiny village, Rarir, in which she had been born, lay south of the Vosk, and near the shores of Thassa.

"Why do you wish to go there?" I had asked Ute.

She had been stolen from that village as a little girl. Her parents, the year before, had been slain by roving larls. Ute was of the leather workers. Her father had been of that caste.

"I do not much wish to go there," said Ute. "But where

is one to go?" She smiled. "In my own village," she said, "they will not make me a slave."

Sometimes, at night, Ute would moan the name of Barus, whom she had once loved.

At the age of twelve, Ute had been purchased by a leather worker, who dwelt on the exchange island, administered by the Merchants, of Teletus. He, and his companion, had cared for her, and had freed her. They had adopted her as their daughter, and had seen that she was trained well in the work of the leather workers, that caste which, under any circumstances, had been hers by right of birth.

On her nineteenth birthday, members of the Caste of Initiates had appeared at the door of the leather worker's hut.

It had been decided that she should now undertake the journey to the Sardar, which, according to the teachings of the Caste of Initiates, is enjoined on every Gorean by the Priest-Kings, an obligation which is to be fulfilled prior to their attaining their twenty-fifth year.

If a city does not see that her youth undertake this journey then, according to the teachings of the Initiates, misfortunes may befall the city.

It is one of the tasks of the Initiates to keep rolls, and determine that each youth, if capable, discharge this putative obligation to the mysterious Priest-Kings.

"I will go," had said Ute.

"Do you wish the piece of gold?" asked the chief of the delegation of Initiates, of the Leather Worker and his Companion.

"No," they had said.

"Yes," said Ute. "We will take it."

It is a custom of the Initiates of Teletus, and of certain other islands and cities, if the youth agrees to go to the Sardar when they request it, then his, or her, family or guardians, if they wish it, will receive one tarn disk of gold.

Ute knew that the leather worker, and his companion, could well use this piece of gold.

Besides, she knew well that, some year, prior to her twenty-fifth year, such a journey must be undertaken by her. The Merchants of Teletus, controlling the city, would demand it of her, fearing the effects of the possible displeasure of the Priest-Kings on their trade. If she did not undertake the journey then, she would be simply, prior to her twenty-fifth birthday, removed from the domain of their authority, placed alone outside their jurisdiction, beyond the protection of their soldiers. Such an exile, commonly for a Gorean, is equivalent to enslavement or death. For a girl as beautiful as Ute it would doubtless have meant prompt reduction to shameful bondage, chains and the collar. Further, on other years, there would be no piece of gold to encourage her to undertake this admittedly dangerous journey.

"I will go," she had said.

She agreed to participate in the group then being organized by the Initiates. The leather worker and his companion, reluctantly, yielding to her entreaties, accepted the piece of gold.

Ute did indeed get to see the Sardar.

But she saw it in the chains of a naked slave girl.

Her ship fell to those of the black slavers of Schendi. She, and the others, were sold to merchants, who met the slavers at a secret cove, buying from them their catch. They were then transported overland in slave wagons to the Sardar, where they were sold at the great spring fair of En'Kara. When she was sold, from the block, over the palisade, she could see the peaks of the Sardar.

For four years, Ute, then a beauty, passed from one master to another, taken from city to city.

Then she was taken by a master, with others of his slaves, again to the Sardar, again to be sold, to defray business debts resulting from the loss of a caravan of salt wagons.

It was there that she had been purchased by Barus, of the Leather Workers.

She had had many masters, but it was only the name of Barus, which she moaned in her sleep.

She had much fallen in love with him, but she had, as

she had told me, once attempted to bend him to her will. To her horror, he had sold her.

She would never speak of him to me, but in her sleep, as I have said, she would cry his name.

"Why do you not go back to Teletus?" I asked Ute.

I did not much favor the idea of living in a village. And it was in Teletus that she had been freed, and adopted. Her foster parents might still be on the island.

"Oh," had said Ute, casually, "I cannot swim Thassa. I do not think I could very well purchase passage, either. And might not the Captain simply enslave me?"

There seemed sense in what Ute had said.

"Besides," had sniffed Ute, "my foster parents might not even be on the island, still."

This seemed possible, for the population of an exchange island, like Teletus, tends to be somewhat more transient than that of an established city, with a tradition of perhaps a thousand or more years.

"But," I had pressed, "perhaps you could find your way back somehow, and perhaps your foster parents still reside on Teletus."

If I were to go with Ute, I would surely prefer to go to an exchange island, with some of the amenities of civilization, rather than to a rude village south of the Vosk.

"Look at me!" had cried Ute, suddenly, to my astonishment, furious.

I was startled.

"My ears have been pierced!" she screamed.

I shrank back.

"They were kind to me!" she cried. "How could I go back and shame them? Should I present myself to them, as their daughter, with pierced ears?" she cried.

I could not understand Ute. She was Gorean.

She put down her head. "My ears have been pierced!" she wept. "My ears have been pierced!" She lifted her head to me. "I will hide myself in Rarir," she said.

I did not respond to her.

At any rate, Ute was adamant. She would seek the village of Rarir.

I kicked at the pebbles in the stream, from where I stood, in front of the ingress to the trap.

The silvery creature began to whip about the inclosure. It frightened me. Once its rough scales struck the front of my leg, above the ankle. I cried out. I closed my eyes, gritting my teeth, my fists clenched, my body contracted. When I dared to open my eyes again, the creature was again at the farther fence of wands, motionless, facing me.

I breathed a sigh of relief. It had not escaped.

If it had not been for Ute I do not think I would have survived.

I seemed so weak and frightened and helpless. Ute, though a small girl, seemed strong, and endlessly resourceful.

She had shown me what could be eaten, and what could not. It was she who had shown how the water trap might be built. She had also shown me how to make snares of binding fiber, bending down small branches, and making triggers of small twigs.

She had also shown me how, with binding fiber, a log and a stick trigger, to make a snare large enough to catch a tabuk, but we did not actually make such a snare. It might have attracted the attention of a huntsman, and provoked his curiosity. The smaller snares would be more easily overlooked. Further, it would have been difficult for Ute and I to have placed the log in such a snare, and, besides, without a knife, and wishing to move swiftly, tabuk would have been heavy game for us. She had also shown me how to make shelters of various sorts and use a small, curved stick for striking down birds and tiny animals. Ute taught me to find food where it would not have occurred to me to look for it. I relished the roots she taught me to dig for. But I was less eager to sample the small amphibians she caught in her hands or the fat, green insects she scooped from the inside of logs and from under overturned rocks.

"They can be eaten," she said.

I, however, contented myself with nuts and fruits, and roots, and water creatures which resembled those with which I was familiar, and, of course, the flesh of small birds and animals.

Perhaps the most extraordinary thing Ute did, to my mind, was, with sticks, a flat piece of wood and some binding fiber, make a small fire drill. How pleased I was when I saw the small, pointed stick whirling in its wooden pit, and saw the dried flakes of leaves suddenly redden and flash into a tiny flame, which we then fed with leaves and twigs, until it would burn sticks.

Over tiny fires, using rock-sharpened, green sticks, we roasted our catches.

We had seen no other human beings since our escape. We had slept by day in Ka-la-na thickets, and moved southwestward by night.

Ute had not wished to build fires, but I had insisted upon it.

We could not eat our catches raw.

"Tal," cried Ute, greeting me as a free person.

"Tal!" I cried, pleased, waving to her. I was very relieved that she had returned.

She had, thrust in her belt, the binding fiber she had used for snares. We always took it with us, of course, when we moved. Over her shoulder she had two small, furred animals, hideous forest urts, about the size of cats, and in her left hand she carried four small, green-and-yellow-plumaged birds.

Tonight we would feast.

I, too, had been successful.

"Ute," I cried, "I have caught a fish!"

"Good! cried Ute. "Bring it to the camp!"

"Ute!" I pleaded, anguished.

Ute laughed and threw her catch down on the bank. She waded into the trap. I remained where I was, blocking the exit to the trap.

Ute approached the creature very carefully, in order not to startle it.

It wavered slightly in the water.

Then, suddenly, very swiftly, Ute struck for it. It backed

into the fence of wands and she caught it there, against
the sticks, and, in a moment, it thrashing and squirming,
she lifted it from the water and carried it triumphantly to
the shore.

"Destroy the trap," said Ute.

Each time we moved from a thicket, if we had built such
a trap, we destroyed it. This, incidentally, is a standard
Gorean practice. He never leaves a trap set to which he
does not intend to return. The Goreans, often so cruel to one
another, tend to have an affection for wildlife and growing
things, which they regard as free, and thereby deserving of
great respect. This affection and respect, unfortunately, is
seldom extended to domestic animals, such as bosk and
slaves. The Gorean woodsman, it might be mentioned, before he will strike a tree with his ax, speaks to the tree,
begs its forgiveness and explains the use to which the wood
will be put. In our case, of course, aside from such general
considerations, we had a very special reason for destroying
the trap. It was a piece of evidence which might betray us,
which might set men upon our trail.

Ute waited sitting for me on the bank, while I pulled up
the sticks of the trap and cast them into the bushes.

I then helped her carry our catch, she bearing the fish,
and the small birds, to our camp.

"Clean the animals," said Ute.

I did not like her giving me orders.

"I do not want to," I said.

"Then build the fire," said Ute.

"You know I cannot manage the fire drill," I said, angrily. I had never been able to master it.

"Then," said Ute, "let us not make a fire."

"No," I said, "I cannot eat raw flesh! We must have a
fire!"

"It is dangerous," said Ute.

"Make a fire, Ute," I begged.

"Then clean the animals," she said.

"All right," I said. I hated that job. It was so dirty, so
sticky and slimy. Ute always wanted me to do it! Who was
she to give me orders? I did not like her. She was stupid.

She made grammatical mistakes in speaking her own language! I hated her.

With a sharp rock and a stick I started to work on the animals.

I no longer needed Ute. She had taught me probably as much as she could. I could now get along without her. Besides, she acted superior to me. I was an Earth girl, superior to Gorean girls! She acted like she was our leader. I had not told her she could be the leader! I hated her.

"What are you thinking of, El-in-or?" asked Ute.

"Elinor," I said, sharply.

"Elinor," said Ute.

"Nothing," I said.

"Oh," said Ute.

After I had worked for a while, Ute, taking up a rock and a stick, began to help me.

I did not thank her. She should have done the work herself. I had spent the day fishing. She had only roved about the thicket, hunting birds and checking her snares.

Ute began to hum.

"Why are you humming?" I asked her, irritated.

"Because I am happy," said Ute.

"Why are you happy?" I asked.

She looked at me, puzzled. "Because I am free," she said.

When we had cleaned the animals, and the birds, and the fish, which latter job I left to Ute, for I did not like to touch the creature, Ute bent over the fire drill.

"Hurry," I told her. I was hungry.

Ute worked for more than fifteen minutes, bowing the drill, sweating, her eyes fixed on that tiny, blackened pit in the wood.

"Hurry," I told her. "Hurry!"

Then, at last, a tiny flame appeared, eating at the flakes of dried leaves wedged about the pit.

In a few minutes, we had our fire.

Because we had more food than usual, we set up two small spits on forked sticks.

When the food was done, we removed it from the spits, placing it on leaves. I was terribly hungry. It was now

dark out, and the evening was chilly. It would be pleasant
to eat by the fire, and warm ourselves, while we enjoyed
our open-air repast.

"What are you doing, Ute!" I cried, seizing her wrist.

She looked at me, puzzled. "Putting out the fire," she
said.

"No," I cried.

"It is dangerous," she said.

"There is no one about," I said.

"It is dangerous," she repeated.

I had no wish to eat in the dark, nor to freeze. "Do
not put out the fire, Ute," I said. "It is all right."

Ute shook her head, undecided.

"Please!" I pressed.

"All right," smiled Ute.

But scarcely more than a Gorean Ihn had passed before
Ute, suddenly, with a look of terror in her eyes, began to
fling dirt on the fire.

"What are you doing!" I cried.

"Be quiet!" she whispered.

Then I heard, far overhead, in the darkness, the scream
of a tarn.

"It is a wild tarn," I said.

The fire was now out.

"We must leave now," said Ute, frightened.

"It is only a wild tarn," I insisted.

"I hope that is true," said Ute.

I felt a shiver course my spine.

Ute began to destroy, in the darkness, the small shelter
of sticks and leaves we had constructed.

"Bring what food you can," she said. "We must leave
now."

Angry, but frightened, I gathered what food I could find.

When she had finished with the shelter, Ute felt about
and, with her hands, scooped together the bones and en-
trails, the fur and scales, left over from our catch, and
buried them.

As well as she could, she destroyed all signs of our camp.

Then, moving swiftly through the darkness, I following, carrying what food I could, Ute fled our camp.

I followed her, hating her. I was afraid to be without her.

We moved southwestward through the great thicket, and then, finally came to its edge.

The night was dark.

Ute scrutinized the skies. We saw nothing. She listened for a long time. We heard nothing.

"You see, Ute," I said, irritated. "It was nothing."

"Perhaps," agreed Ute.

"I hear no more tarn screams," I told her.

"Perhaps they have dismounted," suggested Ute.

"It was only a wild tarn," I told her.

"I hope that that is true," she said.

Together, at the edge of the thicket, we ate the remains of our meal, which I had carried.

We wiped our hands on the grass, and threw the bones into the brush.

"Look!" whispered Ute.

Through the brush, some two hundred yards away, moving in the darkness, we saw two torches.

"Men," moaned Ute. "Men!"

From the thicket, running together, we fled southwestward.

By dawn we came to another large stand of Ka-la-na, in which we, wearily, concealed ourselves.

Four days later, in yet another thicket, one afternoon, Ute requested that I set one of our snares on a small game trail we had found earlier.

We had heard nothing more of pursuit. We had seen no more torches, following us in the night.

We had again escaped.

Swinging the loop of binding fiber, I walked along the trail.

There were small birds about, and I saw a scurrying

brush urt, flowers, even a lovely, yellowish Tabuk fawn. I crossed two tiny streams.

Suddenly I stopped, terrified.

I heard the sound of a man's voice. I slipped from the soft, gentle, green path between the trees and brush, and fell to my stomach, concealed among the brush and grasses.

They were not coming along the trail.

I inched forward, on my elbows and stomach, and then, through a tiny parting in brush, saw them.

My heart almost stopped.

They were in a small clearing. There were two tarns hobbled nearby. The men had made no fire. They were clad in leather, and armed. They were warriors, mercenaries. They seemed rough, cruel men. I recognized them. I had seen them as long ago as Targo's compound north of Laura. They were hirelings of Haakon of Skjern, his men.

"She is somewhere in here," one of the men told the other.

"If we had hunting sleen," said the other, "and could find her trail, we would have her in our bracelets before dusk."

"I hope she is red silk," said the other.

"If she is not when we apprehend her," said the other, "by the time we turn her over to Haakon she will be of the reddest of silks."

"Haakon might not be pleased," said the other.

The first laughed. "Haakon does not know which girl is red silk and which is white silk."

"That is true," grinned the other.

"Besides," pointed out the first, "do you really think Haakon expects us to return white silk girls to his chain?"

"Of course not," laughed the second, slapping his knee. "Of course not!"

"This one has led us a merry chase indeed," said the first man, grimly. "We will make her pay us back well for our time and trouble."

"But what if we do not catch her?" asked the second.

"She is indeed elusive," said the first man, "but we will catch her."

Lying on my stomach in the grass, listening, I moaned inwardly.

"She seems intelligent," said the second.

"Yet," pointed out the first, "we saw her fire."

"True," said the second, "though she seems clever, though she seems intelligent, though she has well eluded us this far, she yet built a fire."

The first smiled. "Any girl foolish enough to build a fire," he said, "will, sooner or later, be caught."

"What is our plan?" asked the second.

"We know that she had a fire," said the first. "One supposes she was cooking. If she was cooking, she must have caught birds or meat."

"At the edge of a thicket to the northeast, days ago," said the second man, "we found the bones of brush urts!"

"Yes," said the first man, "and, nearby, in this thicket, there is a small game trail."

"It is hard to hunt in a Ka-la-na thicket," said the second man.

"More importantly," said the first man, "brush urts tend to use such trails."

"Yes!" said the second.

"Sooner or later, it seems likely, does it not," asked the first, "that she will come to the trail, to hunt, or set a snare, or see if one is sprung."

"There may be other trails," pointed out the second man.

"If we do not catch her now," said the first man, spreading his hands, "we will catch her tomorrow or the day after."

On my stomach, carefully, silently, I began to back away. When I was several yards away, silently, bending over, noiselessly, I slipped away.

One thought was foremost in my mind. That I must find and warn Ute, that we might escape.

But then I stopped.

I crawled into some brush, frightened. They had always spoken only of "she." As far as they knew, there was but one girl to be caught.

I shook my head. No, I must not think such thoughts.

But the men frightened me. They were rough, cruel men, mercenaries, ruthless. I could not permit Elinor Brinton, the sensitive girl of Earth, to fall into the hands of such hardened brutes. I had heard them talk of what they would do to a girl, even though she might be white silk!

Ute had been a slave before.

No, I told myself, no! I must not think such thoughts.

I found myself getting up and, calmly, walking back toward our camp.

The men knew of only one girl. They thought there was only one of us.

I must not think such thoughts, I told myself.

Ute and I must escape.

I smiled.

Ute had thought she was my leader. She had dared to give me orders. She had commanded me, Elinor Brinton, though she was only an ignorant Gorean girl, had dared to act as the leader of a girl of Earth, and one such as I!

She would learn better.

No, I cried to myself, I must warn Ute! I must warn her!

I was now nearing our camp, walking casually.

I remembered clearly what the man had said. "If we do not catch her now," he had said, "we will catch her tomorrow, or the day after."

They had pursued us for days. They would not give up the chase. They would have us.

I smiled.

Or at least one of us.

Ute was stupid, she was ignorant, she was Gorean, she did not matter. She was a crude, simple girl. She made mistakes in speaking her own language. She did not have my fine mind, my sensitivity, my delicate nature, my cleverness. She was, I reminded myself, of low caste. She was less, far less, than I.

Besides, she had dared to treat me as her inferior, ordering me about, instructing me. I hated her! Pretty little Ute, whom men found so desirable! I hated her! I was more beautiful than she. Ute had been slave before. She could be slave again! I remembered she had once thonged me by the nose ring. I hated her. We would find out who was more clever. I hated her!

I threw the piece of binding fiber, which I had been carrying for the snare, which I had not set, into the brush.

"Greetings, Ute," said I, smiling.

"Tal, El-in-or," smiled Ute, looking up from her work. She was trying, with a pointed stick, to round a pit in a new board for a new fire drill. Usually, in our night journeys, we carried with us only the precious binding fiber. Accordingly, Ute often constructed a new drill.

"Oh, Ute," I said. "I set the snare far down the game trail. And as I was going away, I heard it spring and heard an animal."

"Good," said Ute. "What was it?"

"I don't know," I said. "I looked. I had not seen one like it before. It is some kind of brush urt, I think. It is very ugly."

"Why didn't you bring it back with you?" she asked.

"I did not want to touch it," I said.

"Oh, El-in-or!" laughed Ute. "You are so foolish!"

"Please get it, Ute," I begged. "I do not want to touch it. It is so ugly!"

"All right," said Ute. "I will get it." She returned to her work.

I cast a frightened glance backward, down the trail. "Hadn't you better hurry?" I asked.

"Why?" asked Ute.

"Might someone not find the snare?" I said.

Ute looked at me. "Yes," she said. "We must take it down quickly." She put aside her work and stood up.

"Show me where you put it," said Ute, starting off.

"No!" I cried.

She turned and looked at me.

"You can't miss it," I told her. "It is to the left. You could not miss it."

"All right," said Ute, and left the camp. My heart was pounding.

Stealthily, at a distance, I followed her. A short distance from the camp, I knelt down and picked up a heavy rock.

I hid in the brush beside the trail, clutching the rock.

Suddenly, some hundred yards away, I heard a man's shout.

My heart leaped. They had taken her!

But then I heard the shouts of another man, and then of both, and a crashing through brush.

To my dismay, terrified, frantic, her eyes wide, hands extended, fleet as a Tabuk, Ute was fleeing back down the trail.

"El-in-or," she cried. "Slavers! Run!"

"I know," I said.

She looked at me, startled.

I struck her suddenly in the side of the head with the stone.

They must find her, not me!

Ute, moaning, stunned, sank to her hands and knees, shaking her head.

I threw the rock down beside her. The men would assume she had fallen and struck her head.

Quickly I fled back into the brush and hid.

Ute struggled to her feet, but stumbled and fell again, moaning, to her hands and knees.

I saw them seize her.

She was still stunned, half conscious. While she was still on her hands and knees, they cut the camisk from her, discarding it. Then they threw her forward on her stomach, one pulling her wrists behind her back and binding them, the other crossing her ankles and lashing them together.

I was pleased. Ute had been taken.

I only feared that she might tell them that I was about. But somehow I knew that she would not. Ute was stupid. I knew she would not betray me.

I thus, cleverly, eluded my pursuers.

I would continue my journey to the village of Rarir, which I thought I might now be able to find. I could tell them, in that village, that I had been a friend of Ute's whom I hoped they would remember. They would befriend me. In time, I would use the help of the villagers to find my way to the exchange island of Teletus, where I could find, if all went well, Ute's foster parents. I had little doubt but what they would care for me, and be kind to me, for I had been a friend of Ute, their foster daughter, so long ago fallen slave on the journey to the Sardar. I could tell them, and would, that Ute had told me to find them, and had promised me that they would care for me. Ute and I had been desperately trying to reach them, I would tell them, only we had fallen in with slavers and, unfortunately, only I had escaped. Would they care for me? I had little doubt but what they would. I expected that they would beg me, in Ute's place, to permit myself to be adopted as their daughter.

I was much pleased.

I continued the journey toward Rarir.

I moved by night, and, by day, slept in Ka-la-na thickets.

I was stirring in my bed of soft grasses, hidden in such thicket, half asleep. I was drowsy. There were insects about. I had been well fed the night before, for I had stopped, hidden in the darkness, near a peasant village, where, from a pole, I had stolen a piece of drying meat, bosk flesh. It was far superior to what I had been able to snare.

I had not cooked my meat since Ute's capture. I was not confident of my ability to construct or use an efficient fire drill. More importantly, I knew that it was dangerous to make a fire. I had well learned this.

Mostly I ate fruits and nuts, and some roots. Occasionally I would supplement this diet with the raw flesh of small birds, or that of an occasional brush urt, which I would manage to snare. However, last night, and the night before, at another village, I had managed to steal meat. I had resolved that I would feed myself in this fashion. I was surely not tempted to sample the small amphibians or the loathesome, fat green insects Ute had called to my attention. They might have been a source of protein, but rather than touch such things to my lips I would have preferred to starve!

It was easier to steal meat, good bosk meat, from ignorant peasants!

I lay on my back, drowsy, looking up at the bright sky between the interlaced branches canopied over my head. The day was warm. I smiled.

Then, suddenly, far off, I became aware of a noise. It seemed like the shouting of men, and a clanging and beating of metals, as though pans or kettles might be being struck.

I did not much care for the noise.

In a few minutes it became clear that the sounds were becoming closer. I began to grow apprehensive.

In my camisk, I climbed to my feet, lifting my head.

There was a din, coming from the direction of the village, seeming to move towards me, gradually, through the thicket.

Irritated, I shrugged, and, picking up the fibers I had used for snares, began to move away from the din. I picked some fruit and nuts on the way.

The din seemed to be getting louder, which I did not care for. It was coming from behind me.

I walked before it.

It was not long before I realized that if I did not alter my direction I would have departed the vast thicket, in which I had taken refuge.

Accordingly I turned to my left, picking some fruit as I went.

Then, to my irritation, even closer, I heard the din, and now part of it seemed to be coming from before me.

I then became apprehensive and, half running, turned back the other direction.

I had run no more than two or three Ihn when it became clear to me that the din was now, too, coming from in front of me.

I turned again, this time frantically.

The din, the beating on pans and kettles, and the shouting, was now sweeping towards me, in a vast semicircle.

I suddenly realized I was being hunted!

Only from before me was there no sound. I was terrified. I began to run in that direction, toward the edge of the thicket, but then I was afraid. I would lose the cover of the thicket. Moreover, they might be driving me toward hunters, or nets! The silence terrified me as much as the din.

I must slip between their lines.

Some animals fled past me, away from the din, tabuk and brush urts.

Carefully, concealing myself as much as possible, I started back toward the din.

The din became loud, terrible, and the shouting. The noise, the knowledge that I was being hunted, made me suddenly feel irrational, driven. I wanted only to flee from the sound.

The din became insufferably loud.

I pressed toward it.

Then my heart sank!

There must have been two hundred or more peasants, men, children and women, all shouting, and beating on their kettles or pans. The women and children carried sticks and switches, the men spears, flails, forks and clubs.

They were too close together, there were too many of them!

A child saw me and he cried out and began to beat more loudly on his pan.

I turned and fled.

The din now became maddeningly pressing, intolerable, ringing in my brain, closing in on me.

I could do nothing but fly toward the silence.

Then, in the sunlight of the bright morning, late, almost at noon, I fled from the thicket, across the grass of the open field.

I ran irrationally, driven, terrified.

I kept running.

Then, exhausted, I looked back. The peasants had stopped at the edge of the Ka-la-na thicket, in their great numbers. They no longer shouted, they no longer beat on their pans.

I looked ahead of me. There was nothing. No strong peasant lads waited there, to run me down, to strip and bind me, and lead me, my neck roped, back to the village. There were no nets. There was nothing.

I cried out with joy and fled across the grasses.

They had wanted only to drive me from the thicket!

I was still free.

I stopped.

I stood in the bright, knee-high grasses of that wind-blown, flowing field. I felt the sun on my body, the grass touching my calves. My feet felt beneath them the black, warm, root-filled, living earth of Gor. The Ka-la-na thicket was yellow in the distance, the peasants standing at its edge, not moving. The sky was deep, and blue, and bright with sunlight. I inhaled the fresh, glorious air of the planet Gor. How beautiful it was!

The peasants did not pursue me.

I was free!

I put my head back and, standing feet spread, leaned backwards, with my hands spreading my hair in the wind. I felt the wind lift it. I was pleased.

I was free!

Suddenly my hand flew before my mouth. High, lofty, small in the vertical depths of that glorious sky, there was a speck. I shook my head, no! No!

I looked back toward the peasants. They had not moved.

I knelt down on one knee in the grasses, my eyes fixed on the speck.

It was circling.

I saw it far overhead, first to my right, and then behind me, and then to my left, and then before me.

I cried out with misery.

I knew myself, small on the grasses, far below, to be the center of that circle.

I began to run, madly, frantically across the grasses.

I stopped, and turned, and looked back and upward. I cried out with misery. I saw the bird turn, swirling in the sky. I saw the sun, for a brief instant, flash from the helmet of its rider. The bird had wheeled in my direction. It was now screaming, descending, wings beating, streaking towards me.

I screamed and began to run, madly, irrationally, across the grasses.

I heard the scream of the bird behind me, and the beating of its great wings, closer and closer!

I stumbled, screaming, then running again. I might have been a golden-pelted tabuk, but I was a girl!

The scream of the bird deafened me and its wings broke like thunder about my ears.

The shadow streaked past me.

The leather loop dropped about my body. In an instant it had jerked tight, pinning my arms helplessly to my sides, and I felt my body, my back almost broken, jerked from the grass. The grass rushed swiftly past below me, and I could not touch it with my feet, and then it fled from me, dropping way, and then suddenly, in the rushing air, as I twisted and turned, buffeted in the blasts of wind, a prisoner of the forces, the physics, of the braided leather rope and the accelerations and attitudes, it seemed the sky was below me and the grass overhead, and then I lost my breath, as the tarn began to climb, and I gasped, the grass and the sky, and the horizon, now spinning crazily, first one above, then the other, and the horizon turning, spinning, and I screamed, crying out, my arms pinned, my hands helpless, unable to hold the rope, and I felt it slip an inch on my body, and I saw the earth now below, so far below, and the Ka-la-na thicket in the distance, like a patch of foliage on a lawn, and I swung, wildly, helplessly, the captive of that taut, slender leather strand by which I was bound, forty feet below the tarn, now hundreds of feet above the earth below me.

The rope slipped another quarter of an inch on my body, and I screamed!

Then the rope, pressing itself cruelly into my arms and body, lodged itself firmly.

It slipped no more.

I was effectively imprisoned by the weight of my own body. I feared only that the rope might break.

The tarn then began to wheel, and soar, and I swung below it, dangling and bound, hundreds of feet above the grasses below.

It was turning back toward the Ka-la-na thicket, now remote in the distance, far below.

I felt myself being pulled, foot by foot, upward. I felt the rope press even more cruelly into my body, and I felt myself, foot by foot, lifted. My hands felt so helpless. I wanted to clutch the rope, to hold it! But I could not.

Then, looking up, I saw the great talons of the tarn, held in against its body, above me. They were huge, curved and sharp.

I felt my body dragged against the side of the bird, and then I felt my shoulder rub against the metal and leather of the saddle, and a man's leg.

Then he held me in his arms. I could not move, so terrified I was.

I saw his eyes, through the apertures in his helmet. They seemed amused. I looked away.

He laughed.

It was a great, raw laugh, that of a tarnsman. I shuddered.

He removed the tarn rope from my body. On the saddle before him, facing him, I clung about his neck, terrified that I might fall. He coiled the tarn rope, and fastened it at the side of the saddle.

He then removed his tarn knife from his belt.

I felt the knife between the camisk and the binding fiber that belted it on my body. There was a movement of the knife and the binding fiber whipped from my body and, in the rushing wind, the camisk began to tug, snapping away from me, and then it was high, about my throat, pulling at my neck, flapping and snapping. He lifted it over my head and it flew behind the tarn. I felt against my body his leather, the buckle of his tarn belt. My cheek lay against the metal of his helmet. My hair streaked in the wind.

With his two hands he disengaged my arms from his neck.

"Lie before me, on your back," he said, "and cross your wrists and ankles."

Terribly afraid of falling, I did so.

He bent across my body and I felt my crossed wrists lashed to a saddle ring. He then bent to the other side and, in moments, I felt my crossed ankles lashed to another ring.

I lay there on my back before him, my body a bow, bound helplessly across his saddle.

He slapped my belly twice.

He then laughed another great laugh, that great raw laugh, that of a tarnsman, who has his prize bound helpless before him.

I cursed my misfortune, that I had been driven from the thicket when a tarnsman had been in the sky!

I pulled at my bound wrists, and ankles, fastened to the rings.

I turned my head to one side and wept.

I had again fallen captive.

What an incredible misfortune that I had been driven from the thicket just at the moment when a tarnsman had been in the sky!

I then became aware that the tarn was circling, and descending.

It was hard to breathe. I could see little but the sky, and the clouds.

Then, with a jolt to my back, and with a scattering of dust and a snapping of wings, the tarn alit.

I became aware, as well as I could see, that we stood in the midst of a clearing in a peasant village. I could see, my head hanging down, in the distance a great thicket of Ka-la-na. Peasants were crowding about. Turning my head to one side, I could see men with spears and flails, in peasant tunics. Women and children, too, in the dusty square crowded about. I heard some clanging of pans. I saw sticks in the hands of some of the children.

"I see you have her, Warrior," said a large peasant, bearded, in a rough tunic of rep cloth.

I trembled.

"You flushed her well into the field," said the warrior. "My thanks."

I groaned with misery.

"It is little enough for the many services you have rendered us," said the man.

"She stole meat from us last night," said a man.

"Yes," said another, "and before that, the night before, from the village of Rorus."

"Give her to us, Warrior," said a man, "for a quarter of an Ahn, for a switching."

The warrior laughed. I trembled.

"There are men of Rorus here, too," said the man. "They, too, would like to punish her. Give her to us for a quarter of an Ahn, that we may switch her."

Bound, I trembled.

"Let us switch her," cried the women and the children. "Let us switch her!"

Upside down, fastened in the straps, I shook with fear.

"What is the cost of the meat?" inquired the warrior.

The people were silent.

From a pouch he threw a coin to a man of the village, and another to another man, doubtless one of the other village, called Rorus.

"Thank you, Warrior," they cried. "Our thanks!"

"Her first beating," said the warrior, in his strong voice, "is mine to bestow!"

There was much laughter. I pulled helplessly at the straps.

He raised his hand to the crowd. "I wish you well," he shouted.

"I wish you well!" they cried.

I felt the one-strap of the tarn harness jerk tight across my body, and, suddenly, taking my breath away, the great bird screamed and began to beat its wings, and the saddle pressed up against my back, and I, upside down, saw the conical huts of the peasants drop away below us, and the bird, stroke by violent, majestic stroke, its head forward, was climbing toward the clouds.

The tarn streaked through the skies. I could feel the wind on my body. I lay bound over the saddle. My hair fled back in the wind, across his left thigh. I could scarcely move my wrists and ankles. He had lashed them securely. He was incredibly strong. Never before, even in the hut, had I been tied more tightly, more helplessly. I did not know where we were going, or even in what direction we were flying. I knew only that I, Elinor Brinton, a captured girl, was being carried helplessly, cruelly bound, tightly and uncompromisingly secured, into slavery.

It is now clear to me that we were flying southeastward.

Shortly after we had attained the skies, and he had set his direction, he turned me on my flank, facing him, and, with the fingers of his right hand, fingered my brand. "Only a Kajira," he said. Then, with the palm of his hand he thrust me back on my back.

In a moment or two, he reached down and took my hair, lifting my head, painfully, and turning it from side to side. "Your ears are pierced," he said. Then he dropped my head back against the side of the saddle.

I groaned, helplessly.

The tarn streaked on.

Once, he said to me, "We are crossing the Vosk."

I knew then we were within the territory of Ar, and must be high over the Margin of Desolation, a barren area, now recovering itself, which, years ago, had been cleared and devastated, that the northern fields of Ar by such a natural barrier, by such a wall of hunger and thirst, might be protected, presumably from invasion from the north or, more likely, from the incursions of Vosk pirates. In the reign of Marlenus, prior to his exile, and later, after his restoration, the Margin of Desolation had been deliberately left untended, that it might recover. Marlenus had set a swift fleet of light, Vosk galleys to clear the river waters adjoining his Ubarate of pirates. They had been successful, or muchly so. Seldom did Vosk pirates ply their trade where the Vosk bordered the regions of Ar. Other cities, to the north, of course, looked with apprehension on Marlenus' permitting the Margin of Desolation to recover its fertility and shade. He may have been only intending to extend the arable lands of Ar. On the other hand, under Marlenus, it became clear that Ar no longer feared for her borders. Also, the ambition of Marlenus, the Ubar of Ar, said to be the Ubar of Ubars, was well known. If it was now possible, or soon would be possible, to bring a land army easily southward to Ar, once the Vosk was traversed, by the same token, it would be similarly possible for Ar to bring, swiftly a considerable force of men northward, to the very shore of the Vosk. Of tradition, the northern shore of the Vosk was disputed by various cities. Ar, among others, had made her claims.

Ahn after Ahn, the tarn flew.

He did not unbind me to feed me.

"Open your mouth," he said.

He thrust yellow Sa-Tarna bread into my mouth. I chewed the bread and, with difficulty, swallowed it. He then, with his tarn knife, from a piece of raw bosk meat, cut four small pieces of meat, which he placed in my mouth. "Feed," he said. I chewed the meat, eyes closed, swallowing it. "Drink," he said. He thrust the horn nozzle of a leather bota of water between my teeth. I almost choked. He withdrew the nozzle and capped the bota, replacing it in his saddle pack. I closed my eyes, miserable. I had been fed and watered.

The tarn flew on.

After a time I looked up at the warrior who had captured me.

He seemed broad chested, and broad shouldered. He had a large head, muchly concealed within the war helmet. He carried his head proudly. His arms were strong, muscular and bronzed. His hands were large, and rough, fit for weapons. He wore scarlet leather. His helmet, with its "Y"-like aperture, was gray. Neither his leather nor his helmet were distinguished by insignia. I supposed then, that he must be a mercenary, or an outlaw.

To have been taken by such a man, I had no idea what my fate would be.

There seemed something familiar about the strong figure, before whom I was bound.

Somehow he frightened me. I felt I had known him, or met him before.

Perhaps in Laura, near the compound of Targo!

"Are you," I asked, trembling, "a hireling of Haakon of Skjern?"

"No," he said.

"Will you—" I asked, "will you keep me for yourself?" I shuddered.

"A smelly, dirty little Kajira, with pierced ears, who steals meat from peasant villages?" he asked.

I groaned.

"I would not even put you with my women," he said.

I closed my eyes.

I realized then that such a warrior had undoubtedly captured many women, that many beauties, both slave and free, before me, and doubtless after me, would, as bound prizes, helplessly grace his saddle. Among such riches, I, Elinor Brinton, realized that to such a man, a warrior, a tarnsman among tarnsmen, I was of little account, only another girl and perhaps a poor sort of one at that. He had little more interest in me than in a piece of meat, which he had captured and tied.

"You should be sold to a peddler," he said. "Or I should have left you in the peasant village. Peasants know well how to treat thieving wenches."

"Please sell me in Ar," I begged. "I am white silk."

He looked at me. I could see the mouth grinning. I shuddered.

"You are unworthy of being sold in Ar," he said. "Perhaps you might be sold at a smaller town, a village, or a border outpost."

"Please," I begged.

"I will dispose of you as I wish," he said. "Now be silent on the matter."

I closed my eyes.

When I opened them, I saw him regarding me. He was grinning.

"I am white silk!" I cried. "I will bring a higher price if I am sold white silk!"

"You mistake me, Lady," said he, courteously, "if you think that I am interested only in gold."

"No!" I cried. "No!"

He bent to undo the lashings at my ankles.

I screamed, helplessly.

Suddenly, before he had even touched the lashings at my ankles, he turned about, abruptly, in the saddle.

A crossbow bolt flashed by, like a swift, hissing needle in the sky.

In one moment, as I screamed, terrified, thrown rudely against my bonds, he had jerked his shield from the saddle straps and wheeled the tarn, with a cry of rage, a strange war cry, to face his foe.

He was met with another war cry, and suddenly, only feet from us, another tarn streaked past, and I heard the forcible, tearing scrape of a broad, bronze spear blade, its blow turned, sliding across the metal-bound, layered, bosk-hide shield of my captor.

The other tarn streaked away, and its rider, standing in his stirrups, braced in the saddle, held to it by the broad safety strap, was redrawing his crossbow, a quarrel held in his teeth.

My captor attacked, giving him no instant in which to set again his bow.

When only yards separated us, the other man flung away his bow and quarrel, seizing up his shield. My captor, standing in his stirrups, flung his own great spear. It struck the other's shield, piercing it. If the other man had not been fastened in his saddle by the great strap the force of my captor's blow would have struck him from the saddle. As it was, it spun him, tearing the shield from his arm.

He cursed. "For Skjern!" he cried.

The two tarns wheeled again, for another passage.

Again the other's spear struck, and again the blow was countered by my captor's shield. I again heard the terrible, startling scrape of the spear blade diverted by the seven-layered, metal-bound boskhide shield. Twice more the attacker pressed in, and each time, again, the shield turned the blow, once but inches from my body. My captor was trying to close with him, to bring him within the range of his own steel, his now-drawn, swift, unadorned blade.

Again the spear struck, but this time my captor took the point in the shield. I, bound, saw, suddenly, the bronze point, a foot of it, inches from my face, explode through the hide. I screamed. My captor then wheeled away, the other, his blade now drawn, trying to press close. My captor had wished to rid his enemy of the spear, because of its reach, but, to do so, his own defense was impaired. With incredible strength, his sword dangling from its wrist strap, commonly used by tarnsmen in flight, I saw him withdraw the spear from the shield, but at the same time the other's tarn struck ours, and his blade, flashing downwards, struck the heavy shaft of the spear, splintering it, half severing it. He struck again and the spear shaft, with a scattering of wood, split apart. My captor now thrust his shield before him, and over my body. I heard the blade of the other strike twice, ringing on the metal hoops of the shield that guarded me. Then my captor again had his sword in his grip, but the other dragged his tarn upward, cursing, and its long, curved talons raked downwards, clutching for us. I heard the talons tear across the shield. My captor was thrusting upward, to keep the bird away. Then its talons locked over the shield and it smote its wings, ripping the shield straps, half tearing my captor from the saddle, and the tarn was away, the shield then dropping like a penny, turning, toward the field below.

"Yield her!" I heard the cry.

"Her price is steel!" was the answer that met the attacker.

Bound, I screamed, helplessly.

Then the tarns swooped together again, side by side, saddle to saddle, while blades flashed over my head, in a swift dialogue of steel, debating my possession.

I screamed.

The tarns then, rearing up in the sky, facing one another, began to tear at one another with their beaks and talons, and then, talons locked, they began, beaks snapping and tearing, to twist and roll, turning, locked together, falling, climbing, tumbling, wings beating, screaming in rage.

I was thrown one way and the other, violently, helplessly. Sometimes it seemed I was standing as the tarn would veer, or hanging head downwards as it would veer, turning wildly, in another direction. When it spun onto its back, tearing upwards at its foe, I hung stomach downwards, my full weight on the lashings, seeing in terror the earth hundreds of feet below.

The men fought to regain control of their mounts.

And then again, saddle to saddle, they fought, and once more steel flashed about my face and body. My ears, had they been tongues, would have screamed for mercy. Sparks from the steel stung my body.

Then, suddenly, with a cry of rage, of frustration, the blade of the other struck downwards toward my face. My captor's steel interposed itself. I saw the broad blade of his sword but an inch from my face, for one terrifying instant of immobility, the other's blade, edge downward, resting on it, stopped. The blow would have cut my face in two.

There was blood on my face. I did not know whose it was, even if it might be mine.

"Sleen!" cried my captor. "I have played with you enough."

Once more, over my head, there was a flash of steel, and I heard a cry of pain, and then suddenly the other tarn veered sharply away, and I saw its rider, clutching his shoulder, reeling in the saddle.

His tarn spun crazily, and then, a hundred yards away, to one side and below us, turned and fled.

My captor did not pursue him.

I looked up at my captor, the tarnsman whose lashings bound me.

I still lay before him, over the saddle, his.

He looked down upon me, and laughed.

I turned my head away.

He turned his tarn and we continued our journey. I had seen that his left arm, high, above the elbow, about two inches below the shoulder, had been cut. It had been blood from this cut which had struck my face.

Soon, unable to resist, I turned again, in my bonds, to look upon my captor.

The cut was not serious.

It had already stopped bleeding, the fierce wind having clotted the blood in a ragged line. On the left side of his arm, running from the wound, there were several almost horizontal, reddish lines, where, but moments before, tiny trickles of blood, unable to flow downward, had been whipped backward by the wind.

He saw me looking at him, and grinned.

I looked up at the sky. It was very blue, and there were white clouds.

"That was your friend," he said.

I looked at him.

"Haakon of Skjern," he said.

He looked down upon me.

I was frightened.

"How is it you know of Haakon of Skjern?" he asked.

"I was his preferred slave," I said. "I fled."

We flew on, not speaking.

Then, after perhaps a quarter of an Ahn, I asked, "May a girl speak?"

"Yes," he said.

"To be the preferred slave of a man such as Haakon of Skjern, who is rich and powerful, you must understand that I am unusual, quite beautiful and skilled."

"I see," he said.

"Accordingly," I said, "I should be sold in Ar. And, further, since I am white silk, I should not be used. My price will be higher if I am sold white silk."

"It is unusual, I would suppose," said the man, "for the preferred slave of a man such as Haakon of Skjern to be white silk."

I reddened, all of me, before him.

"Say to me the alphabet," he said.

I did not know the Gorean alphabet. I could not read. Elinor Brinton, on Gor, was ignorant and illiterate.

"I do not know the alphabet," I confessed.

"An illiterate slave girl," said the man. "Further, your accent marks you as barbarian."

"But I am trained!" I cried.

"I know," he said, "in the pens of Ko-ro-ba."

I looked at him, dumbfounded.

"Further," he said, "you have never belonged to Haakon of Skjern."

"Oh yes!" I cried. "I did!"

His eyes became suddenly hard. "Haakon of Skjern is my enemy," he said. "If you were truly his preferred slave, it is your misfortune to have fallen into my hands. I shall have much sport with you."

"I lied," I whispered. "I lied."

"Now you lie," he said, sternly, "to save your flesh from the irons and the whips."

"No!" I cried.

"On the other hand," he said, "if you were indeed his preferred slave, doubtless you would bring a high price in Ar, and would be much bid for by rich gentlemen."

I was in anguish. "Warrior," I said, "I was truly, I confess, the favored slave of Haakon of Skjern, but I fled from him, so do not be cruel to me!"

"What is the fate of a slave girl who lies?" he asked me.

"Whatever the master wishes," I whispered.

"What would you do if one of your slaves lied?" he asked.

"I—I would beat her," I said.

"Excellent," he said. Then he looked down at me. His eyes were not pleasant. "What is the name of the lieutenant of Haakon of Skjern?" he asked.

I writhed in the lashings. "Do not beat me!" I begged. "Do not beat me!"

He laughed.

"You are El-in-or," he said, "who was the slave of Targo, of the Village of Clearus, in the realm of Tor. In the pens it was well known that you did not clean your cage, and that you were a liar and a thief." He slapped my belly. "Yes," he said, "I have quite a catch here. What could it be about you that I could have found of interest?"

"You have seen me before?" I asked.

"Yes," he said.

"My beauty?" I asked.

He laughed. "There are many beautiful women," he said.
I felt weak before him.

"Then," I whispered, "it is your intention to put me in your collar?"

"Yes," he said.

I closed my eyes. I knew then that I, Elinor Brinton, of Earth, would wear the degrading, locked metal collar of a Gorean slave girl, this man's, the collar of this brute who had captured me, and that I, Elinor Brinton, though once a free human female of Earth, would soon belong to him, totally, by all the rights and laws of Gor. I would be completely his, to do with as he pleased. I would be his female slave.

I looked again upon him. How strong he seemed.

"You sought me?" I asked.

"Yes," he said. He grinned down upon me. "I have hunted you for days."

I turned my head to the side in misery. Even when I had thought myself most free, after the escape from Targo, after betraying Ute, and escaping in the Ka-la-na thicket, this beast, with his laugh, his leather rope, and his slave collar, had been upon my trail. He had marked me for his collar, and his pleasure.

How could I, a mere girl, have hoped to elude him, such a man, such a huntsman?

"You saw me in the pens of Ko-ro-ba?" I asked.

"Yes," he said.

"Who are you?" I asked.

"Do you not know me?" he asked.

"No," I said, turning to face him.

He, with his two hands, removed his helmet.

"I do not know you," I whispered.

I was terribly frightened. I had not understood his face could be so strong. He was powerful. He had a large head. The eyes were darkly fierce, his hair a pelt of shaggy sable.

I cried out with misery that I had fallen to such a man.

He laughed. The teeth in his darkly tanned, wind-burned face seemed large and white, and strong.

I trembled.

I feared what they would feel like on my body.

I felt again weak. I felt like a golden-pelted tabuk, lying between the paws of the black-maned mountain larl.

I moaned with misery, for suddenly I understood the foolishness of my fantasies in the pens of Ko-ro-ba, and in the caravan of Targo, that I would conquer, that I might, by the withholding of my favors, or the fervor of my favors, reduce a master to bondage, turning him into a needful slave desperate for my smiles and pliant to my will. I realized with a blaze of misery, and self-pity, that to such a man it was only I who could be the slave. He was totally, and utterly masculine, and before him I could be only totally and utterly feminine. I had no choice. My will was helpless. I suppose that a woman, like a man, has buried instincts, of which they may not even become aware, but these instincts lie within them, dispositions to respond, dispositions locked into the very genetic codes of her being, instincts awaiting only the proper stimulus situation to be elicited and emerge, overpoweringly, irresistibly, sweeping her, perhaps to her astonishment and horror, in a biological flood to her destiny, a destiny once triggered as incontrovertible and uncontrollable as the secretion of her glands and the mad beating of her heart.

I knew then that he was dominant over me. This had nothing to do with the fact that I lay stripped before him, wrists and ankles lashed, his prisoner. It had to do with the fact that he was totally masculine, and in the presense of such a stimulus, my body would permit me to be only totally feminine. I wished that he had been one of the weak men of Earth, trained in feminine values, and not a Gorean male.

I felt a mad impulse to beg him to use me.

"So you do not recognize me?" he laughed.

"No," I whispered.

He fastened his helmet to the side of the saddle and, from his saddle pack, withdrew a roll of leather. He wrapped this about his head, covering his left eye.

I remembered then, the tall figure in the blue and yellow silk, with the leather covering one eye.

"Soron of Ar!" I cried.

He smiled, removing the leather, replacing it in the saddle pack.

"You are the Slaver, Soron of Ar!" I said.

I recalled I had knelt before him, as a slave girl, and he had forced me to do it twice, saying "Buy me, Master." It had only been to me that he had said, curtly, "No," so offending me! And he had looked at me, afterward, and I had tossed my head and looked angrily away, but when I had looked again, he was still observing me, nude, standing on the straw of the slave cage, and I had felt vulnerable, and frightened.

And I remembered how, on the night before we left the pens of Ko-ro-ba, I had dreamed of him and had awakened in terror. "Purchase me!" I had begged, in the dream, "Purchase me!" "No," he had said. Then he had captured me. I had awakened, crying out.

Now I lay before him, in reality, fully captured, his, his helpless, bound prisoner.

"When first I saw you," said my captor, "I decided I would have you. When first you knelt before me, and said "Buy me, Master," I resolved to own you. Then, later, when I looked upon you and you tossed your head and angrily looked away, I knew I would not rest until you were mine." He smiled. "You will pay well for that snub, my dear," he said.

"What are you going to do with me?" I whispered.

He shrugged. "I shall keep you for a time, I suppose," he said, "for my interest and sport, and then, when I weary of you, dispose of you."

"Sell me in Ar," I begged.

"I think rather," said he, "I will give you to a village of peasants."

I remembered the peasants, with their switches and sticks. I trembled. I knew, too, that such men often used girls, with the bosk, to pull plows, under whips. At night, unclothed, when not being used, they were commonly chained in a straw kennel with a dirt floor.

"I am worth gold," I said. "Sell me in Ar!"

"I will dispose of you as I please," he said.

"Yes, Warrior," I said.

I looked again up at him.

"Why did you not buy me from Targo?" I inquired.

He looked down at me. "I do not buy women," he said.

"But you are a slaver!" I said.

"No," he said.

"Yes," I cried. "You are Soron of Ar, the Slaver."

"Soron of Ar," he said, "does not exist."

I looked at him with horror.

"Who are you?" I asked.

I shall never forget the words he spoke, which so terrorized me.

"Lo Rask," said he, "Rarius. Civitatis Trevis."

"I am Rask," he said, "of the caste of warriors, of the city of Treve."

14   I MUST SUBMIT

THIS WAS NOW MY SECOND DAY in the secret war camp of Rask of Treve.

When his tarn had dropped, wings beating, into the clearing among the tents, they ringed with a palisade of sharpened logs, some twelve feet high, there had been much shouting, much welcome.

Rask of Treve was popular with his men.

I saw, too, among the warriors, slave girls, collared, in brief rep-cloth tunics. They, too, seemed pleased. Their eyes shone. They crowded near.

Laughing, raising his hands, Rask of Treve acknowledged the greetings of his camp.

I could smell roast bosk. It was in the late afternoon.

He untied my ankles from the right-hand saddle ring. He then unbound the strap that lashed my wrists to the left-hand saddle ring, but he did not untie my wrists themselves. My hands, then, were still bound, before my body. He then took me lightly in his arms and slid from the back of the tarn. He set me on my feet at the side of the saddle. He did not throw me to my belly or put his foot on the back of my neck, or force me to kneel.

I dared not look at him.

"A pretty one," said a voice. It was a woman's voice. She was incredibly beautiful. She wore a collar. Her garment was white, and came to her ankles, in classic folds. She did not wear the brief work tunic of the other girls. I gathered she was high girl in the camp and that I, and the other girls, would have to obey her. It is not uncommon, where several girls are concerned, to put a woman over them.

267

Men do not care to direct us in our small tasks. They only wish to see that they are done.

I hated men!

"Kneel," said the woman.

I did so.

Some of the men murmured appreciatively.

"I see she is trained," said the woman.

I reddened. I hated men! But my body, subconsciously, had been trained to be attractive to them.

"She is a pleasure slave," said Rask of Treve, "though of a poor sort. Her name is El-in-or. Also, she is a sly girl, and a liar and a thief."

I was furious.

The woman took my head in her hands, and turned it from side to side. "Her ears are pierced," she said, in irritation.

Some of the men laughed. I did not care for their laughter. It frightened me.

I gathered that, because my ears were pierced, they would feel free to do anything they pleased with me.

"Men are beasts," said the woman.

Rask of Treve threw back his great head, like the head of a larl, and laughed.

"And you, Handsome Rask," said she, "are the greatest of the beasts."

How bold she was! Would she not be beaten?

Rask laughed again, and wiped his face with the back of his right hand.

The woman was again looking at me. "So, Pretty One, you are a liar and a thief?" she asked.

I put my head down, swiftly. I could not look her in the face.

"Regard me," she said.

I lifted my head, frightened, and looked at her.

"Is it your intention to lie and steal in this camp?" she asked.

I shook my head fiercely, negatively.

The men laughed.

"If you do," she said, "you will be punished, and prompt-ly, and your punishment will not be pleasant."

"You will be beaten," said one of the girls nearby, her eyes wide, "and put in the slave box!"

This news, whatever it meant, did not much reassure me.

"No, Mistress," I cried, "I will not lie and steal."

"Good," she said.

"Yes, Mistress," I said.

"She is dirty and she smells," said Rask of Treve. "Clean her and groom her."

"Is it your intention to put her in your collar," asked the woman.

There was a pause. I put my head down. "Yes," I heard Rask of Treve say.

He then turned away, and, with him, the others.

"Come with me to the tent of the women," said the wom-an.

I arose and, wrists bound, followed her to the women's tent.

The slave girl, with a touch of her finger, put perfume behind my ears.

It was now the morning of my second day in the war camp of Rask of Treve.

This was the day of my collaring.

I was not permitted cosmetics.

Kneeling within, slave girls preparing me, I looked through the tied-back opening of the tent of the women. Outside, I could see men, and girls, passing back and forth. The day was sunny and warm. There were soft breezes.

Today Elinor Brinton would be collared.

I had been coached in the simple collaring ceremony of Treve. Ena, the high girl, who wore the garment of white, had not been much pleased that I did not have a caste, and could not claim a familiar city as my place of origin.

"But it cannot be helped," she said.

Accordingly, it had been decided that I should identify myself by my actual city, and by my barbarian title and name. In the ceremony then I should refer to myself as

Miss Elinor Brinton of New York City. I smiled to myself. I wondered how often, on this rude world, I would have the opportunity to so refer to myself. The proud Miss Elinor Brinton, of New York City, seemed so far away from me. And yet I knew she was not. I was she. Miss Elinor Brinton, incredibly, uncomprehensibly, found herself kneeling in a barbarian tent, on a distant world, myself, being prepared for her collaring. The fact that New York City was of Earth, and that Treve was of Gor, would not even enter into the ceremony. Scarcely anything would enter into the ceremony save that I was female, and he was male, and that I would wear his collar.

Yesterday, by slave girls, under the direction of Ena, who was high girl, I had been washed and combed, and then fed. The food had been good, bread and bosk meat, roasted, and cheese, and larma fruit. I, famished from my trials in the wilderness, had fed well. I had even been given a swallow of Ka-la-na wine, which exquisite beverage I had not tasted since the time of my capture, long ago, by Verna outside of Targo's compound.

I had been frightened, but I had been well treated. I had not dared to speak.

After I had been washed and combed, and fed, Ena had said to me, "You have the freedom of the camp, if you wish."

I had been startled. I had expected to be close-chained. She seemed amused, regarding my astonishment.

"You will not escape," she smiled.

"No, Mistress," I said.

Then I looked down. I did not wish to leave the women's tent.

Ena went to a chest, opened it, and drew forth a folded piece of striped rep-cloth, a rectangle some two and a half by four feet.

"Stand," she said.

I did so.

"Lift your arms," she said.

I did so, and to my pleasure, she wrapped the piece of cloth about me, snugly, and fastened it with a pin behind my right shoulder blade. She then fastened it again, with another pin, behind my right hip.

"Lower your arms," she said.

I did so, and stood straight before her.

"You are pretty," she said. "Now run along and see the camp."

"Thank you, Mistress," I cried, and turned, and sped from the tent.

I wandered about the camp. It was a war camp, lying in a remote, hilly area, covered with trees. I supposed it to be somewhere in the realm of Ar, perhaps to its north-east, among the foothills of the Voltai range. It was a typical Gorean war camp, though small. It had its compound where tarns were hobbled, and its cooking and washing sheds. There were many warriors about, perhaps a hundred or more, the men of Rask of Treve, and perhaps some twenty girls, lovely ones, in brief work tunics, busying themselves with their tasks, cooking, cleaning leather, polishing shields. Treve, I knew, was, nominally, at war with several cities. Strife is common among the Gorean cities, each tending to be belligerent and suspicious of others. Rask of Treve, in his way, as other raiders of Treve, carried the war to the enemy. Earlier, I knew, he had despoiled the fields and attacked the caravans of Ko-ro-ba. He was now in the realm of Ar. He was a bold tarnsman indeed. I expected Marlenus of Ar, its Ubar, said to be the Ubar of Ubars, would give much to know the location of this small, palisaded camp. I enjoyed the smells of the camp, and its sounds. I watched two warriors practicing with their swift, short blades on a square of sand. The ringing of the metal excited and frightened me, the swiftness and cruelty of it. How brave men must be, I thought, to stand so to one another, so close, in combat so near, face to face, wrist to wrist, eye to eye, short, vicious, sharpened ringing blade to short, vicious, sharpened ringing blade. I could not have done this. I would have cried out and fled. What could a woman be but the prize of such men? For a moment I wished myself back on Earth where there was little for a man to do which could not be done as well, or better, by a woman. But then, as I watched the

warriors at their practice, something deep in me did not
wish this. Something deep in me, primitive, helpless, and
vulnerable, rejoiced that I stood not on Earth, but on Gor,
where there were such men. Suddenly my legs felt very bare,
and my arms. I was suddenly frightened. What if they should
finish their sport, and turn to look upon me, and command
me to serve them? Would I not, as a woman, have to give
them immediate response? Could I have helped myself, kept
myself from yielding immediately and completely to them?
When such men command, what could a woman do?

"Ho!" cried one of the warriors, and their exercises were
finished.

I turned and fled away.

I went to examine the palisade about the camp. It was
some twelve feet high and of sharpened logs.

I traced its interior perimeter.

I put my fingers and hands on the logs, which had been
smoothed, and were closely fitted together. I looked up at
the points, so far above my head. I could not have scaled
the wall. I was closed within.

I continued to walk about the inside wall. I avoided this
only where the tarn compound adjoined it.

Soon I had arrived at the gate.

It, too, was of logs, though here they were separated
somewhat. It was a double gate, with, in effect, log bars.
It was shut, two beams in brackets, chained, locking it.
To my surprise I saw that there was another gate, though
of solid logs, beyond that one, and that the camp was
ringed, actually, with a double palisade. The exterior palisade
had a catwalk, for defending the wall. The interior palisade,
on the side of the camp, was without a catwalk. I was
angry. The exterior wall permitted them defense. The interior wall, high and smooth, a quite effective barrier, served
well to keep their slaves within. I was furious.

"You will not escape," had said Ena.

"Girls may not linger by the gate," said a guard.

"Yes, Master," I said, and turned away.

How furious I was!

I continued to walk about the wall. At one point I found

a tiny door, no more than eighteen inches in height. It was such that one man, at a time, could crawl through it. And it, too, was secured, fastened shut with two heavy chains and locks. And it, too, was guarded.

I saw that I could not, even by standing on the chains, remotely approach the top of the palisade. I imagined myself standing on my toes and stretching my arms and fingers. My fingers would have still been several feet beneath the points. It was so futile!

I was well imprisoned within.

"Move on, Girl," said the guard.

"Yes, Master," I said, and again turned away.

"You will not escape," had said Ena.

Tomorrow I, Elinor Brinton, would be collared!

I then began to walk through the camp. I saw the tents and the fires, and the men talking, and the girls about their tasks. I hated men. They made us work! Why did they not do their own cooking, and polish their own leather, and go to the stream or the washing shed and wash their own clothes? They did not do so because they did not wish to do so. They made girls do their work! I hated men. They dominated us and exploited us!

I found, in one place in the camp, a grassy area, on a slight hill. There was a heavy metal ring there, near the top of the slight hill. It was fixed in a heavy stone, buried level with the grass.

In another place I found a horizontal pole, itself set on two pairs of poles, leaning together and lashed at the top. It was, I gathered, a pole for hanging meat. Oddly enough, there was also an iron ring, set in a stone, buried in the ground, beneath the center of the horizontal pole. Off to one side, in an open area there was a small iron box, a square of some three feet in dimension. In the front of the box there was a small iron door, with two slits in it. One, near the top, was about seven inches in width and about a half inch in height; the other, its top formed by a rectangular opening in the bottom of the door, its bottom formed by the iron floor of the box, was about a foot wide and two inches in height. The door could be closed with two heavy, flat, sliding bolts, and locked with two padlocks. I wondered what could be kept in such a box.

I continued to walk aoout the camp.

In one place I found a long, low shed, formed of heavy logs. It was windowless. Its heavy plank door was locked with two hasps and staples, secured by two heavy padlocks. I supposed it a storage shed.

My steps now, inadvertently, took me toward the center of the camp.

I stood before a large, low tent of scarlet canvas, suspended on eight poles. Inside, through the opened tent flap, I could see the scarlet canvas was lined with silk. It was a low tent, and only near its center could a man walk upright. Inside, in a brass pan, there was a small fire of coals. Over the coals, on a tripod, there was, warming, a small metal wine bowl. Warriors of Treve, I had heard, had a fondness for warm wines. I supposed that Rask of Treve might have his wine so. It seemed strange to me to think of such tarnsmen, such brutal, wild men, caring for such a small pleasantry. Too, I had heard, they were fond of combing the hair of their slave girls. Cities and men, I thought, are so strange, so different. I suspected there were few men as fierce and terrible as those of Treve, dreaded throughout Gor, and yet they enjoyed their wine warmed and were fond of so simple a thing as smoothing the hair of a girl. Inside, the tent was floored with heavy, soft rugs, from Tor and Ar, perhaps the booty of caravan raids. And, within, from extensions of certain of the tent poles, there hung, on hooks, burning tharlarion-oil lamps of brass. It was a bit chilly tonight. And it was growing dark now. The interior of the tent seemed inviting, redly warm and dark. I put the thought from my mind that I wished I was within that tent. I wondered what it would be like to lie within such a tent, naked and collared, on its soft rugs, in the light of the small fire, the tent flaps tied shut, completely at the mercy of its master. Against its far wall I could see great chests, heavy and bound with iron, filled doubtless with a raider's abundant booty, gems and golden wire, and necklaces and coins, and pearls, and jewelries, and bracelets and bangles, set perhaps with precious stones, which might serve to adorn the limbs of exquisite female slaves. Much booty was there. And I reminded myself that I, too, as much as any coin or precious cup in such a chest, or in this entire camp, was booty. I, too, was booty. I wondered, too, if those chests might contain the light, precious chains of silver and gold, wrought by slavers so cunningly, to hold a girl in given positions, while she was subdued at a master's leisure. I trembled. And I wondered, too, if they might contain nose rings, and if one would be put on me. I shuddered.

"Whose tent is this?" I asked a passing slave girl.

"Foolish Kajira," she said, "it is the tent of Rask of Treve."

I had known that it would be.

Outside the entrance of the tent, squatting down, leaning on their spears, there were two guards. They were watching me.

I stood outside the tent. Rask of Treve did not wish to see me now.

"Be off with you," said one of the guards.

I heard the flash of a pair of bangles and saw a dark-haired girl, the two golden bangles on her left ankle, come to the opening of the tent. She wore brief, diaphanous scarlet silk. She looked at me, and then quickly tied shut the tent flaps.

The guard who had spoken to me rose to his feet.

I fled away, back to the tent of the women.

When I reached the women's tent, I flung myself down on its rugs and wept.

Ena, who had been sewing a talmit, a headband sometimes worn by tarnsmen in flight, came to me. "What is wrong?" she asked.

"I do not want to be a slave girl!" I wept.

Ena held me. "It is hard to be a slave," she said.

I sat up and held her. "Men are cruel," I said.

"Yes," said Ena.

"I hate them! I hate them!" I wept.

She kissed me. She smiled.

"May I speak?" I asked.

"Surely," she said. "In this tent you are always free to speak."

I looked down. "It is said," I said, "—I have heard—that Rask of Treve is a hard master."

She smiled. "That is true," she said.

"It is said," I blurted out, "that no man on Gor can so diminish or humble a woman as Rask of Treve."

"I have not been diminished or humbled," said Ena. "On the other hand, if Rask of Treve wished to diminish or humble a woman, I expect he would do it quite well."

"Suppose," I said, "a girl had been insolent, or arrogant with him?"

"Such a girl, doubtless," said Ena, "would then be well diminished and humbled." She laughed. "Rask of Treve would doubtless teach her her slavery well."

This news did not reassure me.

I looked at her. "It is said he uses a woman but once," I wept, "and that he then, with contempt, brands her and discards her."

"I have been used by him many times," said Ena. "Rask of Treve," she added, smiling, "is not a madman."

"Were you branded with his name, after he used you?" I pressed.

"No," she said, "I was branded with the mark of Treve." She smiled. "When Rask captured me I was free. It was natural that, after he had used me, had enslaved me in his arms, I should, the next day, in witness to this fact, be marked."

"He enslaved you in his arms?" I asked.

"Yes, she said, "in his arms I found myself a slave." She smiled. "I expect that in the arms of such a man as Rask of Treve any woman might find herself a slave."

"Not I!" I cried.

She smiled.

"If a girl is already branded," I said, casually, but frightened, "she would not be again branded, would she?"

"Commonly not," said Ena. "Though sometimes, for some reason, the mark of Treve is pressed into her flesh." She looked at me. "Sometimes, too," she said, "a girl may be branded as a punishment, and to warn others against her."

I looked at her, puzzled.

"Penalty brands," she said. "They are tiny, but clearly visible. There are various such brands. There is one for lying, and another for stealing."

"I do not lie or steal," I said.

"That is good," said Ena.

"I have never seen the brand of Treve," I said.

"It is rare," said Ena, proudly.

"May I see your brand?" I asked. I was curious.

"Of course," said Ena, and she stood up and, extending her left leg, drew her long, lovely white garment to her hip, revealing her limb.

I gasped.

Incised deeply, precisely, in that slim, lovely, now-bared thigh was a startling mark, beautiful, insolent, dramatically marking that beautiful thigh as that which it now could only be, that of a female slave.

"It is beautiful," I whispered.

Ena pulled away the clasp at the left shoulder of her garment, dropping it to her ankles.

She was incredibly beautiful.

"Can you read?" she asked.

"No," I said.

She regarded the brand. "It is the first letter, in cursive script," she said, "of the name of the city of Treve."

"It is a beautiful mark," I said.

She regarded the mark. "It is attractive," said she. She looked at me. Suddenly she posed as a slave girl.

I gasped.

"It enhances my beauty," she said.

"Yes," I said. "Yes!" I found myself hoping, though I did not admit the thought to myself, that my brand might be as attractive on my body.

Ena once again, gracefully, drew on her garment. "I like it," she said. She looked at me, and laughed. "So do men!" she laughed.

I smiled.

Then suddenly I was furious. What right had such brutes

to brand us? To collar us? The Gorean right of the stronger, I told myself, to mark and claim the weaker as his own, should he choose to do so. I felt weak, and helpless. And then I was angry again, helplessly furious.

I, the prisoner of Rask of Treve, in his war camp, struggled to control myself.

I wanted to know more of the man who had captured me, whose saddle I had helplessly graced, whose locked collar I would tomorrow wear.

"It is said that Rask of Treve," I said, "has a great appetite for women, and contempt, for them."

"He is fond of us," smiled Ena, "that is true."

"But he has contempt for us!" I cried, my fury, my helpless rage, my frustration, uncontrollably bursting forth.

"Rask of Treve is a man, and a warrior," she said. "It is common for them to view us as mere women, and see us in terms of their sport and pleasure."

"That is contempt!" I cried.

Ena, kneeling, rocked back on her heels and laughed merrily. "Perhaps!" she laughed.

"I will not accept that!" I cried.

"Pretty little Kajira," laughed Ena.

I felt furious, and frustrated. I did not wish to be a mere sexual object! But I felt my throat. It was bare now. Tomorrow it would wear a collar. What could a girl be, who wore a collar, but such an object!

"I hate men!" I cried.

Ena looked at me. "I wonder," she said, "if Rask of Treve will find you pleasing?"

She removed the two pins which secured the garment I wore, stripping me.

"Perhaps," she said.

"I do not want to please him!" I cried.

"He will make you want to please him," she said. "You will try, desperately, to please him. Whether or not you will be successful I do not know. Rask of Treve is a great warrior. He has had many women, and has many women. He is a connoisseur of us. He is, accordingly, difficult to please. You will perhaps not please him."

"If I wanted to, I could," I cried.

"Perhaps," said Ena.

"But I shall resist him! I shall fight him!" I cried. "He will never tame me! He will never conquer me!"

Ena looked at me.

"I do not have the weaknesses of other women," I told her. I remembered the weakness of Verna, and of her girls, and of Inge and Rena, and Ute! They were weak. I was not!

"What a defiant girl you are," she said.

I looked at her.

"But we must rest now," she said, getting up and extinguishing the brass lamp in the tent.

"Why?" I asked.

"Because tomorrow you will be collared," she said.

I knelt, naked, on a large fur.

"Am I not to be chained tonight?" I asked.

"No," said Ena. Then her voice reached me in the darkness. "You will not escape."

I lay down and pulled the fur about me. I clenched it in my fists and bit it with my teeth. Then I lay with my head against it, wetting it with my tears.

I lifted my head. "You are a slave, Ena," I said. "Do you not hate men?"

"No," said Ena.

I heard her with irritation.

"I find men very exciting," said Ena. "Often I wish to give myself to them."

I heard her with horror. How shocking that she should speak so! Had she no pride? If such thoughts were entertained by her, surely she should have carefully concealed them, keeping them as her forbidden secret!

I, at least, hated men!

But tomorrow one of them would own me—fully. I would be his, by collar-right, by all the laws of Gor, to do with as he pleased.

I had not been chained. I had expected to be chained, heavily, and in short chains, fastened to rings, but I had not been.

But I was secured, well secured, locked within the tall, smooth palisade. "You will not escape," had said Ena.

Tomorrow I, Elinor Brinton, would be collared. For the first time on Gor I would wear the locked metal collar of a slave girl.

"You are lovely," said Ena.

I knelt, naked, on the scarlet rug in the tent of the women. I had been washed, and my hair had been combed. The slave girl replaced the glass stopper in a small, ornate bottle of Torian scent. "I shall touch you again," she said, "twice, before you are led forth."

Another girl, one of four near me, besides Ena, again knelt behind me and again began to pass the narrow, purple horn comb through my hair.

"She is combed," said one of the other girls, laughing.

"Aren't you excited," asked the girl combing my hair.

I could not answer.

"You know your part in the ceremony?" asked Ena, not for the first time.

I nodded my head.

It could not be I, Elinor Brinton, who knelt in this tent on this barbaric world!

One of the girls ran to the tent flaps and looked out. I could see, outside, through the tied-back opening of the tent, men, and girls, passing back and forth. The day was sunny and warm. There were soft breezes.

I was frightened.

I could smell the scent of the perfume. It was superior to any I had ever worn on Earth, when I had been wealthy and could command the customized attentions of the finest continental perfumers, and yet here, on this barbaric planet, it was used without thought to adorn the body of Elinor Brinton, a mere slave girl. I had not been permitted cosmetics.

I knelt.

I waited. For better than a quarter of an Ahn I knelt, waiting.

"Perhaps he will not collar her today," said one of the girls.

Suddenly the girl at the tent flap whispered excitedly, gesturing back toward us, "Prepare her! Prepare her!"

"Stand," said Ena.

I did so.

I gasped as they brought forth a long, exquisite garment, hooded, of shimmering scarlet silk.

Behind me, swiftly, one of the girls wound my hair into a single braid and then, coiling it, fastened it at the back of my head with four pins. The pins would be undone by Rask of Treve.

The garment was placed upon me. The hood fell at my back. The garment was sleeveless.

"Place your hands behind your back and cross your wrists," said Ena.

She had, in her hand, an eighteen-inch strip of purple binding fiber, about half an inch in width, flat, set with jewels.

I felt my wrists lashed behind my back.

Ena then gestured to the girl with the small, ornate bottle. The girl removed the stopper and, quickly, again, touched me with the scent, behind each ear, a tiny drop on her finger. I smelled the heady perfume. My heart was beating rapidly.

Then Ena again approached me. This time she carried, coiled in her hand, some seven or eight feet of slender, coarse rope, simple camp rope. She knotted one end of this about my neck, tightly enough that I felt the knot. My wrists would be bound by jeweled binding fiber but I would be led forth on a simple camp rope.

"You are very lovely," said Ena.

"A lovely animal!" I cried, tethered.

"Yes," said Ena, "a lovely, lovely animal."

I looked at her with horror.

But then I realized that Elinor Brinton was indeed an animal, for she was a slave.

It was thus not inappropriate that she should find

herself so, as she was, tethered, about her neck, knotted, a simple length of camp rope, slender and coarse, fit for leading verr or girls.

I turned my head to one side.

Ena drew the hood up from my back and over my head.

"They are ready!" said the girl at the entrance to the tent.

"Lead her forth," said Ena.

I was led through the camp, and, here and there, some men and slave girls followed me.

I came to a clearing, before the tent of Rask of Treve. He was waiting there. On my tether I was led before him. I looked at him, frightened.

We stood facing one another, I about five feet from him.

"Remove her tether," he said.

Ena, who had accompanied me, unknotted the rope, and handed it to one of the girls.

I wore the long, scarlet garment, hooded, sleeveless. My hands were bound behind my back with binding fiber.

"Remove her bonds," said Rask of Treve.

In his belt I saw that he had thrust an eighteen-inch strip of binding fiber. It was not jeweled. It was about three quarters of an inch in thickness; it was of flat, supple leather, plain and brown, of the sort commonly used by tarnsmen for binding female prisoners.

Ena untied my wrists.

Rask and I regarded one another.

He approached me.

With one hand he brushed back my hood, revealing my head and hair. I stood very straight.

Carefully, one by one, he removed the four pins, handing them to one of the girls at the side.

My hair fell about my shoulders, and he smoothed it over my back.

One of the girls, she with the purple horn comb, combed the hair, arranging it.

"She is pretty," said one of the girls in the crowd.

Rask of Treve now stood some ten feet from me. He regarded me.

"Remove her garment," he said.

Ena and one of the girls from the tent parted the garment and let it fall about my ankles.

Two or three of the girls in the crowd breathed their pleasure.

Some of the warriors smote their shields with the blades of their spears.

"Step before me naked," said Rask of Treve.

I did so.

We faced one another, not speaking, he with his blade, and in his leather, I with nothing, stripped at his command.

"Submit," he said.

I could not disobey him.

I fell to my knees before him, resting back on my heels, extending my arms to him, wrists crossed, as though for binding, my head lowered, between my arms.

I spoke in a clear voice. "I, Miss Elinor Brinton, of New York City, to the Warrior, Rask, of the High City of Treve, herewith submit myself as a slave girl. At his hands I accept my life and my name, declaring myself his to do with as he pleases."

Suddenly I felt my wrists lashed swiftly, rudely, together. I drew back my wrists in fear. They were already bound! They were bound with incredible tightness. I had been bound by a tarnsman.

I looked up at him in fear. I saw him take an object from a warrior at his side. It was an opened, steel slave collar.

He held it before me.

"Read the collar," said Rask of Treve.

"I cannot," I whispered. "I cannot read."

"She is illiterate," said Ena.

"Ignorant barbarian!" I heard more than one girl laugh.

I felt so ashamed. I regarded the engraving on the collar, tiny, in neat, cursive script. I could not read it.

"Read it to her," said Rask of Treve to Ena.

"It says," said Ena, "—I am the property of Rask of Treve."

I said nothing.

"Do you understand?" asked Ena.

"Yes," I said. "Yes!"

Now, with his two hands, he held the collar about my neck, but he did not yet close it. I was looking up at him. My throat was encircled by the collar, he holding it, but the collar was not yet shut. My eyes met his. His eyes were fierce, amused, mine were frightened. My eyes pleaded for mercy. I would receive none. The collar snapped shut. There was a shout of pleasure from the men and girls about. I heard hands striking the left shoulder in Gorean applause. Among the warriors, the flat of sword blades and the blades of spears rang on shields. I closed my eyes, shuddering.

I opened my eyes. I could not hold up my head. I saw before me the dirt, and the sandals of Rask of Treve.

Then I remembered that I must speak one more line. I lifted my head, tears in my eyes.

"I am yours, Master," I said.

He lifted me to my feet, one hand on each of my arms. My wrists were bound before my body. I wore his collar. He put his head to the left side of my face, and then to the right. He inhaled the perfume. Then he stood there, holding me. I looked up at him. Inadvertently my lips parted and I, standing on my toes, lifted my head, that I might delicately touch with my lips those of my master. But he did not bend to meet my lips. His arms held me from him.

"Put her in a work tunic," he said, "and send her to the shed."

15   MY MASTER WILL HAVE
HIS GIRL PLEASE HIM

"UTE!" I CRIED.

The guard, by the hair, threw me to her feet. I looked up at her with horror. The left side of her forehead was still discolored where I had struck her with a rock.

"I thought—" I whispered.

She stood before the long, low shed, which I had seen before, when I had examined the camp. It was windowless, and formed of heavy logs. It had a heavy plank door, which was now open. When I had seen it before, it had been locked by two hasps and staples, secured by two heavy padlocks. A lovely girl, in brief work tunic, emerged, and went about the camp. I had supposed it a storage shed. I now realized it was a dormitory for female work slaves. And I realized, to my horror, that I would be such a slave.

"You wear a collar," said Ute.

"Yes," I whispered, kneeling before her, my head down. I had seen that she, too, wore a collar. More importantly, about her forehead, tying back her dark hair, was a strip of rep cloth, brown, of the same material as the work tunic. I knew this meant that she had authority among the girls. Ena was high girl in the camp, but I suspected that Ute might be first among the work slaves. I began to shake.

"She is frightened," said the guard. "Does she know you?"

"She is known to me," said Ute.

I put my head down to the dirt before her. My wrists were still bound, fastened by the leather knots of the tarnsman, Rask of Treve. I was still unclothed. I wore only my bonds and, locked about my throat, a collar of steel.

"You may leave us," said Ute to the guard. "You have delivered the slave. She is now in my charge."

The guard turned and left.

I dared not look up. I was terrified.

"On the first day of my capture, at the first camp of my captors," said Ute, "I fell to Rask of Treve." She paused. "Suddenly, from the darkness, he stood before them. 'Yield to me the female slave,' he said. They would choose to fight. 'I am Rask of Treve,' he said. They then did not choose to draw their blades. With their own tarn goads, Rask of Treve then drove their tarns from their camp. He then lifted me, bound, in his arms, and backed from the camp. 'I thank you for the female slave,' he said. And one of them said to him, 'And we thank you, Rask of Treve, for our lives.' Their journey back to the camp of Haakon of Skjern, afoot, will be long. Rask of Treve then brought me to his camp, where he made me his slave."

I looked up at Ute. "You wear the Kajira talmit," I said.

"The first girl of the work slaves," said Ute, "had been sold shortly before my capture. There had been dissensions, factions, among the girls, each wanting one of their own party to be first girl. I was new. I had no allegiances. Rask of Treve, by his will, and because, for some reason, he trusted me, set me above them all."

"Am I to be a work slave?" I asked.

"Did you expect to be sent to the tent of the women?" asked Ute.

"Yes," I said. I had indeed expected to live in the tent of the women, not in a dark shed, among work girls.

Ute laughed. "You are a work slave," she said.

I put my head down.

"You were captured, I understand," said Ute, "southwest of the village of Rorus."

I did not speak.

"Accordingly," said Ute, "you were still seeking my village of Rarir."

"No!" I cried.

"From whence," said Ute, "you would have sought the island of Teletus."

"No, no!" I cried.

"And on that island," she said, "you would have presented yourself to my foster parents, as my friend."

I shook my head in terror.

"Perhaps they might even have adopted you, in my place, as their daughter," suggested Ute.

"Oh no, Ute!" I cried. "No! No!"

"Your life would then have been quite easy, and pleasant," said Ute.

I put my head down, in terror, to her feet.

By the hair, Ute, bending over me, yanked my head painfully up. "Who betrayed Ute?" she demanded.

I shook my head.

Ute's fists were excruciating in my hair.

"Who?" she demanded.

I could not speak, so terrified I was.

She shook my head viciously.

"Who!" she demanded.

"I did," I cried. "I did!"

"Speak as a slave!" demanded Ute.

"El-in-or betrayed Ute!" I cried. "El-in-or betrayed Ute!"

"Worthless slave," I heard a voice behind me say.

I turned, as well as I could, and saw, to my dismay, Rask of Treve. I closed my eyes, sobbing.

"It is as you said," said Rask of Treve, to Ute, "she is worthless."

Ute removed her hands from my hair, and I put my head down.

"She is a liar, and a thief, and a traitress," said Rask of Treve. "She is utterly worthless."

"Yet," said Ute, "in a camp such as this, we may find uses for such a girl, there are many menial tasks to which she might be well applied."

"See that she is worked well," said Rask of Treve.

"I shall," said Ute, "Master."

Rask of Treve strode from where I knelt, leaving me with Ute.

I looked up at her, tears in my eyes. I shook my head. "You told him?" I whispered.

"He commanded me to speak," said Ute, "and I, as a slave, must needs obey."

I shook my head.

"Your master knows you well, Slave," said Ute, smiling.

I put down my head, sobbing. "No, no."

"Guard!" called Ute.

A guard approached.

"Unbind the slave," said Ute.

I lifted my tightly bound wrists to the guard, and he undid the knots. I still knelt.

"You may now leave us," said Ute to the guard, and he left.

"Am I truly a work slave?" I asked.

"Yes," said Ute.

"Am I under your authority?" I asked.

"Yes," she said.

"Ute!" I cried. "I did not mean to betray you! I was frightened! Forgive me, Ute! I did not mean to betray you!"

"Go into the shed," said Ute. "There will be work for you tonight, in the kitchen shed. Tomorrow will be soon enough for you to eat."

"Please, Ute!" I wept.

"Go into the shed, Slave," said she.

I rose to my feet and, naked, entered the dark shed. Ute closed the door behind me, plunging me into darkness. I heard the hasps cover the staples, one after the other, and then I heard the heavy padlocks snapped shut.

The floor of the shed was dirt, but, here and there, under my feet, I felt a rounded metal bar. I fell to my hands and knees and, with my fingers in the dirt, felt the floor. Under the dirt, an inch or so, and in some places exposed, was a heavy gridwork of bars.

Girls locked within this shed would not tunnel their way to freedom.

There was no escape.

Suddenly, locked within, alone in the darkness, I grew panic-stricken.

I flung myself against the door, pounding on it in the darkness with my fists. Then, sobbing, I slipped to my knees and scratched at it with my fingernails. "Ute!" I sobbed. "Ute!"

Then I crawled to one side of the door and sat down, my knees drawn up under my chin, in the darkness. I was lonely and miserable. I felt the steel collar, so smooth and obdurate, fastened on my throat.

I heard a tiny scurrying, of a tiny brush urt, in the darkness.

I screamed.

Then it was silent, and again I sat alone in the darkness, my knees drawn up under my chin. In the darkness I smelled the scent of the Torian perfume.

Ute was not particularly cruel to me, as I had feared she would be.

She treated me justly, as she did the other girls. It might even have been as though it were not I who had betrayed her to the slavers of Haakon of Skjern.

I did much work, but I did not find that I was doing more than the other girls. Ute would not, however, let me shirk. After I had recovered from my fear that she would exact a vengeance on me for betraying her, I found myself, eventually, becoming irritated, somewhat, that she would treat me with no more favoritism than the other girls. After all, we had known one another for many months, and had been together, I recalled, from well before the time when Targo had first crossed the Laurius northward to the compound above the town of Laura. Surely that should have counted for something. It was not as though I were a stranger to her, as surely were the other girls. Yet, in spite of these considerations, I was not treated preferentially! I had some consolation in the fact that certain other girls, who would try to be particularly pleasing to Ute, who would try to insinuate themselves into her favor, were treated with abrupt coldness. She treated us all alike. She kept herself remote from us. She did not even sleep or eat with us, but in the kitchen shed, where she would be chained at night. We respected her. We feared her. We did what she told us. Behind her lay the power of the men. Yet we did not much like her, for she was our superior. We were pleased that she treated others with justice, not giving them advantages and privileges over ours, but we were angry that the same justice was meted out, in turn, to us. We were not given advantages and privileges over them! Surely I, at least, should have received some consideration, for I had known Ute for many months, and we had been friends. Yet she treated me no differently than the other girls, scarcely recognizing me in my work tunic among the others.

When I could, of course, I managed to avoid tasks, or perform them in a hasty, slipshod manner, that I might save myself inconvenience and labor. Ute could not watch all the time. Once, however, she caught me, with a greasy pan, which I had not well scrubbed, but had returned, not clean, to the kitchen shed. "Bring the pan," said Ute. I followed her, and we walked through the camp. We stopped by the framework of poles, which I had seen before. There was the horizontal pole, itself set on two pairs of poles, leaning together and lashed at the top. I had thought, when first I had seen it, that it was a pole for hanging meat. The horizontal pole was about nine feet high. Beneath its center, on the ground, there was an iron ring. This ring was set in a heavy stone, which was buried in the ground.

I stood there, beneath the pole, by Ute's side. I held the greasy pan.

"The girl's wrists," said Ute, "are tied together, and then she is tied, suspended by the wrists, from the high pole. Her ankles are tied together and tied, some six inches from the ground, to the iron ring. That way she does not much swing."

I looked at her, holding the pan.

"This is a whipping pole," said Ute. "You may go now, El-in-or."

I turned and fled back to the kitchen shed, to clean the pan. After that I seldom shirked my work, and I made, generally, much effort to do my work well.

It only occurred to me later that Ute had not had me whipped.

Often during the day, and sometimes for days at a time,

most of the tarnsmen of Rask of Treve would be aflight. The camp then would seem very quiet.

They were applying themselves to the work of the tarnsmen of Treve, attack, plunder and enslavement.

A girl would cry, "They return!" and we, eager in our work tunics, would run to the center of the camp to greet the returning warriors. Many of the girls would be laughing and waving, leaping up and down, and standing on their tiptoes. I did not betray such emotion, but I, too, found myself eager, almost uncontrollably excited, to witness the return of the warriors. How fine they were, such magnificent males! I hated them, of course, but, too, I, like the others, most eagerly anticipated their return. And most of all was I thrilled to witness the return of their leader, the mighty, laughing Rask of Treve, whose very capture loop I had felt on my own body, whose collar I wore, whose I was. How pleased I was to see him bring back yet another girl, bound across his saddle, a new prize. How sceptically, and eagerly, with the other girls, I would silently appraise her, comparing her, always unfavorably, on some ground or another, with myself. Once Rask of Treve, from the saddle, looked directly at me, finding me among the mere work slaves, in their work tunics. I had felt an indescribable emotion, an utter weakness, when our eyes had met. I put my hand before my mouth. How magnificent he seemed, how mighty among those mighty warriors, he, their fierce leader.

Many of the girls ran to individual warriors, their eyes shining, leaping up and seizing the stirrups, pulling themselves up and putting their cheeks against their soft leather boots. And more than one was hauled to the saddle and well held and kissed before being thrown again to the ground.

When the tarnsmen would return, with their captives and booty, there would be a feast.

I would serve at this feast, but when it came time for dancing silks and slave bells to be withdrawn from the ornate, heavy chests, I would be dismissed to the shed, where I would be locked, alone.

"Why am I never belled and put in dancing silk?" I demanded of Ute. I could scarcely believe that it was I, Elinor Brinton, who so protested. Yet I heard the words. "Why am I never allowed, late, to serve the men in their tents?"

"No man has called for you," said Ute.

And so I, my work tunic removed, would be locked in the shed at night.

I would lie there and, through the crack beneath the heavy plank door, hear the music, the laughing, protesting screams of the girls, the laughter, the shouts of satisfaction, of victory of the men.

But no man had called for me. No man wanted me.

How pleased I was to be spared the ignominious usage to which the other girls, my unfortunate peers, were subjected! How I pitied them. How I rejoiced that I did not share their fate. I screamed with rage, and taking up handfuls of dirt, hurled it against the interior walls of the shed, within which I was locked.

At the third or fourth hour of the morning, one by one, the girls, their silks now removed, would be returned to the shed. How stimulated they seemed, how untired. How they laughed and talked to one another! How vital they seemed! We had to work the next day! Why did they not go to sleep? One would sing or hum to herself. Another would cry out some name, that of a tarnsman, to herself with pleasure. "Ah, Rim," she would cry out, twisting in the darkness, "I am truly your slave!"

I pounded my fists in the dirt, angry.

But they would be exhausted in the morning! In the morning they would be miserable enough! In the morning Ute would almost have to use whips to rout such lazy girls out of the shed!

I was pleased no one wanted me. I wept.

Sometimes there were visitors to the camp of Rask of Treve, though, one gathers, these were men in the confidence of Treve.

Generally they were merchants. Some brought food and wines. Others came to buy the plunder of the tarnsmen. Several of my work-mates were sold, and others, captured, brought in on tarnback, took their place, perhaps to be sold as well in their turn.

When I could, I would manage, in my daily tasks, to pass by the tent of Rask of Treve, that large, low tent, on its eight poles, of scarlet canvas lined with scarlet silk.

It was convenient to pass by the tent, you understand, for it was in the center of the camp, and thus often lay on the shortest route from place to place within the palisade.

Sometimes I saw the dark-haired girl, in red silk with the two golden bangles on her left ankle, when I passed by the tent. Sometimes I saw other girls. Once or twice I saw a stunningly figured blond girl in brief yellow silk. It seemed Rask of Treve had his choice of beautiful women.

I hated him!

One afternoon, after I had been some three weeks in the camp, Rask and his tarnsmen returned from a raid far to the north.

He had raided the slave compound of his old enemy, Haakon of Skjern.

Among the new slave girls brought to the camp were Inge and the Lady Rena of Lydius! Lana had not been captured. Inge and Rena were the only ones I knew among the new girls.

The morning following their capture, as I had been, they, and the others, were collared. They, like I, had spent their first night in the tent of the women. Following their collaring, however, as I had been, they were sent to the shed. When Rask had collared Inge he had shaken her blond head with his large hand. He seemed fond of her. And she had dared to put her cheek against his hand. How shameless she had become! Once of the scribes, she was now only a wanton, shameless slave girl! I wanted to tear her hair and eyes out! How pleased I was, and how startled she was, and the others, when Rask sent them to the shed, where they would be issued work tunics and find themselves work slaves in the camp!

How Inge and Rena rejoiced when they found themselves forced to their knees before Ute!

But Ute did not even let them rise.

They looked at her with horror.

"I am Ute," Ute told them, "I am first girl among the work slaves. You will obey me. You will be treated precisely as the other girls, neither better nor worse. If you do not obey me, exactly and promptly, in all things, you will be beaten."

They looked at her, scarcely comprehending.

"Do you understand?" asked Ute.

"Yes," said Inge.

"Yes," said Rena.

"The slave, El-in-or," said Ute, "stand forward."

I had been hiding in the background. Ordered by Ute, I came forward.

I saw Inge and Rena exchange glances of pleasure. I was frightened.

"This is one of my girls," said Ute, "as you are. You will not be cruel to her."

"Ute!" protested Inge.

"Or I will have you beaten," said Ute.

Inge looked at her, angrily.

"Do you understand?" said Ute.

"Yes," said Inge.

"Yes," said the Lady Rena of Lydius.

"El-in-or," said Ute, "take these new slaves and get them work tunics, and then return them to me, and I shall assign them their duties for the day."

Inge and Rena, and the other new girls, followed me, and I took them to the chest at the side of the shed, where I could find them their simple, brief garments of brown rep-cloth, which raiment would constitute their sole work garment in the camp of Rask of Treve.

From the chest I took forth several of the garments, small, clean and neatly folded. I had washed several myself, and, sprinkling them with water, and sweating, had pressed them on a smooth board, using the small, heavy, rounded Gorean irons, heated over fire. I had folded them, too, and placed them in the chest.

I threw the garments to the girls, the new slaves. They were naked, save for their collars.

"But I am a trained pleasure slave," protested Inge. She held the small, folded garment in her two hands.

"Put it on," I told her.

"I was of high caste!" cried the Lady Rena of Lydius.

"Put it on," I told her.

Then angrily Inge and Rena stood before me, clad in the brief, simple garments of female work slaves.

"You make a pretty work slave," I said to Inge.

She clenched her fists.

"You, too," said I to the Lady Rena of Lydius.

She glared at me in helpless fury, her fists, like Inge's, clenched.

I looked at the others. "Put them on!" I cried.

The other girls, too, donned their tunics, and then I led them all, the new slaves, clad for work, back to Ute, who would instruct them in their duties for the day.

Four days after Inge and Rena, and other new girls, had been brought to the secret war camp of Rask of Treve, the tarnsman, and his fierce men, again returned from the work of warriors.

Again there was excitement in the camp.

I leaped to my feet.

"Finish your work," said Ute.

"Ute!" I cried.

"Finish your work," she said.

Behind the kitchen shed, I was ironing. To one side there was a large pile of laundered work tunics, which I had washed in the early morning. The smooth board was set before me, mounted on two wooden blocks. A bowl of water was nearby, and a fire, over which, on an iron plate fixed on stones, there were, heating, five, small, flat-bottomed, rounded, wooden-handled Gorean irons. I had been kneeling before the board, ironing the tunics, which I would then fold and place to one side. Behind the kitchen shed, I had not been able to see the alighting of the tarns. I could hear, how-

ever, the delighted cries of the girls and the loud, warm,
answering shouts of the men.

I heard one of the girls cry out, "How beautiful she is!"

I supposed a new female had been brought to the camp.

Angrily I pressed one of the hot irons down on a work
tunic, smoothing it.

I must remain behind the kitchen shed, working, while
they were permitted to greet the men! I wondered if Inge
would be there, perhaps smiling and waving to Rask of
Treve!

How furious I was!

But I reminded myself that I hated him!

In time the excitement, the cries and shouts, diminished,
and I knew the men had dismounted, and any captives, perhaps bound, would have been sent to the tent of the women.
The girls, here and there, returned to their labors.

I continued to iron.

About a quarter of an Ahn later, kneeling behind the
board, ironing, I became aware of someone standing before
me. I saw a pair of slim, tanned ankles. I lifted my eyes
and saw slender, strong, tanned legs. And then, to my horror, the brief, tawny garment of a panther girl. And in the
belt of the garment there was thrust a sleen knife. She wore
barbaric ornaments of gold. I lifted my eyes to this tall,
strong, beautifully figured female.

I put down my head, crying out in misery.

"She seems to know you," said Rask of Treve.

I shook my head negatively.

"Lift your head, Slave," said Verna.

I did so.

"Who is she?" asked Verna.

Rask shrugged. "One of my slaves," he said.

Verna smiled down at me. "You know me, do you not,
Girl?" she asked.

I shook my head.

Verna wore no collar. In her belt she carried a sleen
knife. Rask of Treve, my master, stood near her. She was
free, obviously free. She was not even a captive, let alone

a slave. By the attitude of my master, I could see that she was, somehow, for no reason I could understand, a guest in this camp.

"We met," said Verna, "first outside the compound of Targo the Slaver, north of Laura. Then, in the streets of Ko-ro-ba, you incited slave girls to attack me. Later, south of Ko-ro-ba, when I was caged, among the prizes in the hunting retinue of Marlenus of Ar, you, with another girl, whose name was Lana, much abused me."

I put my head down.

"Lift your head, Girl," said she.

Again I did so.

"You know me, do you not, Girl?" asked Verna again.

I shook my head, no, no!

"Your slave is a liar," said Verna.

"Shall I have her beaten for you?" asked Rask of Treve.

"No," said Verna. She looked down at me. "She is only a a slave," she said.

I put down my head.

"You are not to lie again in this camp," said Rask of Treve.

"No, Master," I whispered.

"My patience grows short with you, El-in-or," he said.

"Yes, Master," I whispered.

"I know little of such work," said Verna, "but are you not in danger of scorching the garment which you are ironing?"

I hastily drew away the iron, placing it on the fire-heated plate.

Fortunately the garment was not marked, else Ute, discovering it, might have punished me.

"Permit me, Verna," said Rask of Treve, "to show you the rest of the camp."

Verna looked down upon me. "Continue with your work, Slave," she said.

"Yes, Mistress," I said.

Then, together, Verna and Rask of Treve left me. Weeping, I continued to iron.

That night I sneaked away, following my feeding, and before the time to be sent to the kitchen shed, to the tent of women.

"Ena!" I whispered, through the canvas of the tent.

Ena came from the tent and I, only a work girl, knelt before her, putting my forehead to the ground. "May a slave speak?" I begged.

Ena knelt down before me and lifted me, and held my arms. "Of course, El-in-or," she said. "What is it?"

I looked at her, gratefully.

"There is a new woman, a free woman in the camp," I said.

"That is Verna," said Ena, "a panther girl from the northern forests."

"How is it that she is here?" I begged.

Ena smiled. "Come with me," she said. She led me through the camp, until we came to a small, low tent. Before it, about a fire, there sat two brawny, magnificent huntsmen.

"They are from the hunting retinue of Marlenus of Ar," I whispered. I recognized them, both from the streets of Ko-ro-ba and from the merchants' stockade, on the trade route to Ar, where I and Lana had so abused Verna, she then being helplessly caged.

I noted that these two men were served, each by a slave girl. Inge and Rena were fetching in their work tunics. I could see that they were excited by their proximity to such men.

They were shameless!

"Those men," said Ena, "are Raf and Pron, huntsmen of Treve, though they range widely in their huntings, even to the northern forests. By order of Rask of Treve they, by their skill in weapons and their mastery of the techniques and lore of the hunt, and pretending to be of Minus, a village under the hegemony of Ar, made petition, and successfully so, to participate in the retinue of the great Ubar." She smiled at me. "Treve," she said, "has spies in many places."

"They freed Verna," I said.

"Freeing her, they escaped to a preappointed rendezvous, where Rask of Treve, with his men, met them, and brought them, and Verna, here."

"But why should they wish to free her?" I asked.

"Verna is well known on Gor, as an outlaw woman," said Ena. "When it became known that Marlenus, in his hunting, for his sport, would seek her, Rask of Treve gave order for Raf and Pron to attempt to join his retinue."

"But why?" I asked.

"That," said Ena, "Marlenus, if successful, might be deprived of his prize."

"But why?" I pressed.

"There would be glory in the capture of such a woman," said Ena, "and, surely, ignominy in her escaping."

"You mean she has been freed only that Marlenus of Ar might be deprived of his prize?"

"Of course," said Ena. "Treve and Ar are enemies." Her eyes shone, and I had little doubt where her sympathies lay. "Is it not a superb insult to Marlenus and Ar!" she breathed.

"Yes," I said, "it is."

"Too," said Ena, thrilled, "is it not audacious that my master, Rask of Treve, places his war camp, from which he may despoil the fields and caravans of Ar, within the realm of mighty Ar itself!"

"Yes," I whispered. I then sensed something of the points of honor and of the nature of insults which scornful men, mighty warriors, might exchange. I shuddered, momentarily thrilled with the boldness of my master, Rask of Treve. Then I remembered that he had contempt for women, and that I hated him!

"What of the other girls, those of Verna's band?" I asked. I particularly feared that the blond girl, she who had held my leash, might be freed. I had much abused her, throwing dirt on her and poking her with a stick in her cage. I was terrified of her. If she was free I did not know what she might do to me.

"The others remain caged prizes in the retinue of Marlenus," said Ena.

"Oh," I said. I was much relieved.

I observed Inge filling the paga goblet of one of the huntsmen. She knelt closer to him than she needed to. Her lips
were parted. Her eyes shone. Her hands, slightly, shook on
the paga bottle. Rena knelt to one side. She watched her
huntsman, gnawing the meat from a great bone. I could see
that she was eager to leap up to serve him, should he but
speak to her.

What shameless, wanton slave girls they were!

"Rask of Treve hates Marlenus of Ar," said Ena.

I nodded.

"Have you seen the dark-haired girl, who sometimes tends
his tent?" she asked.

"Yes," I said. I had indeed seen her. She was an incredibly beautiful slave female. She was even more beautiful than Ena, who was one of the most beautiful female
slaves I had ever seen. Her hair was glossy and black, and
her master had had her cut it at the small of her back.
Her features, and body, were breath-takingly beautiful. She
had an exciting mouth and lips. She was a stunningly
figured, green-eyed, olive-skinned slave girl. She would bring
a high price on the market. Always she wore only the brief
garment of scarlet, diaphanous silk. Always, about her left
ankle, fastened, were two golden bangles.

"Do you know who she is?" asked Ena, smiling.

"No," I said. "Who is she?"

Ena smiled.

"El-in-or!" snapped Ute. "Get to the shed!"

I leaped up and, frightened, angry, fled through the camp
to be locked in the shed.

I would soon learn who the beautiful dark-haired girl was.

Verna had her own tent in the camp of Rask of Treve,
though often, when he was in the camp, she dined with
him. Sometimes, too, she would range beyond the palisade,
beyond which other girls were not permitted, to walk and
hunt.

It was not infrequently that Verna requested that it be I
who would tend her tent, and prepare her food, and serve
her. I, collared, did so, fearfully. But she was not more cruel

to me than to any other female slave assigned such servile
duties. I effaced myself as much as possible, serving her as
unobtrusively and anonymously as I could. She tended to ignore me, as one would a female work slave. I made certain
I pleased her in all respects, for I greatly feared her.

Then, one night, on a feast night, for Rask had returned
with new fair prisoners, Verna feasted in his own tent, and
I, to my amazement, was ordered to serve them. Other
girls had prepared the repast, which, for the war camp, was
sumptuous indeed, containing even oysters from the delta of
the Vosk, a portion of the plunder of a tarn caravan of
Ar, such delicacies having been intended for the very table
of Marlenus, the Ubar of that great city itself. I served the
food, and poured the wines, and kept their goblets filled,
remaining as much in the background as possible.

They talked of hunting, and war, and of the northern
forests, as though I were not there.

Sometimes Verna would say, "Drink," and I would pour
wine into her goblet, saying, "Yes, Mistress," and sometimes
Rask of Treve would command me, saying "Drink," and I
would then, similarly, serve him, saying "Yes, Master."

Verna sat cross-legged, like a man. I knelt, as a serving
slave.

She threw me one of the oysters.

"Eat, Slave," she said.

I ate.

In so doing this, she, the guest, had signified that I
might now feed. It is a not uncommon Gorean courtesy, in
such situations, to permit the guest to grant the feeding
permission to the slaves present.

"Thank you, Mistress," I said.

Rask of Treve then threw me a piece of meat, that I
might satisfy my hunger, for I had not been fed.

With my hands I ate the meat, a collared slave, while
the free persons drank, and conversed.

Rask of Treve snapped his fingers. "Approach me. El-in-
or," he said.

I bolted down the meat. I approached him, across the low
table behind which he sat on the rugs.

He extended his goblet to me. "Drink," he said, offering me the cup.

I looked at the rim of the cup. I shook with terror. "A slave girl dares not touch with her lips the rim of that cup which has been touched with the lips of her master," I whispered.

"Excellent," said Verna.

"She was trained in the pens of Ko-ro-ba," said Rask of Treve.

He then, from his own cup, poured some wine into a small bowl, which he handed to me.

"Thank you, Master," I breathed.

With his head Rask of Treve gestured me to one side, and I went and knelt to one side, as I had before.

I put back my head and drank the wine. It was Ka-la-na wine. I felt it almost immediately.

"I have a surprise for you," Rask was telling Verna.

"Oh?" she asked.

I put down the wine cup, to one side.

Rask of Treve looked at me. He was in an expansive mood. He cut a large slice of juicy bosk meat. My mouth watered. He smiled, and then he threw it to me. I caught it, happily, and with two hands, began to feed on it.

"What is the surprise?" asked Verna.

Rask clapped his hands once, and four musicians, who had been waiting outside, entered the tent, and took a place to one side. Two had small drums, one a flute, the other a stringed instrument.

Rask clapped his hands twice, sharply. And the black-haired, green-eyed, olive-skinned slave girl stood before him. "Put her in slave bells," said Rask to one of the musicians. The musician fastened leather cuffs, mounted each with three rows of bells, on her wrists and ankles.

"Please, Master," begged the girl, "not before a woman." She referred to Verna. I was only a slave.

Rask of Treve threw the girl one of the oysters, from a silver plate on the low, wooden table.

"Eat it," he said.

There was a rustle of slave bells. She complied with the dictum of her master.

"It was destined for the table of Marlenus of Ar," said Rask of Treve.

"Yes, Master," said the girl.

She stood facing him.

Verna and I watched.

"Remove your garment," said Rask of Treve.

"Please, Master," she begged.

"Remove it," said Rask of Treve.

The beautiful, olive-skinned girl parted the garment and dropped it to one side.

"You may now dance, Talena," said Rask of Treve.

The girl danced.

"She is not bad," said Verna.

"Do you know who she is?" asked Rask of Treve, eating a piece of meat.

"No," said Verna. "Who is she?"

"Talena," said Rask, smiling, "the daughter of Marlenus of Ar."

Verna looked at him, dumbfounded, and then she laughed a great laugh, and slapped her knee. "Splendid!" she cried. "Splendid!"

She leaped to her feet and, closely, moving about her, examined the girl as she danced, now slowly, to a barbaric, adagio melody. "Splendid!" cried Verna. "Splendid!"

Now the melody became more swift, and it burned like flame in the girl's slave body.

"Give her to me!" cried Verna.

"Perhaps," said Rask of Treve.

"I am the enemy of Marlenus of Ar!" cried Verna. "Give her to me!"

"I, too, am the enemy of Marlenus of Ar," said Rask. He held out his goblet and I, the meat on which I was feeding clenched between my teeth, filled it.

"I will well teach her the meaning of slavery in the northern forests!" cried Verna.

I could see fear in the girl's eyes, as she danced. I continued to eat the piece of meat on which I had been feeding.

She was beautiful and helpless as she danced, before her enemies. The firelight glinted on her collar, which had been placed on her throat by Rask of Treve. But I did not feel sorry for her. She was no business of mine. She was only another slave.

"I have taught her something of slavery already," smiled Rask of Treve.

The girl's eyes seemed agonized, as she danced.

"How is she?" asked Verna, who had now again resumed her place, seating herself cross-legged by Rask of Treve's side.

"Superb," said Rask of Treve.

Humiliation and shame shone in the eyes of the dancing slave girl.

"Where did you get her?" asked Verna.

"I acquired her about a year ago," said Rask of Treve, "from a merchant of Tyros, who was traveling by caravan overland to Ar, with the intention of returning her, for a recompense, to Marlenus of Ar."

"What did she cost you?" asked Verna.

"The merchant," smiled Rask of Treve, "was persuaded to give her to me, free of all costs, as a token of his esteem for the men and city of Treve."

Verna laughed.

"I do not buy women," said Rask of Treve.

I shuddered.

"It is marvelous!" cried Verna. "Your secret camp lies within the very realm of Ar itself! Splendid! And in this camp you keep the daughter of your worst enemy, the daughter of the Ubar of great Ar itself, as slave! Magnificent!"

I watched the girl dancing, the slave.

Rask clapped his hands again, twice, sharply. The musicians stopped, and the girl stopped dancing. "That is enough, Slave Girl," he said.

She turned to flee from the tent.

"Do not forget your garment, Girl," said Verna.

The slave girl reached down and snatched up the bit of

red silk she had dropped aside and, holding it, with a jangle of slave bells, fled from the tent of her master.

Rask of Treve, and Verna, laughed.

I had finished my meat.

They again held out their goblets, and I again filled them.

"Tonight," said Rask of Treve to me, "because we have brought in new prisoners, there will be feasting and pleasure."

"Yes, Master?" I said.

"So go to Ute," he said, "and tell her to lock you in the shed."

"Yes, Master," I said.

"Why do you not give Talena to me?" asked Verna, of Rask of Teve.

"Perhaps I shall," said Rask of Treve. "I must think about it."

I left the tent, to find Ute, to tell her to lock me in the shed.

The next day, for the first time, on a leash with another girl, Techne, a girl of Cos, I was permitted beyond the palisade. A guard was with us, and we were charged with filling our leather buckets with ram-berries, a small, reddish fruit with edible seeds, not unlike tiny plums, save for the many small seeds. I had picked such berries before, with Targo's caravan. Indeed, the first fruit on Gor I had eaten had been such berries.

I was pleased to be outside of the palisade. The day was beautifully warm, and I felt happy.

I had often begged Ute to be permitted to go beyond the palisade to pick fruit. But, always, she had, for some reason, forbidden me this permission. "I will not escape," I had assured her, irritably. "I know," she had said. What then could have been her objection? At last, she had yielded to my entreaties and permitted me, leashed with Techne, to go beyond the stockade and pick berries. It was glorious to be outside the stockade, even though fastened by a leather neck strap to another girl. Moreover, today, two more female prisoners had been brought in, girls who had been fleeing from unwanted companionships, arranged by their parents. There would be another feast, as there had been last night, and this time Ute had told me that, if the berry picking went well, I need not be locked in the shed early this night. I would be permitted, late, to serve the feasters. I was very pleased that the two girls had been captured.

"I suppose I must be placed in silk then," I had said to Ute, angrily.

"And slave bells," had added Ute.

How furious I had been!

"I do not wish to serve men," I had told Ute. "Moreover, I do not wish to serve them clad revealingly in a bit of silk and the bells of a slave girl!"

"Well," said Ute, "you may, if you wish, remain in the shed."

"I suppose it is not fair to the other girls," I had said, "that I should be permitted to remain in the shed while they are forced to serve, so clad and belled."

"Do you wish to serve or not?" had asked Ute.

"I will serve," I had said, with an air of defeat.

"You will then be silked and belled," she said.

"Very well," I had said, dropping my head with resignation. I found myself looking forward eagerly to the evening.

I was sure that I would be among the most beautiful of all the girls. I wondered if, in silk and bells, Rask of Treve might notice me. How I hated him!

"But," had said Ute, "if a man seizes you, you are not to yield yourself to him, for you are white silk."

A flash of irritation passed through me. "I am charged with the protection of my market value?" I asked, ironically.

"Yes," said Ute, matter-of-factly. "Though I, if I were a man, would pay more for a red-silk girl."

"I must do nothing," I said, "to diminish the investment of Rask of Treve?"

"That is correct," said Ute.

"What if I am simply seized, and my attacker is not prepared to listen to reason?" I asked.

Ute laughed. It was the first time I had seen her laugh in the camp. I was pleased I had made her laugh.

"Cry out," said Ute, "and the others will take you from him and get him a red-silk girl."

"All right," I had said.

Ute had then said to the guard, "Leash her." And I and Techne, leashed together, had been taken from the stockade. "Be careful, El-in-or," Ute had called after me.

I did not understand her. "All right," I had called back to her.

I now felt a tug on the neck strap. "Hurry, El-in-or," said Techne. "We must be back soon! Our buckets are not half filled!"

I was irritated with Techne. She was young. She was a lovely slave, though fresh to the collar.

The sun was warm and its heat went through me, and I stretched happily.

When neither the guard nor Techne were looking I stole berries from her buckets, to put in mine, handfuls. Why should I work as hard as she? Also, when they were not looking, I placed berries in my mouth, taking care that the juices not stain my lips, revealing that I had eaten them. I had done this sort of thing often before, when I had picked berries for Targo's caravans. Ute and the guard had never seen. I had fooled them all. I was too clever for them!

At last our buckets were all full, and we returned to the camp of Rask of Treve.

The guard handed our buckets to other girls to be taken to the kitchen shed, and he then unleashed us.

"El-in-or, Techne," said Ute, "follow me."

We did so.

She took us to that part of the camp near the horizontal pole, some nine feet high, resting across the two pairs of crossed poles, rather like a pole for hanging meat, or trophies, from. Near that pole, near the iron ring set in the stone, which was buried in the ground, Ute told Techne and I to kneel.

To one side there was a brazier filled with white-hot coals. From the brazier there protruded the handles of four irons. The fire was quite hot, and it had apparently been heating for some two or three Ahn, perhaps even from the time we had went forth to pick berries.

I was apprehensive.

Two or three guards stood about, and some of my fellow female work slaves.

One of the guards who stood nearby was the one who had taken Techne and I beyond the palisade to gather berries.

Some other men, and girls, from the camp, strolled over to the poles.

Ute stood sternly before us.

Techne looked about, frightened. I was not pleased myself, but I appeared calm.

"Techne," said Ute.

"Yes," said Techne, frightened.

"Did you steal berries from El-in-or?" demanded Ute.

"No, no!" she cried.

"El-in-or," said Ute, "did you, or did you not, steal berries from Techne?"

"I did not," I said.

Ute turned to the guard.

"The first one," he said, "tells the truth. The second one is lying."

"No!" I cried out. "No!"

Ute looked at me. "It is not hard to tell, El-in-or," she said. "Sometimes the guard sees you, sometimes he sees the shadow, or he hears what you are doing, or he sees the different amounts in the buckets. Sometimes he watches in the reflection of a shield hoop."

"No," I whimpered. "No."

"You frequently stole from me," said Ute, "but I asked the guard, who also knew, not to inform on you."

I put my head down, miserable.

"I will not steal berries again, Ute," I said.

"No," she said, "I do not think you will."

I looked up at her.

"But this time," she said, "you stole from Techne, who is one of my girls. I cannot permit that."

"I didn't steal from her!" I wept.

Ute looked at the guard.

He shrugged. "She is lying," he said.

"I will not steal from her anymore," I cried.

"No," said Ute, "I do not think you will."

Ute then went to Techne. "Did you eat any of the berries?" she asked.

"No," said Techne, frightened.

Then Ute stood before me.

"Did you, El-in-or, eat any of the berries?" she asked.

"No, Ute," I said. "No!"

Then Ute stood again before Techne. "Open your mouth and thrust out your tongue," she said.

I moaned.

Ute inspected Techne's mouth and tongue. "Good," she said.

Then Ute stood before me.

"Please, Ute," I begged. "Please!"

"Open your mouth and thrust out your tongue," said Ute.

"Please, Ute!" I whimpered.

"Open your mouth and thrust out your tongue," said Ute. I did so.

There was much laughter from the group.

"You may go, Techne," said Ute.

The young slave leaped to her feet and fled away.

I started to rise to my feet. "Not you, El-in-or," said Ute.

I knelt before her, trembling.

"Remove your garment," she said.

Terrified, I did so, and then again, as before, knelt before her, wearing only my collar.

"Now," said Ute, "ask a guard to brand and beat you."

"No!" I screamed. "No, no, no, no!"

"I will mark her," said a voice.

I turned to see Rask of Treve.

"Master!" I wept, throwing myself to his feet.

"Hold her," he said to four of his men.

"Please!" I cried. "No, Master, no!"

Four men held me, naked, near the brazier. I could feel the heat blazing from the cannister. The sky was very blue, the clouds were white.

"Please, no!" I wept.

I saw Rask, with a heavy glove, draw forth one of the irons from the fire. It terminated in a tiny letter, not more than a quarter of an inch high. The letter was white hot. "This is a penalty brand," he said. "It marks you as a liar."

"Please, Master!" I wept.

"I no longer have patience with you," he said. "Be marked as what you are."

I screamed uncontrollably as he pressed in the iron, holding it firmly into my leg. Then, after some two to four Ihn, he removed it. I could not stop screaming with pain. I smelled the odor of burned flesh, my own. I began to whimper. I could not breathe. I gasped for breath. Still the men held me.

"This penalty brand," said Rask of Treve, lifting another iron from the brazier, again with a tiny letter at its glowing termination, "marks you also as what you are, as a thief."

"Please, no, Master!" I wept.

I could not move a muscle of my left leg. It might as well have been locked in a vise. It must wait for the iron.

I screamed again, uncontrollably. I had been branded as a thief.

"This third iron," said Rask of Treve, "is, too, a penalty iron. I mark you with it not for myself, but for Ute."

Through raging tears I saw, white hot, the tiny letter.

"It marks you as a traitress," said Rask of Treve. He looked at me, with fury. "Be marked as a traitress," he said. Then he pressed the third iron into my flesh. As it entered my flesh, biting and searing, I saw Ute watching, her face betraying no emotion. I screamed, and wept, and screamed.

Still the men did not release me.

Rask of Treve lifted the last iron from the fire. It was much larger, the letter at its termination some one and a half inches high. It, too, was white hot. I knew the brand. I had seen it, on Ena's thigh. It was the mark of Treve. Rask of Treve had decided that my flesh should bear that mark.

"No, Master, please!" I begged him.

"Yes, Worthless Slave," said he, "you will wear in your flesh the mark of the city of Treve."

"Please," I begged.

"When men ask you," said he, "who it was that marked you as liar and thief, and traitress, point to this brand, and say, I was marked by one of Treve, who was displeased with me."

"Do not punish me with the iron!" I cried.

I could not move my thigh. It must wait, helpless, for the blazing kiss of the iron.

"No," I cried, "No!"

He approached me. I could feel the terrible heat of the iron, even inches from my body.

"Please, no!" I begged.

The iron was poised.

I saw his eyes and realized that I would receive no mercy. He was a tarnsman of Treve.

"With the mark of Treve," he said, "I brand you slave."

Then the iron, crackling and hissing, was pressed, deeply and firmly, into my flesh, for some five seconds.

I screamed and sobbed, and began to cough and vomit.

My wrists were tied before my body, by a long strip of binding fiber, which was then thrown over the top of the horizontal pole. I felt my wrists pulled above my head and then I was jerked from my feet and hung, suspended by the wrists, from the pole. The free end of the strap was secured to one side. The men stepped back.

I was sobbing.

"Bring the whip," said Rask of Treve.

I hung perhaps a foot from the ground. I felt my ankles lashed together, and then a strap tied them to the ring below, that set in the stone, which was buried in the ground. That way I would not swing much under the blows.

Once, long ago, I had been beaten by Lana, with a handful of straps. I had never forgotten it. I was delicate. I could not stand pain. I was not a common girl. I had always feared, but never felt, the five-strap Gorean slave whip, wielded with the full, terrible strength of a man.

"Please, Master!" I cried. "Do not beat me! I cannot stand pain! You do not understand! I am not a common girl! It hurts me! I am too delicate to be beaten!"

I heard the men and girls about laughing. I hung by the wrists, miserable. My thigh felt as though it were burning. Tears streamed from my eyes. I coughed, and could not breathe. I heard the voice of Rask of Treve. "To begin," he was saying, "you will receive one stroke for each letter of the word 'Liar', then one stroke for each letter of the word 'Thief', and then a stroke for each letter of the word 'Traitress'. You will count the strokes.

I sobbed.

"Count," commanded Rask of Treve.

"I am illiterate," I wept. "I do not know how many to count!"

"There are four characters in the first expression," said Inge.

I looked at her with horror. I had not seen her until now. I did not want her to see me being beaten. I saw, too, now, for the first time, that Rena, too, stood nearby. I did not want them to see me being beaten.

"You made a great fuss when you were branded," said Inge.

"That is certainly true," agreed Rena.

"Count," commanded Rask of Treve.

"One!" I cried out in misery.

Suddenly my back exploded. I screamed but there was no sound. There seemed no breath in my body. And then there was only pain, and I almost lost consciousness. I hung by the wrists. There had been the terrible sound of the leather, and then the pain.

I could not stand it.

"Count!" I heard.

"No, no!" I cried.

"Count," urged Inge, "or it will go hard with you."

"Count," pressed Rena. "Count! The lash will not lower your value," she said. "The straps are too broad. They only punish."

"Two," I wept.

Again the leather fell and I gasped and twisted, hanging burning from the pole.

"Count!" said Rask of Treve.

"I cannot," I wept. "I cannot."

"Three," said Ute. "I will count for her."

The lash fell again.

"Four," said Ute.

Twice in my beating I lost consciousness, and twice I was revived, chilled water thrown on me.

At last the strokes had been counted. I hung, my head down, helpless.

"Now," said Rask of Treve, "I shall beat you until it pleases me to stop."

Ten more strokes he gave to the helpless slave girl, who twice more lost consciousness, and twice more was awakened to the drenching of cold water. And then, as she scarcely understood, hanging half conscious in the fires of her pain, she heard him say, "Cut her down."

The binding fiber was removed from her wrists but her hands, that she might not tear at her brands, were snapped behind her back in slave bracelets. Then, by the hair, she stumbling, scarcely able to stand, he dragged her to the small, square iron box which sat near the whipping pole, and thrust her within.

Crouching inside the box, I saw the door shut, and heard the two heavy, flat bolts sliding into place. I then heard the click of two padlocks, securing them in place.

I was locked inside. I could see a tiny slit of the outside through the aperture in the iron door, about a half an inch in height and seven inches in width. There was a somewhat larger opening at the foot of the door, about two inches in height and a foot wide. The box itself was square, with dimensions of perhaps one yard square. It was hot, and dark.

I remembered that a slave girl, on my first day in the

camp of Rask of Treve, had warned me, that if I lied or
stole, I would be beaten and put in the slave box.

I moaned and fell to my side, my knees drawn up under
my chin, my hands braceleted behind me. My thigh burned
terribly, from the branding, and my back and the back of
my legs still screamed from the cruel flames of the leather
lash. Elinor Brinton, of Park Avenue, had been branded
as a liar, a thief and a traitress, and a bold tarnsman, from
a distant world, her master, had put into her flesh, insolently, the mark of his own city. The girl in the slave box was
under no delusion as to who it was who owned her. He had
collared her, and, with a hot iron, had placed in her flesh
his brand.

In the slave box, she fell unconscious. But that night,
cold, she awakened, still in pain. Outside, she heard the
sounds of pleasure and feasting, that celebration called in
honor of the capturing of two young girls, who had fled
from undesired companionships, which had been arranged
by their parents.

I remained days in the slave box. The door was opened,
when I was braceleted, only to feed and water me. I was
not allowed to stretch my body. On the fifth day the
bracelets were removed, but I was kept in the box. My
brands had now healed. But the box itself, its heat, its darkness, its tiny dimensions, worked their tortures in me.

In the first days, braceleted, I screamed and kicked, and
begged to be released. After my bracelets were removed,
and the food then, and water, would only be thrust through
the hole under the tiny iron door, I pounded, and screamed,
and scratched at the inside of the box. I thrust my fingers
through the tiny aperture and cried out for mercy. I feared
I would go insane. Ute would feed me, and fill my water
pan, but she would not speak to me. Once, however, she
did say to me, "You will be freed when your master
wishes it, not before." Once Inge came by, to taunt me.
"Rask of Treve has forgotten you," she said. Rena, too,
accompanied Inge. "Yes," she laughed, "he has forgotten
you. He has forgotten you!"

On the tenth day, instead of the pan of bread, with the water, Ute thrust a different pan under the door. I screamed. Tiny things, with tiny sounds, moved, crawling over and about one another in it. I screamed again, and thrust it back out. It had been filled with the fat, loathesome green insects which, in the Ka-la-na thicket, Ute had told me were edible. Indeed, she had eaten them. "They are nourishing," she had said. I screamed hysterically, pounding at the sides of the slave box. The second day, too, I thrust the pan away, almost vomiting. I saw Ute, through the slit, take one of the insects and bite it in two, eating it. Then she turned away. I resolved to starve myself. The third day, almost vomiting, I ate five of them. They, such insects, and water, were my food for the remainder of my time in the tiny slave box. I would spend hours at the slit in the door, hoping to see someone walk by. I would call to them, but they would not answer, for one does not converse with a girl in the slave box. Then I was happy, even, to see someone pass by, or birds alight on the grass and peck for seeds. I spent eighteen days in the slave box.

On the night of the eighteenth day, Ute, with Inge and Rena, crouched before the box.

"Does El-in-or, the slave, wish to leave the box?" asked Ute.

On my knees in the box, my eyes at the opening, frightened, my fingers on the slit, I whispered, "Yes, El-in-or, the slave, wishes to leave the box."

"Does El-in-or, the slave, beg to leave the box?" asked Ute.

"Yes, yes!" I wept. "El-in-or, the slave, begs to leave the box!"

"Release the slave," said Ute, to Inge and Rena.

Elinor Brinton heard the padlocks unlocked. She heard the flat, heavy bolts slide back. She saw the small door swing open.

On her hands and knees, painfully, inch by inch, she crawled from the box. She then collapsed to the grass.

"Wash the slave," said Ute, with disgust, to Inge and Rena.

I screamed with pain as Inge and Rena stretched out my

body, and then, with brushes and water, almost vomiting, they cleaned me.

After Inge and Rena had finished their work, even to the cleaning of my hair, a guard, summoned, not much pleased, carried me, helpless and in pain, back to the shed for female work slaves. There Ute, with Inge and Rena, fed me simple broths, which I gratefully drank. The next day, as Ute commanded, I remained in the shed, food and water being brought to me by Inge and Rena. On the following day I was returned to work. My first task was to clean the slave box, to rid it of its filth. After I had done this, naked, and had washed my body and hair thoroughly, I was again given the tunic of a work slave. I found it a very precious garment. I worked at a variety of tasks that day. Late in the afternoon, I was sent outside, leashed again with Techne, to pick ram-berries. I did not steal berries from her, nor did I eat any.

I was regarded in the camp with contempt and amusement. Not only were my ears pierced, but now, in my flesh, I wore penalty brands.

Once, two weeks after my release from the slave box, Rask of Treve passed near me, in the company of Verna, the panther girl.

I fell to my knees immediately, and put my head to the ground.

I was merely a slave girl who had been punished, and would be again, if need be.

They passed me.

Neither of them noticed me.

One day became another in the secret war camp of Rask of Treve.

The tarnsmen, in their flights, did not have much luck, and many were the times when they returned, their saddle packs empty, their saddles bare of helpless beauties lashed across them.

Similarly, one day was much as another for Elinor Brinton, the female work slave in the camp of Rask of Treve. She rose at dawn and, until dusk, with her work companions,

performed her repetitive, servile tasks. After the night feeding, she, with her work companions, would be ordered to
the slave shed, where they would be locked for the night,
only to be summoned again in the morning, ordered from
the shed, for another round of their labors, tasks fit for
such as they, female work slaves.

I learned to iron and sew, and to cook and clean. Verna
could not have done these things. She hunted, and held
converse with men.

It could perhaps be mentioned that such work, cooking,
cleaning and laundering, and such, is commonly regarded as
being beneath even free women, particularly those of high
caste. In the high cylinders, in Gorean cities, there are often
public slaves who tend the central kitchens in cylinders, care
for the children, but may not instruct them, and, for a
tiny fee to the city, clean compartments and do laundering.
Thus even families who cannot afford to own and feed a
slave often have the use of several such unfortunate girls,
commonly captured from hostile cities. Free women often
treat such girls with great cruelty, and the mere word of a
free woman, that she is displeased with the girl's work, is
enough to have the girl beaten. The girls strive zealously in
their work to please the free women. Such girls, also, have
a low use-rent, payable to the city, should young males wish
to partake of their pleasures. Here again, the mere word of
the free person, that he is not completely pleased, is enough
to earn the miserable girl a severe beating. Accordingly, she
struggles to please him with all her might. It is not pleasant,
I fear, to be a public slave. The Gorean free woman, often,
does only what work she chooses. If she does not wish to
prepare a meal, she and her companion may go to the
public tables, or, should they wish, order a girl to bring
them food from the central kitchens.

But I found, perhaps surprisingly, that I did not much
mind the work of the female work slave. I recognized that
it was essential, that it had to be done. I recognized further
that there was something farcical in the thought of the
Gorean male lending his hand to such small, unimportant
work. It would have been like the larl with a broom. I

could well imagine the accommodating, solicitous males of Earth in aprons, puttering about with vacuum cleaners and boxes of detergent, but I could not imagine it of the Gorean male. He is so different from the males of Earth, so powerful, so strong, so uncompromised, so masculine. Before him it is hard for a female not to know herself as a female, and in knowing this, recognizing herself as smaller and weaker, and thus to be given the tasks he does not care to perform.

Similarly the Gorean free woman does not seem appropriately suited to menial tasks. She is too free, too proud. It is difficult for a collared slave girl even to look into the eyes of such a person. Thus, who is to do such work? The answer seems obvious, that it will be done by the slaves. The small, light, unpleasant work will be done by the female slave; the large, heavy, unpleasant work by the draft animal, or the male slave. Why should free persons do such tasks? They have slaves for such work. And I well knew myself to be a slave. It was thus natural that it should be I, and my sisters in bondage, who performed such labors. How else could it have been?

"Hurry, Slave! Hurry in your work!" cried Ute.

I did so.

I did my work quietly, and seldom spoke to the other girls, nor did they much speak to me. Though I often worked with them, I was, it seemed, always alone. When they sang at their work, or enjoyed laughter and sport, I did not sing, nor did I laugh, nor join them in their pleasures. I worked well. I was, I expect, one of Ute's best workers. Sometimes, when I would finish my work, I would help the other girls with theirs.

Once, when I was helping Inge, she said to me, "I thought you were too delicate to be beaten."

"I was mistaken," I said.

She laughed.

I no longer had an interest in lying or cheating, or shirking my work. I suppose, in part, it was that I was afraid of being punished. Surely I had not, and could not, forget the iron nor the whip's hot kiss. I much feared them. I could no longer even look on a slave whip without a feeling of terror, for I understood now the pain of its meaning, and what it might do to me. If a guard even lifted one, I would cringe. I would obey, and with promptness! Do not scorn me, until you yourself have felt the iron and the lash. But, too, somehow, perhaps unaccountably, lying and stealing now seemed to me small, and trivial, too petty to perform. I no longer regarded such behavior as clever, but now, rather, as unworthy or stupid, whether one was caught or not. I had thought much in the slave box. I was not much pleased with how I had found myself to be. I knew that my body was a slave body, and that it was owned, and that it stood in constant jeopardy of fierce, swift punishment by a strong master, whether it might deserve that punishment or not. But, too, I felt that I had, according to Gorean justice, well earned my beating and my branding, and my torturous confinement in the slave box. I did not wish again to earn such punishment, not simply because I feared it, but because it seemed to me unworthy that I should have done the things for which I was punished. In the slave box, alone with myself, I discovered I did not wish to be the sort of person I had been. I had not been pleased to be locked in the box alone with myself, with such a person, forced there to face her and realize that she was your own self.

"Pierced-ear Girl!" cried a man. "Kneel!"

I did so.

With his foot, he thrust me from his path, laughing, and continued on his way.

Sometimes the other girls would trip me when I was carrying burdens, or dirty the work which I had done, that I must do it over.

Once two warriors, for a joke, tied my ankles together and suspended me, upside down, from the whipping pole, spinning me about, and back, until I vomited and cried out for mercy. Laughing they then left, and Ute, with Rena, released me.

"They are cruel," said Ute.

I wept, and kissed her feet.

I found that I no longer desired to serve in the evening,

even should there be feasting. I wanted only my work, and to be left alone. In the evening, I wanted only the silence and darkness of the shed, with its padlocked door.

In my flesh I wore penalty brands.

"Let El-in-or be it!" cried Ute, when the girls were playing tag.

"No," they cried.

"Do it," said Ute.

"Please, Ute," I begged, "let me go to the shed."

"Very well," said Ute.

And I went back to the shed.

The contempt and amusement which greeted me in the camp made me form within myself a core of hardness. I became withdrawn. I no longer desired to serve in the evening, should there be feasting. I wanted only my work, and the silence and darkness of the shed, with its padlocked door.

I wanted to be alone in the shed, behind the locked door.

There was only one thing left to me, in which I might take pride, that I was not as other women. No matter what brands might be fixed in my flesh, nor what the leather might do to my back or the tiny dimensions of the slave box to my body, I knew I did not have their weaknesses. I recalled the circle of the dance in the northern forest, and how even Verna, the proud Verna, had, beside herself with need, writhed helplessly beneath the bright moons of Gor, a female. How I had then despised her, and the others, so helpless and vulnerable and female! How weak they were! How pleased I was that I was not as they. Gradually, in me, there built up a compensating hatred to counter my shame, and the brands that proclaimed me among the most unworthy and miserable of slaves. I began to hate human beings. I was better than they. I would be better than they. I began to do my work with great efficiency and promptness, better than the other girls. I became exact in my speech, and, though I did not much express myself, quite critical of others. In spite of my brands, I would be superior to them all. I began to wear a new morality with a smugness. I became arrogant in my virtue, to the irritation of the other girls, but I did not care, for I was better than they. I would not now lie or cheat or steal, of course, but not now because I did not care for that sort of thing, or did not wish to behave in such a fashion, but primarily because I was not the sort of person who would do that sort of thing. It was beneath me. I was too good to behave in such a fashion. Virtue, I discovered, is one way in which a human being may attempt to diminish and insult others. I used the blade of cooperativeness, of virtue, of diligence, of punctuality to proclaim myself better than the others, all of them. Mostly I prided myself on my moral superiority as a woman, above the self-indulgent, contaminating weaknesses of their piteous needs. I was not as they.

"Tonight," cried Ute, happily, "you will serve, all of you!"

The girls cried out with pleasure.

This afternoon, for the first time in weeks, the raids of Rask of Treve had been successful. Eleven girls had been brought in, and much treasure. Laughing, bloody tarnsmen, with strings of pearls thrown about their necks, and cups and goblets tied at their saddles, and their saddle packs bulging with the weight of golden tarn disks, had brought their tarns down, wings beating, to receive the greetings of the camp. Merchants brought sides of bosk, and thighs of tarsk, and wines and fruits to camp, and cheeses and breads and nuts, and flowers and candies and silks and honeys. There was much bustle and laughter about the camp, much preparation and shouting. In the women's tent, eleven girls, tomorrow to be collared, crouched in fear. Slave girls staggered under the plunder, carrying it to the tents of the warriors.

"Tonight," had cried Rask of Treve, blood on his shield, his eyes like those of laughing tarns, "we will feast!"

The men had clashed their weapons on their shields and the girls had scurried away that the feast might be prepared.

I would not serve, of course, for Ute would excuse me. She knew I was not as the other girls.

In the shed, scornfully, I watched them, eagerly speaking about the evening, laughing and joking. Such might well serve men.

Then, at Ute's call, they went from the shed, happily, to receive silks and bells.

How I scorned them, such pitiful weaklings!

I remained in the shed. I would retire early. I would need rest, for I must work tomorrow.

"El-in-or, come forth!" I heard. It was Ute's voice.

I was puzzled.

I got to my feet and went outside the shed. There was a mirror there, and cosmetics, and silks and bells. There were no men about. The girls were preparing themselves.

I looked at Ute.

"Remove your clothing," she said.

"No!" I cried. "No!"

I quickly, in anguish, removed the garment. There was a jangle of slave bells, wrapped in a bit of silk, as Ute threw me bells and silk.

"Please, Ute!" I wept. "No!"

The other girls looked up from their work, and laughed.

"Ute," I begged, "please, please, no!"

"Make yourself pleasing, Slave," said Ute, and turned away.

I slipped on the bit of silk. I looked in the mirror and shuddered. I had been naked before men, many times, but it did not seem to me that I had been so naked as this. It was Gorean pleasure silk. Not naked, I seemed more than naked.

I waited my turn before the mirror and applied the cosmetics of the Gorean slave girl. I knew well how to do this, for I had been trained.

I buckled the slave bells on my left and right ankles, and then I went to Ute.

"Please, Ute," I begged.

She smiled. "You come to ask to be belled?" she asked.

I put my head down. Ute was adamant. "Yes," I said.

Ute took the other slave bells and buckled one strap, with its two small buckles, like the ankle straps, except smaller, about my left wrist, and then buckled the other strap, with its two small buckles, about my right wrist.

I was belled.

I stood about, miserably, while the other girls finished their primping. How exciting they were in their silk, their bells and cosmetics.

"You are not unattractive," said Ute to me.

I said nothing. I was miserable.

In a few minutes, Ute, who retained her work tunic, and would not serve, reviewed us, commenting here and there, and recommending small changes upon occasion. We were her girls, and she wished us to present ourselves well.

She stopped before me.

"Stand prettily," she said.

Furiously, I did so.

Ute went to the chest of silks and bells and brought forth five more slave bells, which she tied with bits of scarlet ribbon to my collar.

"There is something missing," she said, standing back.

I did not respond.

She went again to the chest. The girls gasped. As I stood there two large, golden earrings were thrust through the piercing of my ears and fastened on me.

There were tears in my eyes.

"And here," said Ute, "lest the ardor of the men become too strong, this!"

The girls laughed. She took a white, silken ribbon and wrapped it five times about the collar, not tying it.

I had been marked white silk.

Inge and Rena laughed. "Do not laugh," smiled Ute, "for you, too, will be so marked, lest Raf and Pron, huntsmen of Treve, in a careless moment, devour my two other white-silk pretties."

The other girls laughed. I could see, to my irritation, that Inge and Rena did not much care to wear the white ribbon. I could not understand this. Did they wish to be used as helpless slaves by the handsome, powerful Raf and Pron? I supposed they did, and I despised them in their weakness. Inge had been of the scribes and Rena had been free. She had been even the Lady Rena of Lydius! Now they seemed to be naught but female slaves. I was pleased that I was not such as they.

But how shamed I was, that I, Elinor Brinton, of Park Avenue, must appear before men and serve them, so clad and so belled.

Ute touched me, and the others, then, with a bit of perfume. I was in anguish.

"Serve, Slaves!" laughed Ute, clapping her hands, and the girls fled to the center of the camp, where I heard the shouting of pleasure of men, welcoming them.

Ute and I stood facing one another.

"Serve, Slave," said Ute.

Angrily I, perfumed and rouged, belled and silked, turned and followed the other girls to the center of the camp, near the great tent of Rask of Treve, of scarlet canvas lined with scarlet silk, on its eight poles.

"Wine! Bring me wine!" shouted the warrior.

I, a slave girl, with a rustle of silk and slave bells, hurried to him, a master, to serve him.

Kneeling, I filled his cup.

The music of those of the caste of musicians was heady, like the wine.

There was shouting and laughter, the pleasurable moaning and crying out of girls used beyond the rim of firelight.

There was much feasting, and drinking.

On the sand, before the warriors, belled, in scarlet silk, the girl, Talena, danced.

Some of them shouted, and threw bones and pieces of meat at her.

I tried to rise, but the warrior whose cup I had filled had his hand in my hair.

"So, you are a liar, and a thief, and a traitress?" he asked.

"Yes," I said, terrified.

He turned my head from side to side, looking at the earrings. He was drunk, and I could tell that he was aroused.

"More wine," he said.

I again filled the cup.

"Your ears are pierced," he said, shaking his head, trying to clear his vision.

"If it please Master," I whispered. "If it please Master."

"Wine!" cried another man.

I tried to rise.

Talena was driven from the sand and another girl, belled, stood forth to please the men.

At the head of the feast sat the magnificent Rask of Treve, in his victory. At his side, cross-legged, sat Verna, the panther girl, who was served by we girls as might have been a warrior. How I envied her her freedom, her beauty, her pride, and even the simple opacity of the brief garment she wore. She was not clad in a bit of silk, a touch of cosmetics, a scent of perfume and the bells of a slave.

The man whom I had served wine reached clumsily for me.

"I am white silk!" I cried, shrinking back.

"Wine!" cried the other man.

I tried to rise, but the man's hand was knotted in the silk. If I moved I would strip myself.

Another girl, on her knees, reaching for him, holding his head, insinuated herself between us. "I am red silk," she murmured. "Touch me! Touch me!"

His hand left my silk and I darted away.

I fled to the other man and served him.

"Wine!" called Verna. I ran to her and, kneeling, filled her cup.

"Wine," said Rask of Treve, holding forth his cup.

I could not meet his eyes. All of me blushed red before him, my master. I filled his cup.

"She is pretty," said Verna.

Another girl, with jeers, was driven from the sand, and another took her place.

"Wine!" cried another man, about the circle.

I leaped up and, carrying the vessel, with a clash of slave bells, ran to serve him.

I tipped the vessel, but the wine was gone. I must fetch more.

"Run, Girl!" he cried. "Fetch wine!"

"Yes, Master!" I cried.

I fled from the firelight. I stumbled over two figures, rolling in the darkness. A warrior cursed. I suddenly saw, rolled on her back, her dark hair loose, under the moons of Gor, Techne, her lips parted, reaching for the warrior. I fled into the darkness, toward the kitchen shed. Before I reached it I felt myself seized in a man's arms, and felt his leather. His bearded face pressed to my softness. "No!" I cried. He took my face in his hands. There were bells on my collar. "You are the slave, El-in-or," he said, "the little liar, the thief and traitress." I tried to twist away. He saw the earrings of gold, and I felt his hands hard on my arms, hurting them. "I am white silk!" I cried. He shook his head and looked at the collar. About it, wrapped there by Ute earlier, was the ribbon of white silk. He was furious. He did not release me. I could hear, from back at the fire, yet another girl jeered from the sand. "Please," I whispered. "I am white silk! I am white silk." Another shout from the fire indicated that a new girl now addressed herself to the pleasures of the feasters, and one, it seems, pleasing to them. "I would like to see you dance, little traitress," he said. "I must fetch wine," I said, and twisted away, running toward the kitchen shed. There I found Ute. "Do not send me back, Ute!" I wept. "Fetch your wine and return," said Ute. I dipped the wine vesssel into the great stone jar, again filling it. "Please, Ute!" I wept. I could hear more shouting back at the fire.

"El-in-or!" I heard shout. "El-in-or, the traitress!"

I was terrified.

"They are calling for you," said Ute.

"Come, Slave, to the sand!" ordered a man's voice. It was the fierce, bearded fellow, who had accosted me as I had fled to the kitchen shed.

"Hurry, Slave!" cried Ute. "Hurry!"

With a cry of misery, spilling wine over the brim of the

vessel, I slipped past the man in the doorway of the kitchen shed, and ran back to the firelight.

When I reached the feasters another girl took from me the wine.

I was thrust rudely to the center of the sand. I felt a hand tear away the bit of silk I wore. I cried out in misery and covered my face with my hands.

"Liar!" I heard cry.

"Thief!" "Traitress!" I heard cry.

The musicians began to play.

I fell to my knees.

The girls began to jeer. The men shouted angrily. "Bring whips!" I heard cry.

"Dance for your masters, Slave," I heard Verna call out.

I extended my hands to Rask of Treve, piteously. I was suddenly aware, behind me, of a warrior, standing. In his right hand, the lashes looped in his left, he held a slave whip. I cried out with misery, my hands extended to Rask of Treve, my eyes pleading. He must show Elinor Brinton mercy!

But she would be shown no mercy.

"Dance, Slave," said Rask of Treve.

I leaped to my feet, my hands held over my head. The musicians again began to play.

And Elinor Brinton, of Park Avenue, of Earth, a Gorean slave girl, danced before primitive warriors.

The music was raw, melodious, deeply sensual.

I suddenly saw, scarcely comprehending, the awe in their eyes. They were silent, their fierce eyes bright. I saw their hands tighten, the shoulders lean forward.

I danced.

Well had I been trained in the pens of Ko-ro-ba. Not for nothing had it been I and Lana who had been among the most superb of the slave females then in the pens.

In the firelight, in the sand, before warriors, I danced. My feet, belled, struck in the sand. The perfume was wild about me, swift in the brightness and the shadows. On my lips I wore slave rouge. I danced.

I could see the eyes of the men, the movements of their bodies.

I realized, suddenly, in the dance, that I had power in my beauty, incredible power, power to strike men and stun them, to astonish them in the firelight, to make them, if I wished, mad with the wanting of me.

"She is superb!" I heard whisper.

I danced toward him, he who had said this, and he leaped toward me, but two of his fellows seized him, holding him back. I danced back, my hands held to him, as though I had been torn from him.

"Aiii!" he cried.

There were shouts of pleasure.

I saw the girls watching, too, their eyes wide, too, with pleasure.

I threw back my head and the bells flashed at my ankles and wrists, and in my body the music, in its bright flames, burned.

I would make them mad with the wanting of me!

I would do so.

Something deep and female within me emerged, something I had never felt before. I would torture them! I did have power. I would make them suffer!

I was white silk!

It was safe to dance before them as I pleased.

And so Elinor Brinton danced to torment them.

They cried out with anguish and pleasure. How pleased I was in my power!

As the music changed so, too, did the dancer, and she became as one with the music, a frightened girl, new to the collar, a timid girl, delicate and submissive, a lonely slave, yearning for her master, a drunken wench, rejecting her slavery, a proud girl, determined to be defiant, a raw, red-silk slave, mad with the need for a master's touch.

And, too, as I danced, I would sometimes dance toward a warrior, sometimes as though begging him his glance, sometimes as though seeking his protection in my plight, sometimes as though I could not help myself, but was drawn to him, helplessly, in the vulnerability of the female slave, sometimes, when I chose, to deliberately, overtly and cruelly, taunt him with my beauty, my desirability, and my inaccessibility.

More than one cried out with rage and reached toward me, or shook his fist at me, but I laughed, and danced back away from him.

Then, as the music struck towards its swirling peaks I unaccountably, boldly, for no reason I understood, faced Rask of Treve, and before him, my master, I danced. His eyes were expressionless. He sipped his wine. I danced my hatred for him, my scorn and contempt for him. I danced to arouse him, to make him mad with the desire of me, which desire I could then frustrate, which desire I could then, in my strength, for I was not as other women, for I did not have their weaknesses, fail to fulfill. I could hurt him, and I would! He had captured me! He had enslaved me! He had lashed and branded me! He had put me in the slave box! I despised him. I hated him. I would make him suffer! How desperately, in my dance, I tried to arouse him! Yet his eyes remained expressionless. And, from time to time, observing me through narrowed lids, he would sip his wine. And then I knew my body was dancing something to him that I could not understand, that I feared. It was strange. It was as though my body would, in its own right, speak to him, as though it were trying, on some level I could not comprehend, to communicate with him. And then again I was as I was before, and could dance my contempt and hatred for him. He seemed amused. I was furious.

When the music finished, I fell to my knees, insolently, before him, my head to the ground.

There were many shouts of acclaim, and pleasure, from the men, and even from the girls, who struck their left shoulders with the palms of their hands.

"Shall I have her whipped?" asked a man of Rask of Treve.

I was frightened.

"No," said Rask of Treve.

He gestured that I should leave the sand. "Bring others forward to dance," he said.

I picked up the bit of silk which had been torn from me and left the sand, putting it on. I was sweating, I was breathing heavily.

Inge and Rena were thrust forward by Raf and Pron, that they might please the feasters.

There was more shouting.

I walked into the darkness.

I encountered Ute, outside the rim of the firelight. "You are beautiful, El-in-or," she said.

I followed her to the kitchen shed. There, with water, and oils, and towels, she bade me clean and refresh my body. I did so, and prepared to go to the shed.

"No," said Ute.

I looked at her.

"Prepare yourself as you did before," she said.

"Why?" I asked.

"Do so," she said.

Again I prepared myself, as I had been earlier in the evening, as a belled, silken-clad, rouged Gorean slave girl.

"Now," said Ute, "you will wait."

For more than two Ahn we sat in the kitchen shed. Then the feasting grew less, and the warriors, taking what wenches pleased them, went to their tents.

Ute approached me and, behind each ear, touched me afresh with perfume.

I looked at her, puzzled. Then I shook my head. "No," I cried, "no!"

Her eyes were hard.

"Go to the tent of Rask of Treve," she said.

"Enter," said Rask of Treve.

I was alone, defenseless in his war camp, his slave.

I entered the tent.

"Tie shut the tent flaps," said he.

I turned and tied shut the flaps, with five cords, fastening myself in the tent with him.

I turned to face him, his girl.

There was a small fire in the fire bowl in the tent, and

the tiny tripod set above it, where wine might be warmed.

The interior of the tent was lined with red silk. The hangings were rich. There were, here and there, small, brass tharlarion-oil lamps hanging from projections set on the tent poles. At the sides of the tent, where it sloped downward, there were many chests, and kegs and sacks, filled with the booties and plunders of many raids. Several of the chests were open, and from some of the sacks, onto the rugs, spilled pieces of gold. I could see the glint of the precious metals, and the refulgence of gems, reflecting the light of the fire and the lamps.

Rask of Treve owned much.

"Come closer," he said.

I heard the bells of a slave girl approach him.

I stopped, head down, several feet from him. My bare feet sunk into the deep, soft, scarlet, intricately wrought rugs which floored the tent. I felt the pile about my ankles.

"Come closer," he said.

Once again there was a rustle of slave bells.

I stood before him.

"Lift your head, Girl," he said.

I looked into his eyes. I wore his collar. I quickly dropped my head.

I felt his large hands part the bit of silk that I wore and, gently, drop it about my ankles.

He turned from me and went to sit down, cross-legged, some feet behind the tiny fire in the fire bowl.

We regarded one another.

"Serve me wine," he said.

I turned and, among the furnishings of the tent, found a bottle of Ka-la-na, of good vintage, from the vineyards of Ar, the loot of a caravan raid. I then took the wine, with a small copper bowl, and a black, red-trimmed wine crater, to the side of the fire. I poured some of the wine into the small copper bowl, and set it on the tripod over the tiny fire in the fire bowl.

He sat cross-legged, facing me, and I knelt by the fire, facing him.

After a time I took the copper bowl from the fire and held it against my cheek. I returned it again to the tripod, and again we waited.

I began to tremble.

"Do not be afraid, Slave," he said to me.

"Master!" I pleaded.

"I did not give you permission to speak," he said.

I was silent.

Again I took the bowl from the fire. It was now not comfortable to hold the bowl, but it was not painful to do so. I poured the wine from the small copper bowl into the black, red-trimmed wine crater, placing the small bowl in a rack to one side of the fire. I swirled, slowly, the wine in the wine crater. I saw my reflection in the redness, the blondness of my hair, dark in the wine, and the collar, with its bells, about my throat.

I now, in the fashion of the slave girl of Treve, held the wine crater against my right cheek. I could feel the warmth of the wine through the side of the crater.

"Is it ready?" he asked.

A master of Treve does not care to be told that his girl thinks it is. He wishes to be told Yes, or No.

"Yes," I whispered.

I did not know how he cared for his wine, for some men of Treve wish it warm, others almost hot. I did not know how he wished it. What if it were not as he wished it!

"Serve me wine," he said.

I, carrying the wine crater, rose to my feet and approached him. I then knelt before him, with a rustle of slave bells, in the position of the pleasure slave. I put my head down and, with both hands, extending my arms to him, held forth the wine crater. "I offer you wine, Master," I said.

He took the wine, and I watched, in terror. He sipped it, and smiled. I nearly fainted. I would not be beaten.

I knelt there, while he, at his leisure, drank the wine.

When he had almost finished, he beckoned me to him, and I went to kneel at his side. He put his hand in my hair and held my head back.

"Open your mouth," he said.

I did so, and he, spilling some from the broad rim of the crater, I feeling it on my chin, and throat, as it trickled under the collar, and body, poured the remainder of the wine down my throat. It was bitter from the dregs in the bottom of the cup, and, to my taste, scalding. I, my eyes closed, my head held painfully back, throat burning, swallowed it. When I had finished the wine he thrust the wine crater into my hands. "Run, El-in-or," he said, "put it back, and return to me." I ran to the side of the tent and put back the wine crater, and fled back to his side.

"Stand," he said.

I did so, unsteadily.

My head swirled. Suddenly, in my body, like a drum, I felt the hot wine. He had made me run that I might feel it even the sooner.

I looked at him, unsteadily, angrily.

"I hate you!" I cried. Then I was terrified that I had uttered this. It was the wine.

He did not seem angry, but sat there, regarding me.

I was emboldened.

I was suddenly conscious of the earrings in my ears. He was looking at them.

"I hate you!" I cried again.

He said nothing.

"You captured me!" I wept. "You put me in a collar!" I wept. I seized the collar and tried to pull it from my throat. It remained inflexibly fastened on me, marking me his slave. There had been only the jangle of bells Ute had tied to the steel.

He said nothing.

"You branded me!" I cried. "You whipped me, and put me in the slave box!"

He did not deign to speak to me.

"You do not understand," I cried, "I am not even of this world. I am not one of your Gorean women, with whom you may do as you please. I am not a servile thing! I am not a piece of property! I am not a pretty animal that you can buy and sell! I am Elinor Brinton. I am of the planet

Earth! I belong in New York City! I live on Park Avenue, in a great building! I am rich! I am educated! On my world I am an important person! I am of Earth, of Earth! You cannot treat me as a simple slave!" Then I put my head in my hands. What could he, an ignorant barbarian warrior, know of such things. He must think me mad. I wept.

Then, to my terror, I realized he was standing beside me. He was so large. I felt so small, and weak.

"I am of the warriors," he told me, "which is a high caste. I have been educated in the second knowledge, so I know of your world. Your accent marked you as barbarian."

I looked up at him.

"I know you are of the world which you call Earth," he said.

I regarded him, dumbfounded.

"The women of Earth," he said, "are worthy only to be the slaves of the men of Gor."

His hands were on my arms. I looked up at him, in terror.

"You are my slave," he said.

I was speechless.

Suddenly he threw me from him, violently. I was hurled stumbling and falling to the rugs. I looked up at him from the rugs, terrified.

"You," he said, "wear on your thigh the brand of a liar. You wear on your thigh the brand of a thief. You wear on your thigh the brand of a traitress!"

"Please!" I wept.

"Pierced-ear girl!" he said, scornfully.

My hands, inadvertently, went to the rings in my ears. There were tears in my eyes.

To my terror I saw him unroll heavy furs and cast them scornfully over the rugs near the small fire.

Imperiously he pointed to them.

"Please!" I wept.

His finger inexorably indicated the furs.

I rose to my feet and, with a rustle of slave bells, approached him.

I felt his hands on my arms.

"You come from a world," he said, "in which women are the natural slaves of such men as those of Gor."

I could not look at him.

"And you are a liar," he said, "and a thief, and a traitress."

I then felt his face near mine.

"Do you know the perfume you wear?" he asked.

I shook my head.

"It is the perfume of a female slave," he said.

I put down my head.

I felt his hands on my head, lifting it. He was regarding the earrings.

I put down my head again.

"Pierced-ear girl," he said.

I could not speak, but only tremble.

I then felt, to my dismay, his hand tear the ribbon of white silk from my collar. He threw it aside.

"No!" I begged him.

"You will be treated as what you are," he said, "as the lowest and most miserable slave on Gor."

I dared not look into the eyes of my master.

"Lift your head, Girl," he said.

I heard the bells on my collar move as I did as I was commanded.

I looked into his eyes, and then, helplessly, thrust down my head. My entire body began to tremble, uncontrollably. Never had I seen such eyes, terrible and dark, keen, those of a warrior.

I stood before him, alone with him in his tent, at his mercy. My head was down. I felt small and helpless.

Then he took me in his arms.

With a jangle of slave bells and a cry of anguish I was forced back on the furs.

16   I AM CHAINED BENEATH
THE MOONS OF GOR

"LET HER BE CHAINED under the moons of Gor," had said Verna.

Rask of Treve had laughed.

I pulled at the chain on my left ankle. It was fastened in the heavy ring, in the heavy block of stone, set deep in the small, grassy knoll. I had seen this small hillock, with its ring, in my exploration of the camp. It was in an isolated portion of the camp. I was alone on the hillock, chained near its rounded summit. I could see, some dozens of yards away, the backs of tents. I could see the points of the double palisade. The moons had not yet risen.

I was angry. I sat in the grass. I was naked. I lifted my ankle and felt the heavy chain on it. How furious I was!

After my work for the day had been finished, I had hoped, breathlessly, vulnerably, that I might be again summoned to the tent of Rask of Treve. I had done my work well, and when I had finished early I had helped the other girls. I recalled that I had sung much during the day, and had been happy in my work. I had laughed much, too, and for the first time in weeks had eagerly conversed and sported, insisting that I be permitted to do so, with my sisters in bondage. Elinor Brinton, the Gorean slave girl, was now different than she had been. The other girls sensed this and, pleased, accepted me among them, as another mere slave, neither better nor worse than they themselves. When Ute and I had been alone I had fallen before her, begging her forgiveness with tears for how I had treated her so long before. She had smiled, and lifted me to my feet. There

336

had been tears in her eyes. "Hurry to your work, Slave," she had said. She had then kissed me. I sprang to my feet and ran to my work, overcome with affection for her. She had forgiven me! I loved her! Ute, only of the leather workers, was the kindest, most generous, most loving girl I had ever known. How I hated myself for having once hurt her. Inge and Rena, I sensed, regarded me in a new fashion. "Slave!" they had said to me. And I had said to them, "Yes—Slave!" and kissed them. I had then sped away. They envied me. I pitied them in my way, for they were mere ignorant girls, white-silk girls. I was red silk! I jerked at my chained ankle, furious.

Why had I been put here?

"Let her be chained under the moons of Gor," had said Verna, and Rask of Treve, laughing, had had it done.

The chain was heavy on my left ankle.

The moons had not yet risen. The night was hot.

As I could, during the day, I had made it my business to pass near the tent of Rask of Treve, that he might see me.

But he had scarcely seemed to notice me.

Last night it had been different!

He had noticed me then!

I lay on my back, chained on the grass of the knoll, and laughed deliciously. I recalled each instant of the hours in his tent, and later, when I had lain at his side, holding him, my cheek pressed against his thigh, my hair about his body. He had slept, but I had not slept, not until morning, for I had wanted to continue to hold him.

At dawn he had sent me from his tent, to the shed for female work slaves.

I had gone.

This evening Rask of Treve had supped with Verna, and I it was who had served them, only as before, their menial slave. Rask of Treve did not look upon me differently than he had before. It might have been as though the preceding night had not existed. I served well, and deferentially.

Would I be again summoned to his tent?

But he had called a guard.

"Yes, Captain," had said the guard.

"Tonight," had said Rask of Treve, casually, "send the girl, Talena, to my tent."

"Yes, Captain," said the guard, and left.

My fingers went white on the plate that I had been holding. For a moment I could not see. I could not breathe. And then my face went white with suppressed fury, concealing the scarlet rage that burned in my body.

"Wine," had said Rask of Treve.

I had poured him wine.

"Wine," had said Verna.

I served her.

I went to the side of the low table, and knelt there. I hated Talena! I wanted to throw myself upon her and scratch out her eyes, and tear her hair and bite and kick her until she screamed and screamed, and fled away! The daughter of a Ubar! She was only a slave! I was as good as she! I hated her! I hated her! I hated her!

"Your slave seems disturbed," said Verna, smiling.

I put my head down.

"Slave," said Verna.

"Yes, Mistress," I said.

"It is said, among the other girls, that you have told them that you are not as other women, that you do not have their weaknesses."

I recalled that once, in anger, I had told them this. I looked at Verna. I hated her. I knew, and she knew, that I had once seen her in the forest, helpless in her need. She was not likely to forget that, nor was I eager that she do so. I smiled. Rask of Treve had given me some pleasure, of course. But, still, I was, I knew, not as other women. I was not as they. I did not have their weaknesses. "I cannot help the way I am," I told Verna, looking down, deferentially.

Rask of Treve smiled.

"Let her be chained under the moons of Gor," had said Verna.

I looked at her, in anger.

Rask of Treve laughed. "Guard!" he called.

A guard entered the tent.

Rask of Treve indicated me. "Chain her," he said, "under the moons of Gor."

"Come, Girl," said the guard.

I followed him.

I could now see the moons beginning to rise over the points of the palisade.

What did I care that the girl, Talena, was tonight sent to the tent of Rask of Treve?

I hated him!

I hated her, even more than him!

I wished the guard had not taken my clothes.

But when a girl is chained under the moons of Gor, she is chained naked.

I did not understand their intention.

I lay back in the grass. I felt it with my hands. I closed my eyes.

I smiled.

I was furious, of course, with what he had done to me, but also, I could not have helped responding to him as I had. He had, cruelly, mercilessly, unfairly, giving me no option, elicited from me fantastic depths of sensation of which I had not even realized my body was capable. His touch, as that of a master, had commanded my body, totally, and I had swum in sensation, clutching him, fearing that I might drown with pleasure in his arms. Laugh if you will, but I could call him nothing but "Master." Do not scorn me, nor mock me, until you yourself, perhaps, on a distant world, someday wear a collar, until you, yourself, as a slave, have known the touch of such a man as Rask of Treve.

I opened my eyes. The moons now reared over the palisade, low in the night sky, looming.

My throat had been encircled with slave steel, and I had been taught its meaning. I recalled, long ago, how, in a motel on Earth, I had regarded myself naked, branded, collared, in a mirror, and had wondered, frightened, what it would be like to lie in the arms of a barbarian, helpless, so stripped, so marked. I now knew! I cried out, and tore a handful of grass from the knoll.

Why did he not send for me?

Had I not pleased him? I could do more for him, more!

The moons were now high in the night sky, the looming three, dominating, fierce moons of Gor.

I felt my nudity beneath them, and the grass.

I cried out with misery.

"Send for me, Rask of Treve!" I whimpered. "Send for me!" I rolled on my stomach in the grass. "I want to serve you," I wept. I bit at the grass.

I looked up at the moons, tears in my eyes.

The lights of the camp were now, for the most part, extinguished. I could see, here and there, in the distance, the embers of cooking fires. In some few tents there glowed a dim redness, through the canvas sides of the tent, the light of the tiny fire bowls within. The night was hot. I heard night insects. I was alone. Far off, in the tarn compound, a tarn screamed, and then there was only the silence, except for the sounds of the insects.

On the grassy knoll I was chained, alone.

If I could free myself I would run to Rask of Treve! I would beg him for his touch! I pulled at the chain, so heavy on my ankle. It was some eight feet long. I could not slip the manacle from my ankle; I could not free the chain from its ring.

I wept.

I threw myself against the chain, running toward his tent, and fell in the grass, my ankle burning, scraped, from the steel that obdurately clasped it. On my hands and knees I tried to crawl to the tent. My left leg stretched taut behind me, held. I cried out with frustration, and pounded the grassy earth, weeping, with my fists.

I rolled on my back and looked up at the moons.

I lay there, my fists clenched.

Then I closed my eyes. I could not dare to look upon them again, the great, white, looming moons of Gor, dominating the sky.

I pounded the grass with the sides of my fists, in misery.

Then I dared to look again upon the vast, looming moons

of Gor. What choice had I? I was only a girl who had been chained naked beneath them.

I screamed and leaped to my feet, my hands extended to the moons. I stood helplessly beneath them, chained, naked, reaching for them.

Then I began to dance the madness of my need, writhing beneath the moons of Gor, clutching at them, turning, stamping my feet, swirling, crying out.

And when I could dance no more I fell to the grass, writhing, tearing at it, whimpering.

And as I gasped, and wept, I saw, suddenly, in the shadows, watching me, Verna, the panther girl.

"It seems your body moves as might that of a Kajira," said Verna.

"I am a Kajira," I whispered, "Mistress."

"You are not as other women," said Verna. "You are strong. You do not have their weaknesses."

I knelt before Verna. I extended my hands to her. "Have pity on me, Mistress," I wept.

Her eyes were hard.

I put down my head. "I am as other women," I said. "I am not strong." I swallowed. "I have the weaknesses of my sex," I said. "Indeed, I am perhaps more weak than any."

"Now you speak truly, El-in-or," said Verna. Her voice was not unkind. "Sometimes," said Verna, "it requires a man such as Rask of Treve to teach a woman this weakness."

"I have been well taught," I whispered.

"I have fought this weakness in myself," said Verna.

"I will not fight it," I said. "I will yield to it."

"Rask of Treve," said Verna, smiling, "has given you no choice."

"That is true," I said. It was true. Rask of Treve, my Gorean master, had not seen fit to permit me choice in the matter of my helpless surrender.

I put my head down.

"You have been conquered," said Verna.

"Yes," I said, "I have been conquered."

"I am leaving the camp tonight," said Verna.

I looked at her, startled.

She indicated a kneeling figure several yards away, bent over, facing the other direction. She wore crossed ankle rings, not permitting her to rise. Her wrists were brace-leted behind her back. About her throat was a light, chain slave leash. Across the back of her dark hair I could see leather gag straps.

"I am taking Talena with me," said Verna. "Rask of Treve has given her to me. I am taking her to the northern forests, as a slave."

'But she is the favorite of Rask of Treve," I whispered.

"No," said Verna.

"Will you not stay in the camp," I asked, "as the comrade of Rask of Treve?"

She looked at me, and smiled. "No," she said. "My place is in the northern forests."

I did not speak.

"Is it pleasant," she asked, "to surrender to a man?"

I put my head down, shamed by joy.

"Ah," said Verna. Then she spoke to me softly. "Once," she said, "long ago, in the city of Ar, I saw a man, and in seeing him, for the only time in my life, I was afraid, for I feared he might do to me, if he wished, what Rask of Treve has done to you. I have never feared this of another man."

I looked at her.

"And so I hated him," she said, "and I resolved, someday, to see who would conquer."

"What was his name?" I asked.

"Marlenus of Ar," she said.

I could not speak, so astonished I was.

She casually indicated the wretched girl bound to one side, beyond the bottom of the hillock. "This wench is bait," she said.

Verna turned away, and then she turned to face me again. "Farewell, Slave," said she.

I extended my hands to her, piteously.

"Should I see Rask of Treve," said Verna, "I will tell him

that there is a chained girl who, beneath the moons of Gor, begs him for his touch."

"I wish you well, Mistress," I called. "I wish you well!"

Verna did not turn again, but went to the kneeling girl and unsnapped the crossed ankle rings, and put them in her pouch. She dragged the girl, wrists braceleted behind her back, to her feet, and led her away, between the tents. I could see the gag straps tight over the back of her hair as she was led away. I had little doubt that the magnificent Verna, leader of the panther girls, would bring her prize successfully to the northern forests.

I knelt alone then, chained, on the summit of the grassy hillock, beneath the vast, looming moons.

I became aware of a figure standing near me. I cried out, and reached for him.

Rask of Treve did not bother to unchain me, but used me as I was, eager and moaning, beneath the moons of Gor.

Rask of Treve held my head in his two hands.

It was near dawn.

We lay on the summit of the grassy knoll, wrapped in his cloak. Sensing his permission, I again touched my lips timidly to his. I was turned suddenly, helplessly, on my back, and again, clutching him, tears of pleasure in my eyes, yielded to the joy of him.

We were silent together.

There was dew on the grass, and the cloak in which we lay wrapped was wet on the outside. The light of the beginning of the morning was tender, sparkling on the stalks of the grass, giving the hill of my domination a sweet, soft sheen. I still wore on my left ankle the heavy chain. Elinor Brinton, of Park Avenue, once of Earth, once rich, once spoiled, and cruel and selfish, now only a conquered Gorean slave girl, lay intimately, lovingly, in the arms of her absolute master.

I looked up into the eyes of Rask of Treve. He looked down upon me.

"How is it that I care for you?" he asked.

"I love you," I whispered. "I love you, Master!"

"I despise you," he said.

I smiled at him, tears in my eyes.

"And yet," he said, "from the first time I saw you, in the pens of Ko-ro-ba, I could not forget you, but must have you as mine."

"I am yours," I whispered, "I am yours, Master. Utterly. Unconditionally yours. Your slave. Your helpless slave!"

"From the first time I saw you," said he, "I knew that to me you could not be simply as other slaves."

I clutched him.

He looked down at me, troubled. He touched my head gently, moving back hair from the right side of my face. "Can it be," he asked, "that I, Rask of Treve, care for a mere slave?"

"I love you, Master," I cried, "I love you, I love you!"

He did not let me press my lips to his. He looked down upon me, smiling. "Were you curious," he asked, "why before I never let you serve the men, when the other girls did so."

I smiled up at him. "Yes," I said, "I am curious."

"I was saving you for myself," he said.

I laughed.

"I kept from you as long as I could," he said, "but when you danced, then I knew I must have you."

I kissed him, and kissed him, weeping.

His hands were suddenly hard on my arms, and he forced me back. He grinned. "You danced your insolence," he said. "You danced your pride, your defiance, your contempt and scorn." He looked down at me.

I looked up at him. "I am not now insolent," I said, "Master." I smiled, tears in my eyes. "I am not now proud. I am not now defiant. I am not now contemptuous, nor scornful." I reached up, and he permitted me to kiss him, gently. I lay back. "I have been humbled, well humbled, Master," I smiled.

"What are you now?" he asked.

"Only your slave," I whispered, looking up at him, "only your humbled, helpless slave, Master."

He laughed.

I smiled.

"I have heard," he said, "that there is an insolent female slave in camp, a proud, unconquered girl."

I shook my head. "No longer, Master," I said.

"Did she escape?" he asked.

"No, Master," I smiled, "she did not escape."

"Her name was El-in-or," he said.

"She did not escape," I said.

He smiled.

"No female slave escapes Rask of Treve," I said.

"That is true," he said, the beast. But it was true.

"Who are you?" he asked.

"That same El-in-or," I smiled.

"She did not escape," he said.

"No." I said. I laughed to myself. I had indeed not escaped.

"Whose slave is El-in-or?" he asked.

"Rask of Treve's," I said.

"Does she love?" he asked.

"Yes," I said, "she loves." I tried to lift myself, to touch his lips with mine, but he would not permit me. "She loves desperately and completely," I whispered.

"Whom?" he asked.

I lay my head back, regarding him. I put my head to one side. "Must I speak?" I asked.

"Yes," he said, toying with his finger on my shoulder.

"But must I speak the truth?" I asked.

"Or you will be lashed, and put in the slave box," he said.

I was startled. Yet I knew, suddenly, that, if I lied, he would indeed whip me, and quite possibly place me again in the hated slave box. He was a Gorean master. I was at his mercy. I wondered if I could have felt so much his, so completely surrendered, if he had not possessed this complete power over my life and body. I belonged to him. But I did not want him to whip me, or put me in the slave box. I wanted only, desperately, to please him. And I knew I must, for I was his slave.

The absolute truth must be spoken to a Gorean master. It is forbidden to a girl to hide her feelings.

I looked up at him.

"It is well known to Rask of Treve," I smiled, "whom it is that the slave girl, El-in-or, loves."

"Speak it," he said.

"She loves her master," I said. "She loves Rask of Treve."

"I am he," he said.

"It is you whom she loves," I said.

"And who are you?" he asked, his finger idly at my hip.

"She!" I cried, suddenly, laughing, with pleasure.

He kissed my throat.

"Has she been conquered?" he asked.

"Yes!" I said. "Yes!" I held him.

He pressed his mouth to my body.

"Conquer me!" I wept. "Again conquer me!"

There were the sounds of the early morning in the camp. It was now light. Far off, I could hear Ute summoning her girls. A tarn cried in the compound. I heard the sounds of pans. Some fires were being lit.

"In your dance, before you fell before me in the sand," said Rask of Treve, "I thought I detected in your dance something other than contempt and scorn."

"Yes," I said. I kissed him.

I knew then what I had not understood before, what, for brief moments in the firelight, on the sand before his warriors and their slaves, my body had danced to him, my need, my desire for him, my readiness and my desperate plea for his touch.

For those moments, briefly mingled with the dancing of my pride, my insolence, my contempt and scorn, I had, not fully aware, yet sensing with fear what I did, in the dance of a slave girl, piteously begged for the love of my master.

He had seen fit to touch me, and had summoned me to his tent.

We heard the sounds of the camp.

My left ankle wore the heavy chain. We lay together on the grassy knoll. I held him to me, my cheek at his waist.

His hand lay gently on the right side of my head.

"It is time for you to be about your work, Slave," he said.

"Yes, Master," I whispered.

From his pouch he took forth a key and sprang open the heavy manacle that had clasped, so perfectly confining it, my left ankle.

He put his cloak about my shoulders. "Go to the shed," he said, "and get a work tunic."

I was being dismissed.

I threw the cloak to the grass and knelt at his feet, as though chained. I looked up at him. He was now standing on his feet, and he looked down at me, tenderly.

"I am chained at your feet," I said. It was a saying of a Gorean slave girl, to express her feelings.

"Yes," he said, gently.

"I love you!" I cried. I thrust my head to his feet. I suddenly began to weep. "Do not sell me!" I begged. "Do not sell me! Keep me for yourself! Keep me forever for yourself!" I could not bear the thought of being separated from him. It would have been the torture of the tearing of my heart from my body. The very thought caused in me excruciating suffering. I looked up agonized. I understood then as I had not before what could be the cruelty, the tragedy, of being a female slave. What if I had not pleased him sufficiently? "I will please you more!" I wept. "More! I will give you everything! Everything! Keep me! Do not sell me! I love you! I love you!" I lifted my wrists to him, as though they wore slave bracelets. I smiled through my tears. "You see," I whispered, "I am chained at your feet."

"Does the proud El-in-or beg to be kept as my slave?" he smiled.

"Yes," I said, "she begs."

"To your work!" he laughed.

I leaped to my feet. He seized me in his arms, and, on the summit of the knoll, held me long, lovingly, in his arms. I looked up, into his eyes. "I love you, Master," I whispered. Then I laughed, and cried out. He, his body tightening, startlingly again mighty with strength, astonishing me, delighting me, lifted me from my feet and lowered me, gently, to the grass, covering me with his cloak. Again he forced me to weep with pleasure.

When I leaped up, laughing, shaking my head and hair, he again offered to place his cloak about my shoulders, that my body might be covered when I went to the shed for the work slaves.

It was much honor that he did me, a mere female slave. How the girls would have cried out with envy to see me, secure in such a cloak, and that, too, of the mighty Rask of Treve!

But I did not wish to wear it. Did I so, it would not have been well concealed that he, my master, had touched with gentleness, and care, a girl who wore a collar. What would his men think? And I wore penalty brands. Surely a girl such as I, after being brutally used, should have been casually dismissed, or beaten and spurned. No, let it not be revealed that he, my master, the mighty Rask of Treve, had been tender with a slave, particularly such a low and miserable slave as I.

I laughed and hurled the cloak back to him. "A steel-collar girl," I said, "should not have so fine a cloak!"

He laughed. "And one with pierced ears!" he said.

"Yes," I laughed, "and one with pierced ears!"

I turned about and sped down the hill to the shed for female work slaves. I was ravenously hungry. I had little doubt that Ute would have saved me a roll from the feeding pan. I loved her! She would also, however, have a full roster of work for me to perform this day. She played no favorites. I was one of her girls. She would treat me no differently than the others. I loved her! And I loved, too, my master.

I turned. He was watching me, from the hill. I smiled, and waved to him. He lifted his hand. I turned again, and ran toward the work shed.

Before I appeared before the shed, I stopped and, secretly, pressed my fingertips to my lips and then to the lettering on my collar, which proclaimed me the slave of a Gorean warrior. I loved him! I laughed. You could read his name, that of my master, on my collar. It was Rask of Treve!

I was not displeased that I had been chained under the moons of Gor. I hurried to the shed.

"I have saved a roll for you," said Ute.

"Thank you, Ute," I said.

"Eat it quickly," she said. "You have much work to do today."

"Yes, Ute," I cried, kissing her, "I will! I will!"

THE PAST FEW WEEKS had been the most happy and beautiful of my life.

"Hands to the rear. Cross your wrists," said the man.

I did so.

I felt the straps through the heavy wicker. My wrists were pulled back, tight against the wicker, and bound there. I shared the tarn basket, my knees drawn up, with five other girls. We were naked. Our ankles were tied together at the center of the basket.

"They will be in Ar by nightfall," said the man.

My head fell forward on my breast.

Yet I had few regrets, for in the past weeks I had been happy, and I had been alive.

I would never forget the face, nor the touch, of Rask of Treve, nor the long walks, and the speakings, and touchings beyond the palisade.

"Will they be sold in the Curulean?" asked a nearby warrior.

"Yes," said the man.

Two of the girls, bound helplessly in the basket, squealed with pleasure.

In the beginning, following my total conquest by Rask of Treve, I had been summoned night after night to his tent. I had served him in a delicious variety of ways, to our mutual pleasure, for I had been well trained. I had feared only that my imagination might fall short of the invention of new and exciting ways to please him. Sometimes, to my fury, he had tried to put me from him, and had summoned other women to his tent, but often he would send them away again, and it would be I, El-in-or, who would again be summoned to the tent of scarlet canvas, red-silk lined, on its eight poles.

"Did master summon me?" I would ask.

"El-in-or," he would say, opening his arms, and I would run to him.

And then he no longer summoned other women to his tent. Then it was only I, El-in-or, whom he summoned. And then I, to the anger of some of the other girls, was the acknowledged favorite of Rask of Treve, his preferred slave.

A heavy, long strap thrust through the wicker, behind me and to the left. It was passed several times about my throat and then drawn through the wicker behind me and to my right. I felt my throat jerked back against the wicker by the strap. The same strap, passing in and out of the wicker, similarly fastened the other girls in place.

Inge and Rena were not in the basket with me. They had been given to the huntsmen, Raf and Pron. In the fashion of Gorean huntsmen, both girls had then been freed and given a head start of four Ahn, that they might escape, if it were in their power. After four Ahn, Raf and Pron, running lightly, carrying snare rope, left the camp. The next morning they had returned, leading Inge and Rena. The thighs of both girls had been bloodied. Their wrists were bound behind their backs with snare rope. Their slave leashes, too, were formed of a loop of snare rope.

"I see you have caught two pretty birds," had laughed Rask of Treve.

About the throats of the girls were locked new collars, again of inflexible steel, but now those of huntsmen, vine engraved and bearing the names of their masters.

No scribe it seemed would own Inge, but she would belong to a brutal and powerful huntsman, the handsome Raf of Treve; and Rena's captain of Tyros, he who had contracted for her capture, must now surely be disappointed, and his gold lost, for his lovely prize has been taken by another, at whose feet she kneels joyfully, the handsome and splendid Pron, skilled huntsman of lofty Treve. The next day they left the camp, taking their girls with them.

We kissed one another good-bye. "I love you, El-in-or," had said Inge. "I love you, too, Inge," I had wept. "I love you, El-in-or," had said Rena. "I, too, love you," I had said. "I wish you all well."

They then, in the brief green tunics of the slaves of huntsmen, shouldered their burdens and followed their masters through the double gate of the palisade. Their lives would be hard, but I did not think them dismayed, nor unhappy. The huntsman lives a free and open life, as wild and swift, and secret as the beasts he hunts, and his slaves, whom he insists on accompanying him, must, too, learn the ways of the forests, the flowers and the animals, the leaves and wind. I do not know where Raf and Pron may now be, but I know them well served by two wenches, the slave girl, Inge, and the slave girl, Rena, who were well trained in the pens of Ko-ro-ba, and who love them.

I looked up.

The heavy lid of wicker was now being placed on the tarn basket. Immediately, on the body of the girl across from me, there was a reticulated pattern of shadows.

I could not free myself.

The lid was tied down.

The man who would fly the tarn then went to the kitchen shed, to have his lunch.

I had sought to please Rask of Treve in many ways, and found, to my astonishment, that I was eager to do so, and took great pleasure in doing so. I wanted to be many women to him, and yet the same, always El-in-or. A man is a strange beast I think, for he both desires one woman and many women, and perhaps most he desires one woman who will be to him many women, others, delicious others, and yet always, too, herself. I became many women to Rask of Treve, fresh females, yet again El-in-or. Sometimes I would be a new girl, frightened, young, much fearing him, as Techne might have been; sometimes I would be as though of the scribes, much as Inge might have been, refined, dismayed at her fate; sometimes as a fine lady, of wealth and position, of high caste, as Rena had been, who now must find herself to be humbled as a mere, rightless, collared wench; and sometimes I would be a lonely slave, or a drunken slave, or a defiant girl, determined to resist, or a cruel red-silk slave, determined herself to conquer, but, in the end, finding herself his conquest, and in all this, always, his El-in-or.

But, too, sometimes Rask of Treve, after touching me, would hold me, and kiss me, for long hours. I did not truly understand him in these hours, but in his arms lay content and fulfilled. And then one night, when the fires were low, for no reason I clearly understood, I begged that I might be permitted to know him. "Speak to me of yourself," he said. I told him of my childhood, my girlhood, and my parents, and the pet my mother had poisoned, and of New York, and my world, and my capture, and my life before it had begun, before he had seen me naked in the cell of the Ko-ro-ban pens. And, too, in various nights, he had spoken to me of himself, and of the death of his parents, and of his training as a boy in Treve, and his learning of the ways of tarns and of the steel of weapons. He had cared for flowers, but had not dared to reveal this. It seemed so strange, he, such a man, caring for flowers. I kissed him. But I feared, that he had told me this. I do not think there was another to whom he had ever spoken this small and delicate thing.

We had begun to take long walks beyond the palisade, hand in hand. We had much spoken, and much loved, and much spoken. It was as though I might not have been his slave. It was then that I had begun to fear that he would sell me.

Oh when his need was upon him he would sometimes use me as a slave girl, with harsh authority, sometimes even making me suffer under his domination, and, too, sometimes when my need was upon me I would beg him for chains and cords, that I might be fully owned, or would present myself to him as a contemptuous, untamed girl, who must be conquered, provoking him to my utter conquest, but, too, now, we would sometimes love tenderly, and at sweet length. It depended much upon our moods. Sometimes we were master and slave, and sometimes we were something else, that I dare not speak, but I feared now, much, that he would sell me. For what place could there be for this other thing in the war camp of Rask of Treve?

But mostly we sported and pleasured, hiding from ourselves this other thing, both of us perhaps not wishing to speak it. In one week I had even begged him to place in my nose the tiny golden ring of a Tuchuk slave girl, and in that week I had served him as such, clad even in the Kalmak, Chatka and Curla, my hair bound back with the red Koora. In another week I had, the nose ring removed, served him as a Torian girl, and in another as a simple wench of Laura, and in another as an exquisite pleasure slave of Ar.

Then one day we had done little but speak to one another, at great length, with much gentleness and intimacy, and in the night, after our lovings, had spoken together, long, lying before the fire. He had held me, sadly. I had known then that he would sell me.

In the morning, after I had returned to the shed, he again summoned me to his tent.

"Kneel," he had said.

I did so, his slave.

"I am tired of you," he told me, suddenly, angrily.

I put down my head.

"I am going to sell you," he said.

"I know," I said, "Master."

"Leave, Slave," he said.

"Yes, Master," I said.

I did not weep until I returned to the shed.

I felt the knots on my wrists being checked, and I winced, as they were tightened. Then my throat, by the straps, was drawn back tighter against the wicker, and this bond, too, was tightened. The other girls, too, winced in protest, some crying out.

I had asked one thing of Rask of Treve, before, stripped, I had entered the tarn basket.

"Free Ute," I had asked him.

He had looked at me strangely. Then he had said, "I will."

Ute, freed, might then do what she wished. She might go to Rarir, or Teletus, I supposed. But I knew that she would seek out one named Barus, of the Leather Workers, whose name she had often moaned in her sleep. I did not even know his city.

"Into the basket," had said the man who would fly the tarn.

"Yes, Master," I had said to him. I was no longer the slave of Rask of Treve. I now belonged to this stranger, to whom I, and the others, had submitted ourselves. It was he, now, who held absolute power over my life and body. There was now a fresh, but locked, steel collar on my throat.

The man now was checking the knots at the lid of the basket. It was tight. Our ankles were bound together at the center of the basket; our wrists were bound behind our back, to the wicker; our throats were independently secured, the knots outside, keeping us in place. He had finished his lunch. We were stripped, helpless slave girls, his.

I had been sold for nine pieces of gold.

The man mounted to the saddle of the tarn. The tarn screamed and began to beat its wings. Then the basket jerked forward, on its leather runners, and skidded across the clearing, and then, swung below the tarn.

I was on my way to the market.

I was sold from the great block of the Curulean, in Ar, for twelve pieces of gold, purchased by the master of a paga tavern, who thought his patrons might enjoy amusing themselves with me, a girl who wore penalty brands.

I served for months in the paga tavern. Among those I served were guards, formerly from the caravan of Targo. They were kind to me. One was the fellow whom I had fought, by the fire, but to whom I must now completely yield. Another was the guard who had escorted me to the house of the physician, whom I had once provoked. Another was the one who had caught me, when I had fled from the hut in the forest, and returned me to Targo. And there, too, were others, even he who had driven the slave wagon in which I had been often confined; even he who had first harnessed me to the tongue of Targo's one wagon, when I had first been captured by him. After serving them completely I would press them with questions of Targo, and the other guards, and their slaves. They told me much. Targo had recovered many girls, and was now rich. He was intending another trip northward, though not to do business with Haakon of Skjern. The men I served, Targo's men, and others, who might have me for the price of a cup of paga, I gave much pleasure, and from them, too, I received much pleasure. But none of them were Rask of Treve. That master had won the heart of the slave girl who was Elinor Brinton. She could not forget him.

Then one night I heard, "I will buy her," and I stood transfixed with fear. I could scarcely pour the paga into his cup. The bells on my ankles and wrists rustled. I felt his hand on the bit of diaphanous yellow silk I wore in the tavern. "I will buy her," he said. It was the small man, who had touched me intimately when I had lain bound in my own bed on Earth, the small man who had threatened me in the hut in the northern forests, who had been the mountebank, the master, I had thought, of the strange beast, the terrible beast. It was the man who had wanted me to poison someone, I knew not who.

His hand was now locked on my wrist. I had not escaped him. "I will buy her," he said. "I will buy her."

The small man bought me for fourteen pieces of gold. I was taken, on tarnback, braceleted and hooded, to the city of Port Kar, in the delta of the mighty Vosk.

In a warehouse, near the piers, I knelt, head down, at their feet.

"I will not serve you," I said.

The small man was there, and the beast, squatting, shaggy, regarding me, and, too, to my surprise, Haakon of Skjern.

"I have felt the iron," I said. "I have felt the whip. I will not kill for you. You may kill me, but I will not kill for you."

They did not beat me, nor threaten me.

They lifted me by the arm, and dragged me to a side room.

I screamed. There, his wrists bound by ropes to rings, stood a bloodied man, head down, stripped to the waist.

"Eleven men died," said Haakon of Skjern, "but we have him."

The man lifted his head, and shook it, clearing his vision. "El-in-or?" he said.

"Master!" I wept.

I pressed myself to him.

He regarded them. Then he said to me, "I am of Treve. Do not stain my honor."

By the hair I was dragged from the presence of Rask of Treve, and his head, again, fell forward on his chest.

The door closed.

"In time," said the small man, "you will receive a packet of poison."

I nodded, numbly. Rask of Treve must not die! He must not die!

"You will be placed in the house of Bosk, a merchant of Port Kar," he said. "You will be placed in the kitchen of that house, and you will be used to serve his table."

"I can't," I wept. "I cannot kill!"

"Then Rask of Treve dies," said the small man. Haakon of Skjern laughed.

The small man held up a tiny packet. "This," he said, "is the poison, a powder prepared from the vemon of the ost."

I shuddered. Death by ost venom is among the most hideous of deaths.

I wondered how it was that they could so hate this man, he called Bosk of Port Kar.

"You will comply?" asked the small man.

I nodded my head.

"Wine, El-in-or!" cried Publius, master of the kitchen of Bosk of Port Kar. "Take wine to the table!"

Numbly, shaking, I took the vessel of wine. I went to the door of the kitchen, and went through the hallway, and stopped before the back entrance to the hall.

It had not been as hard as I had feared to be entered into the house.

I was sold, for fifteen pieces of gold, to the house of Samos, a slaver of Port Kar. Samos himself was abroad upon Thassa, in ventures of piracy and enslavement, and it was through a subordinate that I was purchased. Publius, the kitchen master of the house of Bosk, drunken, in a dicing match, in a paga tavern of Port Kar, had learned that there was an interesting girl, newly brought to the house of Samos, one who had been trained in the pens of Ko-ro-ba, one who wore the brand of Treve. It was also said that she was beautiful.

Publius, who would, upon occasion, need new girls in the kitchen, as others were given away or sold, was intrigued. I suspect he seldom had the opportunity to chain trained pleasure slaves to the wall of his kitchen after the completion of the evening's work.

The subordinate, though in the absence of Samos, thinking to please him, sold me to Publius for only fifteen pieces of gold, which price he had paid. I was thus, in effect, in part, a gift to the house of Bosk from the house of Samos. The house of Bosk and the house of Samos, it seemed, stood on good terms, the one with the other. Both Samos and Bosk, it seems, were members of the Council of Captains, the sovereign power in Port Kar.

I liked the house of Bosk, which was much fortified, spacious and clean. I was not badly treated, though I was forced to do my work perfectly. My master, Bosk, a large man, very strong, did not use me. His woman was the striking, beautiful Telima, from the marshes, a true Gorean beauty, before whom I felt myself only an Earth woman and a slave. There were other beauties in the house: slender, dark-haired Midice, the woman of a captain, Tab; large, blond-haired Thura, the woman of the great peasant, master of the bow, Thurnock; and short, dark-eyed Ula, woman of silent, strong Clitus, once a fisherman of the isle of Cos. Too, there was a young, beautiful girl, named Vina, the woman of a slender, strong youth, a seaman, whose name was Henrius, said to be a master of the sword. There was too a free dancing girl, a beauty with high cheekbones, named Sandra, who much pleased herself with the men of Bosk, and earned much moneys in the doing of it. She had been taught to read by another girl, also free, of the Scribes, a thin, brilliant girl, whose name was Luma, who handled much of the intricate business of the great house. And, too, of course, there were many lovely slaves. I was somewhat uneasy. Only too obviously Bosk had an eye for beauty. But he did not use me. His affections, and his touch, were for Telima. How superb she must have been, to have held him among such girls. A Gorean girl, who has a first-rate man, and wishes to keep him, fights for him. There are generally other girls, collared girls, only too eager to take her place.

"Hurry with the wine!" cried Publius, from the kitchen, looking after me.

Then he disappeared in the kitchen.

I took the packet of poison from my rep-cloth kitchen tunic, and dissolved it in the wine. I had been told there was enough there to bring a hundred men to an excruciating death. I swirled the wine, and discarded the packet.

It was ready.

"Wine!" I heard from the hall.

I hurried forward, running toward the table. I would serve none but Bosk, he first and he alone. I did not wish more blood on my head.

I stopped halfway to the table. The feasters were watching me.

Rask of Treve must live!

I had recalled how Haakon of Skjern had laughed over his captive.

I asked myself, would he, Haakon, such a mortal enemy, release Rask of Treve, even did I keep my bargain.

I feared he would not, and yet what choice had I. I must trust them. I had no choice.

I did not wish to poison anyone. I knew nothing of such work. I had not been a good person, but I was not a murderess. Yet I must kill.

I remembered, briefly, irrelevantly, that my mother had

once poisoned my small dog, which had ruined one of her slippers. I had loved the tiny animal, which had played with me, and had given me the affection, the love, which my parents had denied me, or had been too busy to bestow. It had died in the basement, in the darkness behind the furnace, where it had fled, howling and whimpering, biting at me when I, a hysterical, weeping child, had tried to touch it and hold it. Tears sprang into my eyes.

"Elinor," said Bosk, at the head of the table. "I want wine." He was one of the few men, or women, on Gor who spoke my name as it had been spoken on Earth.

I slowly approached him.

"Wine!" called Thurnock.

I did not go to the peasant.

"Wine!" cried Tab, the captain.

I did not go to him.

I went to Bosk, of Port Kar. I would pour the wine. Then I would be seized, and, doubtless by nightfall, tortured and impaled.

He held forth the goblet. The eyes of Telima were upon me. I could not look her in the eyes.

I poured the wine.

"I am of Treve," Rask of Treve had told me, in the warehouse, where he stood bound to the wall. "Do not stain my honor."

I wept.

"What is wrong, Elinor?" asked Bosk.

"I am all right, Master," I told him.

"I am of Treve," had said Rask of Treve. "Do not stain my honor."

I hated then men, and their wars, and their cruelties, and their frivolous honors. It was we, their women, who suffered in their madness. No, Rask of Treve would not purchase his life for the price I had agreed to pay, but the decision was not his, but mine, mine, and I loved him, and could not let him die!

"Do not stain my honor," he had said.

Bosk of Port Kar lifted the cup to his lips.

I put forth my hand. "Do not drink it, Master," I said. "It is poisoned."

I put my head down in my hands. There were shouts, of fury, of anger, at the table, goblets spilled and men and women leaped to their feet.

I felt Thurnock, the peasant, with his great belt, pinning my arms to my sides and I was thrown to the tiles of the great hall.

"Torture her!" I heard cry.

"Impalement!" I heard cry.

The door to the hall burst open, and in, wild-eyed, ran a man with short-cropped, white hair, with earrings.

"It is Samos!" I heard cry.

"I have just made landfall," he cried. "I have learned that a woman, without my knowledge, has been entered into this house. Beware!"

He saw me, my arms belted to my sides, kneeling on the tiles.

Publius ran forward, the kitchen master. His face was white. He held a drawn sword.

Bosk poured the wine forth on the table, slowly. The vessel of wine I had dropped, and its contents now trickled among the tiles.

"Return to your feast," said Bosk to the table. Then he said, "Tab, Thurnock, Clitus, Henrius, Samos, I would be pleased if you would join me in my chambers." I saw Telima held a knife. I had little doubt she could cut my throat, and might swiftly do so. "Thurnock, unbind the slave," requested Bosk. He did so. I stood up. "Elinor," said Bosk, "we must speak." He then held his arm to Telima, that she might accompany him. I, numbly, followed them to his chambers.

That night men swiftly left the house of Bosk. I had told them all that I knew. I expected to be tortured and impaled.

When I had spoken Bosk had said to me, "Go to the kitchen, for there is work for you there."

Numbly I had returned to the kitchen, where Publius, himself astonished, gave me my work. That night, with double chains, he fastened me to the wall.

"We could not save Rask of Treve," said Bosk to me the next day.

I put down my head. I had known it would be so.

My master, Bosk, was smiling. "He had already escaped," he said.

I looked at him, wild-eyed.

"Those of Treve," he said, "are worthy foes."

I looked at him, trembling. I put forth my hand.

"He had broken free," said Bosk. "When we arrived, he was gone."

"The others?" I said.

"We found three bodies," said Bosk, Merchant of Port Kar. "One, with an empty scabbard, was identified as that of Haakon of Skjern. Another, that of a small man, was not identified. The third body was strange, that of a large, and, I fear, most unpleasant beast."

I put down my head, sobbing hysterically.

"They were cut to pieces," said Bosk. "The heads were mounted on stakes beside the canal. The sign of Treve was cut into each of the stakes."

I fell to my knees, sobbing and laughing.

"Those of Treve," mused Bosk, as though he might have known them as enemies, "are worthy foes."

"What of me?" I looked up.

"I am letting it be known in the camp of Terence of Treve, a mercenary, that there is, in my house, a wench, whose name is Elinor."

"Rask of Treve no longer wants me. He sold me," I said.

Bosk shrugged. "I am informed by Samos, who keeps spies, that Rask of Treve came free to Port Kar, and alone, where he was captured." He looked at me. "What might it have been that he sought?"

"I do not know," I whispered.

"It is said," said Bosk of Port Kar, "that he sought a slave, whose name was Elinor."

"That cannot be," I said, "for when I was brought to Port Kar, Rask of Treve was already captive."

"It could easily be," said he called Bosk, "for it requires only that rumor in the camp of Rask of Treve be spread that you are in this city. And surely it would be preferable, to the plans of some, my enemies, that you not be in this city when Rask of Treve arrives, lest they fail to capture him and he finds you, and carries you away." He looked at me. "Were you in a place where they could have you when they wished, and yet not seem to own you, nor risk identifying themselves with you prematurely, lest others take note?"

"For months," I said, "I served as a slave in a paga tavern."

"They may even have seen you sold," said Bosk. "It was the Curulean, was it not?"

"Yes," I whispered.

"A most public block," he said. Then he looked at me, a bit sadly. "I once saw a most beautiful woman sold from that block."

"What was her name?" I asked.

"Vella," he said. "Her name was Vella."

I looked down.

"It is my speculation," said Bosk, "that only when Rask of Treve fell captive were you then picked up and brought to Port Kar, where you might be confronted with him."

"Rask of Treve," I said, "sold me. He does not want me."

Bosk shrugged. "Go to the kitchen," he said, "there is work for you there."

I went to the kitchen, and put myself at the disposition of Publius. He had wanted to leave the employ of Bosk of Port Kar, so stricken had he been that he had ignorantly purchased me, and that I had nearly brought about the downfall of the house, but Bosk would not hear of it, and bade him remain. "Where shall I find another kitchen master your equal?" he had asked. Publius remained in the house. He would not, however, allow me to prepare or serve food. He watched me closely. At night he would double chain me.

I sang at my work, for I knew that Rask of Treve lived. Further, those who had sought to employ me as a tool to their dark purposes had been destroyed. I knew that he did not want me for he had sold me, but I was content in the knowledge that he, whom I loved, lived. I did not believe that my master, Bosk, was correct in his conjectures that the warrior of Treve had come to Port Kar to find me, for he had sold me. His informants were mistaken, or confused. I tried, from time to time, to put Rask of Treve from my mind, but I could not do so. Sometimes, at night, the other girls would waken me, and scold me, for I had disturbed them, crying his name in my sleep. Rask of Treve did not want me. But I wanted him, with all of me and my weeping heart. But he lived. I could not be unhappy. I could be lonely, and hunger for his touch, his mouth, his words, his hand on mine, but I knew he lived, so I could not be truly sad. How could I be sad when somewhere he was proud and alive, and free, doubtless once again bold and violent, fighting, raiding, feasting with his cup companions and his beautiful slaves.

"Sell me, Master," I once begged Bosk, for I did not wish to remain in the house where I had so nearly committed so great a crime. I wished to go where I might not be known, where I would be only another collared girl, another wench in bondage, anonymous in her submission and degradation.

"You have work in the kitchen," had said Bosk of Port Kar.

I had returned to the kitchen.

It is time now for me to conclude this narrative.

I have written it at the command of my master, Bosk, of Port Kar, of the Merchants, it seems, but, I suspect, once of the warriors. I do not understand all of what I have written, in the sense of knowing its implications, or what knowledge others, better informed, may draw from it. But I have written down much, and, I think, honestly. My master has commanded that it be so written. As a Gorean slave girl I dare not disobey, and, in this case, I would not care, also, to do so. Further, he has commanded me to speak in this my feelings, perhaps, in his kindness, thinking it would be well for me to do so. I have tried to comply.

I am happier now, than I have been, though I still beg, upon occasion, that I might be sold from this house. I have learned that Rask of Treve did indeed come to Port Kar to find me, and this has given me indescribable joy, though it is mingled now with great bitterness, and sadness, for I shall never again be his.

On the piazza, before the Hall of the Council of Captains, Rask of Treve confronted Bosk of Port Kar, demanding that I be surrendered to him. Bosk, I am told, set my price at twenty pieces of gold, that he might, as a merchant, take his profit on me. But Rask of Treve does not buy women, for he is of Treve. My price could have been an arrow point or a copper tarn disk, but his answer would have been the same. He takes women. He does not buy them. But I fear I may not be taken from Bosk of Port Kar. He is said himself to be a master swordsman, much feared, and his house is strong, and there are men here, some hundreds, who pledge their lives and their blades to him. This house has withstood a siege of thousands, within the last two years, in the time of the warrings of the Ubars and the Council of Captains, and the great engagement between the fleet of Port Kar and that of Tyros and Cos, on the twenty-fifth of Se'Kara, 10,120 Contasta Ar, from the Founding of Ar. And surely Rask, a captain of Treve, cannot bring the tarn cavalries of Treve to distant Port Kar, for a mere slave girl, and, too, such action would mean long and bloody war. I am, unfortunately, safe in this house. It is my home, and my prison. When Rask of Treve demanded that I be given to him, Bosk, my master, first sword in Port Kar, drew his own blade and, for answer, drew on the tiles of the piazza, a sign, that of the city of Ko-ro-ba. Rask of Treve, cloak swirling, turned and strode away.

I am now, by order of Bosk, again permitted to serve in the great hall. But, at night, Publius, still, keeps me double chained. He is a good kitchen master, and loves his captain, Bosk of Port Kar. I do not object to his precautions.

I am now finished with this narrative. Each night I must return to the kitchen, by the nineteenth hour, to be chained. Before that time it is my wont to wander the delta wall of the house of Bosk. I look out upon the marshes, which are in the light of the three moons of Gor, very beautiful.

I remember Rask of Treve.

18 THE EPILOGUE OF
BOSK OF PORT KAR

THIS IS NOW BOSK OF PORT KAR, who speaks.

I wish to add a small note to this manuscript, which I shall have transmitted to the Sardar.

It is long since I have served Priest-Kings. I would be free of their service. Samos often speaks with me, but I have remained adamant. Even so, in the arsenal, Tersites, the half-blind, mad shipwright builds a strange ship, to sail beyond the world's end. I wish to be free, and to be left alone. I am now rich. I am now respected. I have much for which a man might wish, the beautiful Telima, considerable wealth, a great house, wines and allegiances, and before me, gleaming Thassa, the Sea. I wish to be free of Priest-Kings, and Others. I want no longer any part of their dark games. Let the world be saved without me, for I have done my work, and want now only peace. But yet the Others have not forgotten me. They know me, and my whereabouts, and have tried to slay me. I endanger all those with whom I am in contact. What should I do? What can I do? My old sword, the blade carried even as long ago as the siege of Ar, hangs still in my chambers, in its worn scabbard. I am not eager to take it up again.

And I have now learned, from the narrative of the girl, Elinor, that Talena, once my companion, may well be in the northern forests. I have heard, too, that the girls of Verna, chief of the panther girls, were freed in Ar, surreptitiously, and are believed to have escaped northward. In this I think I see the hand of Rask Treve, or perhaps even of Verna, a most unusual woman, herself. I have spoken to Telima. Sometimes she comes with me, to the great keep, which once

366

we defended, and we look sometimes toward Thassa, the Sea, and I look sometimes towards the northern forests. Marlenus of Ar prepares an expedition to enter the forests, to recapture Verna and punish her for her insolence. It is not unknown to him, for rumors have been spread, that she, too, holds captive in those forests the girl Talena, his daughter. It is said he is shamed that she has been a slave, and that he intends to free her, and keep her sequestered in Ar, that her degradation not be publicly exhibited. How could she, a Ubar's daughter, hold up her head, when once she has worn the collar of a warrior of Treve.

"Hunt for her," has said Telima. "Perhaps you still love her."

"I love you," I told Telima.

"Find her," said Telima. "Bring her here as slave and choose between us. If you wish, we will fight with knives in the marshes."

"She was once my companion," I told Telima.

"The companionship is gone," said Telima. "More than a year has passed," she pointed out, "and you have not, together, repledged it."

"That is true," I admitted. By Gorean law the companionship, to be binding, must, together, be annually renewed, pledged afresh with the wines of love.

"And," said Telima, "both of you were once enslaved, and that, in itself, dissolves the companionship. Slaves cannot stand in companionship."

I looked at her angrily.

"You have not forgotten the delta of the Vosk?" she asked. Telima was not pleasing in her jealousy.

"No," I said, "I have not." I could never forget the delta of the Vosk, and my degradation. I knew that I had once betrayed my codes. I knew that I was one who had once chosen ignominious slavery over the freedom of honorable death.

"Forgive me, my Ubar," had said Telima.

"I do," I said.

I looked toward the northern forests. It had been so many years. I recalled her, Talena. She had been a dream in my heart, a memory, an ideal of a youthful love, never forgotten, glowing still, always remembered. I remembered her as I had seen her, in the swamp forest, south of Ar, with Nar the spider, and in the Ka-la-na grove, where I had freed her from the chains of a slave, only to put mine upon her; and in the caravan of Mintar, of the Merchants, in her collar, mine, and slave tunic, with Kazrak, my sword brother; and her dancing in my tent; and she upon the lofty cylinder of justice, in Ar, threatened with impalement, and as she had been, beautiful and loving, in the hours of our Free Companionship in Ko-ro-ba, before I had awakened again, stiff, bewildered, in the mountains of New Hampshire. I had never forgotten her. I could not.

"I will go with you," said Telima. "I know well how to treat slaves."

"If I go," I said, "I go alone."

"As my Ubar wishes," said Telima, and turned and left, leaving me alone on the top of the keep.

I looked out over Thassa, and the marsh, in the moonlight. Thurnock climbed the steps of the keep. He carried his bow, with arrows. "The Dorna," he said, "and the Tela and Venna will be ready for inspection at dawn."

"I am lonely, Thurnock," I said.

"All men are, from time to time, lonely," said Thurnock.

"I am alone," I said.

"Except when they are touched by love," said Thurnock, "all men are alone."

I looked across to the delta wall, bordering the marshes. I could see the girl, Elinor, walking the wall, as she did often at this hour, looking out over the reeds and the glistening water. She was lovely.

"It is time she was chained in the kitchen," said Thurnock.

"Not until the nineteenth hour," I said.

"Would my captain care to join me," he asked, "in a cup of paga before we retire?"

"Perhaps, Thurnock," I said. "Perhaps."

"We must rise early," he pointed out.

"Yes," I said, "we must rise early."

I watched her lone, forlorn figure, looking out over the delta wall.

"Most alone," I said, "are those whom love has once touched, and left."

The tarn strike was sudden. I had been waiting for days for it to happen. There was from the broken cover of clouds, like a bolt of dark, beating lightning, the thunder of the wings of a tarn.

The alarm bell sounded almost immediately. There was shouting.

The tarn's talons struck the delta wall, and, wings beating, it clung there, and put back its head and screamed. I saw, for one moment, the helmet of the warrior, and his hand extended downward. I heard the girl cry out and run to the saddle, and seize the hand.

"No!" I said to Thurnock, putting my hand on the arrow, thrusting it to one side.

He looked at me wildly.

"No!" I said, sternly.

I saw the helmeted figure rear up in the saddle, and with an imperious gesture fling a dark, heavy object to the stone walk behind the wall. A crossbow quarrel hissed through the night from the courtyard toward him. Men were running now. I heard more shouts, the clanking of weapons. The quarrel had sped past, vanishing behind him in the night. The tarn screamed and, wings beating, smote the air from its path, and began to climb into the dark, windy sky, streaking toward the moons of Gor. More quarrels fell behind the great bird.

"I could have felled him!" cried Thurnock.

"Is it an attack?" I heard from below.

"No!" I called down. "Return to your rest!"

"You have lost the girl!" cried Thurnock. "She has been taken from you!"

"Fetch me," I said, "the object which was thrown to the walk behind the delta wall."

Thurnock fetched it, and brought it to me. It was heavy, and leather. It was a purse, and it was filled with gold. In the light of a torch I counted the coins. There were a hundred of them, and they were of gold. Each bore the sign of the city of Treve.

"Thurnock," I said, "let us now have that cup of paga, and then let us retire. We must rise early, for the Dorna, and the Venna, and the Tela are to be inspected."

"Yes, my captain," said Thurnock. "Yes!"